THE CYCLE 8

Michael D. Brodsky

ISBN: 978-0-578-95585-8 (paperback)
ISBN: 978-0-578-99370-6 (hardcover)

Contents

ACKNOWLEDGMENTS

When I first had the idea for this book, I pitched my thoughts to my daughter Dani (a terrific writer and artist), and she thought it could be a great story. Because I respected her artistic opinion so much, I barely slept that night, throwing out concepts, thinking about characters, and formulating a storyline. When I awoke, I ran to my laptop to get it all down. Next, I ran the idea by my oldest son, Cory (another terrific writer), and he loved it and wanted to be involved. As the storyline progressed and *The Cycle 8* started coming to fruition, I next pitched it to my three sisters and mother, who I gathered with every Sunday. They loved it as well! I would like to thank all of them for their enthusiasm and encouragement. You see, I had never published anything ever!

Two of my siblings, Staci Klotsas and Sharon Templeton, were my greatest beta readers. They absorbed the verbiage in the chapters I fed them like hungry puppies, asking when I would have more and feeling free to share their invaluable thoughts and opinions. Needless to say, they were my biggest fans, and I am eternally grateful.

Salma Garcia-Nolasco did the wonderful cover art—but only after she read the entire book! Her feedback was extremely encouraging, and the final acrylic painting captured the horror and formidability of the daunting craurchin.

Finally, I would like to thank Cory Brodsky, who wrote Chapter 2 and incorporated the prologue into Chapter 1, making it a more enjoyable read. He was my coconspirator, allowing me to bounce off of him my concepts, ideas, and what a Cycle 8 would be. He is a *huge* part of this book, and I will always appreciate the help he gave me.

I will be there said my friend of a distant life
Covered in greens of a golden age, set in stone
Follow me, "he sounded of dreams supreme" follow me
Drifting within the glow and the after-glow of the eve
And if that firelight, I could match the inner flame
Sacred ships do sail the seventh age
Cast off your garments of fear, replace them with love
Most of all play with the game of the age
Highest of places remain all as one with you
Giving us light and the freedom of the day
And if that firelight, I could match the inner flame
Sacred ships do sail the seventh age
And have always been here
Celestial travelers have always been here with us
Set in the homes of the universe we have yet to go
Countless expansions will arrive and flow inside of us
My friend, he of fantasy, dancing with the spirit of the age
—"Madrigal," YES

PART I

HOW IT ALL BEGAN

CHAPTER 1

SANDOMARS, SEA ISLE CITY AND NOAH LONG

We had a lot of luck on Venus
We always had a ball on Mars
Meeting all the groovy people
We've rocked the Milky Way so far
We danced around with Borealice
We're space truckin' round the the stars
Come on let's go space truckin'
Remember when we did the moonshot
And Pony Trekker led the way
We'd move to the Canaveral moonstop
And everynaut would dance and sway
We got music in our solar system
We're space truckin' round the stars
Come on let's go space truckin'
— "SPACE TRUCKIN'," DEEP PURPLE

THE AGE OF ENTANGLEMENT

The Native Americans saw it coming long before the tides started to rise, and the earth began to crack and shatter. Man's history had begun its sprint along the Earth's narrow shelf eons before our signals blazed radiation against the black night sky.

Was mankind just another failed species scavenging for food? Another passing rain, beating against an unchanging rock? Or were we more? Would we spit in the face of extinction, push past the guards, and rally forth into the abyss?

The twenty-second century would later become known as the Age of Entanglement. In the United States, tornados, hurricanes, and earthquakes evolved and progressed, shaking the foundations of things built in sturdier times. There were only a few options, and people came together and adapted as they always have in the face of a changing new world. The Second Technical Revolution propelled human beings into a new category of species. Capitalism survived another century, and the world's economy boomed with new aerospace and tech industries. Despite robots taking many jobs, an infinite more were created in these tech industries, so unemployment was low and people felt secure. And there were always jobs available for disaster clean-up.

In this age of uncertainty and turbulent weather, who would ever imagine that a twelve-year old boy would propel our entire galaxy into a series of unimaginable events that would span centuries to come. And as fate would have it, this young boy from Sea Isle City, New Jersey was born to make a decision that would change the face of the planet forever. It all began innocently enough, in the prosperous year 2121 when little Noah Long joined his family on a space travel vacation to a distant planet called Sandomars.

By 2120, recreational space travel was as common for a middle-income family as a vacation to Western Europe was for a middle-class twenty-first century family. Life was relatively good and exotic planetary vacations were within reach for many. The cost was reasonable and the experience was second to none.

When Sandomars was discovered in 2045, what interested scientists more than anything was its similarities to Earth. First call *Sandymars* for its hardened sand mountains and comparison to Mars in color, a human could inhale oxygen expel carbon dioxide with minimal mechanical assistance. Thus the "o" in oxygen later replaced the "y" in Sandymars.

On Sandomars these scientists found a spectacular landscape that was very lush, robust and flourishing with vegetation. Many of the plants were similar to tropical Earth plants, such as canna, bromeliads, cacao, and orchids, but much larger and more vibrant. By 2145, one hundred years after Sandomars' discovery, over 50,000 plant species had been identified. And that was only a fraction. The trees grew very tall with wide crowns that provided great shade from the tropical climate. While our world's atmosphere was growing hotter, and its climate extremes more challenging to maintain, Sandomars was a paradise that was hard to find anywhere on Earth these days.

A NEW DISNEY WORLD

Very few storms hit Sandomars and when they did, they were fairly minor. Animals were captured and housed in the United States Science Commission's facility vivarium for study. It was all for the sake of science, discovery, and hopefully, the improvement of life on both Earth and Sandomars for humans. It was truly an endeavor with the best of intentions, and the scientists, lab techies, explorers, researchers, and everyone who worked at the facility were committed to, and proud of the work they were doing. So, it comes as no surprise that the planners of the proposed resorts looked to the USSC facility as a case study. The facility was a testament to the best use of materials and methods of construction employed on this planet, and how they performed in this environment and their longevity and sustainability. In 2112, the first resort, the Sandomar's Omni Grand Resort, opened its doors for guests.

The resorts on Sandomars were not unlike a twenty-first-century Punta Cana or Cancun resort, with lots of glitter and glitz. They were all-inclusive, providing drink, great food, endless partying, an abundance of activities and well-planned excursions into the micro-environment that surrounded them. All tucked away behind high, secured walls. Space travel was on the path to becoming Earth's most profitable and progressive new form of American leisure. Many hard-working citizens spent years saving for these once-in-a-lifetime trips and very few returned home disappointed. In the past several years, plans were being discussed to build theme parks, a zoo, and even vacation homes on Sandomars, and many wealthy investors were eager to invest. Some invested merely for profit. Others invested as a plan B to live when the Earth became unsustainable.

SPACE TRUCKIN' AGAIN

Noah Long was wearing a T-shirt he couldn't live without. It was blue with white letters on the back that read, "I'm a Space Truckin' Fool!" On the front was a picture of the STS Paladin 2. In many ways, Noah was a typical pre-teen boy. He lived for the moment. He was energetic. He was adventurous and a bit unorganized. How could it come to pass, that this very normal American boy would change the world forever?

"Hey, Dad, are we really going back to Sandomars? I cannot wait!" he yelled out to his father, gently piercing the air with his high-charged enthusiasm.

Noah thought he knew exactly what his future held for him. Here, there were no doubts in his mind. He was going to become a marine biologist. The way it rolled off his lips—*Dr. Noah Long, Marine Biologist*—gave him goosebumps. He loved repeating it over and over again. Sometimes, alone in his bedroom, wearing the fake beard he created from an old pair of black socks, he stared in his mirror, pretending to be a scientist studying marine biology for a living. He had been interested in marine plant and animal life since he was a toddler, bouncing about on the Sea Isle beaches, picking up every shell and piece of seaweed he found and taking it home.

"It's true, Noah, we're going back. We're booked on the STS Paladin 3! We're going to the Planet of Two Suns," his father answered.

Sandomars, a circumbinary planet, orbited two suns. As such, it had much brighter days and dramatic dual sunsets that complimented breath-taking views. Mountains formed from hardened sand, similar to a lithified sand dune, and the valleys left by receding oceans and high winds framed the background. Trees and plant life, similar to Earth but much larger, occupied the landscape with effervescent and bold, all-embodying colors. Among these colors were shades of azure, aqua, and violet. Many of these colors had never been seen by human eyes before Sandomars was discovered—intermediate hybrid shades that had yet to be described.

"Aww yeah! Can we do the wildlife excursion this time? You said when I'm twelve—well my birthday is tomorrow and guess how old I'll be, Dad! We're going to see the Crawchin! You said so!" Noah reminded him.

Noah was doing what his mother referred to as the "the vertical worm," the traditional worm dance executed while standing up instead of on the ground. He held his arms straight up over his head while wiggling his hips and torso forward and back, like a crazed, upright caterpillar in a puddle of espresso.

"Stop, stop, before you turn into a Craw Chin." Noah's dad, Benjamin, was towering above his son, tousling his hair. "C'mon Noah, sit down and chill little dude!"

It was a hot and sunny summer's day, and already the sun was expelling its warming and dangerous rays onto the Jersey coast. The two were relaxing on the back porch, watching a group of vacationers slowly waddling to the beach, struggling with their chairs, beach supplies, and numerous beach sundries. Noah's sister, Georgina, was already down on the beach with her girlfriends, too cool to walk down with the family.

"No way, say we can do it, say we can do it!" he chanted. "Gonna do the wildlife excursion, gonna do the wildlife excursion— oh yeah, oh yeah!" The vertical worm dance continued.

"Okay, okay, we're gonna do it. Just stop," Benjamin Long said with a chuckle. "Yer relentless, Noah!"

THE CRAURCHIN

The creatures and plant life that inhabited Sandomars were abundant. Because a lot of the saltwater oceans had begun to dry up, many of the creatures that once lived in the seas, took to the land. Craurchins were one such species. This crab-like animal had a protective shell around its organs and pincers like an Earth crab. But that was where the similarities ended. Unlike an Earth crab, they had a head with large, greenish-yellow mammalian eyes and limbs—six of them—extending from their shell. Their four lower limbs, more mammal-like then crustacean, terminated to long pointy, spiny fingers. These limbs were covered with a fur-like substance that was thicker than animal fur, almost bone-like. Their long upper limbs each had large pincers, oversized like a fiddler crab's. The pincers were lined with razor-sharp serrations. Being carnivores, this was how the craurchin captured and killed its prey. The protective shell of a craurchin was extremely hard and impenetrable to predators. It was, in fact, the hardest substance ever seen by mankind to date. There appeared to be several sizes that scientists believed were different craurchin breeds, but in reality, the various sizes represented their growth cycles. Craurchins lived long lives (160 years on average) and had growth spurts every twenty or so years. In the first five cycles (one cycle equals twenty years), they roughly double their size, and in the last cycles, they increase about 75%. The scientists initially missed this because the ones they had in their labs for study were captive for less than twenty years, so the metamorphosis or "cycling" had never been witnessed.

Cycle 1 craurchins weigh only a couple of pounds and are no more than four square inches in size. Not very intimidating in their first twenty years, but able to reproduce just a couple of months after birth. On Sandomars, scientists noticed that they appeared to live in the sand, almost always near a body of water. The sea plants and fish thriving in the saltwater rivers and lakes provide most of the nutrients they need to survive. Their natural predator, a huge eagle-like bird called the terragull, keep the species from overpopulating and destroying the ecosystem. Terragulls, with their long pointy beaks, can impale their skulls and eat their brain, which is a viable source of protein and other nutrients. Terragulls go for the head because the craurchin shell is almost indestructible, especially in later cycles.

The second, third, and fourth cycles of a craurchin are much the same as the cycle 1. They continue to double in size but still pose no serious threat—as long as they are alone. In the first four cycles, they can bite, sting, and transfer a weak venom, but nothing lethal. It is in the fifth cycle that they become a formidable, extremely dangerous predator. In this cycle, they grow approximately five to eight feet long and weigh anywhere from three hundred to five hundred pounds. They develop horns on their foreheads that can inject a toxic liquid that can partially and temporarily paralyze their victims. These horns help protect them from terragulls and other flying predators. In the seventh cycle, contact with this toxin becomes fatal to most creatures. On Sandomars, the terragull and other natural predators ensure a limited number of craurchins hit the fifth to seventh cycles. They do reach those cycles, mind you, but they are not as abundant as the cycle 1s and 2s.

Because the space commission scientists knew how much they still needed to learn about the craurchin, and Sandomars for that matter, they initially resisted approving Sandomars for habitation. Despite all the uncertainties about this new planet, the business elite pressured the politicians, who in turn pressured the space commission. As a compromise, the USSC agreed to limited development and strict rules as to what could and couldn't be done (i.e., limited excursions, walled-in resorts, etc.). What they got in return was increased funding and grants for studies. As is always the case, money *can* buy anything. Even a resort, on a planet millions of miles from Earth.

HAPPY BIRTHDAY NOAH

Gunther Schmits had a show on Saturday mornings that focused on the wildlife of Sandomars. It was currently Noah's favorite show. It was currently on and could be heard from where Noah and his father sat on the porch. Just inside from the kitchen, they could hear Noah's mom, Laura.

"Noah, turn the show off—and in the future, keep the volume a little lower. You're too young to be losing your hearing, so why so loud?"

"And here we have the terragull, the craurchin's natural enemy. A supreme flyer with talons as big as a basketball. It can swoop down and—" Before Noah could respond, Laura Long popped her head out the door.

"Ben, Noah, come on in for lunch, before the soup gets cold!" Noah's mom was just inside, in the kitchen of their three-bedroom contemporary beckoning them. Ben and Noah could smell seafood wafting its way out.

Yes! Mom made crab soup, Noah thought, *Freakin' awesome!*

He, his sister, and parents lived three blocks from the beach in Sea Isle City, New Jersey, and the crabs used in the soup recipe that his mother had perfected over the years were caught by Noah in the nearby bay, a place he would often go while his parents were at work and his sister off doing whatever older sisters do. His mom and dad both worked for the city. Benjamin Long was one of the town's building inspectors and Laura Jennings Long was the city planner for Sea Isle, a title that once carried local fame and respect, but in the last fifty years, not so much.

"Noah, this is your birthday weekend. Have you thought about what you want for dinner? By the way, those blue claws you caught were the best I've seen this season. How's the soup?" Laura, a very serious and straight-to-the-point woman, couldn't contain her excitement. "Well? well?"

"Unbelievable, Mom! Yes, I want to eat on Mike's glass-bottom boat. I want to eat my lobster while watching the bluefish swimming under the ship! How cool is that?" Noah had some of the white, creamy soup on his cheek as he shoveled in another chunky spoonful.

"Crap, I was hoping you'd forget. That's such a tourist trap! But, even so, I made reservations for tonight, ya little brat." She said this with a smile and threw him a napkin. "Wipe your face."

Dad was deep in his own world of palate-bliss, attacking the savory, rich soup with much enthusiasm. Seeing this made Laura feel good and validated her efforts.

"Seriously, Laura, you should patent this recipe. How do you get it to taste so freakin' good?" Ben joked.

"Well, Ben, first I add a little bit of passion, then a little bit of love, then the best crabs on the east coast, and finally, tons and tons of butter," Laura said this with the silly grin he loved so much. Ben thought it was cute that this was her reply every time anybody complimented her soup.

"By the way, I'm going into the office today. Gotta review the McNimble house some more. I'm not sure the engineer has the house lift quite right," Ben informed her.

House lifts were becoming popular for the billion-dollar residences built close to the sea. In these times of frequent and aggressive super storms, a house lift could raise a structure as high as thirty feet above the ground, protecting it from flooding and flying debris. Benjamin spent most of his workdays reviewing virtual walk-throughs of elaborate beach homes submitted for building approval. Currently, he was reviewing this six-thousand-square-foot steel and glass beauty that could sustain two hundred mile-per-hour winds.

13

"Ben, it's Saturday. I thought we were all going to hit the beach. You promised." Laura was obviously disappointed.

"I know, but I'm getting pressure from the boss to get this approval moving. I had to hear his stupid line about how, in this town, McNimble money talks and—"

Laura finished his sentence, "—and those who don't take it, may as well walk."

In 2120, Sea Isle City was very much a resort community. Folks vacationed in Sea Isle City from late April to mid-October. The town was clean, the beaches pristine, and the nightclubs packed every night. The climatic changes that started in the late nineteenth century and worsened every year, had afforded Sea Isle almost six months of good beach weather and all the activities that go with it. That is, when the super storms weren't striking.

The wealthiest Philadelphians and New Yorkers, like Cameron McNimble, owned beachfront and bayfront homes on this South Jersey shore town. They pumped a lot of money into the community. The days of snow-birding to Florida or South Carolina were becoming a thing of the past for many rich and upper-middle-class citizens who desired the warmer weather. Ben hated giving up a Saturday with his family for the likes of McNimble, but he could most definitely use the overtime pay. The McNimble's, four generations of developers and shady businessmen, hailed from Atlantic City. They were a politically connected, corrupt empire that made their fortune doing questionable business deals with sleazy people in the hotel and casino industry. Their real skill was getting away with barely legal deals, illegal shortcuts and the exploitation of others.

"So, when do we leave Mom?" inquired Noah, tugging at his mother's arm.

"Leave for where Noah, the beach?" she answered.

"No, Momma, Sandomars!" Noah's eyes were wide and bright.

Ben looked questioningly at his son with squinted eyes and scrunched up mouth, then at Laura. He thought Laura had already told Noah.

"Okay, okay, so I sorta saw the message on the house monitor," Noah admitted.

"Sort of saw? No, mister, you didn't sort of see anything. You opened my message," Laura scolded. She was now "Stern Laura" and was now talking in her professional, no-nonsense voice.

"Ben, young Noah here hacked my confirmation letter. Well, Noah, thanks for ruining the surprise. We were going to tell you tomorrow on your birthday."

Ben thought this was a good opportunity to highlight some family values. "Did you know your mom and I saved up money for two whole years for this vacation? We earn a modest living, and saving for this wasn't easy, let me tell ya. We expect you to show your appreciation by continuing to improve your grades and staying out of trouble. Comprende?"

Here we go, Noah thought. "Yesss."

"That's right. We are not wealthy like some of the residents in this town. *We* work hard for our money, and *we* do not take luxury vacations like a cruise to Sandomars for granted." Laura added her two cents.

"I know Mom, I know, Dad. I will improve my grades, and I do appreciate the things you guys do for me. Can we go to the beach now?" Noah begged.

"You want to go to college? You better improve those grades. You wanna be a marine biologist? You improve the grades", Laura sighed, "Okay, fine, let's go to the beach now. Here, put this on," Noah's mother instructed.

She picked up a bottle of sun and anti-cancer spray from the kitchen table and handed it over to him. Noah sprayed it into the air in front of him and watched as a cloud slowly formed. When it formed a volume stretching from where he sprayed down to the floor, he stepped into it wearing his special glasses. In an instant, the cloud particles attached themselves to every part of his exposed skin, forming a colorless body shield that would wear off in about six hours.

"Don't work late, Ben. Reservations are for six-thirty."

"Okay. Have fun guys," Ben replied as his wife and son walked out the door and into the bright, cloudless day.

They walked the three blocks to the beach, with the beach hover following close behind. When they got to the end of the block, they climbed the stairs up to the boardwalk and crossed over to the retinal scanners on the other side. They each looked into the scanner. It flashed green, and they walked down the second set of stairs and onto the beach.

As they stepped gingerly through the hot sand, Laura could not help but notice the trash some vacationers had left behind. It filled her with controlled anger. Currently, she was working on long-term plans to counteract beach erosion. This would involve rewriting zoning ordinances that would make it harder to build near or on sand dunes and certain waterways. Frankly, her job was not easy. She had to satisfy the wealthy citizens who paid their taxes, fueled the lush economy, and contributed money to local amenity projects, while simultaneously fighting to do what was right for the environment. Needless to say, sometimes she made decisions that were not popular with many residents. Some of those residents, like Cameron McNimble, lined the pockets of local politicians, and it worried her that she, or Ben, might one day be asked to do something they knew was unethical. She knew neither of them would ever do anything illegal or harmful, but she worried how they would survive on one income, if one of them were to refuse and lose their job.

"Hover down," Laura commanded when she found a good spot.

They unloaded their beach chairs, coolers, towels, and other items as a warm breeze blew off the ocean. When she settled in, she thought of how lucky they were the winds were blowing hard from the east. Though it would not completely stop the flies, it would help. In the last several years, flies and other insects had become almost unbearable, their population spurt due to the warming oceans. Like his mom, Noah appreciated the shore and its many wonderful, natural gifts. Noah collected and studied fiddler crabs, sea bass, toads, spider crabs, horseshoe crabs, and the sand sharks he would sometimes catch on his father's small boat. He would catch sand crabs for pets and study them using various apps he had on his communicator.

He could not wait to get back to Sandomars! This time, he would bring home an animal to study. Perhaps, it would make a good pet. Some of the creatures he saw last time around seemed friendly enough. He knew there were strict rules against bringing home any plant or animal life from the planets. *But come on, what harm could one of those little Sandomars creatures cause?* he thought innocently.

CHAPTER 2

THE PALE BLUE DOT

Look again at that dot. That's here. That's home. That's us. On it everyone you love, everyone you know, everyone you ever heard of, every human being who ever was…
— "THE PALE BLUE DOT," CARL SAGAN

THE STS PALADIN 3

The endless shadows gave off a sort of distrustful anxiety in the days before a few small lights appeared hopeful in the dark distance. The robant attendant hovered casually up the staircase into the gold metallic hallway and subtly tapped on the arched white door.

"Mr. Long, your children have been taken to their regular Tuesday evening activities."

The door turned green as she spoke, allowing her gentle voice to penetrate the soundproof wall. "Georgina is in Vmax, and as you know, Noah was approved this week for SkyRide."

Benjamin Long pulled a sweater over his thinning blonde hair as the door spiraled open and revealed the silver-skinned new prototype. He'd seen some high-tech robants while inspecting billion-dollar homes, but nothing like this one.

"What's Georgina tuned in to at the Vmax?" Ben asked the robant, concerned.

The robant hovered patiently, holding a tray with two glasses of green chardonnay and two small orange capsules.

"She is currently plugged into PalaSoc3, the ship's social platform."

Ben fixed his collar, swiped up a capsule, and slung it back with a gulp of the green chardonnay.

The Pale Blue Dot was now more than three lightyears behind the Paladin 3 luxury liner, and for Mr. Benjamin Long, it couldn't have been further.

"Honey, come on now before we miss the asteroid belt." Ben had been waiting the entire trip for the belt.

The Johnsons and the Middletons would be waiting at the gravity drop two columns below. He could picture them now with their overpriced bickering and judgmental mockery of the first and second-floor attendants.

Benjamin turned back toward the room, which was spacious, but getting smaller each day.

A petite blonde woman zig-zagged across the suite, rummaging through piles of clothes and empty suitcases. She looked elegant but a little bit frazzled.

"One second, Ben!"

"You know how they are, Laura."

"I found it!" Laura crowed.

Benjamin sighed, turned the dome latch, and secretly imagined an asteroid smashing into the fifth floor.

The airlock lifted, and the group stepped leisurely out of the gravity drop and into the ship's massive ballroom. Tables were filled with colorful laughter, as robots and robants served endless dishes of fresh fish and roasts of chicken alongside fresh vegetables and sparkling crystal glasses filled with amerlot and green chardonnay.

"Welcome! On behalf of Euphoria Cruise Lines, I'd like to thank each and every one of you for saying yes to the trip of a lifetime!" a voice boomed out into the still air.

The tall bearded man in a black tuxedo stood on a small platform in the corner of the room, and his image projected across each table's menu screen.

"For those that have ventured across the cosmos with us before, I say a special thanks for returning to our space transportation systems!"

The huge, metal window shades lifted and revealed a land-scape filled with massive shadows of boulders, shifting and bob-bing around a vast black ocean.

"Don't be alarmed! Although these monstrous space rocks appear close, I assure you we are in no danger at all. This particular vessel, the STS Paladin 3, is a shining example of Euphoria's continuing progress in the new space race and our world leadership in ingenuity."

Laura Long sat uncomfortably at the group's table and took another sip of her wine. She felt a little bit like royalty, a role she was far too humble to play. This was a high level of formality that even the "serious" Laura had trouble adapting to.

"I heard that Zion Delight had a special to Oceanica last year that cost half of what we're paying," Janice Johnson revealed. She scoffed in disbelief. Mr. Johnson fumbled with his napkin, preparing to be embarrassed yet again.

"It's much more pleasant in this system than anything by Proxima Centauri, let me tell you. There's not enough activity there yet to sustain a comfortable quality of living." Mr. Johnson was try-ing to compensate for the Mrs.'s negativity.

Ben put his hand up as a robant exchanged his drink for a brand new one. He, unlike Laura, was getting used to the good life, at least certain aspects of it.

The landing process proved to be the most mundane and time-consuming part of the Long family vacation.

"Why is this taking so long?" Georgina asked a robant secu-rity agent for the fifth time.

"Euphoria apologizes for the inconvenience. We provide premium service and care only for the safety of our passengers."

Georgina moaned. "That's exactly what she said before!" Benjamin rolled his eyes at his wife and flipped on his eye monitor to check the progress reports of the people ahead of them.

"The Middletons made it to their rooms already," Laura announced.

"Yeah, I see the Johnsons are a good bit behind us." The floor whirred and moved underneath them. "I'm sure Henry is just loving Janice right now," Benjamin joked.

Laura ignored him and looked up ahead at the security machines, as their conveyors inched closer and closer to the planet's surface.

"What's your name?" A small tan-skinned boy asked innocently.

"Noah. What's yours?" The lobby filled with more and more young kids as they were directed to their assigned lines to stand and wait to be processed.

"I'm Camir, but everybody calls me Cam for short," he answered.

A tall woman walked impatiently down their aisle and handed each of the boys a small capsule while a man behind her handed out bottles of water.

"Have you ever done SkyRide before?" Noah asked. Camir shook his head.

"I have." Noah proudly exclaimed. "This is my second time."

They had been there for two whole days, but to Noah, it felt like an eternity as he patiently waited for SkyRide to call on him. For him, it was one of the highlights of the trip.

Noah swallowed his capsule and uncapped his water.

"My friend Jimmy that lives on my street did it four times!"

Camir's eyes lit up in amazement. "Four times? Lucky kid!"

"Yeah, I think his dad helped with the original designs or something," Noah stated.

The lines started to move forward and numbers were being called. Directions were playing on their watch screens.

"Please take the red capsules. Please take the red capsules," a robant voice chanted through the frenzied sea of adolescent excitement.

In the lines closest to the entrance of the hangar, kids were being handed compression suits and oxygen helmets.

Noah turned around and looked intently at his new friend. "You ever hear of a craw-chin?"

A PECULIAR ROCK

The nature dome had flourished since the last time Noah had been to Sandomars, and the purple hues of the bamboo-like grass looked just like the dreamvertisements he had seen on the wall screen at home. Camir adjusted his seat belt and gazed off toward the second horizon, staring intently at the silhouette of a distant object. The tour cart hit a bump and slightly shifted in the air, quickly switching its gravity configurations.

"Up ahead, you can see the World Commandment Center! Right on top of that mountain. Does anybody know what that mountain is called?" the captain asked.

A small girl with a black ponytail lit up her buzzer and screamed, "Mount Gaines!" in her helmet mic.

"That's right, Captain!"

The smiley lady stepped down the aisle, happily handing the small girl a space commission windbreaker as a prize.

"Do you see that jet out there!" Camir asked Noah, shoving at his shoulder.

"That's not a jet!" Noah gasped. "That's a terragull!"

Some other kids began looking out the left side of the bus, toward the gigantic figure moving across the tangerine sky. As more and more children became distracted by the massive bird, the attendant flipped her script and began her introduction to the terragull a bit early.

"When General Martin Gaines first came to Sandomars, the shriek of the terragull is what he remembered most."

"I learned about this in school," Camir exclaimed. "That looks way bigger than the holograms we looked at!"

The monstrous golden eagle screamed and pierced the sound receptors even from that far in the distance. A unified sound of awe filled the tour hover bus, as the stunned children sat paralyzed in amazement.

"You just wait until we get to the space commission. That's where they let us get out," Noah whispered to Camir as the first sun of Sandomars set in the west, just like on Earth.

"One at a time, everybody!" the headset speakers announced to all the children simultaneously as they anxiously tried to exit the hover. They were all handed primitive paper maps, as they stepped off the tarmac. It was a scavenger hunt, and they were paired up accordingly. Naturally, Camir and Noah were put together after a robant conducted compatibility and behavioral analysis on all the children while they interacted with one another throughout the day.

In the distance, the purple tower hung on the shelves of the great mountain. A humongous yellow antenna shot up through the thick atmosphere, like a sword in the air of an approaching battle.

"I bet you couldn't climb that," Camir pointed at the tall needle.

"I bet I could! I can climb better than all of my friends. My cousin is a fleet operator, and he taught me how not to be scared of heights." Noah itched his nose and scratched the back of his neck.

"I dare you to climb it then!" Camir urged.

Noah laughed. "I'm pretty sure we're not allowed to leave the safe zone. Even if we could, I don't know how long we could breathe Sandomars oxygen."

Camir looked at his eye monitor and double-checked his air supply. It was still at one hundred percent.

"My dad says that one day we won't even need helmets up here, and there will be all the people living here instead of on Earth."

Noah scoffed and made a doubtful face. "Why would we ever want to leave Earth!"

The navigation alarm went off abruptly and signaled to the two boys that only twenty minutes remained in the group scavenger hunt and so far, they were only one item short. Camir had been carrying the bag full of mostly manmade tinkers the two had collected throughout the afternoon.

"What's left on the list?" Noah asked.

"The sandostone!" Camir yelped. "I haven't seen a single rock anywhere!"

Noah looked to the east and noticed that most of the other kids had taken the road that led to the small crystal-blue pond that lay safely within the artificial boundaries of the biosphere. The adventurous duo, however, had taken the path less traveled, searching for the creatures that science fiction writers had described during the early days of space travel.

A shriek echoed throughout the dome and the galactic shadow of a monstrous bird hustled across the ground. Noah hadn't noticed, but Camir dropped to his knees, shaken with fear at the sudden fly over.

"What if we could ride on one of those things?" Noah wondered.

"I don't think they would let us ride them," Camir answered, clearly embarrassed. The alarm went off signaling a graphic to their eye pieces, sparkling, "Ten minutes left!"

"What if the people that live here ride on them?"

Noah stopped dead in his tracks. "Nobody else lives here. That's what my dad told me."

Camir coiled in disbelief. "Well, my father works for the Earth Force and he told me that they think there might be people like us up here."

Noah suddenly spotted a pile of blackish rubble lying in the shadow of a Maypalmetto oak tree.

"Camir! Look! Sandostones!"

The two ran ahead toward the stand of orange hybrid palm trees. On the sandy ground appeared to be a nest full of fist-sized dark rocks shining in the waning sun.

"Quick, let's grab them and get back so we can have the front seat on the tour hov!"

Camir snatched one and ran off. Noah picked one at random and took off after his new best friend. Running in the foreign gravity of Sandomars sent tingles of excitement shooting throughout his body like fireworks, as he spurted toward the migrating groups of children being herded aboard the bright green transit shuttle.

Noah pulled out the sandostone from the knapsack and studied it vigorously, following the weird green lines that ran up and down the rough edges of the blackish stone.

"Well, we sure got these in the knick of time!" Noah exclaimed. "I wonder how many of the other groups collected every single item on the list!"

Camir seemed more interested in the horizon than the rock in his hand, his eyes anxiously scanning the dimming skies for one last terragull sighting. Suddenly, Noah released a startled gasp as he felt something warm touch the palm of his hands, instinctively dropping the rock on the trolley floor.

"What's wrong?" Camir interrogated.

"Oh, nothing. I just thought I felt something move." Noah's face reddened a bit as Camir quietly giggled. All the other kids started looking over their safe rails at the men in orange suits headed toward the hover as it moved into the quarantine zone.

The adolescent expedition group was right back where they started at the main visitor's port on the southeastern sector of the massive resort. All the children were allowed to bring one item back with them inside, and eventually back to Earth, to take home with them as "a souvenir from a different world."

Noah and Camir chose to bring home their sandostones. Camir thought that the green lines running dimly through the stone looked like a little racecourse. Noah didn't notice the lines, but couldn't stop staring and feeling around a specific part of the rock. The piece at the bottom seemed to fold up a bit into a sort of crater point, which looked like a little hole going into it.

The pair stood in line impatiently, and as they slowly wobbled forward, they heard strange zapping noises up ahead toward the steel hallway that led back inside the safety net of Euphoria's massive tourist center. The familiar lady with the white-blonde hair and the metal visor came strolling through the line, her robant attendant hovering casually behind.

"Everybody, have your one item out and ready for the inspection crew!"

The moment Noah pulled his rock out, he noticed it. There was definite movement in the sandostone! Then, he saw it. The little tentacle-like thing came reaching out, feeling around from the bottom crevice of the rough black rock. It wasn't a rock at all; it was a shell! As he stepped forward in the line, holding back his excitement, Noah tried to reveal the discovery to Camir.

"Camir! Quick look!" It was too late by the time he heard him. They were already being escorted toward the huge metalic hall. They each had to put their hands in the air to be scanned by the machine. One of the robants had taken the rocks and placed them on some sort of conveyor belt that ran through another massive scanner machine.

"Why does everything have to go through that machine?" Noah asked the robant.

"The machine will sanitize the objects using radiation and destroy all foreign microorganisms, effectively preventing anything of danger coming back to Earth."

Noah gulped and felt sad for the creature living inside the rock. It reminded him of the hermit crabs he would catch at low tide, back home. It almost sounded like a scream as the machine whirred and flashed, zapping the object with powerful waves of light. Noah looked over at Camir and whispered, "Did yours have something inside of it?"

Camir laughed and pressed forward through the line of children collecting their items at the baggage claim. "If it did, I doubt it survived the zapper." Noah retrieved his "rock" and searched every crevice for the creature, never finding a single trace of what could have been contact with a real-life alien. Again, he asked his friend about the peculiar movement in the rock. Camir was a bit spooked by Noah's question but tried to hide it.

"Nah, not really. Hey, Noah, why don't you take my rock? I really have no need for a stupid ol' rock, anyway. Besides, two is better than one."

Neither boy, or any scientist for that matter, knew that the two rocks were actually the egg-shell vessel that insured the cycle 1 a most definite birth.

BACK HOME

"Wake up, Noah!" Laura screamed from downstairs. Laura took being on time for school very seriously. Actually, her ulterior motive was to get them all out and have a relaxing cup of coffee and morning news in peace and quiet. "Don't make me sound the alarm!" She walked back to the kitchen and gave the pan full of hash browns a few shakes and shoves. Benjamin walked into the kitchen, fixing his tie.

"That trip really set us back, Laura. I'm not sure about Atlantic City next weekend. Why don't you just invite them over here? It's supposed to be a sunny weekend. We can test out the solar grill Janice got us."

Laura pinched her face up and continued scrambling eggs and scrunching bits of potatoes across the electric surface.

"I knew you were going to say that! Ben, this has been planned for months!"

Benjamin sighed and let the machine fill his coffee cup. Georgina came sulking into the kitchen, rubbing her sleepy eyes. Laura turned toward her daughter.

"Is your brother awake yet?"

Noah heard his mother's voice as it penetrated through his half slumber. Abruptly, he sprang out of his bed and hustled toward the bathroom. The sound, this time not his mother, stopped him dead in his tracks.

Noah looked over toward his bed and the desk by the window. There it was. One of the two sandostones that he had brought home from the trip was moving gently to and fro. A look of sheer astonishment mixed with horror expanded across his face.

What sound was that? It sounded like a mix between a cricket and a bird, maybe even a bit *liquidy*.

"Noah! If you don't get your butt out of bed and into the shower—" Laura shouted.

Noah quickly grabbed his animated souvenirs and put them in one of his many hermit crab cages. He quietly opened the window, figuring they would need more air and placed the cage on the windowsill, then headed toward the door.

"I'm coming!" he screamed as he ran out of the bedroom. That was the last time he saw his "rocks."

CHAPTER 3
STRATHMERE

My sweet, let me tell you about the shark
Though his eyes are bright, his thought is dark.
He's quiet - that speaks well of him.
So does the fact that he can swim.
But though he swims without a sound,
Wherever he swims he looks around
With those two bright eyes, prideful stroke
And one dark thought.
He has only one but he thinks it a lot.
And the thought he thinks but can never complete
Is his long dark thought of something to eat.
Most anything does.
And I have to add
That when he eats, his manners are bad.
He's a gulper, a ripper, a snatcher, a grabber.
Yes, his manners are drab. But his thought is drabber.
That one dark thought he can never complete
Of something - anything - somehow to eat.
Be careful where you swim, my sweet.
— "THE SHARK," JOHN CIAR

DEAD IN A WEEK

"Okay, everyone, listen up."

Brenda Bronkowski was in the front of the family vehicle and spun her seat around so that her three children in the back seat could see and hear her. It was a cloudy, overcast day, a day reeking of anxiety and fatigue because the Bronks were heading back home to Philadelphia.

"Shhhh. Quiet."

Her husband Bob punched a couple of buttons on the steering wheel of their vehicle, then set the navigation. The car was now in self-driving mode. He too spun his seat 180 degrees to face the back.

"So, before we start the game, we have to follow our time-honored tradition and decide on a name for Phillip's pet hermit crab," Brenda reminded them. She had their attention.

Every year on the last night of summer vacation, Phillip and his older twin sisters, Marne and Michelle, were given money to spend on the boardwalk. They could buy T-shirts, get some snacks, play some VR at the arcade, or buy some souvenirs. Phillip always bought a hermit crab. He loved all animals and really tried to take care of his pets, but the hermit crabs never lived more than a week or two.

"I say we name it Virgil."

"Oh Virgil—like that cute boy Virgil who was living in the house next door." Marne turned bright red but held her ground.

"Bite me, Shelly! I just think it's a totally rad name!" Marne said defensively.

"I like Crusty. Crusty the hermit crab."

"That's a good one, Phillip. I like it," Brenda chimed in.

"Really, Phil. Your last one was Crusty. Can't you think of something original?"

"That was two years ago and—"

"Dead in a week. I say name it Dead in a Week," Dad cut in.

Everyone, including Phillip, had a good laugh from Dad's suggestion, and so it was. Phillip's 2124 hermit crab was hereby named Dead in a Week. Phillip really did his best to take care of Dead in a Week. He would prove his father wrong! He never overfed him, kept his tank clean, and did his best to maintain the proper temperature and humidity levels. And DIAW did well. For a little while. Nonetheless, two months and three days later, Dead in a Week lost his battle with life outside of his natural habitat. But at 64 days, he set a new Bronkowski record!

STRATHMERE, JULY 23, 2125 (ONE YEAR LATER)

Young Phillip Bronkowski and his family had vacationed in Strathmere, New Jersey for as long as he could remember. In fact, one of his earliest thoughts was of himself playing on the beach in a diaper and his mother scolding him for eating sand. When the Bronkowski's talked about heading down the shore, they were talking about Strathmere. It was a quiet, small town that one could pass through without ever noticing. It was basically just a stretch of road called Ocean Drive that ran parallel with the beach. There were beaches on the east side and houses on the west. The ocean could be seen beyond the beach and the bay beyond the houses.

Most of the houses had large decks with views of the ocean on the front and views of the bay or marshlands at the back. They had rented the same place, in the last week of July, every year. Most days, Phillip fished and crabbed with his father off of the small dock in the back, while his mother and two sisters lazed away the days on the beach. At night, his parents would take him to the board-walk in nearby Sea Isle or sometimes to Ocean City, which was also pretty close. They occasionally ate breakfast at Uncle Bill's Pancake House or at any of a dozen or more places in nearby Sea Isle. Some years, his parents drove him and the twins to Water World in North Wildwood, while they had lunch and drinks in one of the nearby taverns. If they could squeeze it in, they would try and spend a half-day on a charter fishing boat like the Miss Townsends Inlet or the Miss Avalon.

"Whacha want for dinner tonight, guys?" Mrs. Bronkowski asked her family as she flipped pancakes one by one. The boar sausage patties sizzled as she flattened them with the spatula. It was the first morning of their seven-day summer vacation and the family was in a good mood.

"Chicken divine, Mom, chicken divine!" shouted Marne.

"Okay, that could work." Mom looked around the breakfast table.

"No, shrimp scampi. We're down the shore, so we gotta eat seafood!" Marne lowered her eyes and tossed a look at Phillip. Everyone always conveniently forgot that she hated seafood.

"Okay, Phillip, good suggestion. Shelly, Bob?"

"Don't care." Bob was disinterested as he read the news on his communicator.

"I wanna go out for dinner, Mom!"

"We are going out to dinner on Wednesday night, Shelly. You like shrimp scampi, don't you?"

"Shit, Brenda you read 'bout these craurchins?" Bob interrupted, still looking down at his phone.

"Cray what—who?"

"Cray-urch-in." He now had one hand on the phone screen while the other emphasized his words. "Evidently, some people have reported seeing these crab-like creatures burrowing in the sand. They think they may be some kinda exotic crab from the Bahamas or something that was released on the beach."

His demeanor relaxed again. "It's back-page news. Who cares, right? Now this article is a good one. Listen to this, Philly. *What authorities believe is a 17-foot great white is being tracked along the New Jersey coast. It was first spotted in Beach Haven and is expected to be off the coast of Ocean City by tomorrow.* Whoa, still want to stay home and fish in the backyard, Philmeister?"

Phillip's wide eyes complimented the silly grin on his face. "Hell no!"

DAY TWO

"Phillip, help your father load the beach hover. Bob, you put on the sunscreen. It's next to the chair—and put some wooder in the cooler, not just beer!"

"I'll put it on when we get settled on da beach, Brenda."

He rolled his eyes 360 degrees, then crossed them, hung his tongue out to the side and pretended to be having a spasm as he flapped his arms high-stepping like a deranged bird. Phillip nearly peed himself with laughter. Philly's contagious laugh got Bob laughing.

"What's so funny? Do you think sun poisoning is funny? You think skin cancer is funny? Well, I'm not taking care of either of you when you get burned!" Brenda spat out from the other room.

This only made them laugh harder until they heard the bedroom door slam. When they recomposed themselves, they filled the beach hover with towels, beach chairs, a big beach bag, beach umbrella, toys, games, snacks, the huge cooler, and then finally their dog, Spike. Spike was a chubby little Corgi who loved running in the ocean after balls.

"K, everyone, ready? Lez go." Bob was getting tired of waiting.

"Just go!" Brenda shouted from the master bedroom; it's across the street; I think we'll find you." Brenda and the girls were still getting ready.

"Oh, you'll find me all right. You'll find me, then tell me how the spot I picked sucks, 'n then I'll have to move everything to a new spot. I've been down this road before. No thanks!"

"JUST GO!" Brenda shouted. "Aye yah yah."

"Okay, okay, Goddamn. That first beer's gonna taste good," Bob said under his breath. "Let's go, Philly. Hover, follow," he spoke into the front of the beach hover. The BH-2A rose up five feet off the ground and followed Bob and Phillip out the door, across Ocean Drive and onto the beach, Spike sitting on it like canine royalty.

"Down, hover." The BH-2A lowered itself down and settled on the hot sand. Spike jumped off, tail wagging as he took in all the wonderful beach smells, while Phillip and his father set up the beach chairs and umbrella and unloaded mostly everything off of the beach hover. When everything was unloaded, Bob put the cooler next to him and then plopped into his chair. It was a gorgeous beach day. The sun was bright and hot, but the breeze coming off the ocean made the heat more than tolerable.

"Ahhh, love it. Never gets old, kiddo. We've been coming here since the girls were three or four. Love it, but I'll tell ya—and don't say a word to anyone—but I was thinkin' a taking the family on one of those space cruises next year. I hear Sandomars is da bomb!"

"Wow, you kiddin', Dad?"

"Shhh, our secret, okay," said Bob with his index finger to his lips. "Hey, pass me that tal?"

"Okay." Phillip handed a beach towel to his dad, who used it to open the beer he had grabbed from the cooler.

"Ahh, as we say in Philly Town, it must be five o'clock somewheres!" The beer was ice cold and went down smoothly. As Bob enjoyed the dark brown lager, he thought of just how lucky he was. Good job. Great family. Life was indeed good.

Eventually, Phillip's mother and two sisters arrived. He was sitting in the sand, tinkering with a toy he had gotten for Christmas. It was the remote-controlled "Sand Flea II." Between punching the buttons on the remote and reading the instructions, he would throw Spike's ball toward the water. The Sand Flea was a wireless, torpedo-shaped vehicle with caterpillar track wheels that could drive on the sand and actually burrow into light sand. It was also waterproof and had a built-in video camera, so Phillip could drive it into the ocean and get an ocean floor view from the remote's six-inch screen. Very cool.

Phillip had test-driven it at home in the nearby Pennypack Creek, so he knew how to operate it. He just needed to make a few tweaks. Once he got it going, Spike lost interest in the ball and started chasing the SF2 down the beach and straight into the ocean. Only a few yards into the surf and the Corgi, with his short stubby legs, was nearly under water. He turned and ran back to the family's spot on the beach.

"Leave it, Spike. Dad, check this out. I can see a kid's feet in the water!"

"Yeah, well, you better head the other way where there are no swimmers. That thing cost me a pretty penny, don't need someone steppin' on it."

Phillip did as he was told and navigated the Sand Flea II to an area adjacent to the multitude, where there were no people gathered. It had a range of about a thousand feet so he could go pretty far away from the crowd of swimmers and wave riders. The ocean cam on this high-tech toy sent back some pretty clear video of the grayish-brown ocean floor, which had divots in the sand intermixed with some shells and rock, but mostly sand and greenish-gray water. Occasionally a school of minnows would swim by. Now he was looking at some seaweed, the black kind. *Oh my, something shook up some underwater dust. Wow, a little fiddler crab. Cool!*

"Hey, Dad, you should check this out."

He handed the controls to his dad who, being an IT professional, knew gaming software and had no problems figuring the controller out. He sat fixated on the screen, pushing buttons and toggling the joystick. He was definitely digging this high-tech toy! Suddenly, he jumped up from his beach chair, eyes wide, glaring at the screen.

"My God! Oh God—it's—it's a great white! Phil, it's a white!"

"No way, really!" Phillip jumped up and came tearing toward the controller like a hot white laser beam, tripping twice along the way. "Lemme see. Lemme see!"

Bob, who never expected that intense a reaction, busted out in uncontrolled belly laughter. Gasping to catch his breath and half-choking on the sip of beer he had just taken, he fell off his beach chair onto the sand as he held his stomach, convulsing with laughter and drawing stares from nearby beach-goers. This went on for about a minute and then he stood up, eyes watering and his sides hurting.

"Dad!" By now, the whole family had joined in and were laughing, including Phillip. "Paybacks are hell, Dad, I'm gonna get you back!"

"Awww, Brenda, you should have seen the look on his face. C'mere son." Phillip came over and sat on his lap. Bob gave him a big bear hug and a kiss on the cheek. "I'm sorry, pal."

DAY 3

The next day, Phillip was back at the beach. He was really enjoying the Sand Flea II and had even attacked his sister Marne with it when she was in the water riding waves. She freaked when the Sand Flea bumped her ankle and still had no idea it was Phillip. He did some more underwater exploring and after about an hour, grew bored and walked

45

back to their beach spot where his mom was reading a book and the twins were building a drip castle. It was a little bit after noon, and his dad announced that he was heading back to the house. He had gotten too much sun yesterday but would never admit that to his mom.

"I think I've had enough for the day. I'm gonna head back and make a san'wich. Does anyone want one?" Everyone did in fact want one, so when he got back to the rental, he made a variety of sandwiches, cut them in quarters, added some drinks and snacks, then sent them over with his new drone.

As Phillip sat on a towel in the sand, legs crossed eating his sandwich and sipping his drink, he saw Spike charging toward the water's edge. He grabbed a bucket and shovel and ran to his dog. He was hoping for a blueclaw crab or horshoe crab.

"Hey, Spike, waz going on?"

He was standing behind the dog as he continued to bark and nuzzle something that was trying to scuttle into the water. At first, he was sure it was a crab. Every time the crab would get into the water, Spike would swat it with his paw knocking it back a foot or two. Phillip stepped closer and saw that it most definitely was not a crab. It was about the size of a large blue claw, but its pincers were bigger and it had a head with yellowish eyes and a mouth. In fact, it appeared to be looking directly at him when the other dogs arrived. There were now three of them and Spike. They had the crab thing surrounded and were barking and growling at it when suddenly, out of the blue, Spike bit its head off.

"Spike! No! Gross."

Spike really seemed to be enjoying the thing's head, and before he knew it, the other dogs had ripped the shell open and were gobbling up its innards. When they were done, all that remained was the bullet-shaped black shell.

FRIDAY

The rest of the week went by far too quickly, and when Friday evening unwelcomely arrived, the Bronkowski's had most of their stuff packed for their departure early the next morning. The drone from a pizza shop in Avalon had just delivered their dinner order, and they were sitting around the table as Brenda unloaded pizza, sandwiches, crab fries, and salads.

"So, did everybody enjoy their vacation?" she asked as she handed Marne her cheesesteak hoagie with hot peppers and mayo.

"It was okay, but we never got to Wildwood," Marne exclaimed.

Shelly grabbed two slices of spiced ostrich and onion pizza and dropped them on her plate. She rudely reached over her little brother and grabbed the garlic powder and oregano.

"Marne's right. We were really jazzed about checking out VR 2250!"

Shelly was talking about the new virtual reality attraction on Zelba's Pier. VR 2250 was a virtual tour of apocalyptic Earth in the year 2250. A land that lay in waste and overrun by monsters and aliens. It was basically a sci-fi horror flick that made the audience participants and allowed them to interface in 3-D.

In one scene, you are in New York City running alongside a toppled Statue of Liberty as you are pursued by the most horrible, nasty monsters ever seen. There was a rumor going around that an older woman actually had a massive heart attack while participating. Maybe that was urban legend.

"I had a blast, Mom!" Phil said with a mouthful of chicken tenders. Good ol' Phillip, a kid who really appreciated the nice things his parents did for him. Phillip made Brenda and Bob feel good about the time and money they put into a family vacation.

"So, what did you buy on the boardwalk this year, Philly? Let me guess—a hermit crab?" Dad teased.

"No hermit crabs this year, Dad. But I did buy a new hermit crab cage."

"A cage, but no crabs?" Mom said with a puzzled look.

"That's right. The cage is for Bonnie and Clyde, my new pet crabalurchins!"

CHAPTER 4
BIRTH OF THE BADLANDS

Did you hear the cops finally busted Madame Marie for tellin' fortunes better than they do?
For me this boardwalk life is through, babe
You ought to quit this scene too
—"4ᵀᴴ ᴏꜰ Jᴜʟʏ, Aꜱʙᴜʀʏ Pᴀʀᴋ," Bʀᴜᴄᴇ Sᴘʀɪɴɢꜱᴛᴇᴇɴ

2220, THE FLEA CIRCUS

When the crisis was first recognized fifty years earlier, actions were put in place by the government to eliminate the craurchins. Though the depth and scale of the problem was greatly underestimated, the media managed to keep the story alive and in the public eye on a daily basis. Not only was the story of the first alien species to inhabit Earth of great public interest, but it also captured the imagination of people of all ages and walks of life, and man oh man were they in for a surprise!

"Quiet, Todd! This is important!" Molly, the pants-wearer in the family, scolded her husband.

"And to fund the effort, the entire New Jersey coast will be declared a natural disaster area. FEMA will provide disaster relief immediately and soldiers with the National Guard will be sent to the area as early as next week to begin extermination efforts." Spoken from the talking head projected on their kitchen wall screen, the story caught the couple's attention. *"More news to follow."*

"Shit, Molly. What the hell! A natural disaster area? Last year the crab thingies were causing some people to change their vacation plans, and five years before that they were a simple nuisance! And now the National fucking Guard! Don't *even* ask me to drive to the Outer Banks this Summer! I hate that fucking drive!"

"Yeah, well, know this. I'm not sharing the beach with those nasty things! If you have to work double-time, I don't care. You're taking my fat ass on a vacation somewhere!"

The government did an admirable job killing most of the larger cycle 3s and 4s, but what they didn't realize was that the majority of the cycle 1s and 2s burrowed in the sand beaches and ocean floors, reproducing and remaining protected from seagulls and other predators. They could live on the seafloor for months using oxygen stored in the walls of their complex shells. These smaller craurchins were the real threat because they were the most reproductive.

When people look back and ask, "How was the burrowing thing missed?" they would realize, as usual, that politics played a huge role in the demise. They will be reminded of the debates Americans had on how to resolve the problem. The political right and war hawks wanted to use all funds available for an all-out obliteration campaign of the invasive creatures, whereas the left wanted to use a portion of the allotted funds for researching the craurchins and attacking the problem scientifically as well. It would be another five years before the more formidable cycle 5 would come into existence, and of course, nobody knew this.

"Good evening and thank you for watching Independence News. The main story tonight, 'America and the Craurchin Crisis.' Some feel it is time to declare victory, but others say doing that may be premature. Here is John Bowers reporting from the boardwalk in Avalon, New Jersey. John."

"Thanks, Martha. After six months of diligent efforts by the National Guard and civilian volunteers, thousands upon thousands of these creatures from Sandomars that we call craurchins, have been exterminated."

The camera moved from John to heaping piles of dead craurchins spread across the yellow beach. Workers in orange coveralls were in the background, shoveling them into sanitation hovers. In Molly and Todd's kitchen, 'SmellSense' was on.

"Ugh God, Molly, turn the SmellSense off, that's disgusting! I think—"

"Shhh."

"It is commonly known that these crab-like invaders from Sandomars, which can grow to the size of a large dog, wreak havoc to our beaches, bays, oceans, and marshlands. Some people have even reported being attacked by them. There is no argument that they are a menace and need to be eliminated. However, it is the 'how' that gets people worked up. I am talking with Dr. Felix Sanchez, a marine biologist who has been studying the craurchin for several years now. Dr. Sanchez, why are you opposed to the government's aggressive extermination program?"

"Well, John, I am not opposed to extermination—absolutely not. I just think we need to do it intelligently. We simply need to understand our enemy better. We need to know their eating habits, how they mate, the reproduction process, the growth process, and the species' vulnerabilities. We need to thoroughly understand their biology. We absolutely need to eliminate them, but again, we have to do it thoughtfully. If we miss something, the extermination effort could all be for naught. By the way, this is the view of most of my peers and scientists all around the world."

"Doctor, how does studying the creature assist in removing it completely and permanently? I mean, I don't want to sound crude or brash, but isn't a dead craurchin a dead craurchin?"

"Point taken, John, but consider this. History has shown us time and time again that rushing into a quick response to a complicated problem, without a true, thought-out plan, a plan that follows science, can have devastating consequences. The best example

would be rushing into a war without knowing our enemy—and believe me, the craurchin situation is a war, and make no mistake, they are our enemy!"

"But tell me and the viewers how studying a species can help in its obliteration?"

"Let me answer your question with a question. Do we know we have killed all of them? Are there craurchins hiding in the sand or ocean? I mean, we know they burrow. Do they communicate with each other? What are their vulnerabilities? What are their growth patterns? A little more funding put into research can go a long way."

2230, WHEN EVERTHING CHANGED

Unfortunately, the all-out obliteration campaign was the action taken and the easiest one to sell to the American people. Studies of such attributes as the craurchins unique mating patterns, their twenty-year growth cycles, and their eating habits were initially missed. Toxic gases sprayed by drones and "boots on the sand" kills were the tactics employed, but each year there were still craurchins crawling about the beaches and, in 2230, they all came out of hiding.

They were everywhere—on the beaches, in the bays and marshlands. They sprang up in inland salt lakes and ponds. They ruined the fishing industry by chasing the fish further out to sea. They got tangled up in fishermen's nets and clogged up waterways and inlets. They scurried the streets in clusters, chasing tourist away indefinitely. South Jersey shore towns such as Sea Isle, Avalon and Stone Harbor were now under siege and nobody was doing anything about it.

In their comfortable home in Blackwood, New Jersey, Molly and John were watching a documentary about the high oil yields on Sandomars, and how America was exploiting that resource.

"Molly, did you hear about the Gardners?"

A commercial sounded in the background. *"Were you a worker on Sandomars? Did the government not disclose the dangers of Sando-flu to you? If so, Swartz, Regan, and Swartz Inc., are here for you. Call us for a free consultation and—"*

"No, Todd, I did not." Molly air-swiped her pointer finger towards the floor, decreasing the volume. "What happened?"

"They were asked by the government to consider voluntary relocation from their home last week."

Later that day, Molly called Jan Gardner. "But Jan, you don't need to go into government housing, girl. Move back to Blackwood or further inland. Surely, they will get this situation under control, and you can move back!"

Jan and her husband, Tony, lived in a small rancher, five blocks from the beach in Margate.

"It's not that simple, Molly. We can't sell our house. We can't rent our house, and we can't rent another place without selling or renting our house. We thought about not paying the mortgage, but then our credit would be screwed. All the government can do is offer relocation to the Heartland. There has been no talk of them buying homeowners out."

"My God, Jan. What the fuck? Is it really that bad?"

"It's worse than you can imagine. The 'shore' is no longer what you think. These—things. They are everywhere. And not just the little ones. There are bigger ones now! And they are dangerous!

Last week a man was killed, and a few days before that, a child! Right here, in peaceful, pristine Margate. I don't understand how it happened so quickly. It was as if they were all hiding somewhere and decided to come out all at once."

Jan gathered herself, and with a shaky voice asked Molly, "Is it true what they are saying about D.C.?"

"It is. The Senate is taking a vote next week about moving the capital from D.C. to Bloomington, Indiana. Evidently, this, combined with the water crisis, has made the prospect of keeping the capitol on the east coast unsustainable."

"How is it that this so-called great country of ours could allow our drinking water to be poisoned? How is it they can give up on the east coast so easily?"

"They're putting all resources into the goddamn war! Concentrating everything to the middle of the country. I don't see why they can't work out a treaty like they did with the fuckers that poisoned our groundwater!"

Six months later, there was a mass relocation effort along the east coast, from Long Island, New York, to the shores of Delaware, extending as far as twenty miles inland. People were transported and placed into FEMA housing in the U.S. Heartland until they could be resettled. Many of the population just packed up and moved, but some stayed. Only a few coastal military bases would be kept open to defend the coastline. Relocation efforts continued, until it got too dangerous and ultimately only strategic base locations were allotted resources to stave off the craurchins. The military, who played a huge role in the extermination effort, was fighting an escalating war with Russo-China, so the majority of drones and soldiers were redeployed for that effort.

"Hurry over here, Molly, you've got to hear this!"

"Relocation efforts have begun. The plan is to start with the entire Cape May County shoreline and work north from Cape May to Atlantic City, Asbury Park, and all the way up the north coast to Long Island." This was breaking news and both anchors had a look of concern and surprise on their faces. *"Peter and Martha?"*

"We're here, John. John, who exactly are the folks that are being evacuated, and where are they going? Also, are they expected to return?" Martha's look of concern was now one of downright shock.

"Well, first you have your homeowners who summer at their second homes down the shore. They, I imagine, will stay at their primary residences inland. You have others—year-round residents who will sign up for the relocation program and start a new life in the Heartland or take up residence further inland. The problem is their homes are now worthless and most don't have the money to buy a new home inland. Their only choice is to stay or go into government housing in the Heartland. There is no word on when they can return, but sources tell me it could be years, maybe decades."

"Hey, John. This is Peter Cabana. Did you say decades? How is it one day we are reporting on a craurchin overpopulation issue, you know, not dissimilar to the pythons in Florida, and the next day we are reporting on a major evacuation effort of residents? How did the situation escalate so quickly?"

"Peter, that is the billion-dollar question. Scientists believe that the creatures somehow eluded the extermination campaign.

That, combined with their rapid reproduction biology, caused the crisis we are now facing!"

PART II
THE BADLANDS

CHAPTER 5

ENTER THE BADLANDS

Lights out tonight
Trouble in the Heartland
Got a head-on collision
Smashin' in my guts man
I'm caught in a crossfire
That I don't understand
I don't give a damn
For the same old played-out scenes
I don't give a damn
For just the in-betweens
Honey I want the heart, I want the soul
I want control right now
Talk about a dream
Try to make it real
You wake up in the night
With a fear so real
Spend your life waiting
For a moment that just don't come
Well don't waste your time waiting
Badlands, you gotta live it every day
Let the broken hearts stand
As the price you've gotta pay
We'll keep pushin' till it's understood
And these Badlands start treating us good
—"BADLANDS," BRUCE SPRINGSTEEN AND THE E STREET BAND

TROUBLE IN THE BADLANDS

The year is 2268, and it's been close to 150 years since Noah brought his two passengers back home to Sea Isle City. Since their escape onto the beaches of this small town in southern New Jersey, the original craurchins—we'll call them Adam and Eve—have grown from their original size to almost twenty feet long, weighing close to a ton each. They are cycle 7s and until now have managed to elude capture or even being sighted. The good news is that they are the only two of that size, although the second generation is only twenty years behind and weigh-in at almost 800 pounds.

The bad news is that their descendant's population has grown so large they have completely destroyed the ecosystem along most of the eastern U.S. coastline, leaving a path of destruction and making it difficult for humans and much of the wildlife.

They found out early on that dogs could sniff out these unearthly creatures and kill them with little or no effect from the craurchin's venom. Also, the craurchin's provide dogs with a kind of super protein, which can sustain all of the nutritional needs their bodies require. So, it is no surprise that nearly every home in the Badlands owns several dogs, and the bigger the better. A large dog can kill a cycle 1, 2, 3, or 4 craurchin, and a large pack of dogs can kill craurchins up to cycles 5 and 6.

Living in the Badlands is so dangerous and difficult that almost every day is a struggle to survive. A lot of the food and other necessities that the people need to survive are airdropped from drones or delivered by hovercopters flying in from the Heartland to designated drop zones. Most of the essentials delivered to the drop zones are government supplied and include cheese, bread, milk, baby formula, clothing, and batteries among other things. All non-essentials, which is basically everything else, are paid for using kill points. Kill points, or KPs, are earned by recording craurchin kills. These drops occasionally include dogs bred to kill craurchins. In fact, decades ago, dogs were released into the wild and have since grown in size and number. Forty years later, wild dog packs called "wilds" roam the Badlands, living almost entirely on a steady diet of craurchin meat. But are they enough?

To get to their designated drop zone, Badlanders have to make their way through hostile terrain. Oftentimes, they have to walk because roads are in disrepair and fuel or batteries for vehicles are unavailable. In some of the more organized communities, squadrons were formed to collect the food in large hover vehicles for distribution to the community. Some Badlander's use their own private drones to retrieve this food, but most of their drones are in disrepair, and there are very few people with the skills to fix them.

Many folks in the Badlands live inland, in dwellings far from water because the craurchin populations tend to gather in greater numbers near bodies of water, especially saltwater and the warm Atlantic Ocean. Only the hardest of the hardcore have remained on the beaches and bays flanking the Atlantic.

They have learned how to survive as a community, for very few can make it on their own. They are technically still under the jurisdiction and laws of the United States, but because the Heartland cannot provide the aid they need, they do much of their own emergency management and public works. This helps to not only keep people safer but provides work and a sense of self-achievement and self-worth. In most communities, citizens who do not pull their weight or who are deemed troublemakers are encouraged to move on—or are outright banished. This is the Badlands. And as one can imagine, the people and lifestyles born from it are raw, gritty, unpretentious, unassuming, proud, and sometimes hopeful.

DROP ZONE 15

"Roger that, Drop Zone 15. I am flying down the New Jersey southern coastline right now. I'll be landing in ten. Over."

As Daniella decreased her altitude and navigated the hovercopter southwest, she could see the black-spotted, gray beaches of Ocean City. She took a deep breath and prepared herself for the sight that always caught her off guard. As she came in lower, the black spots became clearer and many were moving. Craurchins. Zipping across the Great Egg Harbor Bay, she could see them burrowing into the soft sand beaches or scattering into or out of the black bay. She could see much destruction. Leveled houses, abandoned diesel engine cars stripped for their parts, and roads and bridges in disrepair. In what appeared to be a striving community, she could see a ring of fire with burning rubber tires, surrounding the town square. It was her fifty-third mission, but seeing the Badlands always shocked her to the core. From her vantage point in the gray sky she could see the failing structures, houses in shambles, suffering from decades of non-use and no maintenance. Metal sheds, roofs, fences and utility poles corroded from the endless, merciless attacks of the harsh salt air. Many of the numerous bridges from the barrier islands to the mainland were in severe dilapidation as the harsh conditions destroyed the protective sealers on the steel and corroded the bolted or welded connections. That, combined with the high winds of the super storms caused many of these bridges to collaspe. As she flew towards Drop Zone 15 she noticed that part of the Stainton Memorial Causeway bridge had collapsed, leaning into the bay like a giant steel dinosaur bending in to take a drink.

"Roger that, Dani. See you soon."

Coming in, Daniella could see that the runway was again in need of repair. It ran between the warehouse building and community building. Beyond the property, on all sides, the terrain was heavily wooded with pine trees. She did her best to keep the aircraft over the flat sections of the runway as she switched the mega fans to landing mode. When the aircraft was safely docked, she hopped out and actuated the cargo doors, which coiled overhead, allowing the ramp to engage. She hopped out and walked toward the young man in the baggy shorts and work boots.

"Mornin', Dani. How was your trip? I patched up the runway as best I could, but once again, I am low on material."

"Not bad, Jacky. I hit a little weather in Ohio, but other than that, no issues. The runway is fine, no worries," she lied.

Jacky managed DZ 15. He was air-traffic control, supply inventory, distribution, stocker, accountant, and everything else required to run a drop zone all wrapped into one. A little on the chubby side, he was a pleasant, handsome man who, beyond anything else, was there to help. He actually loved his job and lived at DZ 15 in a little bungalow behind the concrete block warehouse.

Across the runway, Daniella saw a group of bearded men sitting at a picnic table under the wooden pavilion about a hundred feet away. Many of the pilots who flew missions to the various drop zones would have seen these men as a band of ragged, disheveled low-lives. Not Daniella. She knew each one by name and knew a bit of this and that about most of them. She knew how many kids Isaac had. She knew that RuryAnne lost her boyfriend Christian last year. She had empathy and admiration for each and every one of them and their families.

"I see we have a few early birds." Daniella nodded toward the group. A light warm wind swirled her long, blond-streaked black hair.

"The Stonies got here early this morning." The folks from Stone Harbor were referred to as Stonies by locals.

"They're gonna start setting up for the barbeque in a bit. Will you be staying?"

"Most certainly," replied Daniella.

"Awesome." Jacky could hardly hide his pleasure.

He had more than a mild crush on Daniella, who knew it and liked it—a lot. Daniella felt Jacky was different then the men she knew in the Heartland. He was real, unpretentious, and kind. It also helped that he was not hard on the eyes. His dark wavy hair and beautiful green eyes were enough for her to easily overlook the few pounds of extra weight he carried. The dimples helped as well. The two had been flirting with each other for weeks and they both knew instinctively that tonight would be the night.

The Stonies were setting up for the barbeque they'd been planning for weeks. Slowly but steadily, folks arrived from Avalon, Cape May, Sea Isle, the Wildwoods, and several other places. Hovers and other vehicles were loaded to maximum capacity as

Daniella, with the assistance of Jacky, read the manifesto and called individuals up to collect their supplies. The distribution and loading of supplies went on for the better part of three hours and when every box of cheese, every round of ammunition, and every case of medical supplies was unloaded, individuals slowly made their way to the pavilion where the fire pit was blazing, and the food was cooking.

Jazz juices (a savory concoction of aged whiskey, caffeine, and cannabis), homebrew, and dago red were the drinks of choice. Everyone always had a good time at the drop zone. Information was exchanged about respective communities such as where the larger craurchins had been spotted, the number of casualties in the last month, and who currently had the highest kill points. Jacky had set up horseshoe pits a few years ago, and there was an informal tournament going on.

The day eventually turned into evening, and with it, a cool breeze blew in from the west, stoking the fire pit. Some Badlanders were sitting in beach chairs, either resting before their trip back or settling in for the night. Some set up tents, and others just planned on sleeping under the stars. The final two teams were toe to toe in the horseshoe match, the bright hot flames of the roaring fire pit their only light.

Daniella and Jacky sat by the fire, talking and listening to the stories being told. Daniella was always fascinated. The contrast of these stories and these people's lives were so very different than hers. As people began leaving or settling in for the night, Jacky turned to Daniella then nodded toward the rear of the compound where his bungalow stood. She smiled, and they both stood up and walked hand in hand, the brightness of the fire glow fading behind them. When they turned the corner around the back of the warehouse, Jacky turned on the high-powered spotlight and a couple of cycle 2s ran into the woods. He unlocked his bungalow door and the two of them disappeared for the next eight hours.

CHAPTER 6
DANTE LONG

In the year of the scavenger, the season of the bitch
Sashay on the boardwalk, scurry to the ditch
Just another future song, lonely little kitsch
There's gonna be sorrow, try and wake up tomorrow
—"Diamond Dogs," David Bowie

DANTE LONG OF SEA ISLE CITY

Dante Long was born and raised on the Jersey Shore, in the Badlands, only a few years before they became the Badlands. He grew up there and intended to die there. His Great-Great-Great-Great-Grandfather, Benjamin Long, had settled in Sea Isle City in 2110 at the age of thirty-one, and five generations of Longs followed suit. The shore was in their blood. Salt air and the ocean were in their pores. He had heard the stories about how his Great-Great-Great-Grandfather, Noah Long, was responsible for bringing home the two craurchins who had created the nightmare that was now the Jersey Shore. He had also heard the conspiracy theories — the creatures were planted in his luggage. Noah was not the only smuggler of craurchins. And of course, his favorite, the craurchins had always been here, living deep in the middle of the Atlantic. Not many folks even thought about all that anymore. However, Dante did.

The year was 2265, and it had been 145 years since Noah Long brought Adam and Eve home to Earth. Dante was in his thirty-fifth year and living his life in the Sea Isle Badlands. Though he was of medium stature, he came off as stocky. He was thick, rugged-looking, and in excellent physical shape.

Many years ago, when they started the relocation effort, Dante's father, Elijah Long II, declined the offer. His wife, Anastacia, concurred. Dante was but a fetus. When they initiated voluntary evacuations, his parents again declined. When they enacted mandatory evacuations, his dad said, "To hell with that." Both his mom and dad helped with the evacuations, but along with other hardcores, refused to leave. Besides, he felt an obligation to stay because of what his ancestor, Noah Long, had done.

As the extermination efforts failed, Elijah witnessed the hostile takeover that the craurchins imposed on the beaches, bays, and marshes of his beloved home. He saw the crabs disappear. He saw the fish disappear. And he saw the towns along the Jersey coast turn into the Badlands.

Dante Long stepped out onto his back deck, peering down at the peaceful sand dunes below, as he sipped his morning coffee. He watched the wind blow the loose sand and rattle the marram grass sticking out of the dunes. Out of the corner of his eyes, he saw movement. Craurchin. *So much for the peaceful sand dunes*.

Dante had one of the nicer "jetsam" homes in Sea Isle and the large deck afforded him views up and down the boardwalk, dunes, and beach. Jetsam was the name given to the abandoned homes that had survived the multitude of storms, vandalism, and neglect that most homes in the Badlands experienced. It was his third home and was won in last year's kill point auction. Though many squatted in abandoned houses, the finer jetsam homes had to be purchased. Dante used many kill points for this house.

"Hey guys, we're gonna walk to Bob's, y'all down? Wanna say hi to Felix?"

Springsteen sat up as if waiting for a treat, his ears sticking up stiffly. Nevelle jumped up with a *woof* and then Springsteen followed suit.

"Okay then, let's go."

Both dogs were just a year old and eagerly waited at the door, fluffy tails wagging, while Dante grabbed his backpack. Dante had lost his dog Bullet a year or so ago and replaced him with the two huge Malamutes. He was still training them. They walked down the elegant stairway and out of the two-story beach home's front door and onto the street. Neville ran hastily into the bright morning sunlight.

"Neville, stop!" Dante commanded when the dog ventured too far ahead. The dog obeyed.

The dog waited as his master and brother caught up and they headed up Landis Avenue, and onto Forty-Fifth Street toward Bob Handler's place on the bay. Bob had a nice house on the water, which his parents owned before the evacuations. It had a dock with two boat slips. Bob had his boat moored in one, and he let a friend use the other. It was currently low tide, and Bob was on the dock prepping his boat for the day's outing with Dante. His dog, Felix, was in the bay happy as a clam and looking like a seal swimming in the channel.

On the short walk to Bob's house, the dogs killed and ate a pair of cycle 3s. Dante calmly sipped water from his flask, water purified from a device invented by a young boy, a genius some said, from Cape May. This device made use of craurchin shells to filter the contaminated water that had sickened so many in the Badlands. He capped his flask and pulled out his communicator and touched the screen. He pointed it toward the first dead craurchin, and it flashed a white light.

In red alpha-numeric, "Dante Benjamin Long – SICX23402" popped on the screen, and Dante touched the screen, recording the first kill. He did the same for the second dead craurchin.

They walked a few more blocks and then sprinted the rest of the way to Bob's. Dante made sure his dogs got their exercise.

The last thing he needed was an out-of-shape dog up against a healthy craurchin. Dante trained his dogs, as well as other's dogs, to walk by their masters' sides at all times. When he was in unfamiliar territory, he would give the command, "See," and the dog would proceed ahead and sniff the area for craurchins. A dog was not told to attack a craurchin. It attacked and only stopped attacking when commanded, "Cease." Dante was the alpha, and they moved as a pack. Either of these two dogs could smell a craurchin from two miles away, and the closer the alien was, the stronger the smell. Because a craurchin's scent was like nothing else on the planet, they could easily differentiate them from almost anything else on the planet.

When they arrived, Bob hopped out of the boat onto the deck with a jazz juice in each hand, offering one to Dante. He gave each dog a treat from his pocket. Bob was a large man with long, curly blond hair that he often wore in a ponytail. At six foot eight inches and weighing around 280 pounds, he was a formidable presence. Bob was also a gentle giant. In the ten-plus years that Dante had known him, he had never seen him hurt another human being. Bob downed the rest of his drink, which looked tiny in his large pale hands. Felix climbed out of the bay and onto the dock. He did a water shake-off that seemed to last forever, then ran to greet his master's friend and two dogs.

"So, what's the game plan?" Bob asked, as he loaded the last two fishing rods on the vessel.

"I thought we'd start out bottom-fishing for flounder in the bay. There should still be a few left—the crawdads couldn't have eaten all of them. At least, I hope."

"Fish for flounder says the man with the highest kill count on the east coast. Sure, why not? I do make the best stuffed flounder in the south of Jersey. I guess I can go a day without income." Bob quipped sarcastically. "Luckily, we have the means to decontaminate the fish."

"I'd love to meet that kid someday," said Dante. "My father always told me someday we would be able to eat fish again."

"Hey Bob, we can also hit the marshes for craurchins. I know where a cycle 5 has a lair with a cluster of four. I've been scouting it for a few days."

"Now we're talkin', my brother." Bob's face brightened up a bit. He was trying to collect enough kill points for a new laser. He also needed another dog.

THE MARSHES

They boarded the small solar craft and came to a spot in the bay where the gulls were quite active, swooping up minnows and other smaller fish that were feeding on the surface. They dropped anchor, and in the course of several hours, pulled in four large flounders. As they sat in the small boat talking, they could hear the flat, white fish flopping around in the cooler on the boat's bow. The dogs were sitting quietly on the bow, taking in all the wonderous smells.

"I told you clams were the way to go. Does the trick every time." Bob was convinced that clam was the best bait for flounder. It was unfortunate that clams were scarce these days.

"Well, we'll never know, now will we?" Dante snarked.

"Whattaya mean?" Bob replied.

"Well, who's to say if we used minnow that we wouldn't have caught ten? Anyway, who cares? Let's kill us a big craurchin. We'll scope out the lair 'n see if Big Daddy is home. If he is, here's what we do…"

Dante had devised a plan and discussed it with his friend as they sat anchored in the peaceful bay, under clear skies in the calm, hazel-toned waters. His great skill, and the reason he had the highest kill count in the Badlands, was his talent as a strategist. He was agile, strong, and quick, but his uncanny ability to work out scenarios in his head and quickly assess the risks and benefits of each was his true skill. He was a firm believer of the KISS method—Keep it simple, stupid—and that's exactly what his plan was for today's hunt—simple. Simple but effective.

The two men and three dogs took in their surroundings as Dante steered the solar-powered boat through the network of channels into the murky back bay. It was an ebb tide so the channels were a little deeper with mud sidewalls that were filled with fiddler crab holes and patches of cordgrass sticking out. Every so often, a crab would curiously pop his head out to make their acquaintance. The smell was rough (at least for the men), but they got used to it quickly. As it turned out, Big Daddy and his cluster were indeed home, so they pulled the boat up past its lair and executed the first part of Dante's plan.

"Boys, this is your stop. Let's get to it!"

With that, Felix, Springsteen, and Nevelle jumped out of the boat and onto the muddy marshland soil. The dogs knew what to do as they trotted to the rendezvous, their large padded paws clumping in the mushy soil toward the lair. When they reached an area near the lair, Dante drove the boat forward as Bob monitored the dog's position. They timed it perfectly, and the boat pulled in front of the lair just as the attack from the dogs began.

Felix went directly for the cluster, taking out a cycle 3 with one clean bite then pouncing on a 4, with part of the 3's head still hanging from his jaws. At the same time, Nevelle and Springsteen tore into the surprised cycle 5's pincer arms, both getting a firm grip at the wrists. The 5, in its pain and utter confusion, didn't know which threat to defend—the one from the marshland or the one just beginning from the bay. It didn't matter because its pincers were being subdued by the large canines' strong jaws and sharp teeth. The dogs employed every ounce of strength to prevent the alien from lifting them off the ground.

The only defense mechanism the 5 had left was its two middle feet and of course, its venom, which it shot at the dogs. It shot like a wet, lethal missile just missing Nevelle's left ear. In an instant, and on impulse, Dante lunged from the boat, climbed up on the 5's shelled back, and put a bullet in its brain. He did this just before it whipped its body to the left, throwing Dante to the right and into the nearby brush. The dying craurchin lashed out in pain and defeat, its high-pitched cry echoing through the thick marshland wood. It screeched its final breath as Dante was making his way back from the dense brush. Bob, in the meantime, docked the boat and killed the remaining cycle 4. Dante and Bob recorded the kills and allowed the dogs some feeding time. That's when they noticed the decomposing body in the 5's lair not far from where Dante had been thrown.

It appeared to be a young female. She was sitting on the damp earthen floor, her back up against a red, rotting maple tree.

Brodsky

Her legs were slightly bent, stiff and covered with blisters. Her face and torso were quite bloated, and there was reddish-white foam leaking from her mouth and nose. Her skin was greenish and her dark, dirty black hair had blond streaks in it.

"How long do ya think she's been dead?" Bob asked as he closed her eyelids, then her mouth.

"I know bloating begins like three or four days after death." Dante, who remembered reading this somewhere, couldn't take his eyes off the corpse. "Hey, what's that?" Dante, covering his nose with his left hand, pointed with his right to what appeared to be a three-inch diameter hole just above her flat belly.

"Look, the blood caked around it is dry. Maybe the craurchin impaled her with its claw." Bob was staring intently, a sick feeling starting to form in his gut.

"It must be that young lady who went missing a few weeks ago," Dante said almost to himself. Neither had seen the copter barely in sight in the distance, mangled and half-buried in the marsh, nor the debris line stretching out behind it. It all kind of blended in with the overgrown chaos that was the Jersey marshland.

"Nah, it's more recent than that."

The two men wrapped the body in a blanket that Bob kept on the boat, bound it tightly with fishing line and some rope, and put it on the edge of the marsh peninsula. They marked the spot with Bob's big white t-shirt tied to a stick so that Sea Isle's undertaker could pick it up later. As he was untethering the boat, Bob saw a shadow of movement in the distance. A long black bullet scurrying among the plants and trees. It came a little closer, stood up on its hind legs, and then froze in its position, staring in their direction.

81

Bob nudged Dante and pointed toward the huge silhouette on the horizon.

"*Fuck!*" Dante whispered. "It's massive. That has to be a cycle 6!"

"Hell! Dante, that may be a 7. Let's get out of here. Cease!"

The dogs, about to attack, headed to the boat. The men gathered their gear and along with the dogs, jumped into the boat and sped off, the dark shadow still holding its position, watching them as they moved away.

Later that day, after Bob's stuffed flounder had been consumed, Dante and Bob sat on Bob's south deck, sipping whiskey and watching the orange sun set over the marshes. Bob had stuffed the flounder with crab meat he caught the day before, and the tasty, hardy dish was settling in their stomachs. He handed Dante a sizable Cubacana cigar he had bartered for at the drop zone. The dogs, completely worn out, had had some dinner and were lazing by their owners. Springsteen lay on his back, spread out and vying for a tummy rub. Nevelle and Felix were lying across from each other sleeping quietly. Every once in a while, Felix's paws would flutter as he chased craurchins in his sleep.

"I'll tell ya, Bob, I just can't get that 6—or whatever it was—out of my head. That thing had to be fifteen feet long. Can you imagine the amount of food that guy must consume?"

"I think it was bigger. Hell, that may have been Adam. How many kill points would he bring in, I wonder?" Bob sipped his drink. "What disturbs me even more is that girl."

"Me too." After some time. "Bob, I've been thinking about this, and I don't think that was a pincer wound on her belly."

Bob nodded his head and had a look of concern on his face. Dante had just confirmed what he was thinking. The look stayed there for quite a few minutes. They sat for a long time, sipping their drinks and puffing their cigars as they watched the day turn into dusk and the dusk turn into complete darkness. Dante thought about what life was like here before the invasion. *Was it always this peaceful? So solemn?* He doubted it. *Peaceful didn't always mean safe, now did it?*

CHAPTER 7
CAPE MAY

We walked to the sea, just my father and me
And the dogs played around on the sand
Winter cold cut the air, hangin' still everywhere
Dressed in gray, did he say, "Hold my hand"
I said, "Love's easier when it's far away"
We sat and watched a distant light
We're two ships that pass in the night
We both smile and we say it's all right
We're still here, it's just that we're out of sight
Like those ships that pass in the night
—"SHIPS," BY IAN HUNTER

CAPE MAY

Three generations of Ballies called Cape May their home. In fact, Grammy Bernstein, Auntie Bridget Burns and the Ballies all lived on the same block on the north side of the Cape, one block from Cape May Harbor and not too far from the old Coast Guard Training Center. Other relatives and friends were spread out on the various nearby blocks. Before the craurchin invasion, M.J. Bally always said, "This is our home and we will always live here, for better or for worse." The Ballies and their forebears dined numerous times each year at the Lobster House, a landmark restaurant at the marina on Cape May Harbor. They also fished from their twenty-foot dual-fan hover boat in the Delaware Bay and forever attended the many year-round events in town or at Congress Hall. They worshipped at the Progressive Christian Church. They were not wealthy like many of the residents of this beautiful Victorian town, where John Philip Sousa once spent an entire summer and wrote "Stars and Stripes," but they got by. They knew who they were and where they came from. They worked hard, they played hard, but mostly they cared for, loved, and looked out for one another.

That was another world in another time that seemed long ago but actually wasn't. On the cape, craurchins flourished in and along the Atlantic Ocean, Delaware Bay, Cape May Canal, and the Cape May Harbor. In fact, the Delaware Bay was referred to by most as Craurchin Bay. The Ballies, along with all of the Cape May Badlanders, or "creurcheonites" as many Heartlanders referred to them, dealt with them on a daily basis. Cape May was no longer the quiet tourist town with its lavish restaurants and quaint bed and breakfasts. It was a town struggling to survive. A town struggling to sustain its existence.

On this day, Lonnie Bally was visiting Grammy. It was a warm, sunny March afternoon. Lonnie was a strong-willed thirty-eight-year-old with piercing green eyes, auburn hair, and a petite frame. She was small but tough. She had a nose ring and her entire right arm was a tattoo sleeve of memories, good and bad. She was the one who suggested to her husband M.J. (short for Mitchell Joseph), that they move Aunty Bridge to the house in between the Ballies and Gram. After the move, she, along with M.J., Joey, and Nicole, connected all three houses with an enclosed corridor. This allowed the safe interaction between the three families without going out-side. Later, they built a high stone wall with metal gates. That was Lonnie, always thinking outside the box, especially when it came to another person's safety.

"Listen, M.J., life is not as it was when we were kids. We have to think about security in every aspect of our lives. Especially on the homestead. If we can't think of our home as the safest place to be, then what can we think of as our safe zone?"

In fact, she was drawing up plans to connect to the houses across the street, move in other relatives, and create a sort of com-pound. And, as was usually the case with Lonnie, this would happen sooner rather than later. She saw the future of Cape May as being a place where the craurchin problem would be solved by locals not the government, and she based this off of the efforts that the Heartland had put into alleviating the problem thus far. Sure, the government still helped. It provided the drop zones and sprayed weekly for the bug problem, but it could do a lot more. A whole lot more.

They were enjoying the beautiful, bright cloudless sky and watching the waves crash on the beach as they sat on Grammy's back deck, sipping iced tea with fresh lemons.

"I can remember when we didn't have this great view, when there were two blocks of houses between us and the sea. If the world didn't end, this place would be worth a fortune."

"Well, Gram, wealth and possessions don't mean much these days. What means something is having your family and friends. And by the way, the world has not ended. It's just—different."

"Speaking of family, where is my beautiful Baby Brim?" Gram's face lit up like a night light.

Lonnie smiled, then gave a loud whistle. "Brimmie! Brim come see GG."

There was some shuffling just inside the house, a bang, and then the pitter-patter of five-year-old Brim running through the door out onto the deck and into GG's wide-open arms.

"GG, GG!"

Brim had been playing with her dog Spanky inside, and of course, he was never far behind. The large Labrador was her best friend and guardian angel. He was also the most patient dog in all of dog history.

"How ya doin' baby girl! Hey, Spunky."

"It's Spanky, GG, Span-kee."

Gram always said that.

"If there were angels, and they occasionally fell from heaven, then that's where Brim came from."

She was a blue-eyed little sweetie with light, wavy auburn hair, like her mother, that fell past her shoulders. Her chubby cheeks were spotted with little freckles. She was feisty, energetic, and filled with a special optimistic spirit not common in the Badlands.

"What's the latest on that crablurchian problem, Lonnie?"

"You mean craurchin, Gram?" Lonnie responded patiently to her ninety-two-year-old grandmother. "Crae-urchin."

"Yes, that."

As Lonnie gazed out on the beach, she was glad her grandmother could not see the multitude of black-shelled creatures scuttling about. So surreal, even to this day. It must have been feeding time. That, or something else was holding their attention.

"Still the same. The Heartland and CMAAC are working diligently on the problem."

The Cape May Alien Assault Committee was started by the Ballies and organized the protection of citizens, Badlanders, who decided to stay. They cleared sidewalks and streets of craurchins and repaired damaged houses, streets, vehicles—anything that needed fixing. They also made the run to the drop zone and distributed food, clothing, and other necessities to the people of Cape May.

"Lonnie—Hi, Gram—Lonnie, we're heading out to the beach, something has gotten the urchies going." M.J. and Nicole were outside, just below the deck with their dogs, Temple and Wilson. They each had a rifle.

"So, I noticed—just be careful."

"Will do, babe. By the way, where is Joey?"

"He and Terrell are working at the radio station. Their shift will be ending soon."

"See ya, mom." Nicole cut in.

"You be careful, Nicki!" *My, how Nicole has grown*, Lonnie thought. As Nicki walked off, her rifle strapped over her shoulder, Lonnie was reminded of the stories her grandmother had told her about the adventures of Annie Oakley. An American folk hero, Annie, was a sharpshooter and traveled in Buffalo Bill's Wild West show in the late 1800s. She would have fit in well in the Badlands.

Lonnie and Gram watched them walk off toward the beach. Gram was looking at her with concern on her face. Lonnie knew that look, and it broke her heart to see it.

"Probably just a pack of wilds having some late breakfast, Gram," Lonnie said reassuredly. She was correct.

THE WILDS

Fourteen-year-old Nicole and her father heard the barking and growling, mostly growling, before they stepped onto the sand. Smaller craurchins were running toward the surf. Some were heading toward the sand dunes where they were presently standing. Their intent was to burrow in the dunes, but the father and daughter duet picked them off one by one. They were mostly 2s and 3s.

"Leave some for the dogs, Nicki," M.J. pronounced.

"Will do, pappa." Nicole, who was an energetic teen with natural, frizzy blondish red hair, knew a thing or two about the beach and its many inhabitants. She was also a fair shot with her rifle. She waited for the dogs to finish up, then took her father's communicator and recorded the kill points.

"Dad, have you ever seen a pack of wilds that large before?" She pointed down the beach toward the shoreline. Temple and

Wilson were apprehensive and panting loudly, their long, pink tongues hanging from their snouts.

"Back to the house, guys, go!" The dogs sprinted back toward the Bally home. He didn't want to disrupt the wilds with the presence of domestic dogs. "Nah, Nicki. That is definitely the biggest pack I've seen. There are what—twenty of them, maybe?"

They proceeded carefully toward the pack, killing and recording hits along the way. When they arrived a safe distance from the commotion, they could not believe what they were seeing.

"Grrrr-arrr."

In the middle of the pack of about sixteen were two cycle 5s being torn apart. The wilds had formed into two groups of eight, one group on each cycle 5. You could see that they were trying to topple the beasts so that one of the dogs could get to the head. Their sixteen tails were wagging wildly, and looked like a cirrus backlit by the sand. A few minutes later, the one group achieved that goal. The smaller of the two craurchins came down, and in an instant, two dogs ripped into its head and neck, opening up its vulnerable velvety skin and spilling alien blood on the wet frothy sand. Both groups were now onto the remaining craurchin, and minutes later, he was dead, hitting the salty Atlantic with a shallow splash. Greenish-red liquid mixed with the salty grayish-blue water.

The canines feasted on the soft, tender inner body, ripping pieces out in an orderly fashion. In their uncontrollable hunger for super protein, none had noticed their fallen packmate. She was sprawled out on the sand, whimpering and struggling to stand up.

"Look, Daddy, that one is hurt!" Nicole was pointing toward a dog on the ground a short distance from the rest of the pack. It broke her heart to see it try to stand and then fall right back down.

M.J. made his way tentatively toward the animal. When he got closer to the canine, he could see her injury. He put his hand out to show he meant no harm, and the dog seemed to understand.

"There, there, girl." He took off his coat and removed his shirt, exposing his thick tattooed arms and chest, as well as his dark olive skin. He wore his salt and pepper hair short. His rugged face and squinted eyes expressed deep compassion.

"Her leg got pierced." He pulled out his communicator. "Joey, where are you?" he asked as he shifted his eyes from the injured dog to the pack, feasting just a short distance down the beach.

"A mile or so from home. Why, what's up, Pops?"

"Get down to the beach in front of our house right away. We need the hover! Got a wounded wild!"

Joey had the family hover. He and his best friend Terrell had used the hover to work their shift at the makeshift radio station on the other end of the cape. Families with hovers were rare in the Badlands, and it could take years to save up enough kill points for one. If a person could prove that they were a special asset to the community, such as a medical doctor or if they made the runs to the local drop zone, then the Heartland might give them a hover. The latter is how the Ballies got theirs.

"On my way!" Joey pronounced.

A couple of the wilds had come up for a breath and were eyeing the human father and daughter suspiciously. One let out a low growl and the other, a huge German Shepherd-Husky mix, nudged him with his snout. The growling immediately stopped. He was the alpha male. They continued to watch as M.J. worked on the injured dog.

"Daddy, what are you doing with your shirt?"

"I'm tying a tourniquet to stop the bleeding. I think she'll be all right."

A few minutes later, Joey pulled up with the hover and parked it in the sand next to the injured wild. Both boys jumped out of the vehicle, never taking their eyes off of the pack of wilds just down the beach.

"Dad, Terrell called Dr. Santos. He's waiting for the dog."

"Way to think ahead, Terrell. Okay, get her head and upper torso. I'll get her legs, on three. Ready, one, two—three."

They lifted the dog and placed her in the back of the hover. They did it quickly before she could realize what was happening. By this time, about half the pack was watching. But none made a move. The four humans climbed into the hover with the injured wild and exited the beach, spraying sand clouds as the hover rose. One of the wilds let out a high-pitched howl. A few joined in as the rest followed the Ballies departure into the distance.

JOEY

Three weeks later, Lonnie and M.J. paid Dr. Santos a visit. The kids had visited almost every day. In fact, a couple of times Lonnie had allowed seventeen-year-old Joey to take Brim, who had named the injured wild "Nala." Joey Bally was a handsome kid with long curly, unkempt hair and hazel eyes. He was a very conscientious, thoughtful, and often sensitive young man who had proven to be a responsible and valued member of the community—and of course the Bally clan. You did not let just anyone take your five-year-old out into the Badlands.

Dr. Leonard Santos welcomed the Ballies into his clinic as he adjusted his round, wire-rim glasses and walked them toward Nala's pen. He wore a white smock over his polo shirt and slacks.

"She is doing very well. I really like the way the wound has healed. Also, she is a very pleasant dog. No resistance to any of the shots I gave her—totally submissive. She will be ready to go in about thirty days or so." Dr. Santos was smiling as they walked with him toward the back of the clinic. Lonnie and M.J. looked at each other quizzingly.

"Lenny, I don't understand. If she's doing so well, why thirty more days?"

Leonard was grinning like the devil. "Well, two days ago, she gave birth to six healthy puppies. I have to make sure the pups and Nala are healthy enough to release. Wait'll ya see these pups, folks. Gorgeous!"

Since the rescue of Nala on the beach, Joey and Terrell had been tracking the pack of wilds. Joey noticed that they had not traveled very far since the day of Nala's rescue, and they seemed to have a pattern of seeking out the larger craurchins, which was indeed a good thing. At night, they would return to their various dens, which were usually on the deck or patio of an abandoned home or in a park under a cluster of trees. Dr. Santos had explained to him that during the breeding season, the wilds, like other canids, usually did less wandering, but outside the breeding season, they tended to be nomadic. However, since there was an abundance of craurchins, their hunting patterns required less roaming.

"They do a lot of sleeping, Doc, even more than any of our dogs."

"That's correct, Joey. It's because they are expending so much energy hunting. They require more rest."

Joey was fascinated with the wilds. He would observe certain behavior patterns and then discuss them with Dr. Santos the next day. And Dr. Santos was more than happy to answer his many questions. One day, Joey was asking Dr. Santos about the wild that appeared to be the leader.

"Well, Joey, the aggressive, large canine is what is called the alpha male. He is basically the boss. He tells the others what to do, and he gets to mate with whatever female or females he chooses. He also gets to eat first. But more than anything, he protects the pack and will always do what he feels is best for the pack."

"What if one of them don't want to listen to him or they want to mate with the same female, Doc?"

"Then there is a problem. He will either fight or he will be banished from the pack. If they fight, the challenger usually is on the losing end of the fight. Sometimes, the outlier will form his own pack. In large packs, at least for wolves, you will sometimes see an alpha male and an alpha female."

On this particular day, Terrell was with Joey and articulated some of his thoughts to the doctor and his best friend. "I think they understand that we are taking care of Nala. I think the alpha knew she was pregnant and that it was his offspring in her belly."

"You may be right, Terrell."

This pattern went on for weeks, Joey observing the pack from a safe distance in the hover, writing down his notes and discussing them with Dr. Santos the next day. He was developing an appreciation and fondness for the wilds that he had never had until now.

Eventually the time had arrived, and Dr. Santos was ready to release Nala and her pups. The puppies had gotten big and feisty. There were four males and two females. All of the females had Nala's blue eyes. The doctor, M.J., and Joey were loading them into a cage to carry out to the hover. Nala was fitted with a leash.

"Please! Please! Please, Mommy. Let me take one home?"

"We talked about this, Brim!" Lonnie shot her *the look*.

"Your mum's right, Brim. You don't want to take a wild away from its pack. Besides, the puppies need their mommy." Dr. Santo looked at her parents and extended his hand to M.J. and gave Lonnie a hug.

M.J. and Joey carried the cage of puppies out to the hover with Lonnie, Brim, and Nala close behind. When everyone was in the hover, M.J. started it up and headed home. When they arrived, Lonnie and Brim climbed out of the vehicle.

"Okay, Brim, time to say goodbye," M.J. said.

Lonnie was dreading this moment.

Brim stretched her little arms out, trying to hug all six at once. They chirped, barked, and licked her arms and face.

"Goodbye!" she said with tears in her eyes, then ran to her mom crying hysterically. Nicole came out of the house and walked over to the hover to say her farewells. She knew she might never see the pups again, knew that wilds were mostly migrant and may not be around again for a while, if ever.

"Bye bye, puppies. Goodbye, Nala!"

REUNITED

When M.J. and Joey arrived at the wilds' den, it was early evening and the dogs were resting after their most recent hunt. Terrell was deep into his latest project and could not join them. The pack had worked their way to the far south end of the cape, to an area called Cape May Point. Many were licking their paws and stretching out on the patio of an abandoned beach house enjoying the cool April evening breezes blowing in off of the inlet. The patio provided shade from the sun and shelter from the rain. From their vantage point in the hover, Joey pointed out the alpha male to his father.

"He is the gray and brown one with the white mask. The big one. The biggest one in the pack. Do you see him?"

"Oh, I remember him from that day. He's impressive."

"I call him Mask," Joey whispered.

"Of course."

Suddenly, they had the attention of the entire pack. The wind must have been diverting their scent away from the dogs, but the wind subsided. Several of the dogs were emitting a low guttural growl. Some were baring their teeth. Mask stifled them immediately. All of the scents coming from the vehicle were familiar but one was extremely familiar. Mask knew this scent very well.

Slowly, Joey climbed out of the hover, his hands raised in a display of passivity. "Mask," he whispered, "It's me."

He opened the back hatch of the hover and unleashed Nala who stepped gingerly from the vehicle. She caught the scent of her pack and took a few wary steps toward Mask, who had his head down and eyes up. He now knew what the familiar scent was and began taking calculated steps toward Nala and the humans. He sensed that the humans posed no danger, but he could take no chances. He and he alone was responsible for the pack. The one standing behind Nala had been watching them for weeks but never gave an indication of any kind of threat. Nala took a few more steps and then stopped and looked back toward Joey and her pups.

"Okay, Dad. Let's get the puppies."

M.J. came around to Joey's side of the hover and together they opened the back door and lifted the cage out of the hover. They placed the cage on the sand a few yards behind Nala, who had not moved.

"Not yet, Dad. Let them catch the scent of the pups."

Mask took several more steps forward as did Nala. They split the difference and when they came face to face began sniffing each other for several minutes. Nala gave Mask a playful slap with her paw as she rolled on her back in the sand, in a show of her submission to the alpha.

"Now, Pops." M.J. opened the cage door and the puppies came running out, sprinting toward their parents. In an instant, the entire pack was jumping around paw slapping and playfully biting the puppies. They were ecstatic. This went on for quite a while, and when Mask looked back at the humans, they were gone.

The puppies could not get enough play time with their new family. Many hours later, when most of the adults were sleeping, probably worn out by the pups, the puppies were still as energetic as ever. Mask was lying next to Nala, head between his huge paws, watching the six newest members of his pack. His pack was now twenty-two. He was grateful to the humans who saved his mate and offspring, and he knew instinctively that they needed each other, dogs and humans alike.

CHAPTER 8

DESTINATION DROP ZONE

Bridges burn and castles fall,
and nighttime follows day,
Some do hear the bells that toll
while others waste away.
In the short history of mankind
multitudes have suffered and perished,
at the hands of bands and barbarians,
who only death and war do cherish
…but sometimes you see, the real enemy,
is not always man but aliens from the sand…
UNKNOWN BADLANDER

JUST ANOTHER MORNING IN THE BADLANDS

Dante grabbed his communicator and set it to binocular mode as he stepped onto his third-floor back balcony and into the late December cold and damp. It had been the end of summer when he and Bob had discovered the corpse and unusually large craurchin.

On that sad and chilling day, the weather was warm, the skies were clear and still. Today, however, the skies over the Jersey shores were gray and filled with puffy white clouds as the sharp, bright sun fought to break between and make its presence known. The chilly wind that blew off the Atlantic caused Dante to shiver. Close behind him followed Neville and Springsteen. He had put in a request for more pups and was hoping it would be approved soon. He tracked and photographed every kill on his communicator and was confident his request would be granted. He still had the highest kill count south of Long Island! He treated every dog he ever owned like family and loved them like family because to him, they were family. These two dogs were no different. They were loyal boys and would lay down their lives for Dante. And man, had they grown in the short three months since he and Bob discovered the body in the Sea Isle marshland.

"Hey, boys, look alive!" Dante clapped as he scanned the Sea Isle boardwalk to the north and then to the south. To the south, a block or so up the boardwalk was a cluster of what Dante referred to as "craw-daddies." He found that if he called them by this name, they were not as intimidating. Nonetheless, he was always aware of their danger and never took them lightly.

Scattered all along the beach were craurchins as far as the

eyes could see. They meandered their way to the ocean from their sand dune burrows for some early morning horseshoe crabs or jellyfish. Others absorbed the sun on their shiny black armored shells. Many of the shells had greenish patterns on them and when taken as a whole, one could form images, like we sometimes do with puffy cloud formations in the sky. Dante got lost in those images for a while, then came back to reality.

As the persistent December wind mixed with snow flurries hit Dante's stocky, muscular frame, he thought about that ancient Bruce Springsteen Christmas song.

It's all cold down along the beach

The wind's whipping down the boardwalk

Hey, band!

(Yeah? Hey, babe!) You guys know what time of year it is?

(Yeah!) What time, huh? What? (Christmas time!)

What? (Christmas time!) Oh, Christmas time!

"Yeah, another Christmas. Hip, hip, fucking hooray!" Dante said aloud.

Springsteen let out a low, long growl when he caught the scent of the craurchin cluster down the boards. His head was lowered and the hair rose on his neck. They could stay on the beach, but the boardwalk and streets were off-limits. At least that's what most towns strove for. Dante and his two dog's sole goal in life was to kill as many craw-daddies as humanly—and—caninely possible. Yesterday, he and the dogs killed over sixty. That was a really good day—and that was a lot of kill points! The government provided certain nonessentials in exchange for KPs. Most of their kills were young cycle 1s and 2s—a very good day indeed. He tried to kill mostly cycle 1, 2, and 3s because those are the only stages in which they procreate.

The larger cycle 5s and 6s he tried to kill simply because they were so dangerous (and challenging). In recent years, it had become a thing for rich adventurous hunters to fly into the Badlands and hunt the craurchins. In fact, the government adamantly encouraged it—kind of a thinning of the herd. Dante referred to them as the modern-day shoobies, a name given to twentieth-century tourists from the big cities, who hit the Jersey beaches with their shoes and lunches packed in brown paper bags. This was all fine with Dante. *Bring it on weekend warriors, the more the merrier!*

Today Dante was heading inland to Sea Isle's closest drop zone in Woodbine with his friend, Khim, but first he and the puppies had some business down on the boardwalk.

"Hey, band, you guys know what time of year this is?" Dante said to his two dogs. They sat, heads tilted to the side. "Yeah, you do."

Neville and Springsteen knew the drill for this particular kill. Their training was solid. They lagged behind half a block as he approached the cluster of six or seven craurchins. Halfway between him and the cluster, the boardwalk heaved like a pregnant rum barrel. This occurred intermittently all along the boardwalk as the sand, piled up from under the boards from burrowed craurchins, forced the planks to bellow up. As Dante decreased the distance between himself and the cluster, he realized there was a cycle 5 in the group. He hadn't noticed before because it was lying flat behind the three cycle 2s and one cycle 3, giving the appearance of a larger cluster of smaller craurchins.

Intentional? Dante wondered. More and more he was questioning the intellect of the craurchin. The 5 stood about five and a half feet long and three feet high, small for a cycle 5. As he drew closer, they took their normal defensive stance. A human against a cluster, especially a cluster with a cycle 5 in it, was a lopsided battle. But not when he had two large dogs!

"C'mon, boys!" He let out a shrill whistle. "Get 'em!" screamed Dante.

The dogs closed the half-block within twenty seconds. Two cycle 2 craurchins ran onto the beach and began burrowing into the sand dunes while the three remaining raised their pincers in self-defense. Springsteen went right for a cycle 3, clamping his jaws around its head and narrowly missing a snap from the cycle 5's left pincer. Nevelle went directly for the cycle 2, biting its head off in an instant. All the while, Dante distracted the large 5, swiping at its head repeatedly with his samurai sword, a wall decoration that came with his house.

It was now three on one. "Team Dante" against the cycle 5. They knew the drill—two distracted the creature while one went for the head. Take out the head (and brain) and you take out the crawdaddy. Springsteen clamped his sharp canines onto its left pincer wrist and Nevelle onto its right. In almost perfect unison, each pulled in opposite directions, stretching the cycle 5 out like some kind of freaky Messiah on the cross, leaving its head vulnerable. It shot some venom, but Dante dodged it and wasted no time decapitating the fucker in one quick swipe with his razor-sharp sword.

The greenish-red liquid spilled from the severed head and neck onto the decaying wood boards. The dogs released their grip and the carcass plopped onto the boardwalk, pincers and legs making a few final twitches, before ceasing all movement. Dante took out his knife and cut off the single horn from its head and placed it in his backpack. He flashed the three dead creatures, recording the kill on his communicator. *Just another morning in the Badlands.*

KHIM AND HAKIRA'S FARM

Later that day, Dante Long's two dogs charged across the greenish-brown field toward the massive orange-brown dog. Jax was his name, and he was a Golden Retriever Giant—a breed of Golden Retriever bred to hunt and kill craurchins. Khim opened the door and let out his other two dogs, Pablo and Kaisha, large Siberian Huskies who ran hastily toward the other dogs, tails wagging and barking cheerfully. Dante walked slowly toward the small farmhouse and the vehicle parked in front of it.

"Hey, Khim Nguyen, what's up with the HV25, my friend?" nodding toward the old hover.

The five dogs were barking, rolling in the field and biting each other playfully as Dante and Khim approached each other, clasped hands, and hugged. Khim adjusted his John Lennon style glasses and twisted his tall, slender body toward the large silver-gray vehicle on the lawn. His dreadlocks hung down to his narrow shoulders. He pointed proudly toward the vehicle.

"Fixed 'er up last week. She's ready to go. I salvaged the parts I needed from a shop 'bout ten miles from here. She's been soaking up the sun for about five days now." He spit some chewing tobacco onto the ground. "The batteries are charged 'n she's good to go—for this trip, anyway."

Because the roads were in such bad shape, hover vehicles were a great mode of transportation in the Badlands. "We'll need new solar panels soon; the photovoltaics are close to thirty years old. I requested them from the Heartland weeks ago. I also requested ammo." he said as he placed his rifle in the back of the hover. "I've got four rounds left."

"Maybe they'll be there today," Dante responded as he retied his bandana around his long brown, shoulder-length hair. "I guess we'll see." Both knew they probably wouldn't.

Dante took in the clean, lush air of the farm and the hint of saltwater marshes that wafted by in the intermittent wind gusts blowing from the east. He was taking a breather after their four-mile walk from the beach. After about an hour of rest and shooting the shit with Khim, Hakira walked out with some refreshments and snacks. "How was the trek here, Dante. Any problems? I really wish you'd let Khim pick you up."

Hakira James was a brown-haired beauty with a tight frame, long slender body and dazzling blue eyes that one could get lost in. Dante, like most men, found her very attractive, but he had too much respect for Khim to even think about her sexually. Besides, she was like a big sister to him. Hakira carried an air of love and genuine concern about her that made you just want to be around her.

"It was fine, Hakira." On the last drop, Dante and the Malamutes had some issues at the Sea Isle Blvd. Bridge. The bridge, being in disrepair, had limited access in one spot where the macadam had completely deteriorated. During the course of time, rain, moisture, and the vicious salt air left the unprotected steel deck vulnerable. Eventually, it completely corroded, leaving a large void between the steel girders.

Locals had patched it up with wood planks and rope leaving a narrow, shaky path across. On the east side of the bridge, a cluster of craurchins was blocking the access. It almost seemed intentional, as if they knew this was a vulnerable crossing to the inland. Below a multitude of larger ones swam in the bay, loitered on pilasters and piers, as if waiting for someone to fall down. The bay was filled with smaller cycle 1s and 2s, hard at work destroying the ecosystem.

Team Dante handily took out the cluster, but during the struggle, Dante had slipped between two of the boards, leaving his right leg badly bruised and bleeding. One of the bastards shot some venom into the open wound, infecting it almost immediately. Said bastard lost his craurchin head shortly thereafter. Hakira took care of the nasty wound once they arrived at the farm. For Team Dante, ten legs were their mode of transportation—at least until Dante was issued a hover vehicle. Probably a hover bike.

I have to get that kill count up, he thought.

"No issues at the bridge this time, but we took out three craurchins on the boardwalk. One was a cycle 5! Also, on our trip here, we ran into a pack of wilds."

"Were they a new pack or locals?" Khim wanted to know. He liked to record and track the wilds.

"I believe they were a new pack and a large one at that— over twenty members. Five or six puppies. I never saw them before.

The alpha was a huge fucker with a white face. They were peaceful and followed us almost all the way here." Dante looked thoughtful. "It was almost as if they were protecting us. Weird, right?"

"Yeah, but even though they can be unpredictable. I've never heard of anyone getting attacked. Have you?"

"Nah, just one incident where some weekend warriors were provoking them." It was quiet for a while as the three of them thought about the wilds following Dante. No one had ever seen this before. Hakira broke the silence.

"All right, drink up. I made these drinks myself. Put in some good vodka from our last scavenge! Here's to a safe trip to the drop and hopefully your new pups." Hakira raised her glass.

"And some ammo," Khim chimed in.

"Here, here," said Dante.

"Here, here," said Khim.

"Latest word from the Heartland is that the number of shipments here may be cut. They're saying that the war is not going well." Khim downed a quarter his drink.

"Fuck! Really?" Dante's face scrunched up in disgust. "We need more drops not less! You know, they don't think twice about cutting support to us, but when they need our boys and girls to pay the ultimate sacrifice for their fuckin' war—well, that's another story. It's always the same shit. Cut support to the folks who need it most, but let the rich fucks in the Heartland get richer."

The Russo-China war had been in the making for centuries, but had escalated at just the wrong time. Namely, at the same time as the craurchin population spurt. The war was a mixed bag of contentions on all sides involving the United State's monopoly on super oil from Sandomars, and Russia and China's alliance and joint attacks against U.S. water supplies, oil lines and other infrastructure. This was obviously a bad time to not be focusing on the alien invasion from Sandomars, but as usual, the men in power were too arrogant and stubborn to try and resolve human conflicts and focus soley on alien conflicts.

You could see by the look on Hakira's face that this was a sensitive issue for her. "You know, I saw a group of hunters last week cruising in on their hovers. Nice clothes, good gear. The Badlands might be their fucking playground but it's our home. They disrespect our rules and put our people in danger."

"Weekend fucking warriors!" Khim chimed in.

"But isn't this a good solution to help cut down the craurchin population?" Dante sipped his drink. "How do you figure they're putting people in danger?"

"They are flushing crawdads out of the sand dunes, and then shooting them as they run out," Khim enthusiastically quipped. "I love that they are making high kill counts, and for the most part, I don't care what weaponry they use to do it, but they are using explosives on the dunes. If they start depleting the dunes, that leaves the entire shoreline vulnerable to flooding! And I do believe we have enough flooding already with the fucking super storms!"

"I'm no scientist but if the sand dunes and beaches start eroding, then the bays and marshes flood and take away more land, which will leave the craurchins with more habitable areas," added Hakira. She was correct. Erosion to these areas without reparations could be catastrophic.

Currently, the craurchins were spread out from the coastline of New Jersey to both sides of the Delaware River and as far west as the Susquehanna River. Further south, they were beginning to take over the Chesapeake Bay, whose streams and rivers sustain the states of Maryland and Delaware.

"Hmm." Dante looked thoughtful. "So, what do we do? Have they been asked to stop this? I assume they have."

"Of course, and they're not lis'ning. They don't respect us or our rules. Never have."

Again, silence as all three pondered this ongoing problem. It was just one of many. Again, Hakira broke the silence. "Okay, enough about that—for now." Hakira pointed toward the hover. "Are you dudes ready?"

"Listen, I see a group of them every so often. I'll talk to them. Yes, I'm ready. Let's do it." Dante hopped in the front passenger seat of the old hover.

Khim and Hakira had one of the few working hover vehicles in the area. They were given extra rations to run their small farm and batteries to power the fans that operated the hover and farm equipment. They served as one of only a dozen or so South Jersey ration houses, meaning they collected their area's drop (with the help of Dante) and brought it back to the farm for distribution.

Sometimes, they delivered food to families that couldn't make the trip to their farm. They also bartered for chicken eggs and fresh goat milk with the locals. Hakira volunteered at the local school and being a former nurse, also volunteered at the local clinic. Also, like everyone else in the Badlands, she, Khim and the dogs, hunted craurchins.

"You know what they say, boys!" Hakira shouted as the men made their way to the hover.

"The Heartland provides medicine, weapons, ammo, and shoes. KPs provide everything else, including booze!" Dante yelled back, laughing.

And it was true. Every mother and father, every daughter and son, had hunt time to kill craurchins, log the kill, and report it to Heartland for kill points. Encouragement by the government to kill craurchins for any and all nonessentials, a government that either couldn't or wouldn't help its people.

Dante and Khim climbed into the large hover truck. Dante called his dogs and Khim whistled for Jax, the perpetually happy Golden Retriever Giant. His other two doggies were sitting this trip out. Staying home to help protect their mother. The three large dogs raced to the truck and one by one leaped on board. Khim fired up the vehicle and it slowly rose a few feet above the grass, the fans underneath whirring softly. They hovered off the farm and headed west toward the drop zone. As they made their way toward the Woodbine drop zone, slowly and quietly, the flat open fields and marshes disappeared and were replaced by heavy pineland.

"I may need to hover over Shore Road this trip. I heard there is a huge tree down on Route 9, and I am not sure we will clear it," Khim said.

The truck could only hover five to eight feet above the road surface so the tree could be a problem. Smaller and newer model hovers could go as high thirty feet, depending on the model. There were also the personal aircraft vehicles, or PACVs, but of course, no one in the Badlands could afford one of those.

"I've taken that road before. It shouldn't be much longer," Dante commented. "A little more remote, but it should be passable." Dante thought about the vast wetlands in that area and the numerous craurchin lairs that would exist there, but kept that information to himself. He was confident that they could handle any difficulties they might encounter.

THE TREK

The two men traveled what were once considered the backroads of South Jersey. Long ago, these roads winded their way through one farm after another. Back then, New Jersey, once deemed the garden state, farmed blueberries, cantaloupes, apple orchards, cranberries, the world's greatest tomatoes, spinach, and corn. These backroads also once served (in a time when life was more comfortable) as scenic alternative routes to the highways and parkways that most vacationers took from Philadelphia and Trenton to the South Jersey Shores. The backroads offered vegetable stands, honky-tonks, antique shops, and less traffic.

Today, the roads were ripped up in most places and spotted with potholes. Crabgrass and weeds grew through the holes and crevices in the aged macadam. Only in populated areas were the roads maintained. On each side of the road, the woods were thick with pine trees and saltwater swamplands. On this day, the sun was bright and optimistic as it reflected off of the tattered roadway. They traveled down flat, straight roads with the sun hitting them low from the east, sometimes to their left, sometimes to their back. As they rounded a soft curb, all three dogs sat up at attention and let out a deep, throaty growl.They instinctively knew not to bark.

"What's up, boys? What're you hearing? What're you smelling?" Khim was concerned, then he spotted what the dogs were smelling. "Dante, do you see it? It's a big one! Looks like a 5 or 6. Holy fuck! He's *big*. Gotta be a 6!"

"Okay, quiet, boys. Khim, do you see any others? Do ya think he's alone? Where's his cluster?"

"Naw, looks like it's just him. I've only got a few bullets. I don't think we can hover over it. If it stands upright, we won't clear. We need a plan—and fast!" He wasn't panicking, but he was definitely concerned. Although the two men were not aware, the cycle 6 was keenly aware of their presence.

KAK0O

The cycle 6 craurchin, referred to as Kak0o by her cluster, saw the craft with the lowlanders slowly making their way toward her. She first noticed them when she had come out onto the road, pursuing some large turtles as they crossed the road, making their way to the saltwater pond on the other side. She was not particularly fast, but faster than the turtles, which were currently in her gut.

Kak0o was easily ten feet tall and at least 600 pounds. Perhaps more. She had three horns on her forehead, the middle one being the largest and most venomous. She sensed that the humans in the craft could not fly over her. She also sensed their fear. Craurchins communicated with each other by a form of telepathy, choosing which thoughts were shared and which were not.

Cluster, come forth! she called to her cluster. She needed to formulate a plan. *I must terminate the canines first. They are the larger threat*, she thought. *I can take two of them with pincer left and strike the third with pincer right. At the same time, I must attack the lowlander with my juice.*

She thought about the human she had at her lair, barely alive. He had been there three days now. *I will finish with him tonight, and tonight, I will have a replacement.*

A quarter-mile up the road, the craft stopped its progression forward. Two canines jumped out and then after a minute or two a human as well. Kak0o took it all in, standing on her back four mammal-like legs, her massive torso-shell pointed at a sixty-degree angle, and her two huge pincers raised above her head, snapping at the sky. Liquid oozed from all three of her pointy, long horns. She called again for her cluster.

Two canines and one human out on the road, one canine still on the craft with one human. They walk slowly toward me. What does the human have behind him? The dog's heads are low to the ground, their eyes glaring at me. Where are you, my cluster?

She could feel the slight stinging sensation as the juice engorged her horns. Rage and aggression filled her very being.

Pak0o, Mak0o, come forth! she called again.

She poised herself in an aggressive stance, waiting for the canines to get closer, and as they approached from her left, she prepared herself to attack. The two dogs and human slowly advanced with the craft floating slowly behind them. She watched them closely as she and they, slowly advanced toward each other. She could hear the soft whirring of the hover's fans.

Snap the canines. Juice or pierce the human. Close in canines, close in canines, close in. Pincer left. Pincer left. Horn center human, horn cent—

The human made a noise and the two canines suddenly started racing toward her. Fifty paces, thirty paces, twenty paces, ten, and then, they suddenly stopped. Unexpectedly from her right, the third canine lunged at her right pincer as she was already in motion, striking to her left, guiding her left pincer toward the two canines.

Where did it come from? she thought as Jax connected, clamping his massive jaws on her right pincer arm. She stood upright again, lifting the canine with her, but he held on tight, refusing to release his grip. Springsteen and Neville charged and bit her legs as they avoided her swinging left pincer.

BACK AT THE HOVER

Dante watched the large craurchin stand on its hind legs, raise its pincers to the sky, and release a bone-chilling, ear-piercing screech. It was very unsettling, and he prayed their plan would work. It had to work.

He never took his eyes off the monster as he walked with deliberate, carefully measured steps behind his dogs, while Khim and Jax slowly followed in the hover behind him, all moving slowly and carefully toward the large craurchin.

"Khim, you ready?"

"Ready, man, say when."

"Slow and steady, slow and steady, slow and—now!"

In a loud voice, he had commanded Jax, Springsteen, and Neville to attack. Springsteen and Neville from the right side of the hover, Jax from the left. At about forty paces, he shouted, "Cease, Neville. Cease, Spring!" They did—just ten paces short. Meanwhile, Khim commanded Jax, "Keep going, boy! Fast!" The huge Golden increased his pace and like a shot was on the beast whose full attention was on the other two dogs.

When Dante saw the beast divert its attention to Jax, he signaled his dogs to attack as he sprinted behind them, sword drawn. Kak0o never heard the dogs coming but felt the pain as they each latched onto her left hind leg. The massive creature was now standing semierect, swinging poor Jax to and fro. Dante raised his sword and began slashing at the creature's swinging left pincer. He saw his two dogs attacking the crawdaddy's left side.

Khim used the opportunity to pass by with the hover. He saw an alien creature in obvious pain trying to fling off Jax and maneuver himself away from the biting dogs.

"Come on, motherfucker!" Dante shouted, trying to psych himself up. "Down here!"

Suddenly, the craurchin lowered her body to try and get closer to the dogs, who were causing tremendous damage to her left leg. As she came down, Dante seized the opportunity and swung toward her large neck.

"Ahh—ugh." He missed her neck but hit her right pincer shoulder. The slash, combined with Jax's unfettered grip and weight, severed the pincer clean from her body. Jax went flying with the limb still clutched in his jaw.

Enraged and in incredible pain, she swiped with her remaining left pincer, narrowly missing Dante and Nevelle, but piercing Springsteen in the side.

Springsteen howled in pain as he rolled over three or four times. He limped toward the hover vehicle ahead where Khim was directing him, but then stumbled. "Come on, boy." Khim, standing in the craft, raised his rifle, ready to take a head shot, when he noticed the two cycle 4s, which had emerged from the woods.

"In the truck, everyone!" Dante ordered. He hadn't seen the massive damage done to Springsteen yet. The large craurchin was ready to attack him and Nevelle when he heard the crack of the rifle and then watched the craurchin's head crack open. It was alive but very disoriented and Dante took advantage of the stumbling creature and finished it off with his Z gun. The powerful laser hit the creature square in what remained of its head, splattering brain matter, tissue and bone in all directions, as the dead craurchin hit the road with a loud thump. When he turned his attention to Springsteen, two smaller craurchins were dragging his injured dog into the woods.

The dog was bleeding profusely, his innards hanging out. He raced over along with Nevelle but the 4s were moving fast. Dante's eyes followed the trail of blood where they dragged him along! Enraged, he charged the creatures, but three more craurchins emerged from the shadows. "Crack, crack, crack." Khim discharged his last three bullets. One hit a craurchin, one went into a tree, and the third into Springsteen's head. Dante watched his dog's life leave his body, his world is spinning. His head felt heavy and inflated, like it was ready to explode. Anger, sorrow, fear, and rage rushed through his entire being. Mostly rage. He chased the beasts into the woods, his loyal Neville at his heel.

"Come on, Dante! Leave it." Khim was frantic as he saw in the distance the rest of the dead craurchin's cluster making their way to the road. "*Now*—or I leave without you!"

Dante knew Khim would never do that but decided to head back to the hover before things got too hairy. As they headed back to the road, they met and took out the remaining cluster, which consisted mostly of small craurchins. Dante then lifted up what was left of Springsteen's broken body and ran to the hover. Nevelle would never have allowed him to leave without Spring.

Winded, gasping for air, Dante climbed into the hover after placing Springsteen's body in the cargo bed. Neville jumped in the back seat with Jax. For most of the trip, Dante was quiet and introspective. His silence engulfed the space like a tent. The dogs were curled up, comforting each other as only canines can do.

When they were a safe distance from the cluster, Khim stopped the hover truck, gathered himself, and took several deep breaths. He looked into Dante's eyes as he carefully formed his words.

"When they reach cycle 5, they like to keep their victims alive while they take their blood. They keep the heart beating and pushing warm blood through the veins. They prefer warm blood, Dante. They would have kept Springsteen alive for days—he would have suffered terribly. I know this because it happened to me."

Shocked and unable to find the words, Dante wiped a tear from his eye and used his sleeves to rub the snot and blood from his nose. He nodded in understanding and gave his friend an acknowledging nod, then a hug. "Let's go get those bullets, Khim."

They reached the drop zone a short time later. The place was bustling with activity. Folks from all parts of the South Jersey Badlands were there to collect their rations and cash in on their kill points. Hunters from the Heartland were arriving to begin their hunting trips. There were workers unloading cargo, as food and drink were shared. Stories were exchanged among groups of ragged-looking men and women. Badlanders. Warriors.

Dante and Khim loaded the hover with their territory's rations for the better part of an hour. Dante collected a handgun and ammo with his acquired kill points, and then the helicopter pilot pointed toward a cage in the corner. Inside were two white puppies. On the cage was an envelope of official Heartland stationary addressed to Dante. He opened the envelope and read the letter inside:

Dear Mr. Long,

If you are reading this letter you have probably received the protection canines that the Department of Heartland Security has sent to you. They are yours to train and love. We thank you for your continued service to this country, and we will continue to support brave men and women such as yourself in your fight to preserve the east coast of this great nation.

As the war with Russo-China continues, the Heartland will persevere and eventually defeat our human enemies. We will then turn our full attention to the eastern seaboard and defeat our nonhuman enemies.

Stay strong.

General Martin Gaines II

Department of Heartland Security

December 10, 2265

Dante crunched up the letter and threw it on the ground.

"Fuck you!" he said aloud. He then opened the cage, scooped up both pups in his sweaty, muscled arms, and walked back to the hover, happy for the first time that day.

CHAPTER 9

THE TAKING

Susie is here and Bobby is dead,
A cycle 5 pierced his knobby head.
Sara is fine but Raheem is hurt,
A cycle 6 shot a toxic squirt
Yani was bad, went on the beach w'out his dog
And a cycle 7 happened along
Lin forgot her gun 'cause she was running late
A block down the road she met a cycle 8!
—BADLANDIAN NURSERY RHYME

TALONS OF STEEL

Fourteen-year-old Terrell Williams was not your typical American kid. No, sir, he was not your typical Badlander kid either. He was five foot nine inches tall with a short-cropped afro, smooth brown skin, and soft, pleasant facial features. He was very popular with the teenage girls on the cape. Like every Badlander child, he was in tune with the hostile environment in which he lived, and he was raised to take nothing for granted. He was also an extremely intelligent child, a genius really—an odd combination of nerdy and cool.

He was tagged as nerdy because he was always quoting facts from the multitude of books he had read and the long research papers he wrote that no one would ever read. Cool because he applied his knowledge and skills to real-life inventions and serious solutions. For example, one time he retrofitted a drone, owned by his father's best friend Jackson, to kill craurchins without actually shooting them.

"Listen to this, Dad. It says here that seagulls swoop up clams off of the beach and then fly up high in the sky and drop them on rock beds to break the shell so that they can eat the meat."

"Cool, man, very cool," Mr. Williams replied.

"I thought so, Dad."

Coincidently, that same day, his dad's best friend Jackson was at the house for a visit. Jason Williams and Uncle Jackson were sitting around the kitchen table drinking homebrew and talking about kill points. That's practically all they ever talked about—kill points and the government.

"I've got this drone. Took me almost a year to build up the KPs. I couldn't swing the UMAV-22, so I had to settle for the UMAV-8."

"Oh hell no! The 22 would take five years to save for. That's a badass drone, Jackson."

"Yeah, it's the one you see the shoobies from the Heartland using. I mean the 8 is cool, don't get me wrong. It can fly out to sea and catch me some fish. It can also patrol—the camera on it is amazing, but damn, if It had the capability to shoot lasers, or even bullets, that would truly be goddamn great."

"Yeah, that would definitely bring up yer KPs big time. Can it track craurchins?"

"Unfortunately not, only fish. For some reason, nothing else. But thanks to your son, we can at least eat the fish again. Hell yeah!"

This gave Terrell an idea. The next day, he started working on plans. A week later, when he felt his sketches were just right, he, his best friend Joey, and his brother Zak collected the parts he would need to build his new invention. Within three weeks, he built a pair of hawk-like talons from light metal and aluminum salvage from around the cape. He then attached the hawk talons to the bottom of the drone. It was tricky, and very time consuming, but he got it to work. After that, he altered the drone software so that the talons could be controlled by a communicator. A few preliminary test runs, a few tweaks to the software, and he was ready for the final test run of his new hawk drone.

Once he got the hang of swooping down on craurchins and clutching them with the hawk drone talons, he taught Uncle Jackson how to operate the modified drone. Within days, Jackson had gotten the knack for it and was racking up kill points. In no time at all, he could fly his newly upgraded UMAV-8 onto the beach and snatch up craurchins, sometimes two at a time, then fly it high into the air over the nearest street and drop them onto the hard macadam road below, where they smashed into pieces. It could handle up to cycle 3s, the lighter craurchins whose shells had not yet super-hardened. For his efforts, Terrell received half of all Jackson's KPs. That was young Terrell Williams. Everyone in the Cape Badlands knew he was special, knew that he was a huge asset to the community. Some would even say he was a prodigy.

HOW TO IMPRESS A GIRL

One morning, Terrell was with his two older brothers Zak and James at one of the cape's barter markets. He was outside of the store holding a box of dry goods, waiting for his two brothers to come out. His dog Einstein was lying on the sidewalk, watching out for craurchins. Out of nowhere, she appeared.

"Hey, Terrell. You coming to the bonfire on Friday? I hear there's gonna be marshmallows!"

"Yeah, Tasha, I'll be there."

Tasha, who was just a year older, thought Terrell was cute, and she thought his current blushing was adorable. Terrell had a huge crush on her, and he knew that she knew it. He was not exactly calm and collected when around her.

"Well, you gonna show me how you cook marshmallows. I hear you got a secret technique!"

Be cool, Terrell. Don't be a dork, he said to himself. "I can show you my secret, but it'll cost you," he said with a shaky voice and a goofy grin. *Oh, shit. I'm such a doofus!* he thought. He could feel his face flushing.

"Terrell!" Tasha was having a blast. "Terrell, whatta you mean cost me? You *better* teach me your technique! Whatta ya mean, it'll cost me?"

His brother suddenly emerged from the market.

"Hey, Terrell, who's yer girlfriend?" James knew who Tasha was. Everyone on the cape knew who everyone was. Terrell was now three shades of red and fumbling for a reply when Zak stepped out of the market and saved him.

"Terrell, James, let's go. We need to be back by ten. Hi, Tasha. I hope you're not here alone."

"No, my dad is inside. Bye, Terrell. I'll catch you Friday night?"

"Bye, Tash. See you then." Terrell was excited and embarrassed all at the same time.

He spent the rest of the day thinking about Tasha and working on sketches for a multi-marshmallow cooker. He had some ideas but needed to vet them out on paper. He knew metal conducted heat and wanted to work along those lines. By the time he had his sketch complete and was satisfied with the results, the sun was down and his father was calling everyone to the kitchen table for dinner. His dad was a horrible cook.

"Let's go, boys! Dinner!"

God, I miss Mom's cooking, Tyrell thought.

Two years ago, his mother had died. It was not a craurchin attack, thank God, but it was tragic nonetheless. Martha Williams had a passion for cooking. It was a God-given gift, and she loved nothing more than to share this gift with her family.

One day, Martha had been at the Barter Market on Columbia Avenue, looking for some fresh fish and good ingredients to make a nice fish stew. It was one of the family's favorites. It wasn't always available, but lately, there were stripers coming in from the fishermen who were using drones to carry their lines out past the craurchin cluster line, out to a point in the sea where the fish were running free from craurchin interference.

"Yeah, so when the fisherman gets a hit on his line, the drone, which is hovering above, pulls the line out of the water and brings it back to shore. Pretty slick, huh?"

"Very slick!" Martha started coughing loudly. "Very slick indeed!" She followed with more sickly coughs.

"Martha, are you okay?"

She was not. A week later, the cough was worse. She had chronic pain in her chest and shortness of breath. The antibiotics Dr. Santos had given her were not working. Three weeks later, Jason Williams was loading up his friend Jackson's hover and taking his wife and three sons to the drop zone. There, Mr. and Mrs. Williams would board a hovercopter to a hospital in the Heartland, the closest hospital that had any reasonable hope of treating the disease that was killing her.

"Zak, I know we had our talk, but I'll say it again—I am counting on you to take care of your brothers and the dogs and the house, and, of course, yourself." Jason's eyes were red and puffy. "He'll be fine, Jason. He's a strong young man." Martha began coughing uncontrollably before finishing her thoughts. "I know he'll do what needs to be done. I know he'll take care of his brothers."

They said their teary goodbyes, all four men empathetic and wanting to go with their mother, none of them knowing what the future held for her—or them for that matter. "Sad" did not begin to describe how they felt. The anxiety and fear in their respective hearts held a firm grip on each of them.

"I'll be okay," she assured them. "Just be hungry when I get back 'cause I am cooking a feast! You too, Jackson."

That was the last time the boys saw their mother. Three weeks later, what was left of their father returned home. He had transformed into a broken and depressed man.

Now, two years later, Terrell still missed her immensely. He thought about her all the time and he knew his brothers and father did as well. He knew deep down that a distraction like Tasha was a good thing and that his mom would have approved. And so, he concentrated his efforts on keeping his word to meet up with her on Friday night and impress her with his latest invention.

"Dad, after dinner, I need to scavenge the neighborhoods for some materials for my project." He shoveled some instant potato-noids and ground beef, always overcooked, into his mouth. "I just need to find the right metal and some plastic bushings and some springs."

His father was tossing a salad of lettuce, carrots, and onions from the garden and mixing mayonnaise and ketchup for the dressing. "Only if one of your brothers can go with you. Also, don't stay out for more than an hour. You know the rules." Mr. Williams turned his head toward James.

"Sorry, Terry. I'm staying put tonight, bud." No surprise James couldn't help him.

"Zak, how 'bout you?" Pop now turned to his oldest son. Zak was always there for Terrell and was about as good a big brother as a kid could have. They had a special connection that only grew stronger with the loss of their mother.

"Sorry, pal. I am volunteering with the Cape Action Committee tonight. We're patching up some damaged roadway on Maryland Ave. I'm already committed."

"C'mon, Dad. I can go alone. I'll be fine. I'll have Einstein with me."

"Ab-so-lutely not! Don't ask again."

"Well, I need my parts so I can complete my project by dusk tomorrow for the bonfire!"

"I can take you in the morning, T-man, sound good?" Zak was again to the rescue.

"Sure," Terrell said with obvious disappointment in his voice. He really wanted to work on it this evening. "Thanks, Zak."

The next morning, Terrell was up before sunrise. He fixed himself a bowl of fresh grains and condensed milk, which he ate while reading Heartland USA on his communicator. He was immersed in a story about a growing company called CraTek that developed products from craurchin shells. They already had a line of laser-proof vests that the military was using. They were currently testing a line of safety helmets, commercial building products, and various shell composites.

The article mentioned that CraTek believed that the craurchin shell was the strongest substance on Earth. They'd spent a lot of money on research and believed that their technique for processing raw craurchin shells created a product that was stronger than diamonds, metallic glass, and even graphene.

CraTek still hasn't discovered what I already know, Terrell thought proudly. *Namely that the underside makes an amazing purifier.* Every citizen from Cape May to Atlantic City had one, and it was because of Terrell and his two years of study, hard work, and foresight. *Wow I should work for CraTek. We could do some amazing things together. It really sucks that the space program was defunded. That's where I truly need to work.* Terrell turned his attention to his latest project. He peeked in on Zackary and saw that he was still sleeping soundly.

He whispered softly, "Zak?" got no reply and then tried again. "Zak, hey Zak."

He quietly closed the door. Even Zak's dog Petro wasn't budging. He didn't want to wake his brother because he knew Zak had gotten home late last night. He tinkered with his design a little more, grew bored, and then decided he could scavenge on his own. No need to wake Zak. Besides, he would have Einstein with him, and he wasn't planning on venturing far. He would be back before any of them even awoke. And so, he grabbed his backpack, his Z gun, whistled for Einstein, and quietly left the house.

BAK0O

The cycle 6 that took Terrell was called Bak0o. She was a small 6, approximately ten feet tall when standing upright, but fierce. Bak0o's lair was at the old Cape May wetlands area in South Cape

May. It was lush, damp marshland with tall marsh grass, herbaceous plants, cattails, sawgrass, and many other plants, insects, and wildlife. Although the wildlife population wasn't what it once was, it was still thriving. The lair itself was set on the edge of a peninsula, a mushy, muddy nest of sand, sticks, and saplings. There was plenty of food to sustain her, but on occasion, she would venture to where the humans lived. She knew there was larger, more substantial prey there.

She spotted the boy human and canine in the empty structure just off the beach. She stayed downwind of them so the canine would not catch her scent, and she patiently made her way to the abandoned structure. Slow and steady, she evaded breezes that would carry her scent. Still, there was no reaction from the canine who was sniffing around the kitchen. She crawled closer. She was now within striking distance. It was still dark, but the sun would be up soon.

"Grrr." Einsteen smelled her and attacked.

Come to me. Yes, come to me, Bak0o thought. When the lone dog attacked her hind leg, she struck him with her large pincer, throwing him across the room and knocking him out instantly. It was a miracle the dog was not dead. The boy stood there in shock and horror and before he could react, she lunged forward and pierced his stomach with the sharp tip her middle horn. He stood for a few seconds and then the paralysis took effect. He could not scream. He could not even move his lips. Instantly, his entire lower body went numb, then limp, and then he collapsed. She then wrapped her long tail around his torso and dragged him out of the structure, down the beach, and back to her lair. An old woman sweeping her porch thought she saw a cycle 5 dragging a boy down the beach but thought it could also have been a dead porpoise it was dragging.

"It was all so surreal," she would later report.

EINSTEIN

Jason Williams sat in the kitchen, drinking his bitter coffee and thinking about what he should make for breakfast. The boys were still in bed, or so he thought, and he liked calling them down for a big breakfast to start their day. He opened the cold box door and peered in. The light flashed on and off, on and off, then settled to on.

"Goddamn generator. Man, I hope it isn't going on me," he said aloud. He sat thinking about the lifespan of the GS-20. *Did the Heartland say two years or was it four?* As he stood staring into space, in his quiet kitchen, he heard a scratching sound. It was coming from the front door. He layed the carton of eggs he had snatched from cold box on the table.

As he walked closer to the door, the sound was louder, and he could also hear whimpering—dog whimpering. *Aren't all of the dogs in bed with their humans?* He walked to the front door.

"Einstein. What the hell—*Einstein*? Einstein, is that you?" He swung the door wide open and saw Terrell's dog on the stoop. He was whimpering and visibly upset. The hair on the back of his neck was standing up, and he had his tail between his legs, as he cowered on the stoop.

"Einstein, hey boy. It's okay, bud. It's okay. Where's—hey what's in your mouth?" Panic filled his very being. *Is that a communicator?*

"Give it here, Einstein."

It was, and even worse, it was Terrell's.

CHAPTER 10
THE THIRD ORDER OF BUSINESS

The Negroes in the forest brightly feathered
They are saying, "Forget the night.
Live with us in forests of azure.
Out here on the perimeter there are no stars
Out here we is stoned – immaculate."
Listen to this, and I'll tell you 'bout the heartache
I'll tell you 'bout the heartache and the loss of God
I'll tell you 'bout the hopeless night
The meager food for souls forgot
I'll tell you 'bout the maiden with wrought iron soul
— "THE WASP (TEXAS RADIO AND THE BIG BEAT)," THE DOORS

THE THIRD ORDER OF BUSINESS

It was late October on a warm evening and the council was having their bi-weekly meeting at the community center. M.J. and Lonnie were on the committee and in attendance. M.J.'s cousin Rory Bally had volunteered to host a bonfire on the beach for the community. Joey would forego the bonfire and stay home with Grammy and Auntie Bridge. With the exception of the occasional Heartland defector and other renegades that took up residency in the Badlands, everyone tried to do their part.

"Okay, before we begin, did somebody secure the building? Are the dogs being attended to? Yes? Okay, good. Thanks, Ben. Tonight, we will be covering three main topics."

Freddie May, a large man with a contagious smile, short black afro, and gray beard, was the chair. He emphasized his words using animated gestures with his large arms and hands. "The first—who will volunteer to help the Ballies repair the Elmira Street Bridge? We talked 'bout this two meetings ago 'n MJ pointed out that we needed some supplies from the Heartland. Well they hooked us up with some volunteers from Western Pennsylvania who delivered the materials we needed a couple days ago."

"My two son's and I can help." A voice from the back called out.

"I can help." A female voice from the third or fourth row.

"Thanks Peter, thanks Mira. Anyone else?" Silence. "Mitchell Joseph, will four more bodies do the trick?" Freddy had a habit of calling almost everybody by their formal name, even though almost no one called him Frederick.

MJ shook his head. "That will be fine. Thanks, guys, meet us at the bridge at eight in the morning the day after tomorrow."

"I can bring you guys down some lunch," sweet Mrs. Schmitt volunteered.

"Thanks, Mrs. Schmitt," the bridge repairers replied, almost in unison.

"Thanks, Mrs. Schmitt. Can somebody make sure Emma has an escort to the bridge? Okay. All right, the second order of business—we need volunteers to prepare food for the next drop zone run. Stone Harbor did it last month and from all accounts it was pretty good. They had lots of great food and drink and even brought in some entertainment."

BACK AT THE BEACH

On the beach, Rory and his two sons were creating a no-fly-zone around the bonfire area. The area within the perimeter would be craurchin-free and guarded by five teenagers who would prevent any of the many 1s, 2s, 3s, or 4s from crossing the four-foot-wide ditch they reshoveled in the sand. The smaller craurchins appeared to be apprehensive of fire so the job would not be too difficult. But in the Badlands, you didn't assume anything—nothing was left to chance. As citizens started arriving on the beach, Rory drove that point home to the teenage sentries who had volunteered to stand guard.

"Thanks again, men and women for volunteering. I guess I don't have to tell you how important your job tonight is. We are putting the lives of these people in your hands. Kill only cycle 1s, 2s,

3s, and 4s. Anything bigger than a 4, you call for help. You can also run to the bonfire and grab one of us. Your dogs stay within twenty feet at all times. We have had more and more cycle 5s rearing their ugly craurchin heads, so keep an eye out, and pay attention to your dogs' warnings. As you know, their growl is more intense when they smell a 5. I am happy to let you know that you will get, not only the kill points you earn tonight, but bonus KPs for volunteering. Okay, are we good? Rodney?"

"Yes, Mr. Bally!"

"Monica?"

"Absolutely, Mr. Bally!"

"Sammy?"

"I cool, Mr. Bally!"

"Izzy?"

"Yes, Mr. Bally!"

"And Raul?"

"You betcha, Mr. Bally!"

Back at the bonfire, they had dug a pit and were starting to fill it with kindling. "We need more kindling to get this thing going." They had been piling up firewood all week long but somehow kindling was overlooked.

"No biggie, there's lots of it in the area. We just need to gather it." Rory's oldest boy Raj saw no issue with gathering dead branches from the trees just off the beach. Rory saw it differently.

"Okay, Raj. You do the gathering, and Carson, you cover him. Take that sand slider and fill it up, then come right back—and bring dogs!"

Raj and his best friend Carson, along with their dogs, headed toward the stand of trees just off the beach. The sand slider followed behind them.

"So, Carson, have you seen Terrell? I was looking forward to seeing what crazy-ass invention he came up with for the marshmallows."

"No, come to think of it, I haven't. I know your cousin Joey won't be here. Maybe he's with him."

It was low tide, so there was a lot of beach between the bonfire and ocean. The sun would be setting soon, and they needed to get the fire going in the next half hour. Rory had planned the bonfire around the tides and the timing would be perfect. The tide would be up to the bonfire at just the right time to extinguish it.

"This is one of those situations where a drone would come in handy."

"How so, Rory?" Raheem and Rory grew up together in the cape. Both had started families in the cape and both had decided to stay in the cape when all hell broke loose. Raheem, who was in his early forties, was not the most technically inclined man but made up for it in many other ways. Like Rory, he only had one kid, who happened to be Rory's son Raj's best friend.

"Well, for one, most have programs that, via satellite, can give you not just the locations of urchies, but their cycle size as well. It will literally show you their cycle number and location. You like, see the number 5 moving on the screen as it tracks the movements of the cycle 5. Speaking of which, there's been more and more 5s being spotted and I gotta tell you—I'm concerned. It will be the main topic at tonight's committee meeting.

I'm going to tell you something but you have to keep it quiet just until tomorrow."

"What is it?" Raheem looked concerned as Rory explained.

While they were talking, several more children, teenagers, and adults were arriving, all of course, with their dogs. Nicole strolled onto the beach with her little sister Brim, and their dogs Spike and Spanky in toe. Sitting quietly by herself in the circle of chairs that had formed around the fire pit, Tasha was wondering why Terrell was not there. Had he not picked up on her obvious advancements?

"What do marshmellers taste like? Are they gooey? What is gooey? I'm not sure I've ever had something gooey?" Brim had never eaten a marshmallow, and it was all she could talk about. Lonnie had used a bunch of her kill points to purchase the soft, sugary treats, and the kids were all excited.

Raj and Carson were finally back with the kindling and placed it strategically in the pit along with bits of paper here and there. Raheem struck a match, lit the pack on fire, and started lighting the pieces of paper that were stuck in between kindling. The kindling started igniting, and they put some of the smaller pieces of wood on top. As the kindling and wood started to burn (with the help of the soft ocean breeze), larger pieces of wood were added. Soon enough, the bonfire was crackling to life. In a short while, the bonfire lit up the night sky and shed its warm light out to the perimeter, which Cape Badlanders had created many years ago.

This location of beach, just a half-block north of the Bally homestead, had been established as a community social spot. It was used for meetings, dances, barbeques, and of course, bonfires. The perimeter moat had been dug and filled with rocks and broken glass to slow craurchins trying to cross. There were tiki torches at each corner and in between. They were planning on running barbwire coils around eventually, once their request for them was granted or they salvaged some from a nearby abandoned factory or lumber yard.

Beach chairs were spread around the bonfire. Adults were drinking jazz juice or sipping on homemade wine, chatting it up as the fire crackled in front of them. Every so often, they would hear the sharp *pop* of a .22 or the *zoop* of a laser as the teens secured the perimeter of small craurchins. It mixed in with the crackling of the fire. Children were playing close by, building sand sculptures, or melting marshmallows on sticks in the fire.

"Careful there, Tara," one mother told her child. "Not too close to the fire."

THE THIRD ORDER OF BUSINESS

"Okay, people. Shall we discuss the third order of business? Then we'll open the floor for discussion."

Freddie was a good leader with a natural knack for keeping order, sticking to the business at hand, and being fair and equitable with all. Tonight, his leadership skills would be of utmost importance.

"Tonight, Alonza Bally is going to talk. Lonnie, would you please speak to the third topic tonight?" Nobody ever referred to Lonnie as "Alonza," but coming from Freddie, it sounded proper.

"Sure thing, Freddie." She cleared her throat as she walked up to the podium. "The third topic concerns cycle 5s. We are seeing more and more 5s lately, and it doesn't seem to be leveling. Every day, we hear another report of either an incident or a siting."

She pulled a sheet of paper from her pocket and began reading. "This list is extensive so I'll start in July, almost four months ago. Keep in mind that it goes back much further."

She then read verbatim the timeline of events outlined on her list.

"July second, Jane Langly attacked by a lone cycle 5. She escaped in her hover. July fourteenth, a cycle 5 with a cluster of 2s and 3s was spotted on the banks of the Cape May Creek. July nineteenth, Omar Brown and his dog took out a lone cycle 5 while hunting on Perry Street Beach. Omar owns a Z gun and is a good shot. This was only five days after the creek siting. July thirtieth, a group of weekend warriors took out a large cluster consisting of two cycle 5s, a 4, and a half-dozen 2s and 3s. One of the hunters got careless and was killed. This happened on Diamond Beach. August fifteenth, a pack of wilds were spotted at Cape May Point Park fighting a cycle 5. Jamie Peterson did not stick around to see the outcome but reported that the dogs were winning that battle. September second, a pack of wilds was spotted by Lona Fitzpatrick taking on a cluster with one 5 and several 4s. She owned a Z gun and assisted in killing one of the 4s.

"More and more, the wilds are becoming less aloof to humans and seem to be welcoming our assistance. I believe they intuitively understand how the invasion is all of our problems and that we are all, man and dog, fighting the same enemy. Dr. Santos is working on some theories and will be speaking at our next meeting about how wild animals have been known to break protocol for the sake of the pack. Let me continue.

144

"September twelfth, Roberto Martinez reported a cycle 5 literally walking down Beach Street at four in the morning. Walking down the street, not a care in the world! September twenty-second, Missy Johnson opened her back door to let in her dog, only to find a 5 attacking her dog. She grabbed her shotgun and fired headshots from the doorway. Most of her shots hit its shell but it was enough to scare him off. Her dog Buster was uninjured."

Lonnie stood and took in everyone's reaction. All around the room she saw faces of shock and some of horror. Some knew of these increased incidents with 5s or bigger but most did not. Several started commenting, but she hushed them before they could begin.

"Okay, okay, you'll get to speak your mind and ask questions, but let me finish up this list! I've got one more. Please, please, listen up." The crowd grew silent.

"Thank you. This last item is quite upsetting, so please be calm. On October twenty-first—this morning—young Terrell Williams was carried off by, what we believe was a 5 and its cluster. As you can imagine, his family, and mine for that matter, is beyond distraught, and his father and two older brothers, along with twenty volunteers, have been searching nonstop. This is why we decided to have this meeting a week early."

The audience erupted in questions. Folks wanted to know how they could help. What they could do to prevent this from happening again.

"How did this happen?"

"Where could it have taken him?"

Lonnie was not the least bit surprised at how visibly upset

145

everyone was. Everyone wanted to know what they could do. Everyone.

"How did this increase in cycle 5 craurchins happen so suddenly?" Dave Shah wanted to know. Dave had one of the highest numbers of kill points on the cape.

Freddie May was back at the podium. "Good question, Dave. As we all know, craurchins double in size every cycle. And as we all know, a cycle is twenty years or so from the date of birth. We always want to kill the most 4s because once they reach 5, they become extremely dangerous. Well, it is this simple—we didn't kill enough 4s."

"What are you talking about, Freddie? Cape May County alone took out ten thousand cycle 4s last year." Brenda Chu was a researcher who had moved to the Badlands to collect data for her employer CraTek. She and her partner Leona Wilkes lived on Cape May Point.

"The latest scientific studies from the Heartland indicate that between cycles, craurchins either burrow in the sand or head out to sea. We do not hunt them in the sea, people. When they are going through their change, they may not be on land!" M.J. Bally was making a point. "Getting out of the inlet can be dangerous. This is something the Heartland needs to fund! This fucking war is going to be the death of the entire east coast!"

M.J. was livid. From the moment he had understood this problem, he had spent every waking hour thinking about it. His frustration was reaching its boiling point. "We need hove boats! Hove boats can get over the craurchins clogging up the inlet. If the Heartland doesn't provide exterminators, then they need to provide us the boats!"

THE NORTHERN PERIMETER

Back at the bonfire, everyone was enjoying themselves. The adults were sitting in their beach chairs, some telling stories and some singing as Shelly Martin strummed her guitar. The dogs had formed a pack and were playing in the sand with several balls and old frisbees. There were a couple of children joining them.

Brim adored her cousin Raj, who was showing her how to roast marshmallows on a stick. "The trick, Brim, is to not let it catch fire. You get it just close enough to char and melt a little."

"Like this, Rajie?"

"Yes. Make sure you turn it every so often."

"Look, Uncle Rory, I'm cookin' marshmellers!"

"Good job, Brimmers!"

Raj kneeled next to her and checked her progress. "Now for the best part, Brim. You get to eat 'em!"

Nicole sat on Brim's other side. "Before you eat it, Brim, blow on the marshmallow like this." She demonstrated and then took a bite out of the gooey, melted heap of whiteness. "Yum."

As Brim was partaking in her newfound vice, Carson tapped Raj on the shoulder. Raj looked up, and Carson tilted his head toward their friend Eron, who was waiting near the perimeter. Raj stood up, and the two boys walked toward Eron.

"He's got some jazz juices and some canabites!"

"Yeah, Carson, lez do it!"

As they approached Eron, Raj shouted, "Where'd you get canabites, dude?"

From their location on the perimeter, they waved to their sentry friends further down the beach on each side of them. The sentries waved back, indicating all was clear in terms of craurchins—and adults.

"My pop racked up some major KPs last month, and I guess he treated himself to a little reward. He's one of the best shots on the cape but he's got no skills when it comes to hiding his stash, haha."

The three boys giggled as they shared jazz juice and ate some canabites. It was looking like it was going to be a fun night. Their conversation was interrupted by the occasional *pop, pop* and *zoop, zoop*. The light of the bonfire ended just short of the perimeter, so they were standing in the shadows.

Raj was taking a gulp of jazz juice when Brim, face covered in marshmallow goo, tugged his shirt. "Why aren't you at the bonfire, Raji?"

"Brim! What are you doing here? Go back to the fire, you little marshmallow face. I'll be along soon."

"But—"

"Go, Brim."

She reluctantly started back, Spanky by her side. Raj never took his eyes off of her, until from the corner of his eye, he saw his friend Monica frantically waving to Raul. He briefly turned to see what the commotion was and when he looked back, Brim was gone.

From her position on the perimeter, Monica saw a large, dark spot in the distance, about a block down the beach. She set her communicator to binocular mode for a closer look. "Oh, *shit!*" Heart racing, she yelled to the closest sentry to her right.

"Raul, do you see it?" Raul put his hand to his ear. "Do you see it?" she repeated pointing down the beach. Raul looked and started shaking his head rapidly. "I see it. Call Mr. B!" he shouted.

"Mr. Bally, Mr. Bally? You there?" Silence. "Mr. Bally!" More silence. "Mr. Bal—"

"I'm here, Monica, I'm here. What's going on?"

"We think we see a 5 coming toward us!"

"Okay, Monica, be calm. We're on our way!"

Rory stood up and interrupted the talking, singing, and general cheer that was happening around the fire. The dogs had caught the scent of the 5 and were growling low and long, confirming this was not a false alarm.

"Listen up, everyone. We've got a 5 coming toward us! I need everyone to listen to me. I need Raheem and four other shooters, preferably shooters with Z guns, to head to Monica's post and wait for me. Wanda, can you gather up the children?"

"I'm on it. I'll get them all to the fire." She immediately stood up and ran toward a group of children playing nearby. "Dogs as well!" Raheem yelled to her as he ran with four other men and five dogs to the perimeter.

"Everyone else, stay here at the bonfire—and keep your eyes open. Keep your dogs here. I want to do this in a quick, orderly fashion. No need for anyone to get hurt, not a person or a dog."

The attack was coming from the north, and Rory did not want to leave the south exposed. He waved to the two sentries on the southern perimeter and ran to the one closest.

"Izzy, we are getting attacked by a 5 from the north. I need you to stay at this post and keep your eyes open for others. But first, contact the rest, except Monica and Raul, and tell them to do the same."

With that, he ran down the beach toward the group of men and dogs standing at the edge of the northern perimeter. As he ran by the crowd at the bonfire, his niece Nicole ran to him, screaming and hysterical.

"I've lost Brim! I've lost Brim!"

Rory's heart nearly stopped beating. "What? Where was she when you last saw her? Think!"

Suddenly, he heard Raj. "Dad, what's going on? Where's Brim? She followed me to the perimeter, but I sent her back! I found her communicator in the sand!" His voice was cracking, and he was nearly in tears.

Rory's head was spinning. He pulled out his communicator and called Raheem. "Ralph, you're in charge. You know what to do. Brim is missing! If you see her, let me know. I have to search for her!"

"Fuck! Find her, Rory!"

"I will, Raheem."

Everyone at the bonfire was armed except the children, and everyone had a dog. Brim's dog Spanky was also missing. *That is a good thing*, Rory thought. He split the remaining group in half, one at the bonfire with the children and one with him scouring the perimeter. They started on the west side of the beach, searching the brush and tree line as the dogs sniffed for trouble.

At the northern perimeter, the five men and Monica faced the oncoming cycle 5 and his cluster of four cycle 3s. When it drew close, Raheem gave the signal, and all six dogs were released. The dogs went for the small craurchins and the shooters all fired at the cycle 5's head. The dogs tore into the four smaller craurchins as the large 5 covered his head with his pincers blocking the shots. He stood on his hinds and leaped forward, crushing one of the dogs. The remaining dogs latched onto or bit its legs, while the shooters continued their assault.

"Keep firing! Don't stop!" Raheem shouted.

Zoop, Zoop, Zoop, Zoop.

The cycle 5 continued to block the shots with his two pincers as he twisted from side to side, trying to shake the dogs. Raheem crept up to the 5's blindside, then to its rear. He waited patiently then took his shot. The 5 screamed in agony as the first white-hot laser hit his scaly neck, and then his scream was cut short as the second and third carved into the back of his head. The craurchin fell forward into the moat with a crash.

"Now we need to find Brim," Raheem called out of breath.

CHAPTER 11
AVALON

He felt the cut of a sword, but the pen's mightier
Then he spread his wings and he flew away, Yeah Yeah.
If anything...is happening...I'm comin' back
I'm comin' back
For your ass, mother fuckin' fast is,
How you be running in the day.
Now you're gonna feel how,
how it feels to be running when you can't get away
—"Comin' Back," Citizen Cope

AVALON

The four men set up camp in an abandoned condo overlooking the 28th Street beach. The place was in relatively good condition but smelled stale and rank, like something terrible had happened there a long time ago. It had. They arrived at the drop zone the previous morning and started their day with a good ol' drop-zone-style barbeque, where they met some welcoming Badlanders.

Some of them were disheveled and rough, and others much like himself, wore nice clothes and were well groomed. But all were polite and cordial. They spent a few hours at the barbeque, and then did some hunting in the nearby Cape May Court House area. They had all done pretty well and racked up decent kill points. Afterward, they set up camp in an abandoned, gloomy motel on Route 9, enjoyed some dinner and drinks, then went to sleep. They awoke early the next morning, broke up camp, and then hovered their way deeper into the Badlands, all the way to where the land meets the sea. Mario "Dingo" Capella and Vin Johnson lead the way, riding side by side on their respective hoverbikes. Gabe Marshall and Bryce McPherson rode side by side, slightly behind them.

"Come on, guys. Keep up!" Vin shouted over the wind and hum of the hovers.

"We're right here," responded Gabe. "Right here."

To say his journey thus far was eventful would be an understatement. That first day they had encountered Badlanders, craurchins, and even a pack of wilds. To a seasoned Badlander or seasoned Weekend Warrior this was nothing special. For someone who had never experienced the colorful Badlander, the creepy craurchin or the majestic and formidable Wild, it was…well…shocking.

Shocking and overwhelming. Bryce's first day in the Badlands was more intense than he could have ever imagined. He was really enjoying himself but could do without the constant ranking from his fellow hunters, on this man-cation that he so desperately wanted to be part of. So urgently needed. Well, all but Gabe. Gabe was cool with his cammo coveralls and wavy brown hair. He wondered if Gabe was feeling the same strong connection that he was.

Bryce was a tall, blue-eyed, dark skinned man with a perfectly shaped, shaved head. He was of slight, but strong, stature. He wasn't what you would call a burly man. No, that would be his ex-lover Raphael. He was the one who got the long looks from other men (and women). He was the one who spent half his life in the gym. He was the one who ditched Bryce for that fucking bastard Ricardo. Fuck 'em'em both!

"It's not that far now," Dingo announced. "Just a few more miles."

Along the shore, the Badlands were dark and dreary this morning as the wind smacked them in the face. The smell of salt air was heavy in the air, and he was reminded of the beach he had been to so many years ago when he was a scrawny, blond-haired adolescent.

"Bryce, not too far out. Stay where we can see you." Bryce's parents had taken him and his younger sister to New Santa Monica Pier in California, on a family vacation.

"Joe, he just can't get enough of the ocean." While on this vacation, he had tried his hand at deep-sea fishing, did a little surfing, and ate real Mexican food. It was a fond memory indeed, and he swore he would move there one day and leave the flat, boring life he had in Nebraska, helping out on his family's factory farm.

When Gabe, Bryce, Vinny, and Dingo arrived, they parked the four small hover bikes, all HV-20s, on the roof and climbed down the winding stairs and into the house, gear in hand. They each picked a room, then met up twenty minutes later, except for Gabe, who was announced he was taking a quick nap.

"Hey, Vinny, did you check the building for urchies?" Dingo was fussing with his drone on the condo's balcony. He had a special drone tool in one hand and communicator in the other. He would tinker with the drone then point the communicator at it, trying to sync the two up. Among their vast allotment of expensive toys, the group had brought along a super bat that they would use to charge the drones, the hovers, communicators, various camping gadgets, and their Z guns for the next two weeks. Among their clothing, they had hunting armor, helmets with shields (for protection from craurchin venom), accessory vests, hunting boots, and soft leather shooting gloves.

"Yah, killed two. One on the side wall and one on the rear. I think the one on the rear wall was heading for Brycie boy's bedroom window." He pulled Bryce's earlobe jokingly. Bryce turned a little flush, but nobody noticed.

It was Bryce's first hunting excursion in the Badlands and Dingo and Vin were teasing him nonstop. Bryce had come to terms years ago with his sexuality, but this guy time—this ball-busting, ranking each other bullshit was already getting old.

"Eat my ass, Vin!" He was beginning to wonder why he came

along on this trip but told himself it was normal male rite of passage crap. *I'll get used to it,* he thought. He loved hunting too much to allow a little macho bullshit to get under his skin. *Fuck it, these are basically good guys. They can't help it if they're douchebags.* He didn't think either of them knew he was gay and he doubted they would care.

"Where is Gabe?" Bryce tried not to sound overly interested.

"Still sleeping. Vin. Wake his ass up. I want to see what he can do with that UMV-30 of his."

"Nah, let him sleep. He's fighting some kinda bug. Maybe the flu or something. Maybe just jetlag."

"Flu? Is that the new name for an amerlot hangover these days?" Dingo said sarcastically.

"He didn't touch a drop. Trust me, I was keeping an eye on him 'cause I've seen him in action!" Vin and Gabe were good friends back home, going back years all the way to grade school.

"He does like his amerlot," Dingo mused.

They had just finished eating their breakfast of dehydrated eggs and jerky and were now on the balcony sipping on jazz juice. They chatted about their venture from the drop zone as the mellow drink soothed their nerves and relaxed them before the next day's big hunt. Today was a day to relax and do some light partying.

This may be a great trip, after all, Bryce thought as he sipped his drink and observed the mellow, potent concoction going right to his head.

Dingo finished tinkering with the drone and then hooked it to the super bat. In thirty seconds, it was charged. He set it on the balcony deck, tapped his communicator a few times, and off it went, whizzing toward the sea.

"Okay, guys, watch and see how kill points are racked up!"

On the beach below were thousands of craurchins scattered north and south as far as the eyes could see. Mostly 1s, 2s, and 3s. The low whizz of the sleek aircraft was barely detectable. It flew up toward the sky, did three loop-the-loops—Dingo showing off—then reduced altitude, cruising back toward the beach. It leveled out at about twenty feet above the sand. Then down to ten feet.

Zoop, zoop, zoop. Dingo's fingers were slapping the communicator furiously.

On the beach, craurchins were scattering in all directions, as the hot laser strikes hit sand and craurchin, sending guts and shell and sand flying everywhere.

"Woohoo! Yah! That's how you take out urchies!" Dingo glanced at his communicator, which synced to the drone, recorded every kill. "Twenty-five!"

The beach was now only one-quarter as populated as ten minutes before. The craurchins on the beach scattered into the ocean or burrowed into the sand.

"Twenty-five," he repeated, "in what, less than ten minutes?"

"Gimme a try!" Bryce begged. "Come on, man!"

"All right but don't crash it, or you're walking out on urchie beach to retrieve it." Dingo gave him some brief instructions. Bryce flew the drone for a while and did a decent job flying, but could not manage to make a kill. The laser strikes were off target, and the controls felt awkward to his fingers.

"It'll take some practice till you get the feel." Dingo downed his jazz juice. "Didn't you practice on the simulator I gave you? Keep at it. You'll get the feel. We gonna kill us some urchin my brothers, oh yeah!" The mood on the balcony was quite upbeat.

Vin had his Z gun out and was shooting at the fleeing craurchins. He got two or three smaller craurchins, when suddenly Scout started growling, and then barking incessantly. The men rented Scout for the trip. He was trained to hunt and kill craurchins but had never actually been to the Badlands. He came from a really good hunting stock, had a great disposition, and had been great thus far. The barking and growling coming from this German Shepard mix were intense and filled with deep emotion.

"He's overwhelmed by the smell of craurchin! Chill, boy!" Dingo scolded.

Bryce knew something was wrong. He could just feel it.

"What's up, boy? What's going—*holy fuck!*"

Bryce's face contorted and his eyes grew wide. His heart was pounding! He'd only ever seen what he was seeing on the wall screen. The other two followed his and Scout's gaze. The dog was still barking and growling furiously.

"Oh shit!" Dingo grabbed his communicator back from Bryce and started hitting the controls on the drone like a madman.

"Woah, I never saw one that big. Dingo, have you?" Vin was quickly reloading his Z gun. "Must be a cycle 5! He is actually coming toward us—can't be more than fifty feet away. Shit, he's heading right toward the house! Toward us! Ah, I'll run downstairs and try 'n get a shot from the side door. We'll get 'em from two positions!" Vin disappeared into the house. They could hear Vin's footsteps clopping down the stairs.

Bryce was in a momentary shock and felt as though things were moving in slow motion. That big-ass fucking—thing—was heading toward this house! He snapped out of it and grabbed his Z gun off the table and was aiming up the beast in his sights. Dingo was flying the drone back toward the condo.

"Go for the head!" Dingo shouted excitedly, "Go for the motherfucking head!"

"Look, Dingo, he's got some help!" Four cycle 3s were marching along with the large creature. They seemed to be taking cover behind the large monster's massive body. All were on six legs, scurrying at a rapid pace.

MA0O

Ma0o watched from the surf as the silver-gray bird flew over the sand, shooting blue streaks of bright light from its snout. Many of these blue streaks were hitting his cohabitees and killing them instantly with a short *pop*. He could not allow this slaughter to continue. He worked his way from the cold, choppy sea, surf smacking against his armor, eyes never leaving the silver bird in the sky. Then, the silver bird flew back up into the sky. As Ma0o stepped out of the Atlantic and onto the sand, he scanned up and down the beach. He let out a high-pitched shriek, calling for his cluster. Seagulls and small birds flew from the sand dunes, flapping their wings and flying away in fear.

Who is controlling the silver bird? he thought. He knew instinctively that this bird was controlled by a human. He also knew that the blue streak could not hurt his cycle 5 shell.

160

Where are they? Suddenly, he spotted them. *Three humans and a canine.* As he started crawling his way toward them, his horns became engorged. Four from his cluster joined him about halfway up the beach, about a hundred feet from the structure where the attackers were positioned. *If you get hit, you will die. Your armor is not strong enough yet. Stay behind me. Where is the rest of my cluster?*

"*Dead,*" they each answered.

At about forty paces from the humans, Ma0o was hit on his foreshell with the blue streak. *Pop.* He stood up on his hinds and shielded his head with his large pincers.

Behind me! he ordered his remaining cluster.

There were two more hits on his shell, and one on the pincer protecting his head. He quickly closed the remaining thirty paces and began slamming his massive seven-foot-tall body against one of the posts that supported the deck above. The post started to deflect in the center, shaking the entire deck.

Suddenly, the large cluster king heard the low whizz of the silver bird, and it headed up vertically toward the sky, just a few feet shy of the house. Ma0o turned his head and saw his remaining cluster's corpses. Shells and guts were everywhere, and more craurchin blood and guts stained the sand. He let out a shriek of pure rage that made anybody or anything in earshot cringe. He heard the canine barking. Then human voices. He knew they did not have a clean shot from their position on the balcony.

I must take out this support!

After several more hits, the support post split in half and the balcony partially collapsed, hanging awkwardly like a giant hunchback. Suddenly, to his right, a human emerged from the lower lair.

Zoop, zoop. The first shot hit his shell and the second, an obvious head shot, hit his exposed pincer shoulder, tearing a gaping hole and exposing what could only be described as alien tendons and ripped skin. He streaked in pain and anger as goo oozed from his injured shoulder. He spun around and charged the human at the door.

MAKING A STAND

"Bryce, aim for the head—the head—aim for the fucking head!"

The entire balcony vibrated.

"Inside!" Bryce screamed as he turned and ran toward the door. "C'mon, Scout. Dingo, what are you doing?" Scout obeyed and ran into the condo, still barking and growling.

Dingo was slapping the controls for the drone like a demented bass player. "Hold on, hold—"

The first thump put him on his ass and scrambling for his communicator. The second split the post in the center, leaving him sliding toward the edge of the balcony. The third completely sheared the post. The balcony's entire left corner dropped and Dingo Capella was hanging onto the rail, feet dangling just inches from the cycle 5.

I'm going to die, Dingo thought. *Right here in this shithole world they call the Badlands!*

He looked down, and the beast was not in his sight. *Should I let go? I could drop and try to get into the house from the other side.*

"What the—" Just then, he heard Bryce from above.

"Give me your hand—c'mon!"

Bryce was in a challenging position. He was gripping both hands on Dingo's wrist, holding him with all his strength, while at the same time locking his legs so as not to slide down the sagging balcony. Mario "Dingo" Capella was not a small man. He ate and drank liberally and as a result sported an ample mid-section.

"Hold on!" With all the energy he could muster, he pulled his friend up until Dingo was able to get his elbows onto the deck. Bryce grabbed him under his armpits and pulled and shimmied up the collapsing deck. When they were on fairly level ground, they spider-crawled into the condo.

"Hey! Downstairs! A little help!" came a faint voice from below. Scout was down there with Vin, barking madly. "I'm freaking out here guys, a little help please!"

After Vin opened the door and fired on the cycle 5, he saw something he had never seen before. Not in all his years of hunting in the Badlands. Sure, he had been charged by craurchins before, but the 5 was trying to get into the house! It was looking in the garage window, peering through the sliding doors, investigating the doors and windows for a vulnerability. It appeared to be planning. Looking for a way in. Vin had never heard of such a thing. He faced 1s, 2s, 3s, 4s and even a 5 once, but never—never did one display an act of thoughtful decision making. They, like most animals, acted on instinct.

Ma0o was infuriated. Enraged. *I need to get in. I need vengeance. I need human blood!* The rage engorged his two horns and the thought of warm human blood filled him with desire. Currently, his large gut was filled with jellyfish, a couple of seagulls, and a small

163

wild dog. He heard the human inside the lair yelling. He smelled the canine by the human's side.

He walked under the collapsed structure and saw an opening into the lair. As he attempted crossing into the lair, his body was pushed back, blocked by an invisible force, but the opening shook. *Charge it,* he thought. *Charge it*! He backed up ten paces and lunged into the laminated glass doors with all the force he could muster.

Bryce heard Vin's cries for help and Scout's shrill barking from downstairs. Both men were gathering their wits and heading toward the stairs when they heard the loud crash of the glass doors exploding below. They heard the *thump* as Ma0o landed on the floor. They ran down the stairs, and as they reached the bottom landing heard Vin's screams of pain and horror. They saw the large craurchin's right pincer impaled in Vin's chest plate, blood streaming down like a red waterfall and organs swinging like bloody vines. He was dangling from the pincer, two feet off the floor, eyes wide, feet kicking wildly and fists smacking at the creature's face.

"Agh, help!" Vin screamed. But he was beyond help. Scout was latched onto one of the creature's hind legs biting deep and pulling in a death grip.

Bryce fired two quick shots as Dingo raced toward Vin's Z gun lying on the floor. Ma0o lunged toward Dingo as Bryce's first two shots grazed his head. Bryce fired two more into his head but not before the large black creature impaled Dingo with his left pincer. The large cycle 5 named Ma0o stood there for a few seconds, headless, then dropped backward with Dingo and Vin impaled in each of his two pincers. His head was completely gone. He lay motionless. Dead. As were Bryce's two friends.

The room was filled with the sound of complete silence. Scout let go of the craurchin's hind leg and was lying on the floor, tongue hanging out, breathing heavily, catching his breath. Bryce's head was spinning, and his ears were ringing. He glanced upon the dead beast, his dead friends, the dog named Scout lying on the ground. He was filled with grief for his fallen compatriots. He knew at that moment that the world was dying, and he wanted—no he knew, intuitively, that he had to help stop it. He wondered how Gabe felt about—Gabe! Holy shit! Gabe!"

He ran up the stairs two at a time and raced into Gabe's room, practically breaking the door off its hinges.

On the bed was Gabe in a fetal position, asleep and dead to the world. As he walked to the side of the bed, he could see the sweat on his brow, the shaking of his chest as Gabe shivered in his sleep. He could feel the heat emanating from his flu-stricken body.

This poor bastard slept through the entire ordeal! Bryce thought. Somehow Bryce managed to wipe Gabe's brow, cover him with a blanket, and sponge his overheated body. Bryce knew this flu would either run its course or Gabe would die. Antibiotics were not effective and besides, unavailable. When he awoke, Bryce would have a gallon of water waiting for him.

Several hours and a few jazz juices later, when his heartbeat slowed down and the fog in his head began to subside, he heard Gabe stirring in the bed. Sleep would be his best bet. He walked downstairs and detached his two friends from the dead creature's pincers, laid them on the floor and put clothes from Dingo and Vin's luggage over their lifeless bodies. He tried to drag the dead craurchin out the back door, but to no avail. The fucker weighed at least 500 pounds! Damn, that was going to stink in the morning!

As he lay his beaten body down on the floor upstairs, Scout's large fluffy head resting on his stomach, he thought about his mother and father and little sister at home. He also thought about his next move. He stroked Scout's head and neck.

He passed the next few hours planning. He was not going home, that much he knew. He remembered a man he had met at the drop zone when they first arrived. The man, Donnie Long—no Dante Long, left a really positive impression on him. He said he lived in Sea Isle, the next town north of Avalon. Perhaps he would visit Dante and see how he could help out in the Badlands.

"Hey," came a throaty voice from the next room. "Where are Dingo and Vin? And what the fuck is that smell?"

CHAPTER 12

WHERE THE SEA MEETS THE SAND

It's not the size of the dog in the fight
It's the size of the fight in the dog.
— MARK TWAIN

WHERE THE SEA MEETS THE SAND

Joey was in Auntie Bridges house with Grammy and Bridge when he heard the door open in his house next door. He excused himself from the older women and walked through the connector and into the kitchen. There he saw his little sister washing her face with a towel while humming cheerily. Spanky was lying on the floor at her feet looking at him as if to say, *Whatta ya want from me? I can hardly keep up with her.*

"Brim? Brim, what are you doing here? Where is Nicki? Are you alone? Brim!" Joey was getting upset. In the Badlands, a five-year-old girl did not walk home from the beach, at night (or day for that matter) alone. "Did you walk home by yourself?"

"Yes, I did. I got marshmeller face and need to wash it off like a big girl," she said proudly.

"Are the others all at the bonfire?"

"Yes. Joey cooked 'n I ate marshmellers!"

As Joey entered the bonfire, people were scattered all around the perimeter. Some were scouring the ocean, others in the stand of trees, with their communicators on spotlight. He knew instantly that they were searching for Brim—even before he heard the calls, "Brim, Brim? Where are you, Brim?"

He gave a sharp loud whistle. "Yoooah, I've got her! I've got her!"

One by one, the group would shout the news out to the others further away or call on their communicator. As word got out, the group eventually reassembled at the bonfire, which was now a simple campfire. The light emitted from it was now quite a way back from the perimeter. Nicole and Raj were jubilant. Raj nearly squeezed the life out of her. People slowly made their way back to the bonfire where everyone was gathered. Many sighs of relief all around, all keenly aware of their fragile existence.

"Don't you ever walk off like that again, Brims! Do you hear me?" Nicole tried to be stern and then gave her a hug and a light slap on the cheek. If Spanky could talk, he'd tell them all how he had stayed with her the entire walk and protected her from four cycle 3s along the way. As the group reconvened, a sense of relief mixed with high emotion filled the starry night air. The moon reflected off of the ocean, which was now only ten feet from the dying fire. Some of the Badlanders were packing their stuff and saying their goodnights. The Bally children walked back to their house with their dogs, as did most of the children and their parents.

"Despite the drama, we had a nice night, Rory. Good job!"

"Thanks, Em. I'm just glad we found our little girl. Raheem and company took the 5 out but we lost poor ol' Buzz. He was a great dog. We're all very sad for Taj. Have a safe walk back and stay with the group. I'll see you soon."

In the Badlands, the loss of a dog was felt by everyone. Buzz would have some kind of service that week. He would be buried with a headstone in the dog cemetery in the Emlen Physick Estate on Washington Street, where so many other pets were laid to rest.

About a quarter of the group were still at the bonfire talking, finishing their drinks. The group consisted of ten men, six teenagers and ten dogs.

"Some night, huh, Rory." Raheem took a sip of his drink.

"I hear ya. Well, at least you'll get some decent KPs for taking out the 5."

The way the kill points worked for a group kill was the entire group got points. In a situation like the one with Raheem, where he had the actual kill, he would receive bonus points. If he chose to do so, he could evenly divide all the points, including his bonus points among the group. As the cycle size of the craurchin increased, so too did the KPs, as 5s and better earned high points.

"Just want to let y'all know I will be sharing my bonus points. That was a group effort." Raheem always shared his bonus points.

"Here, here." The group toasted to Raheem and the efforts of others. The adrenaline level of the group was still high.

"Here's to Buzz," Frank Mazzio replied with a tear in his eye.

The men and women were finishing up their drinks, waiting for the tide to extinguish the remaining fire when Raj noticed something in the ocean. It was out in the breakers, wide and black, moving slowly inland toward the group. His first thought was that it was a small whale or large shark. When the breakers rolled past it, he could see that it was making its own set of small wakes. It was indeed that big.

"Dad, Uncle Raheem, there's something in the water! There's something in the water! Do you see it? There!" he pointed.

A few seconds later, the dogs caught the scent and were going absolutely wild, running up to the edge of the ocean, barking and growling hysterically. Everyone was standing in defense mode, Z guns and weapons ready. The black shape got larger and larger as it neared.

"Oh, fuck. It's a craurchin! A big one!" Jake looked terrified.

172

"Guys, this is a 6. Fuck maybe a 7!" Rory shouted. "Too late to run!"

"Everyone, aim for the head! For the head!" Raheem was on one knee, waiting.

"Form a semicircle around his center! Fire when he's in range!" Rory's heart was racing, as was the entire group's. One man, Roy Spencer, not known for registering high KPs, was on the verge of hysteria. "What do I do? What do I do?"

"Be calm, Roy. Just shoot for the head, and don't get close. You'll be okay," someone whispered.

They waited, and the cycle 6 hit the shallow water, walking on its long hind legs as the dogs barked frantically and the men stood poised. Suddenly, it swung sharply to the right and took out four dogs that had gotten too close. It mortally tore them open with the swipe of one pincer. The one or two that survived lay in the shallow ocean water, crying in pain. Suddenly, the 6 stood on its hinds, both pincers swinging like two gigantic scythes. It was easily twelve feet tall—a living, breathing beast! Behind him, tiny 3s and 4s scurried out of the dark water. The dogs attacked these smaller craurchins as everyone opened fired on the enormous cycle 6.

The cycle 6 protected its head with its massive pincers as it stepped forward, cracking a dog with a whip of its tail. This did not deter the remaining five dogs, who latched on to its huge tree trunk legs. This slowed it down a little as the humans continued firing. Raheem glazed its head with a laser shot. It shrieked, but was not in the least deterred.

"Back up, men, back up. It's too dangerous!" Rory could see a bad situation unfolding.

"We're sixteen to one, plus five dogs! Let's take this fucker out!" Bubby Jones shouted. "Let's charge it!"

"Too dangerous—we have to keep our distance and keep up the firepower."

The beast took two more steps forward, dogs latched to its hinds. Bubby came in close for a headshot.

"Cover me," he shouted. "Cover m—"

As if in slow motion, the group watched as the 6, quick for its size, swiped his right pincer, decapitating Bubby instantly. The craurchin raised its four-foot-wide pincers to the dark sky and let out an ear-piercing screech as if to say, "Come and get me, motherfuckers!"

The remaining defenders fired all at once, but the 6 moved forward.

The semicircle collapsed and the group retreated back, continuing to fire their weapons. No one could seem to get a direct head shot, but many laser shots grazed its 3-foot diameter head. The 6's two pincers were like massive shields, creating a solid barrier between the group and its head. Raheem knew that if they could get the craurchin to expose its head, they could get that vital headshot they needed. But they would have to take out both brains.

"We need more people! We have to get him to expose his head longer."

One brave teenager thought he could distract it. He ran toward it, waving his arms and shouting.

"Raul! No!" Too late. In a heartbeat, the 6 moved forward and used his middle body leg to slash the seventeen-year-old. The large craurchins had razor-sharp, finger-like spikes on the ends of their middle legs. The rest of the leg was covered with thin, spiny hairs. Standing on its back legs, this put the middle legs at about five or so feet above the ground. The kid had no chance. The spikes ripped across his torso, causing deep lacerations that left him on the ground, screaming in agony.

The craurchin put an end to his screams as he crushed the boy's skull with a thump of his scaly foot. The dogs still held their grip. They were barely breaking the scaly skin, but they latched on tight and held firm, slowing the craurchin down. The nonstop barrage of lasers and bullets helped slow him as well, but Rory knew that they only had so much ammo and could only slow the craurchin down for so long. The 6 had already proven how well he could sustain an assault from sixteen men and ten dogs for fuck's sake!

"Raj, run over to Uncle M.J.'s house and get him and Joey and the dogs down here!"

M.J. and Lonnie had gotten back from the Committee meeting less than an hour before. M.J. was going to join his brother on the beach but figured he would be gone by now. They had left a meeting that was filled with fear, distress, and confusion only to return home to a house filled with anxiety and unease. The combination of the cycle 5 attack and Brim going missing had shaken up Joey and Nicole. Brim could sense their fear and anxiety and was upset as well. She knew now that she had done something terribly wrong, and she felt sad that she upset everyone. Lonnie had taken her up to bed to try and calm her down and explain things to her as only a mother could.

She will definitely be sleeping in our bed tonight, she thought.

From a distance the father and son heard a high-pitched shreak.

"What was that?" Joey asked his father. "Dad? Did you hear that?" M.J. did hear it and knew only too well what it was. "Gather all of the family dogs, Auntie Bridge's as well. I'll meet you at the entrance to the beach."

When Joey got to the beach entrance, his dad was talking to his cousin Raj. Raj appeared visibly upset and gasping for air, pointing to the edge of the beach.

"What's going on, Raj?"

"We're under attack by a cycle 6!" M.J. cut in.

"Four dogs and two men dead!" Raj added.

"Let's go, Raj. Joey, grab the hover!"

Joey ran back to the nearby hover, jumped in, and caught up to them halfway down the beach. His father and Raj climbed in. The dogs ran ahead and joined the other dogs. M.J. saw instantly how desperate the situation was.

"Joey, hover in behind it, not too close, and watch the waves. The last thing we want is to be in the water." M.J. was amazingly calm. Joey did as he was told. The others continued firing, careful not to hit the vehicle hovering twenty feet behind the cycle 6. The 6 felt the hover's presence behind it and stepped back, swinging his pincer toward the craft.

"Headshot, headshot, headshot!" Raheem shouted from the beach. "While he's turned around!"

At least five shots connected but the 6, though clearly injured and in pain, was nowhere near through. Enraged, he charged the group on the beach, swinging his pincers wildly, as he kicked up sand and shells in all directions. The group retreated in different directions as M.J. and Raj open-fired on the sprinting craurchin. None of their shots connected anything but its massive shell.

The enraged craurchin charged toward the closest man, Roy Spencer, who had fallen on his back. He lay on the sand, firing toward the beast. The 6 slammed his giant pincer down toward his victim. Roy, eyes wide, rolled to his left as the pincer pounded into the beach, shaking the ground like a mini earthquake and creating a deep imprint.

As it returned its attention to the scrambling, horrified man, who was trying to get onto his feet, it heard a commotion coming down the shoreline. The sound had gotten the craurchin's full attention, and it turned from the man toward the sound, which was growing louder and louder.

Howling, and with paws clacking down the beach, raced twenty-three fierce wilds, their trajectory homed on the large craurchin like a heat-seeking missile.

"Mask! Mask!" Joey screamed from the hover. "It's Mask! It's fucking Mask!"

As the headshots continued, the cycle 6 was in his full defensive stance, leaving his head exposed as the wilds charged full strength. Several men got off final shots. Joey noticed that the puppies, in the back of the pack, had grown substantially. They were now fierce hunters. The pack hit the cycle 6 in almost perfect unison, knocking it into the soft sand. The canines went to work biting and snapping at every exposed, vulnerable part of the huge creature's body, the giant craurchin swinging his pincers and kicking all six legs like a spastic cockroach on its back. Several dogs were hit with the swinging pincers and legs but miraculously none were seriously hurt.

From all sides of the craurchin, the only thing one could see was the hind legs and tails of the dogs. Their leg muscles flexed as they ripped off every exposed part of the massive creature. The struggling, defeated craurchin screeched in pain and agony and never stopped until the five or so dogs that had their teeth dug deep into its huge head, severed its skull, and destroyed its two brains.

PART III

FIGHT FOR THE JERSEY SHORE

CHAPTER 13

I'M STAYING

Correct your heads
For there's a new song rising
High above the waves
Go write your time
Go sing it on the streets
Go tell the world, but you go brave
Oh my sweet instant Christian you are such a sly clown
Too many questions, no replies now
'N rejoice for the king ain't lost his throne, oh no
He's still here, you are not alone
—"HYMN FOR THE DUDES," MOTT THE HOOPLE

COOLER BY A MILE

The hoverbikes were more like small cars than bikes. They were narrow with two seats in the front and cargo space in the back, enough space for the luggage of two lightly packed people. There was a glass roof that could be opened or closed. Also, they were made so that as many as three or four bikes could be daisy-chained together, so Bryce and Gabe did just that. They each hooked one of the extra bikes to their bikes. They then divided up and loaded all of their departed compadre's equipment and remaining luggage onto the extra bikes. Gabe tied his three-day bed head into a bandana, did some yoga stretches, and then climbed onto his hoverbike. He had a two-day beard but looked pretty good for a man who had been sleeping for the last 24-plus hours.

Gabe had made a very good recovery from whatever bug it was that he suffered from. The sleep was probably the key to his survival. *But at what cost?* he thought. Two of his friends were now dead. He was certain that, had he been there, at least one of them would be alive today. That said, the decision to stay, not just to hunt, but to actually help these people living in the Badlands, had been an easy one. He didn't experience the rage and violence of the craurchin firsthand, but he saw the results—in fact, he was having a hard time keeping the vision out of his head! The dead, headless beast downstairs didn't help.

Bryce started his hover and called for Scout to sit in the front seat. He and the handsome, black canine were fast becoming best friends. Scout never left Bryce's side. The three of them were heading to Sea Isle, but first they needed to do a little exploring here in Avalon, N.J. They had never actually spent any time here, other than at their house camp. Ahead of them, stretching out into the ocean, was the Thirtieth Street fishing pier. A relic from better days. Even from two blocks away, they could see the hundreds of cycle 1, 2, and 3 craurchins clutching to the rotted pylons like giant black barnacles. It was a nice day, with cool breezes blowing off the sea. If you removed the hundreds of black, shiny creatures crawling about on the beach, added a porpoise or two jumping high in the waves, it would have been a beautiful scene. A digi-card moment!

"Cooler by a mile."

"Excuse me, Gabe?"

"Cooler by a mile. Back in the day, that was Avalon's slogan. 'Welcome to Avalon, cooler by a mile.'"

Gabe saw Bryce's confused look and continued.

"Avalon extends about a mile or so further into the Atlantic Ocean than the other barrier islands along the Jersey coast, hence the motto."

"Well then, I better zip up my coat." Another breeze bordering on cold hit him.

They headed south toward Stone Harbor. Riding through the middle of town, they passed abandoned restaurants, ice cream parlors, and Avalon Virtual Reality and Lazer Golf, a place that offered jet pack rides and the like—all falling apart or boarded up. They saw a few people here and there. A guy removing dead craurchins from his front porch, a couple of kids and their dogs playing in the street, a family heading out for a day of hunting. There was actually one store, in the middle of town, that was open. It was the old bison burger joint. The old compo-brick structure was in decent shape, though in dire need of pointing. The faded, rotting sign read, "Be ny's Bison Burg rs."

They parked in front and walked into the eatery, taking in the wonderful aroma of open flame burgers cooking. Neither realized how hungry they were.

"Good morning, sir. How are you?" Gabe spoke to what he assumed was the owner, a gray man of about fifty-five or so, flipping burgers.

"Mornin', gentleman. Does your dog need some water?"

"Please," Bryce answered. "Thank you."

"Will y'all be eatin' today or just here for coffee?"

Gabe and Bryce shook their heads in unison. "Both," responded Bryce.

"Just to let ya know, we serve anyone or anything that is not a craurchin—and we only barter. No cash of any sort, thank you. I'm John Reynolds, the owner. We've got the best burgers on the Jersey coast, prob'ly the only burgers on the Jersey coast, ha."

Gabe knew that bartering was the norm in the Badlands, where, in most places, cash was useless. The closest place cash had any use was Atlantic City or Philadelphia.

"How about kill points, John?"

It was most common to transfer KPs to a vendor for services rendered. The Heartland treasury department had a simple application for that.

"I'd prefer to barter if you have something to barter, but if not, KPs 'r fine."

They ordered, then took a window seat near the entrance, where they could keep an eye on the hovers, as Scout lapped his water. John placed two steaming cups of coffee on the table, which they sipped while they waited for their food. The coffee was a bit bitter but totally enjoyable. With the exception of a slightly mussed but attractive middle-aged women reading her communicator, they were the only customers in the place.

"So, Gabe, how do we let Dingo and Vin's family know that they have passed on? Do we get word to one of the pilots at the drop zone? Do one of us need to go back to the Heartland? Sending a message via the communicator seems awfully cold."

"No, no, I can use the communicator. I know Vin's sister, in fact I've known the family most of my life. I still can't believe he's gone, man. That was like my third trip with those two. He and Mario went every year. He could be a twat, but he was basically of good guy." At this moment, Gabe was getting a little choked up. "I'm sorry, man."

"Are you kidding? Shit—they were your friends!"

"Anyway, I can contact Vin's sister, let her know what happened and ask her to notify the rest of the family. She is actually Dingo's sister-in-law. Her husband and Mario were brothers. That's how Vin hooked up with him."

They smelled the greasy, wonderful aroma of the burgers before John even reached the table. "Here y'go gentleman, enjoy." The woman dropped off some burger condiments, smiling at them but not saying anything.

"Thanks, John."

"Yeah, thanks, John." Bryce took a bite of the burger and chewed it a bit. "Delicious burger. John, do you have a minute? Can you tell us a little about what it's like living here?"

187

John stopped mid-stride and turned around, "Well," he said as he spun a chair around and sat, arm on the back of the chair. He was obviously eager for some conversation.

"Honestly, must say, I never had a weekend warrior roll in here and actually give a fuck about what it's like livin' here. I don't mean to sound bitter, but we live a hard life here. We are the only thing standing between the craurchins and the rest of the goddamn country. You folks from the Heartland never seemed interested, let alone appreciative."

There was some shadowy movement outside the store, and as if this were something as simple as a drink spilled or a customer who wanted some water, John Reynolds whistled and pointed to the front of the store. The red-haired, middle-aged woman got up and walked casually behind the counter, picked up a shovel, and walked out the door.

From outside, they could hear a commotion. They heard the bang of the shovel then the scraping as she scooped something into the street and the clang as she leaned it up against the store's façade. Then footsteps as she came through the door and walked behind the counter where she appeared to be washing her hands, lost in her own thoughts.

"Thanks, Tanesha. Anyway, we see folks like you, and pardon me if I seem judgmental, but we see folks like you two all the time. Coming in here with your expensive gear, your hovers, and having the time of your life. Do you have any idea what a Badlander would give for a hoverbike? That's like a year's worth of KPs. You guys come down here, have your fun, and then go back to your cushy lives. Here, every day is a struggle. That's what it is like here!"

Both men were a little flabbergasted. Neither had really thought that that was how they were perceived by the locals, especially not Gabe. Gabe had been here three times and never caught that vibe. Both had the same mindset, namely that they were having some enjoyable hunting time and at the same time helping to rid the country of a major problem. With the exception of the war, it was *the* major problem.

"Is that the opinion of all of the Badlanders?"

"Yes, Gabe—it is Gabe? Correct?"

"Yes, Gabe and Bryce."

"That is the general opinion of most of us," John concurred.

Bryce was stroking Scout's head as he asked, "Tell us everything. Tell us what a normal day is like for the typical Badlander?"

John got up, walked to the back of the store, and returned a short time later with a bucket of jazz juices. He handed each of the two men one, and called Tanesha over to the table. He cracked one open for her and one for himself.

Two hours later, the four of them were shaking hands and saying their goodbyes. The chance meeting had gone really well, impromptu as it was. All four humans were feeling better about each other then when Bryce and Gabe first walked in the shop. A lot better.

"John, thanks again for the insight. We're gonna do our part. You will see. Oh, and thank you for taking care of the bodies. I had no idea that that was how it worked." John had explained to them how there was a group of volunteers that collected the bodies of fallen weekend warriors and prepped them for shipment back to the Heartland. The leader was a local undertaker.

"No problem, I am truly sorry for your loss. Before you go, I want to share something with you."

He stepped behind the counter and walked out with a rectangular black box. It had a steel stick pointing out of the top. He placed it on the counter and turned the circular knob on the front of the box. It crackled and hissed as he twisted the knob left and right, left and right, until finally they heard a static voice.

"This, my friends, is a radio. They haven't been used in over a hundred years, maybe more. We use them because the communicators can be so unreliable. There are Badland volunteers who work shifts broadcasting local news from Cape May to Atlantic City. For the last two days, they have been broadcasting news of a taking in Cape May."

"A taking?" Bryce inquired.

"Yes, just what it sounds like. Listen up, the story is repeated like every twenty minutes." Sure enough, after about four minutes of small talk between the group, a voice popped out the big box.

"In Stone Harbor, the SHC killed a cycle 5 at its lair in the back-bay marshes." *Zzzhisss*. "In Cape May, fourteen-year-old Terrell Williams is still missing. Terrell was dragged away two days ago by a large craurchin. Search parties have been organized, and the community is calling on anyone with a drone with craurchin-tracking capabilities to—" *Zzzhisss*. "—again anyone who can provide advanced tracking tools or drones please help this desperate community, and of course, Terrell's family."

"So, this kid, his name is Terrell. He is actually one of the broadcasting volunteers. In fact, he is the one who got the whole thing going. That, and quite a few other things. Great kid! His family and friends are fucking going nuts! As you can imagine."

"Oh shit, that's horrible!" Bryce was again flushed.

"Bryce! We have a drone! It has tracking capabilities! We can find that kid!" It just so happened that Gabe's profession back in the Heartland, was master drone pilot. He'd been getting paid to operate drones for the better part of eight years, from mapping to spraying crops to tracking. There and then, without even having to utter a word, the two men knew that they had to help.

They left John and Tanesha, promising to come back at their first chance. *How could we not come back for one of those juicy burgers?* Bryce thought, then they climbed into the hovers and headed north toward the Townsends Inlet Bridge. There they would find Dante Long and convince him to come along to Cape May with them.

Five minutes after Bryce and Gabe left Benny's Bison Burgers, John sent a message on his communicator. Ten minutes after that, he turned up his radio.

"This is a special announcement to Dante Long. If Dante, or anyone who can get word to Dante, hears this message—" *Zzzhisss.* "—are two men looking for you. Meet them at the Promenade." *Zzzhisss.* "I repeat, meet them at the Promenade. They are on their way there now from Avalon."

CHAPTER 14
THE SEARCH

On the way to Cape May
I fell in love with you
On the way to Cape May
I saw my dreams come true
I was taken by your smile
As we drifted through Sea Isle
My heart was gone
When we reached Avalon
On the way to Cape May
Stone Harbor skies were blue
We were naming the day
When Wild Wood came in view
—"ON THE WAY TO CAPE MAY," MAURICE "BUDDY" NUGENT

SMILE…YOU'RE IN SEA ISLE
OCTOBER 22, 2271, 4:05 P.M.

Bang, bang, bang.

"Dante?" from a distance. "Dante!"

Bang, bang, bang.

"Honey, Honey, I think someone's at the door."

Dante was lying on his stomach, face buried in a pillow, arm wrapped around his current girlfriend Alexa's thin waist. The puppies, almost a year old, were now awake, jumped up on the king-size bed and were burrowing friskily in between Alexa's body and the pillows. They still had that endless puppy energy, with their long lanky bodies and giant awkward paws. Alexa would playfully slap one of them on the head, and then duck her head under the covers.

Nevelle, on the other hand, was at the front door sniffing out the human on the other side. Right after the first knock, you could hear his large paws pitter patting across the hard floor toward the door. It was cool. He knew the scent and knew it was a friend. Two of them actually. The large malamute let out a friendly howl.

"Ahh, come on, guys. Can't a guy get some sleep?"

Bang, bang, bang.

"Dante, open the fucking door!" pronounced a muffled voice from the outside.

Dante pushed himself up, gave Alexa a peck on the forehead, and slipped out of bed. He walked over to his dresser and pulled out a pair of boxers.

"Hold on, I'm coming." He worked his right leg into his draw-ers and then his left. Alexa laid back, admiring his ripped flat abs and fine tush.

"Are you expecting a visitor today, hon?" she asked.

"No, Alexa, not really."

It was just past four in the afternoon, and he wasn't sure who would be calling on him. He had been with Alexa since last night, woke up and made breakfast for her, and then ended up back in the sack. They had met a few months ago and had been inseparable since. The voice at the door sounded familiar.

"Bob, is that you?"

"Yes, open the goddamn door!" Bob Handler sounded a little impatient. He hadn't seen Dante since he had started dating Alexa and was a little upset that his friend had not called on him in three weeks.

Dante shuffled over to the front door, unlocked the three deadbolts, and swung the door open. Bob Handler stepped in with Felix. Neville jumped up on Bob, greeting him with his hot, stale dog breath and then ran around in circles with Felix as they sniffed each other's asses.

"Bob, what's up? Why the urgency?"

"You haven't been listening to your radio, have you?"

"Ah nah, I have not. Been a little preoccupied, Bob." Dante tilted his head toward his bedroom.

"Gotcha, bud. Well, you're being beckoned to the Promenade, and I am going to take you."

"Promenade? What for? What is—"

"Dante, there's been a taking—a young boy in Cape May. Calls are out for a search. They're looking for someone with a tracking drone!"

"Oh, shit. How old, Bob? And why me? I don't have a drone."

"No, but the two men who do have asked specifically for your help. The poor kid is fourteen. Snatched from his neighborhood early in the morning, two days ago."

THE SEA ISLE PROMENADE

It was approximately 4:30 p.m., and on the Promenade, Bryce and Gabe were sitting on a bench under the old gazebo. The composite wood structure had seen much better days. The Promenade was once the center of many of Sea Isle's social activities. It was the site of numerous summer concerts, community picnics, the judging of the August Baby Parade and most famously the annual winter Polar Bear Plunge. There was shopping on the boardwalk, dining at the many restaurants, and games to played at the arcades. There was all of this, or one could just sit, relax, and take in the ocean view. It was once located approximately where the waves were currently breaking and was moved two blocks in as the beaches continued to erode and become part of the Atlantic. What the Atlantic giveth, the Atlantic taketh back.

When Dante and Bob arrived, both men stood and presented themselves to Dante. Scout was happy to hang out with two other dogs. He'd seen mostly humans and craurchins for the last two days.

"We met at the drop zone two days ago, Dante. I'm Bryce McPherson." Bryce extended his right hand, which Dante shook.

"Yes, I remember."

"This is Gabe Marshall." The two men shook hands.

"I'm out, Dante. I'll catch ya next week." Bob shook hands with the two Heartlanders, climbed into his hover, and flew off with his dog.

"Before we talk about how you figure on finding this kid, I need to know what your motives are. Why are a coupla Heartland yahoos, no offence, interested in finding a missing Badlander boy?" Dante got right down to business.

"Dante, we've got the firepower. We've got the best equipment. We've got four bikes, charging for weeks, and two drones. One is a UMV-22 and the other is my personal UMV-30. The 30 is a commercial-grade drone that I use for my business back in the Heartland where I am a registered professional drone operator."

"Our motives are very simple. If anyone can find this kid, it's us three. We have the 30 and you know the territory and have the highest kill count on the Jersey coast!" Bryce added.

"Fair enough, but what you mean is the *four* of us."

"The four of us?" Gabe looked confused.

"Yes, we need to pick up my friend Khim Nguyen on the way. Khim knows about craurchin lairs. He may be essential in getting that kid out alive."

THE FARM

When they arrived on the farm at 5:30 p.m., the first thing Khim noticed was the four beautiful hoverbikes. With their limited cargo space, they were not much good for pickups, but man, they flew nice—or so he heard. He read that they could reach heights of 25 feet and could easily reach speeds of 120 mph. They would be in Cape May in twenty minutes tops.

Dante and Khim had talked earlier, and Dante filled him in on the situation. They were lucky, the signals were clear today so the communicators were functioning. Khim had been more than eager to help. In fact, Hakira wanted to help as well. She felt she could be of use once the boy was rescued.

"Okay, boys, eat up." Hakira had prepared a dinner of fresh tomato and cucumber salad, pumpkin soup, sliced apples with a cinnamon dipping sauce, fried chicken, and fresh goat's milk. There was enough food set out to feed ten men.

"Hakira, this is the first real meal I've had since I've gotten to the Badlands. Simple but truly delicious—and everything is so fresh."

Hakira really liked the two Heartlanders. They were different than the other weekend warriors she had encountered. Unlike many of them, they were not cocky or condescending. She also sensed something between the two. Something, she was sure Khim and Dante probably didn't notice. They had a thing for each other. She was not even sure that Gabe and Bryce knew it, but it was clear to her. Call it a woman's intuition.

"Thanks, Gabe. Well, here in the Badlands, less is definitely more. The key is keeping it fresh. Use fresh ingredients and every-thing tastes better. So, what brings you two here today—I mean other than the taking?"

"We were here on a trip with our two other friends, Dingo and Vin. As it happened, we lost them to a cycle 5. Bryce over here," Gabe nodded toward Bryce, "eventually took the 5 out."

"But, unfortunately not before it got our two friends," Bryce added.

"As fate would have it, I slept through the entire ordeal," Gabe said defeatedly.

"He had a virus. A virus that probably would have killed him had he not slept."

Hakira could see Gabe was choking up a little. She took his hands into hers and squeezed them softly.

"I'm very sorry. We don't need to discuss that right now but you let me know if there is anything we can do to ease the pain." Gabe could tell she was being a hundred percent sincere and nodded appreciatively.

There was a long minute of awkward silence before Khim broke in. "Gabe, if you ride with me, can you operate the UMV-30 while on the move? That way we can get a jump on the search."

"I can do that, but we need to go to the young boy's house and collect DNA. One of the amazing things about the 30 is it can track his DNA."

"Holy fuck, are you serious? It can track DNA! We'll have that boy in no time!" Dante was feeling very optimistic. He was thinking they'd be in and out in no time.

"Not so fast, Dante," Khim exclaimed. "The lair is a tricky place. A very dangerous place."

"How so?" Bryce wanted to know.

"Well, you must first consider the lair. Only cycle 5s and up construct lairs. Anything smaller burrows in the sand or water or is part of a cluster that lives in a lair. They are large, but they know they cannot leave themselves vulnerable. The lair will be remote and heavily wooded with thick brush and other vegetation. It will be near the water's edge, maybe even surrounded by water to limit direction of approach for attack—and make a quick getaway if necessary. The boy will be in the nest, which may or may not have a roof. The nest will be constructed of tree limbs, vegetation, mud, and anything else the craurchin can find in the woods. Second, he will have a cluster of anywhere from three to six cycle 1s, 2s, 3s, and 4s. They are easy to kill, but they still have to be dealt with quickly, especially the 4s."

"The dogs will be best for that," Hakira added.

"Yes. We bring in dogs, and we go in on foot. The hovers will be useless in there."

"Khim, how do you know so much about the craurchin lairs?" Bryce wanted to know.

Khim lifted his shirt, exposing his thin upper torso. On the left side, just below the rib cage was an ugly circular scar about the size of a small fist.

"I was taken. This scar was where the 5 that had me, inserted its feeding tube. I was in his lair for four days. When they rescued me, I was minus almost four pints of blood. He was taking almost a pint a day from me. When we find young Terrell tomorrow morning, it will be three days. He is a lot smaller than me, so he will be in pretty bad shape. We have to get him tomorrow morning. He will not last past then. Tell them, Hakira."

Hakira was a full-time nurse in another life not so long ago. She had also treated Khim on the scene as a volunteer. She had not known Khim at the time. It was one of the most harrowing experiences of her life.

"It gives me chills to think about the condition that child will be in. If the craurchin has taken that much blood, probably more than twenty percent of his body's blood, he will be in hypovolemic shock. His heart will not be able to pump enough blood and eventually his organs will start to fail. He will be very weak, and if he is conscious, he will be very light-headed. You will need to get him out fast and to that hospital in northern Maryland. I will ride with him and try and keep him alive," Hakira explained.

After hearing all this, Dante now understood what happened to the young woman at the marsh. *That poor thing went through all of that, scared and alone.*

The group spent the next three hours planning. They agreed that they needed to travel by twilight and be at the lair at sunrise. They would leave the farm at 5:00 a.m. and travel to the Williams' house by way of the shoreline. That would be the clearest route. Hakira had already contacted Jason Williams and updated him with the plan. This would put them in Cape May with plenty of time to get Terrell's DNA, input it into the drone, and start the tracking. It would also give them time to coordinate with the Williams and M.J. and Rory Bally, local volunteers who would be helping in the rescue effort. They could not plan the rescue until they tracked Terrell from the UMV-30 and knew from which direction they would be coming in, what cycle craurchin they were dealing with, and how many.

"I hear they have been seeing a wave of cycle 5 attacks on the cape for months now. I even heard they had a cycle 6 attack the night of Terrell's taking." Hakira stayed on top of all news from up and down the New Jersey coast. She could tell you what was happening on any given day in Atlantic City and all the way up to Sandy Hook.

"Fuck me!" Dante let out. "A fucking 6! I have seen exactly

two in my life. Not easy to take out. Not easy to fight. You've got to be really smart in dealing with something that big! What happened?"

"Well, it's an amazing story, in many ways." Hakira took a sip of her tea. "The event started with a cycle 5 attack. They took out the 5 and then a short time later, after half the folks had left the beach, the 6 came out of the ocean. By the time it was spotted, it was too late to have an orderly evacuation, so they fought it. They lost a few lives and then a pack of wilds showed up and took it out."

Bryce and Gabe were amazed. It was surreal to them—like life on another planet. Especially Bryce, who had only been in the Badlands a short while.

Bryce thought, *Wild dogs and humans fighting together to kill a monster. Cycle 5s or 6s taking humans and drinking their blood! These folks are dealing with this every day while I live a lifestyle of sashimi lunches and MegoCattle steak dinners."*

OCTOBER 23, 2271, 5:00 A.M.

Bryce awoke at first light to the crowing of the farmstead rooster. He could not believe where his journey had taken him. It was only his fourth day in the Badlands and here he was on a farm awakening to a rooster's crow. He had battled and killed a cycle 5 craurchin, watched two friends die, and was about to embark on a mission to save a young boy's life. Hopefully. Not bad for a middle-American country boy.

"That's Charlie, our resident rooster. Did you sleep well, Bryce?"

"I wish I could say I did, Hakira."

By 5:20 a.m., the humans and dogs were leaving for the cape. All, with the exception of Hakira, had donned the protective hunting gear and prepared their weapons. The hoverbikes were all charged up. Khim and Hakira were in a hoverbike, the back seat fixed with pillows and blankets for Terrell. Bryce and Scout boarded another hoverbike, Dante and Neville in the third, and Gabe and Jax in the last bike. Dante was the lead. He gave a hand wave, and they headed back toward the shore, over the JFK Boulevard Bridge and onto the beach. They then turned south toward Cape May.

Gabe programmed the drones to follow the bikes. He believed that, like humans, rust never sleeps. Get them into the air to assimilate with the environment. He peeked at his communicator, which had a special device snapped onto it. This device was an accessory that provided a more refined control with the UMV-30. He hit craurchin track mode and in a couple seconds, the screen blinked and was filled with thousands of black dots of various sizes. He tapped the screen a couple times and the dots got bigger, then became numbers. Thousands and thousands of 1, 2, 3, and 4s populated the screen, and apparently the beaches below. Every once in a while, a 5 would appear amid the lower numbers.

"My God," he said aloud. "I had no idea!" The bikes were all interconnected with hand-free audio and video.

"No idea what?" Hakira responded.

"Here, I'll connect you all to the UMV-30. See it?"

"Shit, there are that many? Is that drone accurate?" Bryce also had no idea there were that many craurchins.

"I'm not surprised by the lower numbers. It's the number of

5s I'm seeing—oh crap, did you see that? It was a 6! Oh, there's another 5 and another." Even Dante, with probably the highest KPs in the state, was amazed.

They flew down through Sea Isle over Townsend's Inlet, through Avalon, Stone Harbor, and across the Grassy Sound Bridge. They flew through Anglesea, North Wildwood, Wildwood, Wildwood Crest, and across the Cape May Inlet into Cape May.

5:45 A.M., CAPE MAY

Jason Williams, his two sons Zak and James, along with Jackson, were at the Williams' kitchen table. Jason was just beginning to fill them in on the plan when they heard the knock.

"That would be the Ballies" Jason remarked. "M.J. and Rory will be helping out. James, answer the door."

James walked back into the kitchen moments later with the Bally brothers, and they all exchanged greetings.

"We're gonna get your boy, Jason. I've got a good feeling about this. Joey was beside himself, wanting to help out, but I need him home with the women. Let me know what we can do."

"I hope to God you're right, M.J. We've got part of the plan down. I'll fill you in."

For the first time since Terrell's taking, Jason had hope. The nice lady from the farm had explained everything. She and four men would be arriving on hoverbikes.

"They will be here any time now and thanks to the two week-end warriors, will have top notch gear, fully charged Z guns and, of course, the drones. Her partner believes Terrell is in the craurchin's lair. He has experience with such lairs and feels we can get Terrell out without harming him."

"Dad, how the hell are we going to find the right—what did you call it? Lair?"

"Yes, Zakary, lair—it's basically the nest where the craurchin lives."

"Yes, and here's where our friends from the Heartland come in. They have a commercial-grade drone that can track not just craurchins but DNA. When they get here, they will send off the drone to find Terrell. But first, we need to give them Terrell's DNA. Once we find him, we'll figure out the specifics of the rescue based on live aerial video that the drone will send to us."

The five men were looking at each other with shocked, hopeful faces.

"Zak, run up and get Terrell's toothbrush." Jason thought for a second then added, "Grab his dirty socks from the hamper as well—I always have to fight with him to brush his teeth. Can't take any chances!"

CHAPTER 15

THE LAIR

When you believe you have exhausted all possibilities,
Remember this:
You haven't.
—THOMAS EDISON

THE LAIR: DAY ONE

When Terrell awoke, it took a few seconds for him to realize his predicament and then—full blown panic. His heart was racing, and he was still mostly paralyzed from the waist down. Even though his head felt like it was too big for his neck, it didn't take him long to remember what had happened early that morning.

The nightmare all came swirling back to him in a giant overwhelming wave of horror and regret. Getting pierced by the craurchin. Getting dragged to the cold, damp place—to this—swamp.

Oh God, why didn't I listen to Dad? he thought. He was lying on a bed of sticks and brush and leaves—a giant ground nest? He thought of how being of higher intelligence is not always such a good thing. Not good, because the absent-mindedness that seems to come with it, allowed him to be caught off guard, and particularly not good because he knew, better than most who might happen in his situation, how desperate his predicament truly was.

Even though in his current state of paralysis, he could not feel it, he could see the mark just below his rib cage where the craurchin had taken his blood. He vaguely remembered the long greenish-red—tongue? It came out of its mouth and attached to his body just before he passed out. He remembered the sharp pain of the piercing as it broke the skin of his stomach area.

He also remembered something else. Something he only had the vaguest memory of. A conscious connection? Yes, that was it. Anyway, somehow the wound cauterized because it was not bleeding. He could also see, on the other side of his body, the wound on the side of his stomach from the craurchin's pointy horn. It stung but didn't look infected.

This creature is taking my blood. This place is its home, its lair. It will take my blood until I am dead.

Terrell tried to wipe that thought from his mind. He knew this kind of thinking, though likely true, was not helpful. But it was no use, the panic was setting in again, bubbling up like one of those homemade volcanos about to erupt.

No more than ten feet across from him the creature appeared to be sleeping. He heard a movement and turned his head to the side. There, a couple of cycle 3s were scurrying into the lair from the algae-covered pond. They cozied up next to the 6, like a horrid litter of pups, as they stared at him with their beady, glittering eyes. To his right lay a dead dog, his blood completely drained from its limp body. He knew this because he could see the laceration—no the port, just like his, where the tongue thing went in. The poor thing was starting to rot and the smell was unbearable. Thank God it wasn't Einstein.

"Help!" he cried in utter panic. "Help—help!" Tears filled his eyes as complete and total hysteria took grip, his heart beating fast and his upper body shaking as dirty tears and snot streamed down his face. He could only bob back and forth as his lower body was asleep.

"Someone please, help me—please!" The cycle 6 stirred. The cycle 6 stood on her six limbs and turned toward him, her large round head with four spiked horns and mammalian eyes staring down at Terrell. It raised its pincers and released a loud, high-pitched shriek that echoed across the pond and through the woods—and then, Terrell passed out again.

BAK0O

The boy human has gone to sleep. Tomorrow, we will feed from him again. Tonight we hunt.

Bak0o and her cluster left the lair on their nightly hunt. Lately, the wild dogs had been causing them problems. Two nights ago, they had barely escaped an ambush. The large pack with their white-faced leader were particularly troublesome. They had surprised her on the beach. She and her cluster were scavenging along the shoreline when the pack attacked from the sand dunes. She had barely held them off as she strategically backed her way into the sea, slashing at them with her pincers until she was halfway submerged and the canines were less of a threat.

We will be more cautious tonight and hence forward.

She sent two of her cycle 4s out to scout the nearby beach. It was filled with thousands of other craurchins, but only one other cycle 6. Sometimes 6s would fight for territory, but only when pickings were slim, and these days pickings were far from slim.

Over the last fifteen decades, as the craurchin population flourished and grew, they had managed to nearly deplete their food source of fish, crabs, shrimp, and many other local saltwater species, which had been forced further out to sea. Some had been wiped out completely. As a result, the craurchins had to seek new food sources. Humans and dogs would not cut it as a staple of their diet because they put up too much of a fight. But of course, they would take advantage when an opportunity presented itself, the boy being one such example. With their natural food sources becoming more and more difficult to come by, they did the only thing they could do to survive. They ate their own. Currently, that was just the sick, weak, and dead, but in the beginning, it was common to fight to the death. This didn't last long because when the crabs and other larger crustaceans started disappearing, the barnacles, snails, worms, clams, mussels, and sea urchins that they preyed on grew in numbers and eventually became a large part of the craurchin diet.

Those along with the always-thriving insects, such as mosquitos, anopheles, beetles, and moths became the craurchins new staple. Smaller prey such as this was fine and abundant for cycle 1s, 2s, 3s, and even 4s, but not for cycle 5s and higher. Not even close. Their large size and insatiable appetite had them continually looking for larger more substantial prey, such as land mammals. Their blood, rich in nutritious proteins and lipids, could sustain them for hours, even days.

So, on this starry, chilly night, BakOo and her cluster roamed the beaches outside of their wetlands home and collected several dead cycle 3s, dug up clams and oysters on the sandbar, and stole a sizable horseshoe crab from a feisty cycle 4. The beach was crowded but there was plenty for everyone.

The real payday, however, was what they happened upon as they entered the wetlands on their way back to the lair. In the shallows, a large snapping turtle was preying upon a thirty-inch water snake. As the turtle grasped the snake in a death grip with its large jaws, BakOo crushed both reptiles with her right pincer. The snapper, shell caved in, provided meat for the entire cluster. The snake was just a bonus.

THE LAIR: DAY TWO

Terrell awoke slightly after midnight. The first thing that hit him was the rancid stench of the craurchins, the wetlands—and death. The second was the damp sand, twigs, and grass between his toes, which meant the paralysis was starting to subside. He must have lost his shoes when he was dragged here. The third was the cold— God it was cold! The cycle 6 and its craurchin cluster were sleeping in the shadows, half of the decaying, dead dog was still there to his right, and it appeared as if the cluster had brought home some new dead guests.

Agh, is that turtle shell and guts over there?

He could see all of this from the full moonlight reflecting off the pond. *Is this Bunker Pond?* He had been there a few times with his brothers, crabbing. As he lay there wiggling his toes, he realized once again his dilemma and thought, *I'm going to end up like the dog! The large cycle 6 craurchin is going to awaken and take more of my blood.* He didn't know how he knew that, but it was obvious to him. Just like it was obvious to him that that was the demise of the dead dog to his right.

That said, he had to get out before they awoke. He had to quietly leave the lair—and fast! And so, he stood up on his shaky legs and took a step forward. As soon as his left leg took on the weight of his body, he collapsed, hitting the lair floor with a thud. When he fell, he bounced off the ground and his head came down on a large rock. Lights out yet again.

When he awoke some time later, shivering in the cold night, he realized that paralysis still partially possessed his legs. *No shit!*

he thought. When he looked up, he saw five sets of eyes glowing in the darkness. Five sets of eyes reflecting cold light off of the hazy moonlight. It was a horribly surreal sight and again the panic set in. He was frightened. He remembered an old twentieth-century novel he had read a few years ago. A line from the book stuck with him. *What was it?* he thought. And it hit him. *Fear is the mind killer.* That was it. He took those words to heart and this time he did not pass out. This time he was only filled with anger. He thought of the cancer that took his mother. He thought of the depression that strangled his father on a daily basis, and the anxiety he was going through over the disappearance of his youngest son right this minute. Filled with panic and rage, a spate of angry words left his quivering lips.

"Fuck you, you fucking skanky swamp fucks! When my father and brothers find me, you are dead mother fuckers—*dead.*"

The 6 raised its pincer as if to say, *Bring it on, kid. Bring it on.*

Terrell awoke at first light, shivering. The 6 was again inserting his tube-tongue into the port below his ribcage. A little blood trickled down his stomach from the insertion point. The initial attachment was very painful but nowhere near as unsettling as the feeling of his blood leaving his body. Blood and—and something else. *I will not pass out. I will not pass out,"* he thought. He didn't think there was ever a time when he was so thirsty. He knew he was dehydrated, and he was beginning to feel very light-headed and weak. His heart was pounding.

These—are—just symptoms of blood loss. You—will—get through this, then you will get out of here and your body—will make new blood. Then the geeky boy genius in his head added,

Approximately 2 million red blood cells a second. As his head was growing heavier and the blood drained from his body, he felt as one with the craurchin.

He saw the craurchin. Bak0o was her name and he saw her life flash by in his head like a lightning fast movie. He saw her as a cycle 2 scavenging in the gully for food, as a 4 hunting in the dunes for toads, saw her cycle to 5, then to a 6. He saw all of this in seconds and the entire time he felt a strong, overwhelming theme in her being. Live to be an 8! Live to be an 8! And then, once again, his world went black. He would swear later that the passing out was his mother taking him away from the pain and horror, that it was all she could do to help him.

OCTOBER 23, 2271, 7:15 A.M.

As the Williams, Ballies, and Uncle Jackson continued talking, discussing the rescue plan and anxiously sipping coffee, they heard a knock on the front door.

"That will be our new friends." Jason was clearly nervous. It was now showtime. "Zak, bring them in please."

Zak brought the rescuers and their dogs into the kitchen where introductions were made around the table. The same table where the William's shared so many meals together. Jason poured coffee for the men and filled water bowls for the dogs, as he sized up his new guests, the five from Sea Isle.

The young, handsome, well-groomed men from the Heartland would be those two. Look at those nice clothes and sleek armor. Dante the rugged, muscular warrior, highest KP count in the state, that one, and Hakira and Khim, the community organizers and all-around humanitarians."

It immediately became clear who was coordinating the rescue effort.

"I want to tell you again, Mr. Williams, how truly sorry I am about your son, but also how extremely hopeful I am that we will get him back. My partner Khim over here," Hakira nodded toward Kim, "was taken by a craurchin many years ago. I was on the scene to treat him when he was rescued, just like I will be there when they bring Terrell out. Also, I've been part of more than a half-dozen similar rescues, all successful." What she didn't tell him was that most of the victims were never the same afterward. Many had chronic nightmares and one had even later committed suicide.

"I believe you, Hakira, I do."

"You and I will be with him on the hover taking him to that hospital in Maryland."

"Towson General, I contacted them. They will be waiting," Jason quipped.

"Excellent! Okay, so this is how it's gonna go down. Gabe, are you there yet with the DNA? Can you run through how we are going to use the drones?"

"Almost there, almost there. Ok, we're good." Gabe finished tapping on his controls and brushed a hair out of his eye. "Yes, we will use both drones. The 30 is now programmed to search for Terrell's DNA. I suspect that as it works its way to the lair, the drone will send us DNA from the beach or street near where he was taken, but the DNA we're looking for is in a wooded, secluded area, correct, Khim?"

"Yes." Khim was shaking his head knowingly. "Yes, most definitely in a wooded area. On Sandomars, craurchins need cover from the sky. The terragull is their only predator, so they build their lairs in heavily wooded areas."

Gabe continued. "Once the 30 finds Terrell's DNA in an area that most resembles a craurchin lair, we will send in the 22, which along with the 30, will hover above and wait."

Hakira picked up from there and continued. "Not just hover, but send us back intel. Lots of intel. Once we receive the data, which will be mostly photos and location coordinates, we will then rely on you guys." Hakira nodded toward the Williams, M.J., Joey, and Jackson. "You men will help plan our best route to the location and into the woods. Whatta ya say we launch the drones?"

Hakira nodded and Gabe and Bryce walked out the door to where the drones were sitting in the hovers. Within minutes, the 30 was off into the early morning sky. Bryce marveled at its aerodynamic beauty framed against the gray-blue sky.

"Why two drones?" Jackson asked Gabe when he came back inside.

"Ah Jackson, the 30 is an amazing drone. Truly amazing. Once it finds the boy it will send back crystal-clear images and spot-on coordinates. It will be able to zoom in on Terrell for a positive ID and close-ups for Hakira to assess his medical condition. Also, I have programmed it to do a basic medical analysis. It will check his vitals like blood pressure, heart rate, and body temp."

"Why not just have it take out the craurchin then and there?" James wanted to know.

"It is used in the commercial sector for many tasks that involve pinpoint accuracy; however, it is not a military combat drone. It will not have the maneuverability to man a close attack. I have it set up with a high-caliber gun to take out cycle 6s, but it is too dangerous to use with the boy nearby. That's where the UMV-22 comes in with its lasers and excellent maneuverability."

"Well, when this is all over, Terrell and I only ask that you let us fly it just one time." Jackson said hopefully.

"You can count on it! Let's make it happen!"

"I have a UMV-8 that Terrell retrofitted with what he calls Talons of Steel; do you think we could use it today?"

"My feeling is that as long as you know what you are doing, bring it along. With the 8 you will need human visibility of the scene, but sure. Steel talons?"

"That my friend is a story for another day. As you will hopefully find out, Terrell is an amazing kid!"

Ten minutes later, Bryce jumped up from his seat, "Ahh!" He had been looking at the aerials that the 30 was transmitting to the three screens that Gabe had set up on the kitchen table. "Okay we've got activity, there." He pointed to a green dot on the screen. Everyone stopped what they were doing to look at the green dot. The mood in the room was uneasy and tense.

"Okay, that's Terrell's DNA on the beach, just like we thought. Bryce, zoom out. There. See the trail of intermittent green?" Gabe had a knowing look on his face.

"That must be the route which the cycle 6 carried or dragged him." M.J. was amazed. "Look! It's heading right into the old Cape May wetlands area! Toward Bunker Pond."

"The wetlands make perfect sense, given all you've told us about a typical craurchin lair." Rory Bally added, looking at Khim.

Five minutes later, the 30 was hovering over Bak0o's lair. Gabe keyed some information into the controller and in a short time the drone was sending back photos and live video. He could see the green dot that represented Terrell's DNA, but the photos and video only showed treetops.

"Bring it down—there. There's a clearing."

In fact, all around the pond's edge, there were spots where the extremely dense trees had a clear opening to the sky. Gabe brought the hover down and shot photos and video through the clearing. Soon, the screens were filled with photos and video of the boy along with all his vital statistics. Jason and his two sons made a positive ID.

"That's him, Dad. It's him!" Zak and James were ecstatic, but what the father saw was his son's paleness, his extremely chapped lips, the bruises on his head, and abdomen and his battered half-naked body. *But what is that look on his face?* he thought. *Is that a smile?* Then it hit him.

"He hears the drone! I think he hears the drone—look at his head and face. He's looking up at the sky! Smiling!"

"Hakira, we are getting his vitals." Gabe interrupted. The brothers moved apart to allow her a closer look at the screen.

"Okay, here we go. Body temp ninety-five, not good but not hypothermia. Blood pressure ninety over sixty—very low. It should be around one-twenty over eighty for a boy his age, but considering his probable blood loss, that is to be expected. Heart rate is a hundred beats per minute and should be around seventy-eight. Here's the deal, men. We've got to get to him right now. He is likely on the verge of hypovolemia."

While all the data was coming in and being responded to, Gabe had gone out to the lead hover and plugged the coordinates of the lair into the navigation system. They were ready to go.

"Time to finalize the plans," Hakira finished.

"I know the area." M.J. announced. "And I can see from the aerial the exact location of the lair. We used to fish there many years ago. The woods will be much thicker now."

"Yes, but the 6 will have created a trail with its large body," Rory pointed out. "Gabe, can you see if the drone can locate a trail to the lair?"

THE PLAN

They came up with a fairly simple plan. From its entrance off of the beach, Dante, Khim, Gabe, and Bryce, with their armored vests, gloves and coveralls, would enter the trail and conduct a direct assault on the lair. They would be following Neville and Scout, the only dogs used for the rescue, as they were the best trained to sniff out craurchins. The men all had lasers, and Gabe had control of the drones, which he would use to prevent the cycle 6 from escaping into the pond. They had verified via aerials from the 30, the exact location of the cycle 6 and its cluster. There appeared to be five or six craurchins in the cluster.

M.J. and James would come in from the northeast and Joey and Zak from the southeast, both heading at angles toward the lair. Jackson would lag a little behind the trail team, flying Talons of

Steel close behind him. The first with an opportunity to grab Terrell would do so.

Hakira and Jason would wait on the beach, at the trail entrance, hovers waiting to whisk Terrell to the hospital.

"Dr. Brady! Dr. Brady, what are you—"

"We're a small community, Jason. Word gets around."

"Hakira, this is Norm Brady, our community MD."

"Nice to meet you, Ms. Hakira, I heard you're a nurse."

"I am. Let me fill you in on the logistics here and Terrell's condition."

When she was finished, Dr. Brady pointed to a small cooler he had placed on the sand.

"In that cooler, I've got three units of moo mix. That will hold him over until he gets to the hospital. We'll get the transfusion going as soon as we get him in the hover."

Moo mix was the slang name for synthetic blood made from bovine plasma. This synthetic blood had been used extensively over the last two centuries, mostly on the battlefield for injured soldiers in desperate need of blood. Soldiers who, far from any hospital, haven't the time or luxury to wait for their blood match. Moo mix provided temporary replacement of the lost blood until it could be replaced.

"A cow can yield as much as fifty pints of blood and once the plasma is processed, the synthetic blood has a shelf life of over two years." Dr. Brady nodded confidently toward the cooler. "The Heartland sends me about a hundred units a year. It will keep him alive until he gets to the hospital. Also, these leechings can have devastating psychological effects on a victim. Terrell may need help when he recovers from his physical injuries. He will need help with his head, and the person who can give him that help is Dr. Marcus DiFillipo."

THE LAIR: DAY THREE

Terrell awoke at dawn, almost a full day since the craurchin last took his blood. A slight breeze off the pond made his never-ending chills worse than ever. His heart was racing. He felt light-headed, weak, and he knew he was in the early stages of hypovolemia. He knew that when the craurchins awoke, the cycle 6 would take another pint or so of blood, and after that he would be on his way to death's doorway.

Yes, being a genius really sucks, he thought. He looked over at his shiny black friends across the way, sleeping off their early morning cocktail. They would be active in about an hour as Terrell's precious blood made its way through their sophisticated biology.

The light-headedness was getting worse. The light buzzing in his head was turning into a humming outside his head. Like he had left his body and was looking and hearing from outside of it.

But it was real—coming from the sky. Terrell looked up and saw it. The most beautiful, graceful, eloquent drone he had even laid eyes on, and that's when the smile appeared on his face.

THE RESCUE

Gabe coordinated M.J.'s group and Rory's group via coordinates transmitted to him from the UMV-30. When his group was within sixty feet of the lair, he stopped them. They could actually see the lair below at the bottom of the trail. Dante put his pointer finger to his lips and whispered to the dogs, "Scout, Neville, quiet, boys." He knew they could smell the craurchins even this far away.

Gabe whispered into his communicator as he looked at the screen. "We're now at our sub-rendezvous point. I repeat, we are now sixty feet from the lair. Rory, you are at seventy-five feet and M.J., stop at my command—now. Good, stay put. Rory, you are at seventy, sixty-five, stop." He was now speaking to all three groups. "Okay, gentlemen, are we ready?" Nods and thumbs went up all around. It was amazing how, in challenging situations, certain people seemed to step up. This was most definitely such a day for Gabe Hanson Marshall.

"Okay, on three. Ready, one, two, three. Let's go!" Gabe shouted into his communicator.

Nine men, two dogs, and a UMV-8 drone retrofitted with talons of steel, charged into the area of the lair in almost perfect synchronicity. They came in from every direction but that of the pond. All of the men came in firing their weapons at the craurchin, trying for that all-important headshot. The dogs went right for the smaller craurchins and Zak went right for his brother.

The cycle 6 assessed the situation, realized she didn't have a chance of winning this battle, and immediately raced toward the water, lasers, and bullets hitting her hard, impenetrable shell. There was a split second where she thought of going for the boy human but aborted that thought quickly. Once she got into the water the men would have an extremely hard time getting a shot at her head. And when she submerged and got out to deeper waters, she'd be safe.

Meanwhile, Nevelle and Scout were taking care of the remaining cluster. "Nevelle, Scout, get the legs!" Dante commanded. He was confident that Neville knew what had to be done, and was hoping Scout would follow suit. Nevelle immediately charged and latched onto the 6's hind leg as it crawled toward the pond. Scout latched onto the other leg, and the craurchin screeched in pain but continued retreating toward the pond, her pincers covering her head. She was getting close to the pond, dragging the dogs with her, but the dogs were slowing her down.

The men all came in closer for a shot, but the craurchin was only twenty feet from the water's edge now. They needed to get between it and the pond. Dante pulled out his samurai sword and was slashing its other two legs, but that only slowed it down a little. He dropped the sword and was about to jump onto the creature's back and climb up for the critical headshot, when Gabe shouted to the group.

"Everyone, fall back. We'll take it out with the drones. Bryce, you've got the 22. I'll control the 30!" Bryce immediately brought the 22 in for an attack as Gabe was putting on his motion sync suit. This special suit would allow Gabe to control the drone via his body motions.

Zoop, zoop, zoop. The laser shots were getting close to the head but none actually hit.

Zoop, zoop, zoop—a head graze, but then the 6 descended into the pond.

"Everybody! Back! I'm bringing in the 30. This is our last shot at killing this motherfucker!" Gabe had the suit on, swooping to and fro like some kind of deranged exotic bird, mimicking with his body the maneuvers he wanted the drone to perform, like a master pup-peteer performing his grand finale.

While Gabe was positioning the 30 for the kill, Jackson flew in the 8 and was trying desperately to keep the craurchin's large bleeding head from submerging. He had it grasped tightly in his drone's steel talons as he frantically pounded the buttons and joy-sticks on his controller, trying to build up linear force. He knew he couldn't rip the bitch's head off, but if he could hold it out of the water long enough, one of the other drones might get a headshot.

"Hold onto it, Jack. Hold on. I'm coming in!" Bryce was in better position as he looped the 22 up and around and was swoop-ing in for another attack. *Zoop, zoop, zoop—zoop, zoop, zoop.* Six solid shots all landed near the head and one actually hit the head. Unfortunately, one of the shots took out Jackson's UMV-8.

"Get the boy out of here. Take at least four men with him! Go!" Khim, more than anyone, knew how important it was to get him out of the woods and to the hospital. Terrell was semicon-scious, mostly oblivious to the frenzy happening around him.

As the Williams brothers, M.J. and Rory, carried Terrell up the trail toward the beach, they heard a humming noise growing louder and louder. Still moving, they turned around just in time to see the UMV-30 as it came in low and launched what appeared to be a mini-missile. The missile slammed into the large dark shadow in the shallow water with an explosion that shook the entire lair and embankment, sending birds and other fowl squawking into the morning sky.

The craurchin, wounded from the mini-missile that had just penetrated its large skull, continued moving and twisting, turning the water a bright reddish-green. Then, finally Bak0o's struggling ended, and her body lay lifeless in the shallow waters by the edge of her lair.

CHAPTER 16

THE KNOWING

In my recovery
I'm a soldier at war
I have broken down walls
I defined
I designed
My recovery
In the sound of the sea
In the oceans of me
I defined
I designed
My recovery
—"The Recovery, "James Arthur

TERRELL'S RECOVERY

The latest cyberattack by Russo-China had knocked out the UniNet for almost 24 hours. It was not the first time, and most Americans realized it wouldn't be the last. This time, however, was the longest anyone had gone without it. It was an entire day. Billions of dollars lost. Tons of files and information gone. It affected business, entertainment, multimedia, communication, and every other conceivable aspect of ordinary human life.

It was just another sacrifice that Americans were asked to make in the name of a war that seemed to have no end. A war that made little sense. It was also another point scored for Russo-China. In this war, attacks on infrastructure were the rules of engagement. Drone pilots, computer hackers, robots, and high-tech programmers were the first feet on the ground, not the Marines.

"The Net is back; the Net is back!" An assistant nurse was marching up and down the corridors of Towson General Hospital and Organ Farm, sharing the news with the doctors, nurses, and patients. One by one, the wall screens in the patient rooms came to life. In Patient Room 307, Mr. Jansen, who had just received a new heart, jumped eight inches off his bed. Seemed his new ticker was working just fine.

"Welcome back to Independence News, America. Hopefully, you were following us through other news mediums during the outage. After a long day of interrupted service, the Net is back online, and the U.S. military feels they can block any further attacks."

The wall in front of Terrell's bed flashed its bright, brilliant light, and the news of the day into his eyes. He had been lying awake in the dark room for almost two hours, thinking about his ordeal of two days ago. It was taking him some time to adjust to the sudden intense light. Thankfully, the volume was not up too high or his ears, accustomed to the silence, would have been assaulted as well.

"Had she not stabilized you with the fluids and synthetic blood, your organs would have begun to shut down and you may not be here right now, Terrell." Doctor Bryson had high praise for Hakira and all that she had done.

Terrell was enormously grateful for the woman, a woman who didn't even know him, and what she had done to save his life. Her, and the others from Sea Isle. Doctor Bryson told him all about the moo mix IV, the stabilization of his spine during the journey to the hospital, and the dressing of his wounds, but it was what the nurse on the day shift had told him, that kept him awake most of the night.

"In your sleep, you spoke nonstop of the connection. You were going on and on about the connection with the cycle 6. Was it communicating with you, Terrell?" Nurse Bonnie seemed to be a very perceptive person. It was almost like she knew what Terrell had experienced at the lair. That, or she was really curious. What Terrell didn't know was that she'd treated taken victims in the past. Mostly, the recent past. But right now, right here in this hospital bed, Terrell could not recollect what exactly that connection was. He remembered something vague, like a common knowing, but it was becoming grayer and grayer, fading away like the embers of a campfire recently doused with water.

"And now, some news from the Badlands. Two days ago, we reported on a young fourteen-year-old boy who, in a masterful plan executed by a group of Badlanders and the boy's family, was rescued from a cycle 6's lair. The Badlanders used drones to track the child and—"

"TV off," Terrell spat at the screen. "Off!"

The last thing he wanted right now was to relive those terrible days in the cycle 6's lair. In the darkness once again, he felt oddly calm, at ease and focused. Focused on the one thing.

What was the connection? he thought. Out of nowhere, it hit him like a fighter's surprise left hook. *The blood taking. It was during the blood taking when I was physically connected to the 6, that the knowing had occurred.*

It was then that he realized the overwhelming knowledge he possessed. The lights were back on, brighter than ever, and everything was oh so clear! Terrell now knew what the craurchin takeover was all about. He just—knew. He had to warn his fellow Badlanders. Not the Heartland. They were not to be trusted, and even if they were, they would not take the news seriously—not from a fourteen-year-old boy and not from the Badland leadership either. He suddenly had this overwhelming desire—no, need—to be home in the Badlands with his family, his community, and his dogs. He knew now that the dogs knew what he knew. He knew now why they were the craurchins' natural enemy. Why the dogs needed to destroy each and every craurchin they came upon. Needed to prevent them from moving on to their next cycle, especially the 7s! For some reason, he knew, and the dogs knew as well, that the craurchins could not be allowed to reach cycle 8. Bak0o had lived and breathed that ultimate desire. It filled her very being and the very being of all craurchins. This Terrell knew.

His father and Hikira were camped out in the third-floor lounge down the hallway from Terrell. Jason had another rough night, only sleeping a fitful few hours. The first night, he was deeply distressed that his son may not survive. Hakira had assured him that statistically Terrell had a high chance for a full recovery, but Jason's anxiety would not allow him to process that positive news.

All his mind would allow him to believe was the negative information the doctor had discussed. He knew that the doctor was obligated to discuss, namely that due to the blood loss, there was always the possibility of organ failure, and of course, he could not get that notion off his mind. And even though Terrell had pulled through with no evidence of any long-term damage, Jason's anxiety would not allow him to accept that.

"Jason, are you awake?" Hikira stretched her long legs out on the leather sofa. "Mr. Williams?"

"Ya. Would you like some coffee?" He had gotten two cups from the nurses earlier.

"You didn't sleep again, did you?" She accepted one of the cups and took a sip. Jason shook his head no.

"Hakira, you can leave today if they decide not to release him. You've done so much for us. You and Khim and the others. We'll find a way back to the Badlands somehow."

"Jason, I am going nowhere, and if you mention me leaving without you and Terrell again, I will be obliged to smack you in the back of yer big ol' bald head. We are family now, motherfucker, whether you like it or not."

"I'm sorry, Hakira. I'm just not used to putting people out. Do you want to go and meet the boy genius now?"

In Terrell's room, the front wall was lit up with the morning news. The polished middle-aged man on the screen looked at the camera and then to man on his left. *"And now business news with Dwight Perry. Dwight."*

"Thanks, Don, in business news today, the U.S. Military has signed a ten-trillion-dollar contract with CraTek Corporation to manufacture unibodies, frames, and other parts for the proposed Strike Drone III assault drone. The raw material used by CraTek to manufacture these components comes from the shells of cycle 5 craurchins and is considered by many scientists to be the strongest material on the planet. Not only is the material super strong but it is lightweight as well. Many of these scientists believe that the higher the cycle, the stronger the shell. The product that will be used for the Strike Drone III, is a modified version of the material used on the Volvo Safeguard, the world's safest hover."

CraTek? Where did I hear that name before? Terrell shoveled in his hospital breakfast of eggs and fruit. Since he had awoken that second day, his appetite had been ravenous. Just as he was wondering where his father was, Jason walked in with a younger, pretty woman with long jet-black hair.

"Hey, kiddo! Good morning. Terrell, I would like you to meet Hakira. She is—"

"I know all about Hakira, Dad. Thank you, Miss Hakira, thank you with all my heart!"

Terrell offered Hakira his right hand but she was having none of that. She came right in and gave him the biggest hug he had received since the death of his mother. In that embrace, Terrell knew he had a new friend, as did Hakira. When they released each other, Hakira patted her wet eyes with the sleeve of her shirt. She was overcome with emotion. Deep unexplainable emotion.

"You are one special kid, Terrell."

"That he is." Jason tugged his right ear, a quirk he perpetrated when nervous. Right now, he was nervous. He knew his son, and he could sense something was wrong.

"Terrell, are you in pain? Is everything okay? Where is the doctor?"

"Dad, it's okay. I'm fine."

Hakira took Jason's hands in hers. She looked into his eyes and spoke softly to him. "Jason, you have been through an ordeal and it is all catching up to you right now. Listen to me. Terrell is okay. His young body has performed its magic and will continue to do so. I am sure the doctor will confirm this when he comes in. Shall I go find him?"

Jason nodded his head. "Would you mind?"

Hakira returned, and ten minutes later, Nurse Bonnie waltzed into the room, bright and alert as ever. She was just starting her shift, and Terrell was her first patient. "How's my superhero and cutest patient doing today?" Terrell blushed uncontrollably as she took his temperature, checked his IV, his blood pressure, heart rate, and other vital stats and recorded them in his profile from her ePad.

"Looking good, kiddo. All of your vitals are right where they wanna be. Now, we just wait and see what Dr. Smith has to say. He should be in shortly. In the meantime, do you need anything?"

"I'm good, thanks," Terrell replied in a high-pitched voice that again left him blushing.

"Okay, well just push the button if you do." She looked and nodded her head at Hakira and Jason, confirming what she had just told the boy about his vitals, then left the room.

"So, Dad? Hakira? I have something really important to tell you two. I mean this is, like, pretty huge."

Hakira and Jason exchanged glances, and Jason nodded his head to Terrell. "What is it, son?"

"What I am about to tell you is going to sound a little crazy, but I assure you it is true. It is not something I dreamed. It really happened."

"Please, go on," Hakira chimed in. Terrell had Hakira and his dad's full attention.

"Well, when I was connected to the craurchin—you know when I was its little human IV bag—there was this, this more than physical connection. It was more like a telepathic connection. I could feel its thoughts, feel its—uh, her being."

"I don't understand. If we were to assume a craurchin communicates in a certain language, wouldn't its thoughts be in that language as well?"

"I know, Hakira, maybe telepathic wasn't the best description. It was more like a knowing—I knew what it knew, and it knew what I know. It was like a mutual download. But its the information I downloaded from it that I want to talk about."

"I remember Khim mentioning a type of connection when he was taken, but he could not remember anything specific and what he could remember he couldn't articulate. Eventually, the memory just faded away. But he does suffer from PCLS, post-craurchin leeching syndrome."

"What is that information you want to talk about?" his father asked. "That you downloaded," he added.

"It's really quite simple. We can't allow craurchins to reach cycle 8."

CHAPTER 17

THE ADVOCATE

In the field of opportunity
It's plowin' time again.
There ain't no way of telling
Where these seeds
will rise or when
I'll just wait
around 'til springtime
And then, I'll find a friend
In the field of opportunity
It's plowin' time again.
—"FIELD OF OPPORTUNITY," NEIL YOUNG

THE ADVOCATE

The sleek, self-flying hovercopter landed on the roof of Casa Azteca, next to a small fleet of other flying machines. A few seconds later, a sturdy, middle-aged man with short, thinning brown hair and a salt and pepper close-cropped beard climbed out. The well-dressed man was more distinguished looking than handsome, but handsome nonetheless. He was talking into his communicator, which was in his right hand and he held an ePad in his left. He walked across his roof, peered into the pupil reader on his door, where the red light turned green, and the door opened. The door then closed behind him followed by three solid clicks as the light turned red again.

Jonathan A. Pendleton, AKA "Aztec" was the wealthiest man in the Badlands. Hell, he was one of the wealthiest men in the country. He was known by his peers as the Liquorjuana King, making his fortune as a distiller of various hemp-liquor infusions. His most popular brand, Tequillajuana Agave Bold, was a Pendleton Distilleries top seller. Aztec lived in the Badlands and ran his company out of Buena, a small city in southwest New Jersey. His company motto was "Pendleton Distilleries, quality products from the Heart of the Badlands." Aztec was not ashamed of where he came from.

"Deirdra stop—stop Deirdra and listen. Deirdra, my friend, please—please just stop jabbering for five seconds and let me say my piece!" Aztec's face was bright red but he remained calm.

Deirdra Monaghan was New Jersey's state representative to the Heartland. She was a fifty-five-year-old career politician who spent more time in the Heartland wining and dining with

Bloomington dignitaries than she did with her own constituents in the Badlands. In fact, not a single person living in the Badlands can actually recall her ever visiting the Badlands. Rumor had it she wasn't even from New Jersey.

A few years ago, while giving an interview, she slipped up and called the Badlands the Cralands, a derogatory slur that most Badlanders adamantly despised. Sure, she had constituents in other parts of New Jersey, actually many more, but they were doing okay. They didn't live with the day-to-day challenges that the typical Badlander endured.

"Deirdra, I am simply asking that you talk to the commission about keeping the streetlights on an extra two hours longer—that's all, two additional, God-loving hours my dear, come on! Excuse me—really? Well, how much did I contribute to your re-election campaign last year? You don't remember? Well, I remember quite clearly, love. It was five million. What was that? Okay, fine, great, let me know how it goes. All right, you know I love you." Aztec disconnected and plopped onto his plush sofa with a thump and long sigh.

"Like hell, she's gonna see what she can do! Godddamn fucking liar! Dweezle, bring me a drink, please."

"De usual cooming right up," replied his robant.

Aztec had two main robots managing his homestead. Dweezle the robant controlled the staff of domestic robots and humans that kept the house and grounds in order. They maintained the grounds, cooked, cleaned, served, and attended to any and all domestic needs both inside and outside. Slash was the Milibant. He controlled all security. He was actually a combination drone and robot and was fitted with two pinpoint accurate lasers for defense, if and when needed.

A few minutes later, Dweezle returned with a fifty-year single-malt scotch in a crystal tumbler with one tiny ice cube. "Here you are, Meester Aztec, eze dere anything else I kin get for you?"

Aztec took a sip. "Ah."

He stood up and walked to the large window overlooking the beach. "I'm good Dweezle, thank you, kind sir. Oh wait, I forgot. Put it in my calendar to call Senator Johnson tomorrow afternoon—oh, and make sure I have one of these when I do so." Aztec raised his glass. "I'm gonna need it."

Dweezle nodded. "Yez, Meester Aztec." He then began his way out of the room as Aztec thought, as he often did, why he had had Dweezle programmed with a heavy Hispanic accent.

Aztac stood at the window, admiring the remarkable ocean view. "It's just Aztec. Lose the 'Mister,' Dweezle. Lose the 'Mister.'"

Below, his private beach was as pristine and beautiful as ever. He could even see some noncraurchin activity. This was because it was devoid of craurchins for a half-mile in each direction and barricaded off with electrified, heavy-gauge steel fencing that ran for a mile into the sea. And so, the wildlife prevailed.

To keep his beach clear, he employed several of his staff, who used a machine that Aztec had developed himself. This was a state-of-the-art machine that raked up the craurchins, sifted out the sand, then threw them one by one into his patented cra-chipper. Like a regular chipper, it ground them up and shot the remains through a hopper onto the beach, providing a tasty snack for the seagulls and other marine wildlife. Unfortunately, the machine only worked on cycles 1 through 4. The rest were too large. He also had a pack of wilds, which he allowed to run free on his land. Not only were they a beautiful site to observe from his beachfront perch, but they provided further security from any craurchin trespassers. He fitted them with special override collars that allowed them to migrate off of the property at will, without getting electrocuted.

Finally, he had the ocean cleared of craurchins and had sturdy nets installed a half-mile north, south, and east into the sea. This provided a double barrier, which allowed him to surf the waves craurchin-free. In fact, he was just about to get up and don his wetsuit for some early evening surfing, when his girlfriend, Phoebe Watermark walked into the room.

Phoebe was also director of Pendleton Philanthropy. She was a stunning and bright thirty-five-year-old who had an affinity for vintage 1960s fashion, like the tight denim skirt and paisley halter top she was wearing now. She filled it out perfectly and looked quite wonderful with her hair tied up in a matching velvet headband. As always, she brought a radiant infusion of warmth and "this is what life is all about" to Aztec's often hectic world.

"Where do you think you're going, Meester Aztec?"

"Funny Phebes, real funny." Aztec put a hand on each side of her hips and gave her a passionate kiss on her full lips. "How is the light of my life today?"

"Meester Aztec is feelin' quite feisty tonight. I am wonderful, Senor Azteca. Did you have a good day, sweetie?"

"Ugh, not really. I just got off of the phone with that bitch, Representative Monaghan. She sure knows how to pull my levers!

She makes big promises but does nothing—nothing for the Badlands! Quite aggravating, to say the least."

"Well, we may have given her five million last time, but she is up for re-election next year, and we will give her opponent triple that. How are you doing with Peters?" Phebes also managed his political affairs.

"He wouldn't take my call, but I'm calling Johnson tomorrow."

"Vince Johnson? Why, to offer condolences?"

"Condolences? Condolences for what?" Aztec had no clue what she was alluding to.

"You haven't heard?"

"Heard what, Phoebe?" He used her proper name when matters were serious.

"Oh my! Vince Johnson Jr. was killed last week by a cycle 5 right here in the Badlands. He and a group of friends were hunting in Avalon and were attacked by a large 5. Two survived and Junior and another man were impaled by the craurchin. Horrible ordeal, horrible."

"That's quite terrible. When is the service?"

"Not sure, they are waiting for the body to be returned to the Heartland."

"Dweezle, hey Dweezle." Aztec called for his robant. "Phebes, what will you be drinking?"

"Bourbon. After the day I've had, I need bourbon."

"Hello, Miz Phoebe. Aztec, did you cull?"

"Yes, Dweezle. Please send flowers to Senator Johnson's house. Also, find out the status of his dead son's body. I hear a storm is coming, and we need to make sure Vince Junior makes it home unscathed. He was killed two days ago in Avalon along with a friend. See what you can dig up about the incident, but first get Phoebe a bourbon on the rocks." He glanced over at Phoebe who nodded approvingly.

Later on that evening, after the love making and pillow talk were done, Aztec and Phoebe took a moonlight stroll on Aztec's private beach. Aztec had his architect site the house on the northern tip of Ocean City to capture views of the old Ocean Drive Bridge, the Great Egg Harbor Inlet and the volatile Atlantic Ocean. As they walked, Aztec fixated on the ominous night sky. The winds were just starting to pick up a bit.

"The storm will hit here tomorrow. I should activate the lifts and buckle everything down tonight. This is going to be a bad one." Aztec squinted, and his eyebrows were squished down, his look of concern and deep thinking.

They walked along the beach line all the way to the north fence, then turned around and walked to the south fence and then back toward Casa Azteca, where Aztec built a fire halfway down the beach. They sat in the sand holding hands and sipping wine by the crackling fire. Phoebe sprinkled some wine assist, another Pendleton Distilleries product, into each of their glasses. They toasted to another day. They toasted to having found each other. Then they sat by the fire, hand in hand, allowing the relaxing additive and wine to fill their senses, as they gazed at the crashing waves at the edge of the beach.

I don't know, Phebes. It's like they are deliberately neglecting the Badlands, you know? They are making less drops, providing less medical care, ignoring my calls—your calls. Just showing no regard for the people. Christ Phebes, these are American citizens for fuck's sake. My contact told me that the government is no longer providing tax credits for Badland hunting trips and that he sees less and less commercials advertising for these trips. I heard from a reliable source that they have stopped breeding wilds. Now why, by God, would they do that?"

"Jon, you don't see it, do you?" She was waiting for the right time to broach this subject. She got right to the point. "They want the craurchins to thrive. To grow. The bigger the better."

"Thrive? What? Why the hell would they want them to thrive?"

"Two words Jon—CraTek Industries."

Aztec's eyes grew large as it hit him hard and clear. How did he miss that?

Phoebe's eyes answered his questions, and unfortunately that answer was a resounding yes.

CHAPTER 18

THE WILDWOODS

Sun streaking cold, an old man wandering lonely
Taking time, the only way he knows
Leg hurting bad as he bends to pick a dog end
He goes down to a bog and warms his feet
Feeling alone, the army's up the road
Salvation a la mode and a cup of tea
Aqualung, my friend, don't you start away uneasy
You poor old sod, you see it's only me
— "AQUALUNG," JETHRO TULL

DUNGY DON, END OF SUMMER 2272

It was quite chilly for an early September morning, so the tired old man with the long white beard, matted, dirty hair, and filthy clothes pushed open the door to the old souvenir shop on East Garfield Avenue and the boardwalk. The store signage had long since fallen down and blown away. It was about two blocks down from Morey Mariner's Pier, where Don, known by all as Dungy Don, and his dog Dusty had slept last night. He had found them a warm, cozy spot at the top platform of the haunted pirate ship. Safely elevated from any craurchins, he had settled in for the night with a bottle of Jack Daniels and ten or so cigarette butts he had gathered outside of the Skulls clubhouse. If you had been standing near Don, you would have identified a combination of pungent odors, all mixed together to form a bouquet, which included whiskey, tobacco, piss, and foul breath. Don and Dusty walked into his most recent favorite shop, still partially stocked with merchandise from forty years ago. A store the Skulls had apparently overlooked and not looted after the evacs. He made his way to a rack filled with colorful hoodies and found an XL in aqua green. The front of the hoody sported a picture of a sexy, devilish-looking woman with large breasts and a multitude of colorful tattoos.

Below the woman were the words "Wild Child" written in cherry red. On the back in white letters, "Wildwood, N.J.—Because I Couldn't Afford Cape May." He put on the jacket, which was too big for him, and ventured back out onto the windy boardwalk and it hit him. Hit him hard this time.

"What da fuck. What da fuck!" he yelled as he bobbed up

and down, up and down, across the store. The stomach pains were back with a vengeance. "Fuck. Fuck, fuck!" He doubled over, then he retched up the whiskey that was in his belly. "Fuck."

He stood back up, still slightly hunched over as he stared into space, waiting for the pain to subside. His skin was very pale, almost yellow like the sclera of his tired eyes. His nose was red and bulbous. He was actually not an old man at all, only fifty-eight years old. Don, who had been a homeless runaway during the evacuations at the age of eighteen, remembered a time when being homeless was not so difficult. In the years preceding 2230, food was plentiful. There were hundreds of pizza parlors, hot dog stands, hamburger joints, restaurants, clubs, bars, ice cream parlors, and various boardwalk stands that threw away tons of food at the end of each day. In the summer, there was always the beach, under the boards or somebody's couch on which to crash.

In the winter, you had your pick of unoccupied summer cottages and vacation homes. In that last year in Wildwood, before everyone left and the Skulls and craurchins took over, Don had actually had a job and his own place. Well, he squatted there, but it was home nonetheless, and at least he wasn't transient. To him, at that moment in time, life was indeed good.

I thought I could go a little longer today, Don thought, but the pain was just too much. He needed to go to his hiding spot and grab a bottle. Dusty, a mid-size Australian Shepherd with glaucoma in his left eye, growled softly. They had been friends for almost twelve years now. Dungy stepped out of the store and looked each way up, and then down the boardwalk. About four blocks away, Don could see a big one slowly heading their way. He had to watch out these days because he was not nearly as quick as he used to be, especially in his current state.

Out on the beach, you could barely even see the sand. They were everywhere. So, he walked down the ramp toward the street. The beaches in Wildwood were so large that craurchins rarely roamed the streets. Rarely but not never. About halfway down the ramp, he heard a steady whooshing sound coming from the direction of the beach. It grew louder and louder. He turned and walked back up the rotting wooden ramp to take a look at the source. The large craurchin was nowhere in sight now. He stood on the edge of the boardwalk, leaning against the rickety rail, gazing down upon the beach.

"Holy fuck!" he said aloud, as four large drones, flying side by side and ten feet above the beach, whooshed by. He knew the white fog they were spraying down upon the beach would kill him, or at least make him sick, if he did not get indoors. And so, he ran-staggered into the souvenir shop and closed the door. Once inside, he grabbed a few t-shirts, rolled them up, and draped them over the gap between the door and the floor. He then grabbed two more shirts and wrapped one around his nose and one around Dusty's. Then, he waited.

He awoke to Dusty, at the window, barking loudly. *How long was I asleep?* He got up and stepped back out onto the boardwalk.

"What the fuck?" he said to himself, half-whispering the words.

Below, men were walking the beach in a single column, side by side. They wore white camouflage coveralls, white gloves, ankle-high boots, and gas masks. Also, they were armed. Dusty knew to keep quiet.

What the hell are they doing? Don thought, *Shit, they are shooting the craurchins that didn't die from the spray. No wait, they are only shooting the big ones. I guess they were too big to die from the spray.*

Then Dungy Don noticed something. Further down the beach, perhaps two or three blocks, in the direction that the drones had flown in from earlier, another group of men operating large trucks with giant heavy-duty beach wheels were loading the big, dead craurchins into the bed. Also, some of the smaller ones had awoken, and the men were allowing them—no, actually herding them—off into the sea. Some just burrowed into the sand. Just before one of the camouflaged men had spotted him, he noticed the logo on one of the trucks. CraTek Industries.

"Ey, you! Come 'ere!"

"Fuck that, come on, Dusty!"

Did he just shoot at me? Shit.

Don ran like he had never ran before, pain or no pain, off the boardwalk and toward his spot. He ran down Garfield to Atlantic, where he turned left and ran for a few blocks before dipping into some overgrowth at Fox Park. He lay quietly on the ground, trying to catch his breath. Dusty was right next to him. After a few minutes, he peeked out and peered up and down the streets. It was all clear.

He then got up and took off down East Burk Street toward his spot. For the next two blocks, he walked quickly, trying to catch his breath, constantly looking behind him. Just before he reached

Artic Avenue, he looked all around, then cut down a narrow path, basically a small alley, that ran between two houses. Dusty was at his heels. At the end of the alley, to his right, was a narrow set of stairs that led down to a wine cellar.

"Okay, no one followed me. No one followed me. Please, no one followed me," he whispered to himself. "Let's go, Duster!"

He and Dusty descended the three stairs. At the bottom, Dungy Don pulled a key out of his pocket and opened the metal door to the wine cellar he had discovered last year, his refuge and personal paradise in a world that had forgotten him.

CRATEK: THE WILDWOOD CAMPAIGN

The dozen or so fumigation drones started their Wildwood campaign on Diamond Beach, at the south end of the Wildwoods and flew north all the way to Anglesea. A four-and-a-half-mile trek of craurchin infested beach and sand dunes. They then circled back and repeated the same route a couple more times before landing in Diamond Beach for recharging. CraTek Team One immediately started their run, marching down the beach in full gear and gas masks. Their job was to attach tracking devices and blue tags on 5s and larger. A red tag was placed on certain craurchins of cycles 1, 2, and 3. One hour after their descent, Team Two started out on the same route, in the same regalia, armed with shotguns.

"All righty, Team Two, let's move! Remember just shoot 5s and larger. If you come upon a 6, make sure you kill it dead! Make sure you put one slug in each brain. Also, do not shoot craurchins with a red tag. I repeat, don't shoot red tags. If a blue tag is still alive, call 555 for fumigation. Tillman will take care of it. Okay! Let's go!"

Former Marine Staff Sergeant Robert "Rusty" Cohms was hired by CraTek a year ago. He was serving today as Lead Field Operations Manager for the Wildwoods campaign.

"So, do you think the Rust Man's gonna lose his shit again today? There, Jo! Kill that 5. It's starting to move!"

Blam, blam. "Probably. When doesn't the bastard lose his shit?" The 5 stopped moving, blood splattered all over the whitish-gray sand. Three smaller Craurchins, probably part of its cluster, ran into the sea.

"Run, little fellows, run. Freedom, freedom," Jo sang. "He fucking runs this operation like we're fucking Marines."

Mohammad, a lover of old rock classics, started singing one of his favorite Who songs, cleverly, or so he thought, substituting his own lyrics.

You're free. You're free. And freedom tastes like a Cra-urchin spree. You're free, you're free." On cue, he shot a 5 attempting to stand up.

"Hey, Mo."

"Yeah."

"Shut the fuck up."

"Sorry. Oh, shit. I almost shot a tagged 5. Damn, that was close. By the way, what do we do if a blue tag wakes up?"

"Don't you listen? The Rust Man said that Tillman will be manning fumigation. You call Tillman, 555!"

They continued along the beach, shooting mostly 5s and the occasional 6, leaving the ones that were tagged with red stickers.

Tillman was a few blocks behind, hitting the red tags with the portable fumigation tank he had hovering along with him.

"Team Three, let's go!" The command rattled the air.

Manny put the old nitrogen-operated truck into gear. *In about an hour, this thing's gonna stink to high hell.* As he came upon his first dead 5, he engaged the levers in the truck and sucked the craurchin into the bed. There were four trucks just like his, all moving in line. When full, the enormous trucks would head to the de-shelling station. Behind them, another row of trucks would gather the red-tagged craurchins for reproduction acceleration and the blue tags for study.

Manny lit a safecig as he performed the monotonous work. *Get used to it, Manny,* he thought. *The union said if I play my cards right, I could be doing this for the next five years.*

CHAPTER 19

OCEAN CITY

'Twas in another lifetime, one of toil and blood
When blackness was a virtue the road was full of mud
I came in from the wilderness, a creature void of form
Come in, she said
I'll give ya shelter from the storm
— "Shelter from the Storm," Bob Dylan

AFTER THE STORM

Dweezle did his research and reported his findings to Aztec and Phoebe on a beautiful morning three days after the fifth super storm of the year, and twelve days after the taking of Terrell Williams. The storm was a bad one, hitting most of the Jersey coast and feeding many occupied and unoccupied structures to the hungry Atlantic Ocean.

In Ocean City, the boardwalk took a pretty good beating, with about half of it being washed away, but all in all, it faired pretty well. With the exception of a breach in the south barricade, Casa Azteca stood up against the elements and was still jacked up thirty-five feet in the air. Before any big storm, Aztec always offered up his home to anybody who desired shelter and the last of his guests had left yesterday.

On the south deck, the two humans and robant were conducting business as the light breezes hit them, cool and invigorating. The sun blanketed the ocean, which was calm as a lake right now, leaving an orange glow on the water and the almost absent surf.

Down on the beach below, Slash was patrolling the grounds, taking out craurchins who had entered the property where the storm had breached the barricades. So far, he had killed two cycle 5s and a dozen or more lower cycles. Occasionally, you would hear the distant *zip, zip*, like a giant insect zapper from the beach, among the sounds of a flock of gulls scouring the beach and ocean for food.

"De men from da Heartland; Vin Johnson's friends Gabe Marshall and Bryce McPherson spearheaded de Cape May boy's rescue. Day recruited Dante Long who recruited Khim Nguyen an heez partner Hakira James. Da five of dem, along wit de boy's father and two brothers, as well as some family friends rescued de young man, Terrell Williams, from a cycle 6 craurchin's lair."

As usual, Dweezle's reporting didn't miss a beat. He described the rescue mission down to the uttermost detail, all from information he gathered from sources both on the ground and in the media. Like any good reporter, he vetted every word prior to reporting to Aztec. He reported on the other takings that had happened over the last several years, most, unfortunately, not ending as well as Terrell's. He also brought Aztec up to date on local politics, social events, craurchin attacks, citizens with the highest KPs and local gossip. What really caught Aztec's attention, however, were the rumors floating around concerning Terrell Williams, the young boy taken in Cape May, and his important information.

2272

For the last year or so Aztec and Phoebe, with the enormous help of Dweezle, put their conspiracy theory to the test, studying the trends and statistics in the South Jersey Badlands. They concentrated strictly on South Jersey because it had the highest concentration of craurchins.

Aztec worked on many politicians in the Heartland but particularly Senator Johnson. He felt that somewhere in that cold heart there was a soft spot that he could penetrate. He desperately needed an ally in the Heartland. Dweezle had arranged the transport of the two bodies home safely and Senator Johnson was moved by Aztec's efforts and empathy of a year ago. Dweezle set up interviews with Terrell and many of the others involved in the rescue. To date, Phoebe had met and spoken with Terrell no less than four times. Initially, the family was reluctant, but eventually due to her down-to-earth persona and obvious genuine concern, she gained their trust. His cycle 8 theory was always on her mind.

She was pretty sure he had a little crush on her, and she did not want to exploit that, so she tried to be more motherly and wear more conservative outfits when visiting. She'll never forget that first interview with Terrell, his protective and handsome brother Zak sitting next to him, explaining the "knowing" to her.

"Terrell, when you were connected to the 6, I know the constant theme was cycle 8, but was there anything else?" Terrell looked at his brother, who nodded his head in approval.

"There was, Miss Watermark. I saw images—well, not clear images exactly—more like articulated thoughts in the form of blurry unclear images, of what I think was the future. Or perhaps its vision of the future."

"I don't understand. How do you know those thoughts were of the future? By the way, please call me Phoebe." Phoebe was confused. Could craurchins actually see into the future?

"Well, some of the images I recognized. They were definitely in Cape May but—different."

Now over one year later, looking at the trends and stats Dweezle gathered, Aztec and Phoebe saw a pattern that shook them to the core.

"Jonathan, take a look at this report Dweezle just gave me. These go back the last five years." She handed him her ePad. Today, she was wearing her vintage 1962 leather mini-skirt, silk blouse, and silver leather go-go boots. Her auburn hair was tied in a bun. "These are stats relating to the South Jersey Badlands."

Aztec took the ePad and interpolated the raw data aloud. "Government assistance down one percent each year. Huh, sneaky. Monthly craurchin sprayings cut back to every two months."

On the second Friday of every month, the government would send out drones, which sprayed the beaches and marshland with a deadly chemical. Residents had to stay indoors for twenty-four hours after taping their windows. The following day, known as clean-up day, dead craurchins would be gathered, disinfected, cut up, and fed to the seagulls and wilds. Large 5s and higher were rarely part of the clean-up.

"Alcohol imports up twenty percent. Alcoholism up ten percent—no surprise there. Drug abuse up. Fuel the dregs and cause more crime. Craurchin assaults up fifty percent. We knew that. Human assaults up twenty percent—goes hand in hand with alcoholism and drug abuse. Okay, and lastly, value of kill points is down twenty percent. Holy Fuck, Phebes!"

"Startling, huh? I never realized the Badlands had so many human-on-human assaults by the way." Phoebe was in her fifth year in the Badlands and was still discovering much about Badlandian culture.

"Oh yeah, not only did many of the dregs of society stay here after the 2230 evacuations, but the Badlands are the perfect hiding place if you are wanted in the Heartland or running away from something—law or otherwise. As long as you're hard enough to survive, the Badlands are a safe haven from the law. Phoebe,

I been mulling this over for a while, and I think its time we have a Badlandian version of the Continental Congress. Dweezle come hither."

Together, the three of them spent the next week planning the specifics. There would be a delegation of men and women, representing towns and areas stretching from Cape May Point to Atlantic City. They would meet at Casa Azteca. They drew up a meeting agenda, which would be hand-delivered to each of the delegates. Each town could send up to two delegates. For Cape May, Aztec insisted on one of them being Terrell. He didn't care how old he was. He had something critical to say.

"Listen, if what the young man is saying is true, we need to find out what happens at cycle 8. Dweezle, when would any craurchins reach cycle 8 based on what we know about the history of craurchins in the U.S.?"

"In 2130 Noah Long, a twenty-three-year-old man from Sea Isle City, New Jersey admitted dat when he was thirteen years of age he smuggled a pair of craurchins home from da Sandomars. He called dem Adam and Eve. Da year was 2120. Based on de size and description given by Mr. Long, scientists believe they were cycle 1s. Since records show multiple craurchin sightings in various areas as early as 2121, it is safe to assume de were not necessarily Adam and Eve. Knowing dat craurchins begin reproducing in their fifth year, one can assume they were at least four years old da year dey come to Earth. Dat said, both de first generation, Adam and Eve, and the second generation, their children, would be reaching cycle 8 in de next twelve to fourteen years. Scientists do not know how many cycles craurchins advance to."

"Thanks, Dweezle. Phoebe, if something monumental happens at 8, every cycle 7 must be hunted down and killed."

"And if what we believe about CraTek is true, their mission would be to allow craurchins to thrive and perhaps grow to cycle 8 or larger, since the shells get stronger with each growth cycle! According to Terrell, however, 8 is the last cycle."

CHAPTER 20
ATLANTIC CITY

Finished with my woman 'cause she couldn't help me with my mind
people think I'm insane because I am frowning all the time
All day long I think of things but nothing seems to satisfy
Think I'll lose my mind if I don't find something to pacify
Can you help me occupy my brain?
— "Paranoid," Black Sabbath

THE DREGS

There were many people, mostly young men, who took advantage of the wild-west-like lawlessness that existed in the Badlands. Most communities were well organized and operated a working, though fragile, local government. In most towns, this government took care of keeping the roads open, banishing hardened criminals, caring for the sick, providing security (from both craurchins and humans) and most importantly keeping the lights on and fresh water flowing. These communities always got a lot of support from the federal government. Unfortunately, in the last decade or so, this support was waning, and there were elements that existed outside of these communities that took full advantage of the weak and unsuspecting at every opportunity. These rogues and dregs lived in abandoned houses or farms all over the Badlands. Many formed communes inland. Some formed cults. Most were bad news, and along with the craurchins, contributed to the Badlands' namesake.

Sally sat in her chair, staring blankly out the window. She was tracing her index finger along a scar on her left forearm that ran from just below the elbow, and stopped just short of her wrist. Outside on her front lawn, she could see the long, brown needles on the pine trees just starting to fall, and it reminded her of her child-hood. A sudden wave of sadness overcame her. She fought back the tears and anxiety building inside. God, she longed for home. In fact, she longed for it more and more lately, as she came to realize that she could never accept this place as her true home. She snapped out of it when she saw her mate pull up, trailer attached to the back of his old hover.

She quickly ducked away from the window and plopped the fish dinner she had just spent the last two hours preparing, onto a plate. About fifteen minutes later, she heard the front door of their rancher open, and then slam shut. *Shit.* The anxiety, now mixed with fear, came back.

"Hi Charles, how was your—"

He looked at the food on the table then back at Sally.

"Fuck, Sally, I told you no fish tonight, bitch, and what is on this fucking plate in front of me? Fish! *Fucking fish!*" Before she could utter a word, Charles "Scurge" Corbin punched Sally right in her left temple, emphasizing the word "fish" as he swung. It was a small miracle that Sally, who was now on the floor, had not suffered brain trauma from the number of temple shots she had received over the years. Maybe she had.

Scurge was not what you would call a huge man, but he wasn't small either. He had an air about him that intimidated even the largest of men. Perhaps, it was that his entire body, face, and shaved head were covered in satanic tattoos. Perhaps, it was that his 220-pound, six-foot frame was nothing but solid muscle. He had large biceps, triceps, and pectorals.

He had piercings on every pierceable part of his flesh. The tattoos on his back and chest mimicked that of a craurchin shell, done by a local artist whom Scurge supplied with drugs. Perhaps it was the long red beard that hung to his chest. Perhaps it was the fury in his gray-brown eyes. Whatever it was, it was a good thing that he was intimidating, because the last thing in the world you wanted to do was accidently fuck with Scurge. He would kill you without a moment's thought. And in the badlands, he would likely get away with it.

"I'm sorry, Scurgie. It's all I could barter for. They had no meat." She was careful not to make him angrier. "Come on, let me fix you up. Let me give you a bump, then maybe I can make you a san'wich or something."

Scurge half-grunted, half-spoke some unintelligible words, and Sally, eager to satisfy him, poured out some powder on a plate and chopped out three long lines. He snorted them quickly, then walked out of the tiny kitchen and into the next room. Sally could hear the cycle 5 he had captured this afternoon shrieking from outside where it was caged. It was sunset, and she peeked out the window and could see the cage that was secured to a large tree. It was surreal seeing this caged wild animal—a wild alien—silhouetted by the sun melting in the western sky beyond it. Tomorrow morning, they would drive it from their home on the outskirts of Atlantic City to the trainer in town.

"Cisco, it's Scurge. I've got the 5 you wanted, and I plan on delivering tomorrow."

"What are its dimensions? The Skulls are looking for a big one."

"Seven-three, four-fifty."

"Not bad, male or female?"

"You know it doesn't matter, asshole. Look I don't have time for this shit. What time you wanna take delivery?"

"It does matter, Scurge, I have an easier time training the males."

"Is that what you call what you do? Training?" Scurge let out a rare chuckle. "Are you gonna train 'em how to jump through a fiery hoop?" Scurge pictured a big awkward craurchin jumping

268

through a ring of fire and laughed even harder. "Climb on a giant beach ball? Walk a tightrope? Haha, you piss 'em off by torturing them so that they go in the cage and beat the shit out of the other one. Plain and simple, dude!"

"Whatever, Scurge. Listen, the cycle 5 match is tomorrow evening. Can you get it here tonight? I need more time with it."

"It'll cost you an extra twenty-five percent of what I quoted for delivery tomorrow."

"Fine, but I have to give you the extra in kill points."

"You know I can't do that, Cisco. Don't make me explain why."

"Okay, okay. When can you get it here?"

"Give me two hours."

Atlantic City was one of the few places on the northeast coast where U.S. currency was still accepted. When he needed something AC could not provide, he simply traded his cash for kill points in Sally's name. Using his name to claim kill points would guarantee his capture and ultimate conviction by the U.S. government.

NIGHT ON THE TOWN

The following night, Atlantic City was booming. The lights were bright, the bars and clubs were packed, and there was money to be made placing bets on one's favorite craurchin. Of all the Badlandian shore towns, Atlantic City was that one that retained something of its former self—something that existed before the evacuations. Tonight was no exception. The town was filled with people from

New York City to Bethany Beach, Delaware. The deluge of visitors was in town for the craurchin matches and an endless night of partying and hedonism. This month's event, labeled Cycle 6: Death Match 2272, was a battle between a local South Jersey cycle 6 and a north Badlands cycle 6. The arena in which the twelve-foot, 800-pound giants would be fighting was part of the old Monarch Hotel and Casino, one of several casinos to survive after the evacuations. The craurchins would be fighting to the death. The event would be televised worldwide, so Scurge and many like him would need to lay low.

Fittingly, Scurge and Sally were watching the event in a local bar called the Cross Examination, where on all of the vidwalls, Scurge's craurchin, one of the undercards, was getting prepped to fight. They were getting ready to announce the two opponents after a brief message from Atlantic City's mayor, Roger McNimble. Scurge threw some bills on the bar.

"Two beers and two shots of Tequil-juana. Whadda you want, Sally?" It was more of a statement than a question.

"A jazz juice on the rocks, please," she said directly to the bartender.

The bartender was a seasoned Badlander named Doug. The bar was the local dive hangout of mostly undesirables—outlaws, drug addicts, petty criminals, and scumbags like Scurge. Doug engaged in as little conversation as he had to with him.

His woman is nice but that guy scares the fuck out of me, he thought. Unfortunately, the bar was not crowded yet, and he felt he had to talk to his two regulars.

"So, do you have a cra-urch in the fight tonight?"

"Yeah, it's up next. I caught it yesterday. Fucker gave me a good fight too. I've got a lot of money on it for sure. You'd do the same if you were fuckin' smart."

"Well, I hope it wins. Maybe I will put in a bet."

On the wall, the mayor was finishing up his little speech. He was wearing an expensive suit that fit badly on his chubby frame.

"And so, it is with great pleasure that I welcome you to America's Playground. America's longest existing refuge for adult fun and entertainment. Home of the Miss Badlands Pageant. And the home of the 2272 Craurchin Matches, Atlantic City! Tonight's events are sponsored by CraTek Industries and AC Events, Ltd. So, without further ado, let the matches begin!"

As Doug, Scourge, and Sally stared at the screen above, some other locals walked in, thankfully, and saved Doug from further painful conversation with Scurge. The bartender wasted no time attending to his new customers.

Several minutes of silence passed. This was normal for the couple since Scurge said little and Sally was afraid to say anything. After shooting his two shots and downing his beers, Scurge turned to Sally. His eyes were red and a little puffy. Sally thought he didn't look like his usual self. He looked solemn. *Yes, solemn. Strange.*

"I don't know why I'm the way I am, Sal". He almost sounded apologetic. "I don't mean to be the bastard I am but I just can't help myself. I'm sorry for the way I have treated you over the years. Sometimes I feel like the voices in my head are not mine. But tonight, it's crazy, but tonight, I feel like I'm the voice in my head. Does that make any sense, Sally?" This was the most he had spoken to her in two years.

Sally was speechless. The last time she heard Charles talk in this tone was many years ago when they first met. She thought about leaving him many times. No, she thought about leaving him every, single, day. But she knew—knew without any doubt whatsoever, that he would hunt her down and either kill her or beat her to within an inch of her shitty life.

There was a time, and it seemed like a lifetime ago, that Charles Corbin was just your average, shit-kicking bad boy. Just a stupid kid with no prospects, who always seemed to find trouble, basically a good person who was dealt a bad hand, blah blah blah. We all know that familiar story, but in his case, it was true. He really was dealt some bad playing cards. They had gone to the same high school in Seymour, Indiana, where they attended a few of the same classes, and they met in detention one rainy Tuesday afternoon. They walked home together that day, smoking some weed and sharing an umbrella that they stole from the school lobby, and they hit it off instantly.

Charlie was a good-looking young man with curly brown hair and big brown eyes. Sally always loved his long eyelashes and the brightness in his eyes when he smiled or was happy. Sally was an attractive tri-racial girl with beautiful olive skin and long, silky black hair. They were very attracted to each other. They went to the prom together, then shared an apartment. Then, five years later, Scurge was facing a prison sentence for jacking a hover and resisting arrest. He was high and thought the police officer was the owner of the hover trying to kill him. Violent crimes were treated very harshly in the Heartland, but he made bail, thanks to Sally, who convinced her aging parents to mortgage the house. About a week later, a friend of Charles, who lived in the Badlands, convinced him to flee before trial. He promised him work if he came east to Atlantic City.

Charles packed his few belongings, kissed his grandmother who had raised him goodbye, and took off for New Jersey. Sally kissed him goodbye and they held each for a long time. Charlie told her he would be back for her once he settled in. She honestly didn't believe him, but as luck would have it, he snuck back into the Heartland several months later and convinced her to join him. It was by far the worst decision she had ever made.

"Scur—uh Charles, you're just a little drunk and high. The voice in your head has always been you. I'm not sure what you're saying. Just try to enjoy yourself. It's looking like your craurchin is getting ready to fight. Maybe it'll win. Let's watch."

She wasn't sure what else to say. *Voices in his head? Something was off—the gentleness in his voice just now? Totally out of character for the Badlands version of Charles.*

"Hey, Scurge! I've got a hundred kill points on your craurchin, bro! We gonna get a win?" Skeeter and Pudge were seated across the bar.

"You know it!" Scurge replied with an upbeat but shaky voice. Something was definitely off. His normal response to that would have been, "Hey, fuckwad, can't you see that I was talking to my old lady."

Sally thought about how frustrated he was back in their first year in the Badlands. He had hated the godforsaken craurchins that seemed to be everywhere and the fact that he could not find a way to support them. He could not adjust. She thought about how he started drinking and partying too much, sleeping late, and was just deeply depressed. After a year or so of this unsustainable lifestyle, the heavy imbibing, the drug abuse, he awoke one afternoon and decided to reinvent himself.

"Scurge, yer scaring me a little bit. I've never seen you like this." *And I really like it*, she thought.

"Don't be afraid, Sal. I think I'm finding myself. I think I've put my finger on why I've been such a shit for so long. Let's have a great night!"

Sally decided she would just go with it. *What the hell? Why not just have a great night? God knows I deserve it.*

I can do this, he thought. *If I want to, I can reinvent myself.* Back in the early days, Scurge had heard about the craurchin matches and how trappers were in high demand to provide craurchins for the fights. With that fact in mind, he procured a job with a nasty old guy named Trapper George, who drank old-school whiskey all day, farted nonstop, picked his nose, scratched his balls, and from time to time actually spoke to him. But he was damn good at catching cycle 5s.

Scurge was a quick learner and learned all he could from George. He got really good, almost had a natural instinct for catching craurchins, and before long, he was contracting on his own. He started lifting weights, running, and basically keeping himself fit for his challenging new profession. He had also developed several techniques for capturing cycle 5s and 6s. He and Sally were doing pretty well for a while. They were still drinking and doing some drugs, but nothing out of hand. But then it happened. She couldn't quite pinpoint the exact date when the change occurred, but she could trace the scars on her body back at least fifteen years. She remembered one incident about three years into Charles's new business. He had already earned the nickname Scurge because he was considered by everyone in AC to be the biggest scourge to craurchins in the area.

"All right, Sallio, just keep digging. It'll be worth it when we get that pile of cash. I've been tracking this guy for a good week now and he's an unusually large 5, so we've got to dig it deep! I get three hundred for catching him and a two-hundred-dollar bonus if he wins." In AC, $500 went a long way.

"Don't worry about me, Scurgie, you just keep digging yer-self!"

Scurge's favorite technique was to dig a large pit on the beach. A pit large enough to fit a cage that was large enough for a craurchin. He would dig the pit, then place the heavy-duty cage, which he built himself, into the pit with the door side up and open. He would then place long sticks or scratch lumber across the short side of the opening, place heavy cardboard on the sticks, and then cover it all with sand. To attract the beast to the camouflaged pit, he would have a dog, and later, Sally, hang out in front of the pit while he hid in the sand dunes. Eventually, the craurchin, hungry for meat and blood, would take the bait and attack. Scurge would then jump out of his hiding spot and lure the beast onto the trap. Sometimes, it would not cooperate, and he had to lasso and drag it there. Once it fell into the cage, he would then band the pincers and mask the face, so it couldn't hit him with its poison.

On many occasions in those early years, before he learned how to render them unconscious, Scurge had close skirmishes with big craurchins. On one particular encounter, after he had banded his catch and was struggling to mask it, the big monster latched onto his upper stomach, just below the ribcage with a long tongue-like tube that came out of its mouth.

"What the fuck?" This was a first for Scurge. "What the hell is this?" Once he regained his composure, he tried to cut the tube thingy off with his knife, but before he could, the world went black. When he awoke, the creature was still in the cage, banded and sucking out his blood. He grabbed his knife and finished the cutting that he had started. *How long ago?* He then masked and caged the fucker.

"Sally? Sally?"

"Huh—oh hey, Scurge."

"Call me, Charlie, Sal. Charlie. Let's do a bump. Hey, Doug, two more rounds."

Sally poured the white powder on the bar and cut out two long lines. They each snorted one of the long lines of brown pow-der. The bar was now two rows deep as people began to venture in for the main sporting event and crowd up to the bar for a drink. The old Scurge would make it very clear where the boundaries were. You did not want to impede those boundaries, let alone brush up against or touch Scurge. Tonight, it didn't seem to bother him. "Come on up. Get a drink."

Across the bar, Pudge was whispering in Skeeter's ear. "Twenty kill points he slaps her by ten." Skeeter looked annoyed and a little scared. "Careful, Pudge, careful." They rented a room atop the Cross Examination, and like Scurge, were in the Cross Exam almost every night. The last thing Skeeter needed was to be on Scurge's bad side.

On the screen, Scurge's cycle 5 was being introduced by the announcer. A few patrons patted Scurge on the back, wishing him luck. Everyone seemed to know that he had a dog in the fight.

"In this corner, we have the home favorite. Hailing from Margate, New Jersey, and weighing in at four hundred and fifty pounds—"

NAPKO0

The fight would consist of ten-minute rounds, and the fight would end when one of the fighters was dead. Napko0 was the craurchin that Scurge had trapped. He was ninety-five years old and very strong. He had a cluster of six, which represented a high level of respect and stature in his colony. He knew he would be killed either by the humans or his opponent and had no problem taking out another craurchin if it ensured his survival. Every day, he survived was a day closer to cycle 8. He knew his fight was about to begin, and he was prepared.

I will destroy this brother and then, if given the opportunity, I will destroy as many humans as possible. The beach is only a hundred paces behind me, and beyond that the entire ocean. My cluster, if you can hear me, do not attack. It would assuredly be your demise. Here's how you can help me defeat the enemy 5—

Both craurchins were in cages on each side of the giant domed cage in which they would be fighting. The domed birdcage was in the center of the Monarch's large arena. The bell rang long and ominously, and the doors of each cage were raised. As soon as he stepped out into the ring, Napko0 started telepathic chatter with his cluster. Their voices were in his head and the northern craurchin as well. It could not hear what he was thinking and thus did not know the moves Napko0 was planning.

For two rounds, they faced off at the center of the cage, slashing at each other with their pincers, sometimes on their hinds. Both were getting angrier as their trainers zapped them with their cattle prods from respective corners. The northerner shot venom that missed Napko0 and hit the cage. Some of it went between the cage bars and hit a man in the front row, numbing his left arm. He would later tell a friend that, nonetheless, he still got his money's worth.

Two minutes into the third round, Napko0 pinned his formidable opponent, grasped his right pincer arm with his two pincers and did a death roll onto the floor. The craurchin's arm stretched out with the roll, straining the shoulder joint as the large craurchin's own weight continued the momentum, snapping the arm clean off at the shoulder. The opponent shrieked in agony, and the audience cheered with delight. Napko0, still holding the detached limb, swung it around the cage, spraying the audience with the blood and bodily matter flowing from the severed end.

He then grasped that same end in his own pincers and began beating the northern craurchin mercilessly as it cried and shrieked in pain. All the while, the cluster's chatter continued filling both fighters' minds as the crowd cheered wildly. They were truly getting their money's worth!

THE CROSS EXAMINATION

Scurge and everyone else in the Cross Examination watched the fight and most were extremely satisfied as Scurge's craurchin gave the other a beating. Scurge was in great spirits and was actually holding Sally's hand.

"Another round, Doug!" He pointed his finger to the bar top in front of him.

The crowd was cheering their hometown favorite, many high-fiving Scurge and Sally. Many were on their way to winning some money or kill points.

"A round on me for everyone, Doug! Get 'em what they want."

"As you wish, Scurge." Doug had never seen Scurge buy anyone a drink, not even his closest friends, let alone a bar full of strangers.

By the end of the fifth round, NapkoO's opponent was battered and bleeding, running from NapkoO, who patiently stalked him around the ring, waiting for his opportunity. The opponent was snapping his remaining pincer aimlessly and shooting some venom to no avail.

You will not make it to 6, let alone 7 my friend. Until we meet again.

With that, NapkoO dropped his 450-pound body on the demoralized beast and slashed his head clean off with his razor-sharp pincer. As if choreographed, the head bounced across the white ring floor, rolling to a stop at the edge of the cage, leaving a trail of greenish-red blood.

"Oh! Somebody lost their head!" one patron in the Cross Exam yelled.

Scurge and Sally were ecstatic. Scurge had just won a large amount of money. They spent the rest of the night partying with the crowd, buying shots, high-fiving, and snorting more and more of the brown powder. At one point, they had sex in the bathroom—and then more brown powder. Normally, Scurge would take a local in there, whether Sally was with him or not. Tonight, however, it was just Sally. She could hardly remember the last time she had had such a great time.

If this is the new Scurge, maybe we really can have a better life. Maybe the abuse will stop. Maybe I can help him quit the powder. Maybe we can live a more decent life and hang around with decent people and not the dirtbags that are currently part of our lives. Sally, in her current bliss and euphoria, actually believed these things were possible.

When the night finally drew to a close and the dawn closed in, Scurge and Sally left the bar and climbed onto Scurge's hoverbike. They miraculously drove home without killing themselves, climbed into their bed, and made love for the better part of an hour. Afterward, they lay there, exhausted and barely able to keep their eyes open. Sally laid her head on Charles's chest and fingered the ugly red, circular scar on his upper belly. He kissed her on the forehead, and they both fell into a deep sleep.

Many hours later, Charles Andrew Corbin from Seymour, Indiana, sat up in bed, his eyes wide and bloodshot. The scar on his belly was throbbing and oozing a little bit of blood. Calmly, he rose from the bed and walked into the kitchen where he grabbed a bottle of water and downed it. He was extremely dehydrated. He then took a long knife from the cabinet drawer and walked back into the bedroom where he stabbed Sally over a hundred times, slashing and stabbing deep, deadly anger-filled stabs until there was almost nothing left that was recognizable. And with that, Sally's sad, impossible life, all her anxieties and fears, as well as her new-found hope, died with her that night.

CHAPTER 21
STONE HARBOR

A lovestruck Romeo sang the streets of serenade
Laying everybody low with a love song that he made
Finds a streetlight, steps out of the shade
Says something like, "You and me, babe, how about it?"
Juliet says, "Hey, it's Romeo, you nearly gave me a heart attack"
He's underneath the window, she's singing, "Hey, la, my boyfriend's back"
You shouldn't come around here singing up at people like that
Anyway, what you gonna do about it?"
— "ROMEO & JULIET," DIRE STRAITS

DATE NIGHT

Haley and Romeo were both thinking about what they were going to do on the 105th Street beach. They both knew it was going to happen, and they both needed it. It was their monthly date night ritual, and they both had enough pent-up lust and desire in them to ignite a small explosion. Every Thursday evening, they would take their only child Aidan to his Aunt Sherry's house on 112th Street, and then walk to their favorite beach hand in hand. In front of them, Biscuit, Charlie, and Jenny led the way, watching for craurchins. When they completed their seven-block trek, Romeo dug a pit in the sand and gathered kindling and wood for the fire while Haley spread out a large blanket, poured their favorite wine, and put out some snacks. Living in a community of only 240 people had its perks. Tonight, that perk was privacy.

"Did you pack the strawberries, Haley?"

"Yeah, and the wine, and the cheese, and—of course—the condoms." She smiled that crooked, sensual grin that drove him absolutely crazy.

"That's my girl!" Just the mere thought of making love with this gorgeous woman stirred up a passion in Romeo that set his heart beating madly.

They cozied up on the blanket, sipped the wine, and nibbled on cheese under the beautiful July moon. It was drop zone cheese, but it complemented the wine. They could hear the waves crashing in the distance as the fire crackled and spread its warm glow on their firm, young bodies. A warm breeze hit Romeo's bare chest and mussed up Haley's short blond hair. She was wearing a pair of cut-off jeans and a bikini top.

"I live for these nights, Haley. Absolutely live for them." He held up his glass for a toast.

"So do I, babes. You make life in this place worth living. Cheers!" That smile again.

With that, they embraced and kissed long and passionately, their hands exploring each other's bodies as if it were the first time they ever felt one another. Before long, they were both naked and making the most of their short break from being Mom and Dad. Romeo climbed on top and entered her, kissing her mouth with a desperation that only first-time lovers usually experience. After a while, she performed a flawless love-roll and was on top of her husband, riding him cowgirl style.

The dogs were playing in the sand nearby, and Haley was starting to climax, when suddenly the dogs began growling with what seemed to be a dire concern. Before the two lovers could break away from each other, the growls quickly became intense, urgent barks. It happened so fast. A quick-striking cycle 4 attacked his wife. It came out of the darkness quietly and with extreme malice. He'd never seen a 4 move so fast. He never saw a 4 so vicious. So violent. The dogs and Romeo removed it from her fairly quickly but it was too late—the damage was done. The 5 that was hanging out in the shadows had made its move toward the blanket and was almost upon them before the dogs caught its scent and turned their full attention toward the creature approaching from the darkness.

It took out Charlie almost instantly, crushing his neck with its razor-sharp pincer. Biscuit and Jenny, large Goberian Giants, attacked it aggressively, each latching onto its hinds and dropping it to the sand. The 5 lashed out with its deadly pincers but was not quite in position to strike either dog. This gave Romeo enough time to look for the gun in the large bag that Haley had packed. As he glanced toward his wife, he saw a lot of red sand.

"Haley! Oh my God, Haley!"

"I'm okay. Just kill the fucking thing!"

As the dogs hung onto the 5s struggling legs, they somehow managed to avoid its swinging, sinister pincers. Romeo ran carefully and quietly behind the 5, took aim, and got several headshots in. All hit the mark, and the 5 collapsed in the sand with a thud. From the distance, they could hear the high-pitched screech of the dead craurchin's cluster. As the dogs worked on the lush protein from the 5's underbelly, Romeo ran back to his wife. *Why was she not talking?* he thought.

When he got back to his wife, she was passed out, blood spilling from the stump of her right leg. The 4, which they later determined was a small 5, had pincered her leg just below the knee, cutting it off clean.

ONE YEAR LATER

"Hari, I swear you never saw a cycle 5 that vicious, and I have no doubt the entire attack was planned out. The small 5 was a distractor so the large 5 could come in and kill us all!"

"Well, that part of the plan didn't work out so well for it, thank God. Fuck, can these things actually plan? Are they getting smarter or have they always been so and were just waiting for the right moment? Or, did we just not notice?"

"Let me tell you, having Dante Long train those dogs of mine was the smartest thing I ever did." He patted Jenny, who was lying next to his chair, on her large fluffy head. "I really miss Charlie."

The two men were sitting on the back deck of Romeo and Haley's house on 116th Street, sipping vodkas and gapple juices. Hari took a drag of his safecig as Haley limped onto the deck from the house.

"Hey, Haley. How's the new leg?" Hari asked with genuine concern.

"It's not bad, for a prosthetic. How's Reno and the kids?"

"They're good. Tallie's dog is not doing well. We may have to put him down. He's almost twenty-five, you know." Something about a diet of craurchin seemed to increase the life span of many dog breeds.

"Aww, I'm so sorry to hear that. Please give Tallie and her doggie a kiss for me and tell her how sorry I am. When is Reno coming over?" she said in a monotone voice.

Haley had lost much of her desire to socialize since the attack. In fact, she had become a little bit of a recluse. She stopped going to committee meetings. Stopped volunteering. Partly because of her fear of leaving the house and partly because of her handicap. She kept Aiden in the house most of the time and had anxiety attacks whenever he was out with Romeo. To help relieve her fears, Romeo obtained two new puppies. They only helped a little.

She was supposedly on a waiting list for a leg transplant but she knew that Badlanders were on the bottom of any transplant list. It could take years or even decades.

"Haley, can I make you a drink? I want you to relax and have fun tonight."

"Sure, hon. I guess it's about that time. While you're at it, can you put Aidan to bed?"

After Romeo walked into the house, Hari moved into the seat next to Haley.

"Listen, Haley. I know this has been an incredibly tough year, and I appreciate what you've been through."

"I'll stop you right there, man. You can't appreciate what I've been through. I was scared to death every day of my life right up until the attack, but do you know what? I knew if I had to—and a few times I did—defend myself and my child, I could. Growing up in the Badlands taught me how to be tough, how to be—steely. Knowing I had a fighting chance helped alleviate that fear."

"I know but—" With her eyes red and tearing, Haley stopped him again.

"Let me finish. Now that I am disabled, survival just got twice as difficult. We need more kill points than we needed before and only have one earner now. And those KPs don't go nearly as far as they once did. You know, and I know, that I will never get my leg. We are getting squeezed by the Heartland, and I feel like we are on our own. All of us." She wiped her eyes and continued.

"If Aiden and I were attacked, how could I defend him? I couldn't even swoop him up and run for fuck's sake!"

"Point taken, but you do understand that we are all looking out for you, that we all care."

Haley sat quietly for a few minutes, deep in thought. She was staring out toward the field between their backyard and the sand dunes, deep in thought. She had a blank expression on her face that livened up after a while. Her sour mood was lightening up a bit.

"I'm sorry, Hari. I know."

"How come you gave up on the committee meetings?"

For many years, Haley was a councilwoman on the Stone Harbor Committee. She was very active in the community and helped with a variety of tasks, from organizing care for the elderly to arranging transportation for the children to the local school. Her father, Jack, had gotten her involved when she was just a young girl of twelve years old. He took her to monthly meetings, and she helped him with various volunteer activities. When she was twenty, her parents decided to leave the Badlands. Her mother, Martha, who had never really adapted to living with craurchins, developed a rare skin disease. Jack knew he had to relocate her further west for her to get the best care.

They started in western Pennsylvania, where life was much easier than the Badlands and eventually ended up in the Heartland. It was central Ohio to be exact. Both were heartbroken that Haley, who had fallen in love with Romeo, would not be joining them. Jack remained active in Badland politics. To this day, Jack petitioned the government on behalf of the Badlands. Jack and Martha still visited their daughter and grandson several times a year, and Jack was still beloved from Sea Isle to Cape May, where he made numerous friends in his fight for the South Jersey Shores. On his last visit to Stone Harbor, Jack had pulled Haley aside. He looked her in the eyes and she noticed for the first time that her father had elderly eyes, hazy and bags underneath but filled with wisdom, knowledge, and pain.

"Haley, I hate seeing you like this." Jack was on the verge of tears. "You are in pain now, but things will get better. I understand why you are still here and I won't try to convince you to come to Ohio, but if you stay you have to be strong. You cannot let this setback hold you back. There are great things that you need to be a part of."

"Haley? Haley, why did you stop coming to the council meetings?"

"I don't want to see anyone, and I don't want to put myself or anyone else in danger. Please, Hari, I don't want to talk about it." She was getting upset again.

"I'm sorry, Haley, I'm not trying to upset you. The committee is just not the same without you." Haley was looking down at the ground, stifling tears and anguish. "Have you heard about Aztec Pendelton?" Haley shook her head. "No? Have you heard about Terrell Williams? They are forming a delegation. Haley, we need to talk."

That night, Haley lay awake for hours in her bed, thinking. They had just had a really nice night with the Santiagos, and she was wondering why she had been having such a hard time getting back into the rituals of her former life. She could not stop thinking about the things Hari told her. His story about the boy Terrell had really moved her. It wasn't very often that someone taken was actually found and rescued, and these incidents seemed to be happening more and more often.

The government certainly didn't have a great track record helping out. Since the incident, the team had actually rescued two more people. They would have had three but they got there too late. They killed the cycle 6, but it was too late for the elderly woman taken from her front porch in Cape May Courthouse. She remembered Hari telling her how the boy had made a connection with his captor while being blood-sucked.

He spoke of the craurchin's overwhelming desire and how it was one simple thing—get to cycle 8.

She didn't know why that intrigued her the way it did. Anyone who could do simple math, knew that at cycle 8, a craurchin would be huge—twenty feet or longer and thousands of pounds. But that wasn't it. She felt as though something monumental happened, a metamorphosis.

"Something spectacular, something dangerous," she whispered.

"It was a spectacular night, hon. You were spectacular. A spectacular night for sure." Romeo half-drunk, half-asleep, slurred.

She was also amazed that a delegation had formed for the betterment of the South Jersey Badlands. And by all accounts, the movement was being fueled and financed by a legit friend of the Badlands. At some point during the long night, Haley realized what it was that she needed to do for herself and her family. She would talk with the committee Tuesday night at the next meeting. She would overcome her phobia. And she would do her part in making their home in the Badlands safer. But, first, she and Aiden would go see Tallie and her sick dog.

CHAPTER 22
THE DELEGATION

The said States hereby severally enter into a firm league of friendship with each other, for their common defense, the security of their liberties, and their mutual and general welfare, binding themselves to assist each other against all force offered to, or attacks made upon them, or any of them, on account of religion, sovereignty, trade, or any other pretense, whatever.
— THE ARTICLES OF CONFEDERATION, ARTICLE 3

OCEAN CITY

It was ten days before the big meeting and Phoebe and Aztec were in Ocean City, preparing an agenda for what was jokingly dubbed the Badlands first constitutional convention. It was, in fact, no joke. Part of the agenda actually discussed the idea of secession—independence from the United States. Dweezle was in the process of confirming where the invitations should go and if they had representatives yet.

"Aztec, why would you even suggest secession? We wouldn't last a week without the homeland. We need them more than they need us, even with the continued reductions."

"Agreed, Phebes, but it's the eighteen-hundred-pound craurchin in the room. We have to address it, to put it out there and see what the reaction is. It's just part of the process. Besides, if we become a territory, we will lose all representation in Congress. Secession is a real possibility."

They would send the invitations and agenda to each of the representative communities of the South Jersey coastline. For most of these small towns and communities, the only local government was in the form of a committee, most of whom met once or twice a month to discuss and address local community issues. These issues almost always centered around craurchins and their impact on the town, but also, sometimes dealt with minor issues such as maintaining roads, repairing infrastructure, and getting support from the Heartland.

Some of these committees were voted in by the community, and others, due to lack of interest, just formed on their own. For the Badlands, there was no real representation. Sure, there were state senators who were supposed to represent the entire state, but because most of the Badlands paid little or no taxes and were just an inkling of the vote, they were virtually nonexistent in terms of representation. For years, rumors circulated that the Jersey Badlands were on the verge of becoming a U.S. territory.

Unbeknownst to most, the U.S. Congress was putting together a bill to send to the president proclaiming just that, and many believed he was willing to sign it. Aztec and Phoebe knew of this bill and suspected that Mayor Roger McNimble had this knowledge as well. Atlantic City, still an incorporated town with a mayor and city council, would be immune from this bill. Aztec and Phoebe knew that making the Badlands a territory was the first step in exploiting the people and land for the cultivation of craurchin shells, and they needed to know if McNimble was involved. They suspected he was.

CAPE MAY HALL

In their monthly committee meeting in Cape May, Freddie May brought the topic of Aztec's invitation to the floor. He was looking as jovial as ever in his bright and brilliant collared shirt and disheveled Jheri curls, but his voice and demeanor tonight were all business.

"Quiet, please. Okay, quiet, please. So along with several other communities along the coast, we have been invited to Aztec Pendleton's mansion in Ocean City. Aztec, as most of you know, is the owner of Pendleton Distilleries. I have here the agenda for that meeting, and we are asked to think about these items and perhaps provide answers or at least be ready to discuss them. Each community is allowed two delegates; however, for Cape May, one of them must be Terrell Williams. He was emphatic about that. We need to vote on the second. I guess before we do that, we need to vote if we want to participate at all, so all in favor say aye."

The ayes overwhelmingly had the vote. Cape May would participate.

"Now for the second delegate?" Freddie asked the large group.

"I nominate you, Freddie!"

"Me too."

"I nominate Lonnie Bally!"

"People, people, please understand something. The person we will send is merely a representative of all of us. We all have a say. Now, let's take a vote. M.J. will collect the ballots." Freddie made it clear that the cape would speak as one voice. They cast their votes, over four hundred men and women, a little under the eighth of the population that stayed after the evacuations. It was agreed that the representatives would be Freddie May and Terrell Williams.

THE WILDWOODS

The Wildwoods would not be sending delegates. Wildwood, which included Anglesea, North Wildwood, Wildwood, and Wildwood Crest, was a land in turmoil. After the evacuations, very few stayed. Less in fact than any of the other shore towns along the coast. Because so few stayed, there was no organized government of any sort. As such, buildings, roads, and bridges fell into disrepair and eventually Wildwood eroded into the wasteland it is today. After fifty years, the five bridges onto the island were uncrossable, so the few who stayed were now alienated from the rest of the state, unless of course they had access to a boat or hover.

The reason for Wildwood's demise was the huge craurchin population—the largest concentration in the Badlands. The reason for that was simple. The Wildwoods were a five-mile barrier island with huge beaches stretching almost a half-mile from the boardwalk to the ocean's edge. Even in the twenty-first century, the Wildwood Beach, at five hundred yards wide, was the widest on the Jersey coast. For reasons probably due to its topography, global warming, which eroded most coastal beaches, the Wildwoods were left with even wider beaches. This huge expanse of beach and sand dunes created the perfect environment for craurchins to thrive.

Long gone were the days of the crowded, lively boardwalk and its many amusement piers. Hunts, Morey's, and Adventure Pier were all now just rotted skeletons of what they once were, greenish-brown masses of rotting piles, rails, and deck planks, stretching out awkwardly toward the sea. Long ago, the piers that descended into the sea were mostly washed away. Long gone were the numerous clubs and hotels. And long gone was Bill Haley and the Comets "Rocking Around the Clock" at the Hofbrau Hotel.

THE OTHER DELEGATES

Stone Harbor and Avalon each sent two delegates. Stone Harbor sent Haley Dani and Hari George. Avalon sent Gay Paxton and Sonny Patel. Sea Isle, which included Strathmere, sent Hakira and a Sea Isler named Shana Jacuzzi. Shana was very much involved in local politics and was an articulate, energetic forty-year-old who had some progressive ideas for the Jersey coast. She and her girl-friend Alyssa, like most of the delegates, were born in the Badlands, just after the 2030 evacuations. Like most of the younger delegates, she knew no other life but that of the Badlands.

Longport, Margate City, and Ventnor City, the three of which had consolidated governments in 2240, would be sending Emerlito Castillo and Gruman Hamm, two local leaders very active in Badland politics. Emerlito had once spoken in front of Congress regarding the future of the Jersey coast. During this speech, he had harshly criticized Deirdra Monaghan for her lack of effort concerning aid to the Badlands. Shortly after her re-election in 2268, Castillo and Hamm worked together to try and have a recall election, claiming that her indifference to the Jersey coastlands severely prejudiced her ability to introduce bills that would serve all New Jerseyians fairly. The recall failed.

Finally, Atlantic City, land of decadence, the poor man's Las Vegas, would be sending Mayor Roger McNimble and Councilman Robert Connors.

"Tweedle Dee and Tweedle Dum. These two clowns care about one thing and one thing only—money. The word decency is in neither of their dictionaries. McNimble, who is not stupid when it comes to making money, is not smart enough to understand that gaining and keeping power is more important."

"He *is* mayor of AC, Aztec."

"He is, but it's not really what he wants to do at this point in his life. What he wants is to leave a legacy for himself, an empire for his family and a fortune for his lover Robert Connors."

"So why invite them? Do you think they'd take not being invited as some kind of power move on your part?"

"Exactly." Phoebe was really starting to learn how politics in the Badlands, or anywhere for that matter, worked. "We need to control him, or we will get nowhere."

McNimble, now in his mid-sixties, had lost most of his father's fortune when the craurchin shit hit the fan. He could have made a fresh start elsewhere, Vegas for instance, or built from what remained of his AC empire. He chose the latter. First, he liquidated his struggling hotels, then he reinvented his few strong hotels. He would eventually reinvent all of Atlantic City, a city that had a long history of reinvention. He claimed bankruptcy on the businesses he decided to let go and poured a lot of his money into a monumental marketing campaign, which touted Atlantic City as a kind of Sin City where everything goes. It worked. The lowest of the low lived in AC and respectable people with "hidden" agendas sought their vices in AC.

THE FIRST MEETING

On November 17, 2272, the twelve original delegates along with Aztec Pendleton and Phoebe Watermark sat around the long custom-made wood and stainless-steel table that Aztec had installed in his large dining room just for this occasion. They all carried with them a serious and somewhat formal demeanor and were anxious to voice the opinions of their respective communities. Dweezle had arranged pick up for all of them in hover limos provided by Aztec. That is, with the exception of McNimble and Connors who had their own transportation. A limo headed north for the Longport, Margate, and Ventnor representatives and another headed south, for the Strathmere, Sea Isle, Avalon, and Stone Harbor Group. A third was sent straight to Cape May for Terrell and Freddie May. Terrell was now the closest thing to a celebrity in the Badlands.

"Hey, Terrell, it appears your limo awaits you. Knock 'em dead, little man!" Zak was probably more excited than Terrell. He could not believe that one of the wealthiest men in the world had specifically requested the presence of his little brother!

The two remaining Williams men and Jackson were also there for the sendoff. Patting Terrell on the back and wishing him luck.

"Thanks, guys!"

Terrell climbed into the hover's spacious back seat where Freddie, Jheri curls gleaming in the bright sunlight, was waiting with a huge grin and a high five. He was wearing a nice suit, tie, and burgundy shirt. Terrell hit him up and then waved excitedly out the window to his family.

"What's your poison, kiddo? Look at all the choices!"

Directly in front of the rear seats of the plush hover limo was a table, and on that table were a couple of dozen buttons. From these buttons, you could request your destination, adjust your seats, get a foot or back massage, or order a variety of drinks and snacks. The choices ran from a strawberry milkshake to a jazz juice with a slice of limon-orange. There were also lots of snack choices. There was a screen almost the entire width of the limo to view movies or live news from the Heartland. The entire interior of the limo was clad in extra reinforced glass, which provided a panoramic view when in flight.

"Wow, let's see, chocolate milkshake, spinach chips, ah, and cashews from the United Republic of Iran!" Terrell had the intellect of the smartest adult in any room, but at heart was just a fifteen-year-old kid who loved to eat and loved old 1980s rap music. He pushed joyously at the buttons, his eyes wide and tongue hanging out like a Golden Retriever puppy.

"Good choice, Terrell! Here, here!" Freddie toasted Terrell with his double brandy on the rocks.

"Are you gentlemen ready?" asked the self-driving limo.

"We are indeed, chap. Please take us to Casa Azteca, my good fellow." Freddie turned his head toward Terrell, his mouth covered as he giggled into his hands. Terrell stifled a giggle as the limo rose several feet vertically then flew off.

When Freddie and Terrell arrived in Ocean City, all of the other delegates had already arrived and were mingling in the Great Room. Freddie had the back massager on for the entire trip and though sweaty, his back had never felt better. Aztec and Phoebe split the room, talking with their guests and making introductions.

Dweezle, along with one of his staffers, and a young person named Charlene, were serving drinks and appetizers. Charlene was an exuberant transgender woman who helped keep the conversation lively and flowing.

"Now, you have got to tell me all about that wilds incident that happened in Cape May last year, Mr. May. Has anyone been tracking the pack? I just have to see them sometime."

"We have, and it has, in fact, grown to twenty-eight. Mask sired another litter. They all appear to be healthy and happy. Come visit, and I will see to it that you get a firsthand view."

About an hour after the arrival of Freddie and Terrell, Dweezle ushered everyone into the Conference Room. It was 3:00 p.m. on what was turning into an overcast Friday. They were on the third floor and looking out of the large windows, one could see six-foot-high waves crashing on the shore, the aftermath of the super storm that had hit a week earlier. Aztec would love nothing more than to don his wetsuit and paddle out into the surf. Nothing except this. His true passion in life was helping people and seeing his labors come to fruition.

"Please grab a seat next to your city's other delegate. In the future, we would encourage you to mix it up with your shore neighbors, but today, we need you all paired up. We will spend the next three hours discussing and reviewing the agenda with a couple of breaks, and then there will be a cocktail hour followed by dinner, which will be served at 7:00 p.m., Aztec?" Phoebe was wearing a pencil-shaped dress with a short hemline and a pair of matching high heels. As usual, she looked smart and beautiful.

"Thank you, Phoebe. Before we start, I would like to go around the table. As we go around, please tell everyone your name and a little bit about what you care about most, family and lovers excluded. Okay?" There were nods all around. "Great, let me start. I am Aztec Pendleton, and I am interested in restoring the Jersey Shore to the beautiful place it once was—what it was before the craurchin invasion to be precise. Shana?" Shana Jacuzzi was sitting to his left.

"Hello, everyone. I am Shana, and I am representing Sea Isle and Strathmere, and my greatest concern in life is helping the poor folks living in what the rest of the world refers to as the Badlands."

The question made its way around the table and everyone, for the most part, elaborated on Shana and Aztec's vision. Then the question came to McNimble.

"What I care about is making the Badlands a viable part of United States business." A viable part of U.S. business? There was nothing about people suffering. Nothing about eradicating the craurchins.

For the next two hours, the group of fourteen discussed the agenda bullet points. They talked about how they could leverage support for the Badlands and where, and in what form, that support would come. They talked about which members of Congress or the Senate supported the Badlands.

Unfortunately, the party in power was against handouts to the Badlands or any U.S. citizen for that matter. All participated spiritedly except McNimble and Connors. Sure, they threw out an opinion or two, but at the end of the day, they were pretty quiet. Phoebe and Aztec didn't think anyone, other than themselves, noticed.

Phoebe, who had strategically planted herself across from the two, inconspicuously observed their emotional reactions to every topic. For the past year, she had studied with an expert on microexpressions. Flown in compliments of Pendleton Distilleries, James Akeman taught Phoebe how to read facial responses to the seven emotions that all human beings express, namely, anger, fear, sadness, disgust, surprise, contempt, and happiness—and they happened within one-twenty-fifth of a second! She was a quick learner and within months was using her newfound skill to evaluate everyone from the Casa Azteca chef to the farmer out on Route 50.

"Okay, everyone, it's five o'clock. Let's take a ten-minute break and then we'll come back, wrap up, and have some dinner." Aztec took Phoebe by her arm and escorted her into his office down the hall.

"Just as we suspected, Aztec. They are in on it."

"I concur, but please indulge me with your observations."

"Every time the words 'support for' or 'support from,' as in support from the Heartland were uttered, his reaction was utter disgust. When the topic of secession came up, he displayed strong emotions of fear and surprise. When Terrell made his negative comment about CraTek Industries, the anger response was off the charts," Phoebe explained.

During a conversation the group had regarding private industries providing jobs in the Badlands, Terrell had innocently stated, "There is this giant corporation called CraTek that manufactures products from craurchin shells. It would be nice if they could provide jobs and fair trade for craurchin kills, but I get the sense that they are only interested in their shareholders and not so much their employees."

Aztec knew that if a major corporation started pumping cash into the Badlands, it would greatly impact or even destroy the whole kill point system and that, Aztec and Phoebe believed, was the exact opposite of what CraTek, the government, and McNimble wanted!

"Okay, so now we go with plan B?"

"Yes, Phebes, just like we discussed." He said this with a knowing smile and a squint of those deep-set green eyes that she loved so much.

"So then, for the next hour, we steer clear of government conspiracy theories, CraTek and generally any negativity toward the Heartland or Corporate America, then we eat."

At precisely 6:00 p.m., Dweezle announced that the meeting would conclude and ushered the delegates into the Great Room for cocktails.

"Hey Terrell, Dweezle makes hands down, the greatest Bob Dylan you ever tasted!"

"With real cherries, Charlene?"

"Oh yeah, straight from the Smith family farm!"

At 7:00 p.m., Dweezle hovered into the Great Room and announced that dinner was about to be served. Everyone gathered around the hand-crafted oak table and sat in the plush velvet upholstered chairs. Five servers brought out plates of food in a never-ending culinary parade. There was ox-tail soup, hearts of palm salad with avocado, barbequed ostrich fillets, smoked alligator andouille, mushroom ragu, garlic-infused spinach, and an assortment of mussels, clams, shrimp, and lobster tail dishes both raw and steamed. Most of the group felt they had accomplished something today, and they all had the feeling that this was just the beginning.

McNimble and Connors were another story. They masked their disdain very well, but Phoebe read them instantly. They were itching to get out but didn't want to make it obvious. They worked their way through dinner, enjoying the delicious fare and constantly, Connors in particular, having their wine replenished.

"Pssst, hey, Roger, how long do you suppose we need to hang out with these pathetic peons? I'm not sure I could handle another minute of that nerdy nigger kid, and that dike Shana, ugh. Come on, our suite on the tenth floor is beckoning us," Connors whispered flirtingly.

"Shhh, we'll ditch dessert, okay?"

"Fine, but if that gimp in the sexy skirt keeps staring at me, I might have to scratch her eyes out."

It was 8:35 p.m. and the servers were clearing plates and serving coffee and tea. Dessert was going to be buffet style, so Charlene was ushering the guests into the next room. McNimble and Connors took the opportunity to stand up and excuse themselves.

"It was very nice meeting all of you, but the councilman and I must be going. Got some business in AC we need to attend to." Phoebe saw hints of humor and joy on Connors' facial reaction to this.

"Mayor McNimble, Councilman Connors, it was a pleasure having you. We will notify you of the next meeting." Dweezle escorted the two men to the roof where their hover was parked, and saw them off.

While the guests were enjoying dessert, Aztec, Phoebe, and Dweezle regrouped in Aztec's office. Phoebe's eyebrows were raised and she had a sober, concerned look that Aztec knew all too well. He waited for her to speak.

"Next move?" Phoebe genuinely had no idea where they should go from here. Aztec, on the other hand, seemed to know exactly what the next move should be. Even so, he needed Phoebe to be on the same page.

"I feel confident that all of the delegates here tonight, with of

course the exception of Mr. Ding and Mr. Dong, have the Badlands—
err—South Jersey Shores and the people's best interests in mind.
Even so, we need to spend the next couple of weeks vetting them
out to be sure. We then have the real meeting, a meeting devoid of
McNimble and his little friend."

"I'm down, Aztec, but how do we have a meeting without
those two finding out?" Phoebe wanted to know.

"We start by getting the mayor's schedule. Dweezle, I'll leave
that to you. When he is out of town, preferably sucking up to his
friends in the Heartland, we call for an emergency meeting of the
remaining delegates."

CHAPTER 23

THE COLLABORATORS

I'm the fear that keeps you awake
I'm the shadows on the wall
I'm the monsters they become
I'm the nightmare in your skull
I'm a dagger in your back
An extra turn on the rack
I'm the quivering of your heart
A stabbing pain, a sudden start
— "WHEN YOU'RE EVIL," VOLTAIRE

THE SECRET MEETINGS

When the War broke out in 2230, the craurchin extermination pro-grams came to a screeching halt all along the eastern coastline. The U.S. had long suspected foul play both domestically and on Sandomars by her enemies. Diplomacy had failed miserably. The entire world—U.S. allies and enemies—were fed up with American nationalism, its greedy hold on the world's only oil reserves, and the out-of-control price gouging. America was on its own against Russo-China. There would be no allies. When the national oil and gas facility on Sandomars was bombed, the generals and warmon-gers had their motive. Time to teach the world a lesson.

Nobody noticed right away, but much of the extermination efforts on the Jersey coast were shifted to the western parts of Pennsylvania, Maryland, and West Virginia. The rest of the troops were deployed in the Russo-Chino War. It appeared the govern-ment was now in defense mode regarding the craurchin invasion, and pulling troops basically isolated the coastlines of New Jersey and thus created the Badlands. Their new mission was to eradi-cate the craurchins that had popped up in the rivers, lakes, and tributaries further west, a mission that was more feasible to accom-plish—and with less troops. A mission that effectively quarantined the Badlands and planted the seeds for poverty, alcoholism, drug abuse, dilapidation of structures, disrepair of infrastructure, and the growth of craurchin populations.

During this time, Pendleton Distilleries saw its workforce of three thousand workers diminish to less than two thousand. One-third of his employees commuted from the areas that would eventually become the Badlands. Instead of moving the company headquarters west like so many of his competitors had, he encouraged his former employees, many of whom had moved to, or planned to move to, the Heartland or further west, to stay or move closer to the plant in Buena, New Jersey. He knew that deep inside they had no desire to leave their homes and the lifestyle they cherished.

He would help them move into new homes with low mortgage rates, which he would back. Nicer homes, closer to work. He would provide security, maintain the roads to and from the plant, and he would provide other benefits above and beyond the ones they already had. If they wanted to stay, Aztec would do what he could to make it happen. He did all of this on his own dime, knowing that the government would not help.

Aztec, like his father, had always been loyal to his employees and in return they had always tended to finish their careers at Pendleton Distilleries. They didn't let him down this time either. Ninety-five percent of them moved back or decided to stay. He gave many of them part-time jobs at Casa Azteca and other ventures he was involved in. Many such people were working at Casa Azteca today on this chilly September morning, helping to extend his craurchin-free perimeter another half-mile in each direction. Next year, he would add another mile. And the year after, that another.

The work group sang songs as they labored in the early morning cold. A sort of twenty-third-century chain gang on the beach, in a land occupied by alien crabs. The cool breezes off of the Atlantic Ocean made their labors tolerable.

"Come on, Jake. The netting goes over there. See where they're stringing it up?" Nefertiti impatiently asked.

She was dressed in light green coveralls, her dreadlocks tied up into a green and yellow knit cap, and was pointing toward the west end of the beach where a half-dozen men and women were using backhoes and shovels to dig ditches for the posts and netting that would be buried in the sand. Nefertiti, a foreman at the plant and a natural leader, welcomed the opportunity to earn some extra money or kill points to help support her family. She was employing those same leadership skills on the grounds of Casa Azteca today.

When personally approached by Aztec about the part-time job, Nefertiti did not hesitate. "For sure, Mr. Pendleton. I can use the work."

The work continued as the delegates, hovered in one by one, started arriving at Casa Azteca. The delegates were sort of local celebrities. Everyone knew who they were and the good work they were doing for the Badlands. Nefertiti looked at her communicator. It was 10:33 a.m., time for their first morning break. Some ominous clouds had settled in, and the surf was getting a little choppy. *Please, not another super storm*, Nefertiti thought.

"Break time!" she called out to the group. "Let's take thirty."

She walked with the group to their break area. When they arrived, she was happy to see her friend stepping out of the hover limo, just as she and the crew arrived.

"Good morning, Haley. How y'all on this nippy-ass morning?" Nefertiti waved her gloved hand pleasantly, prior to pulling each one off. The break area was on the south side of the mansion where the guests entered the mansion. She and the woman with the prosthetic leg had grown quite friendly over the last couple of months, often talking about their children and promising each other they would get together socially, a not-so-easy thing to do in the Badlands, USA.

"Fine, thanks. How are Joshua and Maria doing?" Haley asked as she limped toward Nefertiti.

"Not bad. Joshua is teething, so that's been a little tough. Maria turns five on Monday. How 'bout Aiden?" Nefertiti had lost her husband about six months after the birth of Joshua. He died unexpectedly from a seizure in the middle of a cold, dark February night. Nefertiti awoke the next morning and realizing he wasn't responding to her efforts to get him to attend to Joshua and called in Doc James, who pronounced him dead.

Nefertiti fought postpartum depression and battled the unexpected loss of her best friend and soulmate with valor. She combatted her depression by throwing herself into her work. Support from family and friends was a huge factor in her coping. Her parents sent money to her from their cushy home in the Heartland, but provided little if any, emotional support. They resented her for staying.

"Really good, Nefertiti, thanks. Romeo is going to take him to play with his cousins today. We've got to have that playdate with Maria and Aiden soon." She laid down her bag, stepped forward, and gave Nefertiti a long, tight hug. "Well, listen, girl, you stay strong. If you want to hang after work one day, maybe we can talk some more."

"That would be nice. Let's do that. Aztec said we could hang at his lower-level bar if we wanted."

"Yes! Let's do that! Hey, I know Aztec supplies y'all with coffee and such, but I've got some of the best coffee cake you've ever tasted. Made it myself. Tell the crew to help themselves."

"Umm, that looks delightful, thanks, dear." Nefertiti went in for a piece. "This will work nicely with my third cup of coffee! Have a good meeting, Haley!"

The meetings had been going on for about eleven months now. Some had been postponed for one reason or another, but Phoebe, currently wearing a green and black striped turtleneck sweater, slim fit black pants with stirrups and flats, had made sure that they had met once a month.

The anniversary of that very first meeting in November of 2272 was only two months away. They had six meetings without the Atlantic City boys and four with. *Keep your enemies close,* she thought. *Truer words have never been spoken.* That first secret meeting without McNimble went really well. Aztec had explained to the delegates how he and Phoebe had discovered that McNimble was conspiring with the Heartland. No one was surprised. They all agreed to play it coy in the farce meetings that McNimble would be attending. They would feed him misinformation. They would create bogus agendas that had nothing to do with the real one. Everyone was more than happy to oblige. And it was working.

"We need to open Atlantic City up to Badlandians as well," Freddie May suggested at one farce meeting. Freddie was dressed to impress in a pin-striped suit and purple bow tie. "They deserve entertainment as much as everyone else. Perhaps we can create a bus line from Cape May to Atlantic City." In reality, very few Badlanders would waste their time, let alone their hard-earned kill points, on the vices in AC, but McNimble and his lover seemed to buy it. In fact, Freddie did such a good job selling it, that at first most of the delegates bought it. Phoebe could see from McNimble and Connors microexpressions that they were believing every word, and in fact, loving what they were hearing. It stunk of more business for the McNimble Empire.

In that first secret meeting, Aztec presented his case. "Friends, we are at war. Let's lay this out plain. First, we know CraTek and the government are working together to harvest craurchins on our beaches and shoreline. We know this because the campaign has already started full force in the Wildwoods."

There were some gasps among most of the group. However, the Stone Harbor delegates, Haley and Hari, were not surprised. Hari had heard firsthand from several of his constituents.

"Several folks in Stone Harbor Point told me they could see drones flying over Anglesea. Big drones, flyin' fast. Also, a fisherman I spoke with said he saw a lot of men on Anglesea Beach, across the Hereford Inlet from Stone Harbor. He said they were wearing white uniforms and were workin' on the beach."

"Yes, Hari, we have a man in the field. He infiltrated the Skulls about two months ago, and he can confirm that CraTek had feet on the ground, killing 5s and larger. They were allowing the smaller ones to survive. He found out from one of the workers that they have set up a de-shelling facility in Voorhees. Also, they evidently have no qualms with killing civilians when they need to. The CraTek worker was not thrilled about that, and said he would quit before killing anybody."

Phoebe brushed a strand of hair from her face as she peered among the group. "We also have a mole in CraTek management. She has been giving us some great intel."

"It is obvious that they are using the Wildwoods as their pilot operation. They'll work out the bugs in Wildwood and then incorporate a refined operation on the rest of the shoreline. Then, they'll move inland. The fact that they are allowing cycle 1s to go is proof enough for me that CraTek is advancing craurchin proliferation. We all know cycle 1s are the most reproductive!" Emerlito Castillo's insight was always invaluable. "They'll spin it as an extermination effort for the welfare of the Badlands, and they will make every effort to conceal the de-shelling operation. Motherfuckers!"

"That's correct, except Atlantic City. In AC, they will exterminate the larger craurchins and drive out all the rest. McNimble will get his craurchin-free Atlantic City in exchange for his unfettered support of the Heartland. He will help the government to try and convince the citizens of the South Jersey Shores to either relocate to AC or to the Heartland. If they stay, they are on their own," Aztec explained.

"Like always!" someone chimed in.

"Like always," Aztec repeated. "We also have intel that McNimble wants to provide tours of our beaches and waterways. McNimble's Badlandian Craurchin Tours will be the new attraction, so the more overrun we are with craurchins, the better business will be for good ol' Roger."

Now here they were, real meeting number seven, and they were actually getting ready to talk about the actions they would take. Things had moved so fast. They had to be careful because once they started, there was no turning back. As always, Aztec started the meeting off on a high note.

"Thanks, everyone, for attending. Not sure if you all have heard, but the young girl who was taken in Margate last week has been rescued and the craurchin that took her—another 6—was killed. Team Dante's training is starting to pay off. The lair and some of the lairs in the vicinity have been destroyed. The team has been doing amazing work and the SJS is rapidly becoming a viable opponent to the craurchin, and CraTek for that matter. Remember, when we kill a craurchin, we save the shell. It is our new currency."

"We need to ensure that only limited people know where our shells are being stored," Gay Paxton pointed out.

"Good point, Gay. Yes, at this point, they are the new gold standard," Aztec responded. "Okay, so let's move on, but first, in appreciation for her exhaustive efforts on this committee and for just being a generally wonderful person, we have arranged a leg transplant for Haley, compliments of Pendleton Distilleries."

Spontaneously, cheers and clapping erupted, and Haley sat, stunned and speechless, completely overcome with emotion, so much so that she put her hands to her face and quietly wept. One by one, the delegates came over to her and embraced her. She hadn't seen this coming, and it was truly the best thing that happened to her since joining the committee. Haley could not wait to tell her good news to Nefertiti—and of course her husband.

Aztec moved the meeting forward.

"Now, onto the business at hand. The POTUS has signed the bill and the following towns are now incorporated into the eighteenth territory of the United States." Aztec waited for the grunts, groans, and general displays of disgust that filled the room to dissipate. It was the really bad news that everyone was hoping wouldn't come but nonetheless expected. Yet, when it came, it was still shocking and disturbing.

It was the final dagger in the heart of the South Jersey Shore. It wasn't every day that you found out you lived in the first area to go from being part of a state to a territory. To go from having the full rights of a U.S. citizen to having the limited rights of a U.S. territory. To top it off, it was a law written and passed by the corrupt Heartland government. The Badlands were truly on their own.

"They are Cape May, North Cape May, the Villas, Erma, and then everything east of the Garden State Parkway, including all of the Wildwoods, Stone Harbor, Avalon, Sea Isle, Strathmere, Ocean City, Longport, Margate, and Ventnor. It will not include Atlantic City. They will rename these areas the South Jersey territories. We now officially have no representation in Congress and cannot vote. To add insult to injury, Roger McNimble has been appointed territorial governor! "

"Unfucking believable!" Terrell grunted, to the surprise of everyone in the room.

THE SCOURGE OF ATLANTIC CITY

"Agh." Scurge lay in his bed, head spinning, face buried in his giant, fluffy pillow. He always demanded Sally keep his pillows clean and fluffy. *Oh shit, Sally.* His head was killing him, and he was hoping that what he remembered was just a nightmare. He was perspiring profusely and had three days of stubble on his face and head. His long beard was greasy and filled with crud. He suspected the night-mare he had was not a nightmare at all. "Fuck!" He was not ready to detach his tattooed head from the pillow. Not ready to face his new reality. His right shoulder was killing him. *My slashing shoulder?*

Some time later, he finally rose from his bed, placed his feet on the floor, and sat on the edge of the bed, holding his forehead in his large tattooed hands. The scar below his ribcage was puffy and bleeding slightly. When his sweaty, bald head cleared, and the blur in his eyes subsided, he lifted his head and glanced around his bedroom—their bedroom.

What he saw shocked and terrified even Scurge. On the walls, on the ceiling, the bed, the windows, the door, the wood floor, and all of the furniture was blood. It colored everything with a dark red hue.

At first, he thought he was seeing double vision, so he blinked a few times and looked around again. No change. He was horrified, and then the pungent odor hit him. It was a combination of the smell of twenty rotting, raw pork butts mixed with cheap per-fume and skunked beer. Behind him on the bed, lay what was left of Sally. The skin on her face, neck, shoulders, and what was left of her abdomen were a pasty green with splatters of red. On her face, the eyes and tongue were bloated and protruding. *How long was I sleeping in that bed with the corpse of the woman I loved and lived with for the last two and a half decades?*

Scurge bent over and puked on the floor. When the smell of his own vomit mixed with Sally's rotting body hit him, he puked again. *What have I done?* For most of the morning, he battled the worst hangover he ever had. He still felt physically drained and sick, and he figured he had been sleeping-comatose for at least forty-eight hours. As the day dragged on, the guilt and regret slowly dissipated. Sure, he would miss Sally, but he'd find another piece of ass. The Badlands version of Scurge was back.

Later that day after cleaning himself up, getting a fix and pouring a long, strong whiskey, Scurge walked into the bedroom. He packed his few belongings, then made several trips to where they parked their hovers, where he loaded his things onto Sally's hoverbike, then daisy-chained her hover to his. He walked to the shed and pulled out two gallons of gasoline, a precious commodity in the Badlands. He then walked back into the house and poured it all over Sally and the home's interior. He lit a match, threw it on the floor, and ran out of the house, drink still in hand.

MCNIMBLE THE TERRIBLE

By the fourth farce meeting, McNimble started to get suspicious. Phoebe, who was monitoring him carefully, saw it. Aztec, Emerlito Castillo, and Gruman Hamm, all experienced with the seedy game of politics and reading people, saw it as well. It was subtle enough but there nonetheless. If McNimble found out that he was being duped, nobody expected him to react calmly. But nobody saw what was coming when he did react. The fact that he was mortified was an understatement.

"Goddammit, Bob. How the fuck could we have missed this?" McNimble shouted. He was in a rage. Livid. His face was bright red and his hands were shaking. Bob had never seen him this angry. Never. The two men were spending the night in the mayor's private tenth-floor suite where they had hashed out McNimble's suspicions over drinks and dinner. Both concurred that they were being conned. Sex that night was not going to happen; however, revenge was.

"Calm down, Roger. Here, have another scotch. We'll take care of this."

"Fucking right, we will!" McNimble yelled. "Goddamn fucking right!"

Cisco Florenzo sat at the bar in the Paradise Lost Tavern, one of McNimble's stripper bars. The interior was nice. A stark contrast to the decrepit neighborhood outside. Although it was in one of the seediest neighborhoods in Atlantic City, it was his most popular by far. Perhaps the burned-out buildings and overgrown lots that surrounded it gave a feeling of danger. A feeling to customers that with the lawlessness and disorder all around, anything goes. His large, fleecy Malamute Maji, sat on the floor next to his stool. The bartender walked over to him with a bowl of water for the dog. "What will you be having today, Cisco? Drinks are on the mayor."

"I'll have a shot of Tequila and a beer please."

As he sat sipping his beer one of the two dancers made his way to Cisco's end of the bar. He was wearing nothing but a yellow jockstrap. A literal banana hammock. When he got to Cisco, he flexed his biceps and twitched his large fan-shaped pectoral muscles. Cisco politely shook his head, then looked down at his drink. The bar was pretty crowded for 11:00 a.m. As he sat sipping his beer, and thinking about what the hell Mayor McNimble could possibly want from him, he heard a low cough. When he looked up, a beautiful light-skinned black girl wearing nothing but a g-string was standing behind him. She had tiny breasts with large, dark areolas. She did an exaggerated bend-over, sticking her ass high in the air, as she petted and talked to Maji. Maji rolled his large body onto his back, legs sprawled out as the woman gave him a belly rub.

"Who is this beautiful boy? Isn't he a handsome doggie!" She was still scratching Maji's belly as he purred with delight.

Cisco rubbed the girl's firm buttocks a couple of times and then swiped her left cheek with his communicator. *Zoop.*Ten kill points.

"Feel like a quickie in the back?" she asked with a seductive smile.

"Why are you still doing this, Rocky?" Cisco asked emotionlessly. "Why don't you go to the Heartland? Why don't you pursue a better life? You're an intelligent woman."

"Why Cisco? Why? Here's why…because I don't want to live in a society of self-righteous religious fucks! Why don't you move to the fucking Heartland?"

"You know why, Rocky."

"Yeah, well—" Rocky suddenly grew silent as the mayor entered the club. She moved on to the next customer as the mayor stood in the lobby, glancing around the club. When he spotted Cisco, he walked toward him, waving enthusiastically.

"Cisco Florenzo, greatest handler in AC! Sorry I'm late, buddy."

"Not a problem, Mr. Mayor. How are you this morning?"

"Good." He snapped his fingers and pointed to the bar top in front of him. "Listen, I'll get right to the point. Who is your number one trapper?"

"That would be Scurge, Mr. Mayor."

"Scrooge? Is that what you said?"

"No Sir, Scurge, S-c-u-r-g-e. Charles Corbin is his birth name, but—"

"Okay, Scurge, I got it. How do I contact him?"

"Mr. Mayor, you know I procure my prize fighters exclusively for the Skulls. I can't—"

"Fuck the Skulls, Cisco, you're not procuring me a prize fighter. How do I contact Scurge?"

TROUBLE AT CASA AZTECA

"Perimeter One, this is Perimeter Two, do you copy?"

"I hear you loud and clear P-2. What's up, Dyl?"

"Just doing a check Mitch. All good?" Dylan Page responded.

"Copy that. All good."

"Perimeter Three, do you read me?"

"Loud and clear, Dylan! Visual is good here as well."

"Perimeter Four, is all clear in the sea?"

"So far, Mr. Page." Joey Bally was not only working at Pendleton Distilleries now, but he was rapidly becoming one of Slash's most reliable security guys. It was not a coincidence that Joey, who had witnessed the cycle 6 invasion from the sea on Cape May, was on beach duty today. He stood on his hover-glide, gun in hand, gazing out at the gray horizon for any movement whatsoever.

Slash had given specific orders to the team to report any-thing out of the ordinary. "If you see anything—a school of dolphins, a piece of driftwood, a hermit crab scurrying in the sand—I want to know about it," he had told them. Currently, Slash was in the control room, monitoring all actions.

"This is the control center. Gentleman, please don't use your names when communicating. Stick to the deployment names, please."

Slash did everything by the book. He was a military robot, a milibont, and deployed all security as if it were a military operation. Use of names could compromise their safety. There were eight security men on the beach, Slash at the control center, and two drones in the air. The water drone was currently in for repairs. There were fifteen workers putting up fencing, and of course the delegates and staff inside the mansion. It was 4:00 p.m. and the limo-hovers were preparing to take the delegates back home.

"Code Red, Code Red!" Slash announced to his beach sentries. From Drone A1's cameras, he could see a man and a large flatbed truck parked to the northwest of the property on the sand, just off the long driveway that led to the gates of Casa Azteca. On the bed of that truck was a large cage. He zoomed in on the cage and could see that inside was a large craurchin. "Perform analysis of target," he said as he placed the craurchin in the crosshairs.

"Cycle 5 craurchin, male, seven foot one, approximate weight four hundred fifty pounds," announced the drone.

"Control, do you read me?"

"Go ahead, Perimeter Four," Slash said calmly to Joey.

"There is some activity about three hundred feet out to sea, just beyond the breakers. Appears to be a boat or hovercraft."

"Copy that, Four. Perimeter One and Sentries Two and Four move to the shoreline. Space yourselves out. All remaining sentries and perimeters be on alert. We are being attacked from the west. Perimeter Two, escort the workers to the mansion immediately."

Slash sent Drone A2 toward the boat, then looked at the activity happening below Drone A1. The man was now on the truck bed and appeared to be unlocking the cage. He accelerated, leaving the cage tumbling off the back of the truck. It hit the ground, flipped over, and the door sprung open just like he planned.

"Drone A1 prepare to fire." As he homed in on the cycle 5 struggling to get up, he caught some movement on his other screen then turned back. "Drone A1—fire!"

Slash switched to the other screen as the cycle 5 collapsed on the driveway, overwhelmed by the hail of bullets. One hundred bullets per click. It didn't have a chance. *A distraction*, Slash said to himself. "Drone A2 give me a visual. Drone A1 fly north-south along the middle of the property." Slashes responses were instant, devoid of any hesitation whatsoever.

Slash peered at the screen, as Drone A2 transmitted images of the craft out in the ocean. It was a calm sea this afternoon and what looked like a hovercraft was hovering just above the bluish-green sea, the sun high overhead to the west. Slash could see a couple of men on the craft and another cage, this one larger, on the stern. They were pushing the cage, which appeared to have casters, toward the edge of the craft and the sea beyond.

"Drone A2 prepare to attack. Zoom in on the cage." Too late. The second man opened the cage as it was rolling, then the two of them quickly tipped it into the ocean, and in seconds, the craft sped off.

"Attack the craurchin, A2, attack." One thing about robants—

they didn't get excited. The white-hot lasers hit the water and sizzled in the ocean, but the craurchin had gone under. Slash could see the dark mass slowly disappearing as it submerged into the deep waters.

"Sentries on the shoreline back up thirty-five feet. The craurchin, which appears to be a cycle 6, is heading your way."

On the south perimeter, Dylan Page gathered the fifteen workers and began the mile walk back to the mansion. All were calm. Evacuations were common. As they moved along, feet plopping in the sand, Nefertiti asked Dylan, "What is going on, Dylan? Why are both the drones on the shoreline?"

Dylan answered honestly. "We were attacked from the west and now it looks like we're being attacked from the east!"

"Craurchins?"

"Yes. The 5 from the west was taken out. The cycle 6 from the sea is being dealt with."

When the cycle 6 emerged into the shallows, the two drones and security detail were ready. The drones hit it with a barrage of hot lasers and heavy-gauge bullets, but it blocked most of the shots with its pincers as it lumbered on, using its remaining four legs. The five sentries on the beach maintained a constant hail of lasers, all aiming for the head. Each time it attempted to move forward, it would advance about five feet before the drones circled back and let loose their fury of firepower. One came in low and the 6 nearly took it out before it buried its head inside its pincers.

To slow it down, Joey jumped in a mini-dozer and began digging a ditch between them and the 6. This was a tactic he had learned from Cape May, only in the cape they used shovels. It worked. The craurchin was having trouble navigating the ditch and protecting its head at the same time. They took advantage but still no headshot. It was, however, bleeding profusely from a shot that had grazed its pincer arms. One of its arms was partially detached. They all waited as it stood on four legs, protecting its head with its pincers.

"It will rest a little and then make a full sprint charge, so be ready men." Slash was watching the entire encounter from the control room. He was part of many craurchin encounters, and this was a common tactic it used. Again, and again, it would lumber forward, protect itself, repeat, then charge. "The drones are getting into position."

They waited for the craurchin to show its head. Nothing. Slash was wondering what had drawn the craurchin to the beach. Craurchin attacks were usually stealthier, and besides, it knew it was under attack.

"Drone A2 scan the beach." Slash looked at the video and saw a group of what looked like a cluster of 3s and 4s. The cycle 6's cluster. He was contemplating the idea of putting a missile through its shell when suddenly the large 6 started burrowing into the sand. In an instant, it was in the sand and then it disappeared. Was it heading toward the sentries or back out to sea? The sentries stood ready, guns drawn and anticipating an attack. Five minutes turned into ten, and everyone was wondering where the large cycle 6 had gone.

Slash was thinking of leaving the control station, but his computers calculated that he was most useful in controlling the situation from above then leaving his command post and participating. After all, the attack appeared to be from multiple directions. To leave would put others in danger.

"All remaining sentries, there are a cluster of two 3s and three 4s—take them out. I am sending their coordinates now." Slash was monitoring all cameras, looking for the craurchin to emerge. Then, he saw something and reacted instantly.

"All sentries head to the mid-beach—thee hundred yards southeast from base. I repeat, three hundred yards southeast of the base."

Slash sent the drones to those coordinates, then released Aztec's trained killers, six huge Dobermans trained to destroy craurchins. They were in their large beach pen and when the gates opened, they charged toward the cycle 6's cluster.

The four sentries on the shoreline turned to the northeast. What they saw was fifteen workers and one sentry in the distance, walking toward Casa Azteca. Then they saw the beach rising and heaving, leaving a concave line of sand that was heading straight toward the group. The drones were heading toward it, guns readied.

"To the rendezvous point!" Joey shouted, and the four sentries, all on hover-boards, headed toward the workers.

"What the fuck is that?" Jake Owani shouted, "Shit!"

"Everyone, stop! Back up behind me!" Dylan commanded. He had barely uttered those words when the beach exploded twenty feet in front of them. Sand, water, shells and seaweed flew everywhere as the thirteen-foot-tall cycle 6 craurchin emerged from the ground. Sand poured off of it like a white-gray waterfall. It shrieked a high-pitched battle cry, slashing with its two huge pincers at the air and sand as it charged toward the group of workers. Its cluster,

328

two cycle 3s and three cycle 4s, gathered around it like a coven of witches.

"Fuck you!" Shouted Dylan as he fired upon the attacking monster. *Zoop, zoop, zoop, zoop*. Five of the six shots connected. One hit its massive shell, two hit pincers, one grazed its head, and the fifth connected with its large head. Blood burst from the left side of its head but only slowed it down for a moment. It continued its charge and the group scattered in all directions. The cluster split up as well, attacking the various retreating group members.

The dogs arrived as the group split up, each taking on a cycle 3 or 4 before they could do any harm.

The drone flew in low and released its hail of bullets and lasers. *Zoop, zoop, zoop, zoop.* The cycle 6 stumbled but regained its composure and slashed at the closest human. Its massive pincer decapitated Nefertiti in a single swipe. Her head rolled across the beach under a retreating Dylan's feet, tripping him up. Dylan rolled onto the sand, gun drawn but not quite in firing position as his body settled on the soft sand. The six ripped his torso open exposing his ribcage and intestines.

"A2, fire missile," Slash commanded. Drone A2 flew in, twenty feet above the beach and launched a missile that hit the craurchin in the upper part of the shell where the head became exposed from the shell. The explosion knocked the four sentries, who had just arrived at the scene, on their backs. All four of them were covered with bits of skin, guts, claws, and horn, but the shell of the craurchin remained intact. When the smoke and air-born sand cleared, the craurchin lay nearly lifeless on the beach. The head was half on its neck. The dogs arrived and finished off what was left.

The group all stood mesmerized. Shocked. Two of their comrades had just been slaughtered for absolutely no reason. Both had children who depended on them. *How could this have happened?*

CHAPTER 24
ASBURY PARK

Though his mind is not for rent
Don't put him down as arrogant
He reserves the quiet defense
Riding out the day's events
—"TOM SAWYER," RUSH

GREETINGS FROM ASBURY PARK, 2231

Asbury Park certainly had its share of diversity and changes over the last several centuries, but they always pulled it together and somehow pulled through. From the riots of 1974 to the government scandals in 2105, Asbury Park managed to keep it together. In 2186, the barrier island towns of Lavallette, Seaside Heights, and Seaside Park were swallowed up forever by the Atlantic when Hurricane Sidney hit—two thousand lives snuffed out in what would be forever referred to as Huracan's Revenge, one of the deadliest hurricanes in American history.

It was definitely the most destructive, but unfortunately did not wipe out the craurchins, which were still no larger than cycle 4s at that time. Asbury Park, only nineteen miles to the north, survived, although it was hit hard. A city of over twenty thousand before the craurchin invasion, it still maintained nearly half of its original population and was still a thriving, sometimes striving, town.

In 2230, when the federal government announced it was pulling out of the South Jersey Shores, Asbury Park had the collective foresight to reinvent itself from a tourist and music town (the greatest talents from New York City and Philly came to play AP) to a fishing, then fishery, town. This happened because the much higher craurchin populations to the south had chased many of the fish and marine life up the northern coast. Asbury Park and some of her barrier island neighbors were the beneficiaries of this. Some took advantage of this, but none to the degree of Asbury Park. They were the only town on the New Jersey coast to actually prepare for the invasion. They accepted the invasion for what it was, expected little support from the federal government and held long, detailed meetings as to the fate of their beloved town.

They saw the cancer that was spreading its way from Sea Isle City to points both north and south. It would arrive in Asbury Park. It was just a matter of time. When the craurchins arrived, they would be ready. To fund this, they would convince the New York City elite that Asbury Park was the first real line of defense before it hit the Big Apple. In one of the last and most important hearings they would have, the board assembled at Convention Hall on Ocean Avenue to vote for AP's future. Elisha Yamamoto, a young energetic and aspiring politician, led the meeting.

"Members of the board, we are at a crucial juncture in our long and proud history. Last week, we all decided. We took a vote and a choice was made that will affect each and every one of us. Some of you may not be here in five years, or maybe even two for that matter. You will have moved away. And that is okay. You are doing what you feel is best for yourselves and your families. We all understand. But for those who choose to stay, I believe life will become harder. Much harder and more difficult." There was some chatter from the audience of over two hundred people. The cameras and reporters were recording every word and every reaction. Elisha waited until the crowd grew silent.

"Difficult, but worth preserving. Let me say this—the craurchins are heading this way. We can try and stop them, and believe me, we will certainly try, but without the support of the federal government it will be difficult. As you know, they pulled out of the southern shores a year ago, so we don't expect any help here. Forget federal help. For the last eight months, the committee has discussed extensively what we will do when the government comes down to Asbury Park with their relocation program. Well, most of us will tell them to stick their relocation plan up their bureaucratic asses! That we have decided to stay!" The crowd cheered wildly and Elisha continued. "Here is the plan."

Elisha had invited several professionals to help her roll out the plan. Among them were a life-long commercial fishermen, a fishery expert, several scientists, an architect, a structural engineer, and a young entrepreneur named Aztec Pendleton. They talked for the next three hours. Aztec went first. Aztec was born and raised in Asbury Park and felt his loyalty and money could help. The plan was quite simple. They would take advantage of the fish and crustaceans that were being chased away by the craurchins, forcing them their way. Aztec explained how, as the craurchin crisis grew, the supply of fish would decrease, driving up the demand and thus the cost of seafood.

"It's Business 101, in its simplest form. Supply and demand. As the fish become depleted or head further out to sea, the demand throughout the nation will rise. The west coast can only supply so much."

A commercial fisherman, a gray-haired gentleman named Robert Bayler, explained how the city could take advantage of the large populations of fish while the fishery was being built, and how they could catch the fish in a sustainable way.

"We take advantage of the influx of fish, especially those inside our territorial waters, but we set our own strict rules as to those we keep and those left to reproduce. We also have to maintain a balance of species for the future. Striper, fluke, bluefish, bluefin tuna, weakies, and sea bass will be the main groups. But there will be many more. The market is very hungry and will only get hungrier. We can be the ones to feed that hunger!"

The fishery expert, a mousy woman with big, round eyeglasses named Amanda Winslow, explained how they would need to build the fishery facility before the craurchins hit their waters. Naturally, as their food sources in South Jersey become depleted, the craurchins will follow the fish. Everyone wanted a fishery that was built directly in the Atlantic and not an inland farm-type fishery. This had been achieved successfully in other places, but not to the level they were proposing. After all, this fishery needed to protect itself from craurchin breeches, as well as the super storms that now hit two or three times a year.

"Amanda is correct," the architect said. "Construction will need to start as soon as possible. It will be a logistics nightmare to try and build the fishery while trying to stave off craurchins at the same time. The engineering of this facility will make construction challenging enough."

The meeting went well. There was some resistance to the plan, but all in all, very little. Many questions were asked and answered to most folk's satisfaction. The majority of the town knew this was happening and tonight was just a meeting to get further into the weeds. Three months after the meeting, floor plans for the facility were already at the end of the concept phase and about to move into detailed design. This was to be a massive design effort on a fast-track schedule.

One night after a long day at work, Elisha, fresh out of the shower, was drying her hair and getting ready for bed when her husband called to her from downstairs. It was a windy Tuesday night in February and she could hear the wind groaning from their bathroom window. *Please, not another storm,* she thought.

"Elisha, turn on the smartwall."

"Video on," she spoke, staring at the blank bedroom wall. "Video on," repeated the house unit.

"And that is why more troops and most importantly, more computer programmers, will be needed."

"Okay, thank you, Petro. All right, now to another war story. This would be our other war, namely the craurchin war on the east coast. We'll go to Amanda Lemone, reporting on how one shore community in New Jersey is dealing with the craurchin crisis. Amanda, what've you got?"

"Deon, I'm here in Asbury Park, New Jersey, outside the famous Stone Pony, where I am speaking with Elisha Yamamoto. If you remember, Elisha chaired the Citizens for a New Asbury Park Committee. As she mentioned in the big announcement just a few short weeks ago, Asbury Park will be taking on the craurchin crisis in their own, special way. Elisha can you elaborate?"

"I sure can, Amanda. Here in Asbury Park, we are proud of our long history and the city we have built. And to put it bluntly, we are not going to give it up to the craurchins! No, ma'am, we are going to fight. We are going to reinvent ourselves. Adjust and align ourselves to deal with the craurchin problem and tackle it head-on. Architects and engineers have already been contracted and are working on plans for the proposed AP fishery works as we speak. Funding has been procured. The entire operation will employ thousands."

"How so?" Amanda wanted to know.

"All labor will be local. Positions will be needed for construction workers, divers, security, fishery plant workers, quality control positions, fishermen, scientists, drone operators, distribution, packagers, shippers, office workers, and probably a lot of other positions that I am not even thinking of right now. Unemployment will not be an issue in Asbury Park. Also, anyone who wants to donate to our cause can commune with me at 232E55."

EROL AND THE AP FISHERY WORKS, 2250

By 2250, Asbury Park was doing quite well. As predicted, the craurchins had expanded their territory all the way up the coast to central New Jersey and beyond. The AP fishery works was the success everyone had hoped it would be. Two of the greatest challenges had been keeping the craurchins from compromising the fishery, and the town for that matter, and keeping the ocean from destroying the fishery. Both were constant struggles that demanded constant attention. To counteract the former, defenses were set up a few miles from Asbury Park's southern border, where drones continuously fumigated the beaches with Craurchicide X25. Fighters stood by to shoot the ones that survived, and Aztec's Cra-Chippers ground up the smaller craurchins into seagull feed—and it was working. The AP fishery started production on schedule, though substantially over budget. But it was worth it. The town had very few craurchin incidents. In the twenty years since it opened, the facility had sustained no less than forty-five super storms and had fared very well. Modern-day engineering techniques and a little out-of-the-box thinking had proved to be successful.

The fishery was breeding and selling tons of fish each day. The facility was also a case study for similar ventures like the desalination plant in Monmouth Beach. In Asbury Park, life was almost as it had been during the pre-craurchin days. Sure, there was the occasional attack, but Asbury Park was basically a safe place. Because of this, it was one of the only shore towns, really the only Jersey Shore town, that actually had vacationers that still visited each year. They could safely hang out on the beautiful, clean beaches, eat at the fine restaurants, drink and listen to music at the best clubs around, and partake in all kinds of water sports in the ocean and bay. Hell, they could even hunt craurchins to their hearts' content, only a few short miles away outside of AP. In contrast, shore towns to the south and north were quite a different story.

Eight years ago, a local man had been ambushed by a cycle 6 while hunting in nearby Neptune. Erol Windsong, a worker at the fishery, had always enjoyed hunting craurchins. Even though he didn't need the KPs, he still liked to hunt and kill urchies, as he called them. But Erol broke the number one rule: Never hunt alone. As fate would have it, a huge cycle 5 craurchin surprised him, paralyzed him, and then dragged him off to its lair where it leeched him for three long, excruciatingly painful days.

When he didn't show up to work two days in a row, his mother Dolly, who also worked at the fishery, checked in on him at his apartment on Memorial Drive. Neither he, nor his dog Fudgie were there, and his hunting gear was missing. Erol, who was intellectually challenged, was supposed to report in with her whenever he went hunting. He was also never to hunt without a human companion.

"Shit!" Dolly thought aloud. "This is not good. Not good at all." She immediately organized a search party. They found Erol using Fudgie's chip, but poor Fudgie was dead. Also, they lost one volunteer and two dogs while executing his rescue. To add insult to injury, the cycle 5 escaped, virtually unharmed into the bay. Truth be told, the group was very lucky—they were not equipped to take on a cycle 5.

Erol had barely survived. He spent three weeks recovering from his physical injuries at the University of Philadelphia Medical Center, seventy-six miles away in Philly. When he got out, he was not the same man. After only two short months, he lost his job at the fishery due to excessive absenteeism and, on occasion, showing up intoxicated. He was drinking heavily and abusing painkillers. He eventually lost his apartment and embarrassed to move in with his mother, moved into an abandoned home in nearby Avon-by-the-Sea. Dolly did her best to get him food and clothes, but could not convince him to move back home where she could take proper care of him.

Erol was a very stubborn man. He was also suffering from a mental illness that Dolly believed was either caused by his abuse of drugs and alcohol or the ordeal with the craurchin. Some kind of mental trauma seized him. She certainly didn't know which. What she did know was that there was nowhere to go for help. The government wouldn't help and the town couldn't help. It just did not have the resources. As the years went by, his condition grew worse. He was often seen in Asbury Park, either downtown peddling for booze money or sleeping on the beach.

In the last couple of years, he was often seen talking to himself, sometimes in what appeared to be another language. He was in dire need of medical help, proper nutrition, and a bath. Dolly was desperate. She was deeply concerned for her poor son, but just as much, her safety and that of others.

DR. MARCUS DIFILLIPO GOES TO THE BADLANDS

In 2242, the same year Erol Windsong was leeched, Dr. Marcus DiFillipo, a well-known craurchin researcher, was hearing more and more reports of craurchin leechings along the Jersey coastline. To him, this upsurge made perfect sense. He recognized the fact that, around the year 2220, the first generation of craurchins were hitting cycle 5, and that by 2245, three short years from now, they would become cycle 6s and even worse, the second generation, which was exponentially greater, would become cycle 5s. Also, as food became scarce, this first generation of cycle 5s was becoming more emboldened and attacks were increasing. He got a call from Jon Pendleton who, like him, was concerned about the increase in attacks. He was also concerned about the mental health of the survivors who had been taken. Like Dr. DiFillipo, he thought there was a connection.

"Dr. DiFillipo, my name is Jonathon Pendleton. I read your latest book and I am impressed with your work. As you know, attacks here in the Badlands are becoming more frequent, but even worse, more and more of our citizens are being taken."

"Taken? I'm sorry, who did you say this was?"

"Jonathon Pendleton. I am president and CEO of Pendleton Distilleries. When I say taken, I am referring to citizens being taken by craurchins—taken and having their blood sucked. In the Badlands, we refer to this as a 'taking'."

"Leeched—oh my!"

"Yes, that's correct, Dr. DiFillipo. Listen, I'll get right to the point. How can I convince you to open a clinic here in Asbury Park? We could really use your help. We have no idea what to do with these poor victims. We think Asbury Park would be the best location because it is by far the safest place in the Badlands for you to work."

The two men spoke for nearly forty-five minutes and, one very receptive Dr. Marcus DiFillipo, agreed to meet in person, in the Badlands. Dr. Marcus had never been there and Aztec wanted him to experience it live and in person. Two weeks later, Aztec had him flown down directly to Casa Azteca where he spent several days touring the Badlands with Aztec and discussing plans for a clinic in Asbury Park.

They began the tour-journey, flying in Aztec's three-man chopperjet across the inland to Pierces Point on the Delaware Bay. Aztec's pilot, an ArtEng named Wallace, landed the vehicle and walked with them along the beach, where they observed crurchins from a short distance, lazing in the sun or hunting for the sparse crabs and other crustaceans. Marcus took lots of photos and SciDat scans. They then flew south along the coast of the Delaware Bay over the Villas and North Cape May until they came to Cape May Point where they landed once again.

In Cape May, they met with several councilmen and talked to some PCLS (post-craurchin leaching syndrome) sufferers. They talked with a teenager who was years ahead of her actual age, named Lonnie Bally. She explained to them how the wilds in the area helped keep the craurchin populations down and how they all depended on their domestic dogs for protection. Marcus had never seen a group of dogs, or wilds for matter, engage with a craurchin.

"Lonnie, have you ever actually seen a dog or group of wilds fight a craurchin?"

"Oh, yes, Dr. DiFillipo, many times!" She had her dog Rascal with her like she always did. "If you want, we can walk down the beach, and you can see for yourself."

Marcus looked over at Aztec who nodded his head approvingly. Rascal, an extra-large white Collie mix who had been lying on the ground at Lonnie's feet, jumped up when he heard "walk down the beach."

"Come on!" They walked the short block to the beach where they saw several dozen cycle 1s, 2s, and 3s going about their business. When the craurchins noticed Rascal, they began scurrying in all directions. Rascal, breathing heavily, his tongue hanging out and tail wagging, looked around, keen to make sure there were no larger craurchins in sight. Lonnie did the same, and when she was comfortable it was clear, she clapped her hands.

"Go, boy!" Rascal took off toward the nearest cycle 3. Within seconds, he pounced on the retreating 3, knocked it on its back, and bit off its softball-sized head. He was about to work on its underbelly when he heard his master.

"Okay, we need to go now. Rascal! Come!" Lonnie pointed to the 5 walking upright out of the surf. "We have been seeing more and more of them lately," she said, pointing to the 5. As they walked off the beach, Dr. Marcus looked over his shoulder, intrigued by a cycle 5 in its natural earthly habitat.

When they left the cape, they flew over the Wildwoods where Marcus saw firsthand the chaos that existed there. Wallace flew in low, and what Marcus saw chilled him to the bone.

"I knew it was bad, but seeing it in person is just—just surreal!" said a flabbergasted Marcus. Below was a sea of black. There were so many craurchins blanketing the beach that you could only catch glimpses of white sand. The warped boardwalk was in dire disrepair. Some portions were completely collapsed, and others were washed away. The town looked like a bombed-out European city from an old World War II movie. It was a decrepit mass of dirty, filthy decay. Crumbling buildings lined the streets and overgrown trees and weeds pushed their way through the macadam of once tidy streets. If the South Jersey Shore was the Badlands, then the Wildwoods were the Wastelands. There was to be no landing here.

They toured Seven Mile Island, the barrier island that encompassed Stone Harbor and Avalon. Once a beautiful stretch of island with lush tall sand dunes and natural sanctuaries, it was now overrun with craurchins. You could still see its beauty if you looked hard enough. Flying over Stone Harbor, the ArtEng pilot pointed out a pack of wilds running down the beach. They flew slowly above them for a while, taking in their natural beauty and eloquence.

"Do you see the large one leading the pack?" Wallace said, pointing a pale finger toward the canine. "He is the pack leader. The alpha male. He is most likely leading his pack to a safer location down the beach. A pack of six, like that, can take out a cycle 5."

In Avalon, they landed on Twenty-First Street and the beach, where the boardwalk once started its twenty-nine-block journey from Twenty-First Street to Fiftieth Street. There, they viewed the erosion of the beaches due to the tri-yearly super storms. The sand dunes were gone and the waves were crashing only a few yards from where only the pylons from the boardwalk remained, sticking out of the sand, black, rotted, and crooked. And it was low tide! The rest of the boardwalk was gone. Just off the shoreline, they saw large rusty dredgers, sitting idle like frozen steel, Loch Ness monsters. Abandoned skeletons now almost thirty years old, since the government halted all environmental operations and pulled out of the Badlands. They flew over the jetties spilling into Townsends Inlet, the waterway connecting bay to sea and dividing the barrier islands of Avalon and Sea Isle City.

In Sea Isle, they landed and walked around the JFK Boulevard area, the town center. There, in New Excursion Park, they met a young zunkie. A zunkie was the name given to people addicted to zeskolyne. In the early days of post craurchin leeching syndrome, zeskolyne was often given to people suffering from it. Although PCLS didn't have a name yet, this synthetic drug, called Z on the streets, was developed to combat hallucinations. The problem was, these so-called hallucinations, which doctors thought were caused by trauma, were really the craurchin telepathic communication that occurred after a leeching. The powerful narcotic was extremely addictive and took hold quickly.

"Sir? Sir, is it okay if we talk to you?" They approached the zunkie, who was just finishing dispensing the potent drops in each of his eyes. He looked up at them from the park bench upon which he was affixed. His remarkable red and hazel eyes were extremely glassy and the whites, a bit yellow—spooky yet intriguing.

"Hey, ya. Wazzup, guys? What can I do you for?" He knew they were not cops. The Badlands had no cops. He was not threatened because he didn't care about his well-being. He only cared about getting high.

"Do you live here, in Sea Isle?"

"I do. In fact, most of the time I live right here in this beautiful park." Marcus scanned the park. It was overrun with weeds, broken bottles, empty Z droppers, and cracked or missing marble tiles. "'Cept in the winter when it's too cold. If you wanna talk to me, it'll cost you," he said matter-of-factly.

"Okay, sure. Here's fifty KPs. Will that work?"

"It most certainly will, my good man. Yes, sir."

"Okay, good. I'm Marcus, and this is Jon." He nodded toward Aztec. "What's your name?"

"My name?" he was temporarily distracted as he looked up at the bright, blue July sky. It was extremely hot—ninety-five degrees and very humid. The only relief came from the occasional ocean breeze. "My name? My name is Rodeo. I don't remember my birth name. I only know that everyone calls me Rodeo."

Marcus got right to the point. "Rodeo, do you hear voices in your head?" Marcus looked him directly in his eyes. Eyes that communicated far more than Rodeo could ever articulate verbally.

"I do, sir. I do. But the good news is they go away when I do Z."

Before they left the town, a town whose slogan was once, "In Sea Isle City the forecast is fun!" Marcus made a mental note to get Rodeo into his clinic once it opened. *So, you have already made your decision?* he asked himself.

All along the South Jersey coast, Dr. Marcus and Aztec spoke with local families and merchants. They spoke with drifters trying to find their place in the Badlands or trying to get out. They spoke with weekend warriors fresh from the Heartland, yahoos in town for sport, oblivious to the pain and suffering happening in their happy little retreat from the real world. They went from town to town, from the barrier islands of Sea Isle and Strathmere and Ocean City, to the barrier islands of Longport, Margate, and Ventnor.

In Margate, they saw Lucy, the six-story elephant that had somehow survived almost four centuries of abuse from coastal weather conditions. Two of those centuries included numerous super storms, and of course, the craurchin invasion. She had one missing tusk, and her steel reinforcing was exposed on both of her hind legs. Nevertheless, Margate, a proud town with proud people, did their best to keep her maintained, for she was a symbol of what Margate once was and could still be.

When they arrived in Atlantic City, Wallace stayed in the vehicle. It could not be left unattended. Aztec and Marcus climbed out and walked the half-block to the boardwalk. When they ascended to the top of the ramp and onto the boardwalk, Marcus could not believe what his eyes were seeing. An intellectual through and through, Marcus rarely spoke what many in the Heartland referred to as the vulgar language of the Badlandians, but upon seeing Atlantic City, he gasped.

"Holy fuck! Holy fucking shit!"

The contrast between what he was now looking at and what he had just seen was startling. Although ugly and somewhat run-down, Atlantic City was bustling. People were walking the streets, drinking beer and cocktails. Some were smoking an odd and strong-smelling cannabis. The noise emanating from the various outdoor clubs was loud and boisterous. Almost immediately, a prostitute propositioned Marcus. Dr. Marcus DiFillipo, a forty-six-year-old nerd with premature graying hair and a salt and pepper unkempt beard, turned six shades of red and a couple shades of purple. Aztec shooed her away and guided Marcus down the boardwalk.

About two-thirds of the boardwalk stores and shops were operational. The rest were shooting galleries where dope of all shapes and forms were being taken, shared, and sold. In one abandoned shop, a couple was having sex on a mattress for all the world to see. In another, a legal house of prostitution, women, men, and transgender people were soliciting passers-by.

"Hey, cutie, twenty KPs for a hand job, thirty for a blowjob, and fifty KPs will get you anything you want, sweetheart!"

They continued on toward the loud noise coming from a large casino on South Kentucky Avenue. A crowd was gathered on the boardwalk, at the entrance, where a large screen was live streaming some kind of event. When they got there, vendors were selling beer and cannabis. There were a few high-top tables, but most of the crowd was standing. As they approached the high-spirited crowd, they could see that the casino was the the Badlandian Hotel and Casino and the event, written in large black letters on the marquee was CRAMATCH 2242 – CAESAR VS THE GHOST. Caesar, a local

349

cycle 6, was the hometown favorite and his odds for winning the match were ten to one.

"Are they cold?" Aztec asked one vendor.

"I got cold ones, but they're more money."

"Give me two of the coldest you have."

"Sure thing, bud—hey are you the Liquoruana King?

"No, but I've been told I look like him. Come on get me those beers. We're hot and thirsty!"

The crowd suddenly started cheering louder and a spontaneous chant broke out.

"Cae-sar! Cae-sar! Cae-sar! Cae-sar! Cae-sar! Cae-sar!"

On the screen, a large cycle 6 was piercing another 6 again and again with its two long horns. The recipient of the horns, the ghost, an albino craurchin, was on the floor, on its back, screeching in agony as its blood stained the ring. They were both at least twelve feet long and were in a huge birdcage hanging from the roof structure of a large arena by eight steel cables.

"Cae-sar! Cae-sar! Cae-sar! Cae-sar! Cae-sar! Cae-sar!"

Caesar, the piercing cycle 6, suddenly fell back, caught with a surprise slash from its downed opponent's right pincer. The Ghost didn't stop. It was as if it had this second wind, snapping both pincers at Caesar like an insane barber who had finally bugged out. He flipped off his back onto four legs.

Caesar, slightly wounded and caught off guard, stood upright, backing out of his opponent's snap zone. Unfortunately for Caesar, he was too slow. The Ghost, not letting up with his snapping, razor-sharp pincers, caught the hometown favorite's hind leg, taking it off above the ankle. Caesar, now off balance, missed with his defensive strike and stumbled and fell onto his side. The crowd gasped as one.

"Get up, motherfucker!" A ratty-looking female in ripped jean shorts and a bikini top shouted. "Get the fuck up!"

The Ghost, still on all fours, continued toward Caesar, pincers snapping wildly, and as Caesar attempted to right himself, jabbed his left pincer into Caesar's brain. Then he slammed his right one into Caesar's other brain. The crowd erupted into a near riot. Screaming and shouting ensued. One man slammed his beer on the ground. It shattered and a piece of glass bounced off the boardwalk and hit another man in the face. A fight started when the bloodied-face man punched the glass-bottle thrower in the nose. In seconds, people were throwing drinks and bottles and punches. Aztec guided Marcus by the arm to a safe distance from the mayhem.

"Now watch how fast this little fire is extinguished," Aztec said calmly. Less than five minutes later, six milibonts arrived and surrounded the crowd.

"Cease and desist! I repeat, cease and desist!"

The majority of the crowd began walking away in different directions until there were only thirteen men fighting in the middle of the boards. They were drunk, pissed off, and bloodied.

"Last warning, gentleman, then I will tell you what will happen next."

"Fuck you!" one shouted just before he lost three teeth.

"Watch this, Marcus." Aztec was grinning ear to ear as the six milibonts, who had them circled, moved in a few more feet.

"Gentleman, you have been warned and have not heeded the mayor's warning. We will now subdue you and deliver you to the city limits per AC Ordinance 2242-A-215. You will not be allowed back for one year. If you violate this penalty, you will be banned from Atlantic City for life. Beyond the city, the craurchins run free, so don't do anything to make us take your weapons. You will need them."

With that, the milibonts moved in and quickly apprehended and cuffed twelve of the thirteen. Number thirteen, who was newly missing three teeth, resisted and was knocked out cold and carried to the hover patrol car where all thirteen of them were given retina scans and then carted off.

"McNimble allows almost anything in Atlantic City, but he is smart enough to understand that it cannot be a place where people fear for their safety. It cannot be the old wild west. At the end of the day, that is what is most important to him, keeping the people coming in so that he can separate them from their money."

They left Atlantic City and continued north, finishing their tour of the Badlands just in time to see the sun set over the tree line at the edge of Sunset Park in Asbury Park. If the contrast between the Badlands proper and Atlantic City was shocking, the contrast between the Badlands and Asbury Park was astonishing. He did not expect it to be so—so beautiful. Beautiful and so old-shore normal. He'd been to Rehoboth Beach, Delaware, many years ago as a kid, and this was very similar to how he remembered it. Quaint old shops in the downtown, beautiful beaches, a vibrant and bustling boardwalk and happy well-groomed people going about their business. On Lake Avenue, the homes were still large and well kept. They were clad with rustic wood shingles and had front yards of the greenest green grass and white-washed wood picket fences.

Aztec and Marcus walked slowly down Kingsley Street, admiring how well kept the shops and restaurants were. One shop-keeper, a chubby man in his early sixties, was sweeping the side-walk in front of his store, getting ready to close up for the day.

"Evening, folks."

They continued down another block, and waiting at a yellow painted building with white shutters, was a man with a set of keys.

"Come on in, gentleman. I think you're gonna love this place!"

A MURDER IN BRUCE SPRINGSTEEN PARK

Three weeks after Aztec and Marcus toured the yellow building, floor plans were drawn up for the clinic. Two months later, the ren-ovations were complete. A week after that, the DiFillipo Clinic was officially opened. Marcus welcomed his first patient on a warm day in early November 2240. He was a local man named David Essington. He was only thirty-four years old, and as Marcus walked him in, he noticed that he had the gait of a seventy-five-year-old. He was unshaven and disheveled and already had deep crow's feet at the corners of his eyes. Everyone in town knew Davy. Davy had been leeched three years ago and was in the late stages of PCLS. He had no family and often roamed the streets, talking to unseen entities.

"I will *not* break the gates! No. No. No," he always said. He was a little scary, but most of the time was harmless and in control. Everyone figured he had some kind of mental illness. Schizophrenia maybe. Asbury Park was not like most small towns where the locals stigmatized the mentally ill, the addicts, the alcoholics, and transients. No, Davy was one of them, and they took care of him. And they would have taken care of him even if he wasn't a local. They were Badlanders and weren't going to let a mentally-ill man suffer or starve to death. After only a few months with Dr. D, people could see the change in him.

"Hey, Dr. Marcus, what's shaking, Daddio?" Davy was currently into 1950s lingo and culture. This was an exercise Marcus had given him to help occupy his mind and battle the voices. Dr. Marcus had already begun working on his craurchin blood theories and was giving Davy mini-transfusions. They seemed to be working. The exercises were merely to keep the brain thinking and divert attention from the voices, and Davy was really into it. He would read mystery books or surf the eNet in the local coffee shop.

"That chrome-plated cat cruisin' down the street yesterday had all the ankle biters upset and the dollies crooning, Daddio."

"Right on, Davy! So how are you feeling today? I see you are still paying homage to the 1950s. Well, that is totally groovy, my main man, totally groovy." With that, Davy laughed a long, hearty, contagious laugh.

"Oh, Dr. D. That's the sixties man, the sixties."

Davy was his first patient, and he continued to see Dr. Marcus for many more years. That same year, Dolly took Earl to see Dr. Marcus.

"Your son most definitely has PCLS, Mrs. Windsong. I have no doubt. When was he leeched?"

"A year ago. Can you help him, doctor?" Dolly pleaded.

"I can, but he has to follow my instructions and take his medication."

It was now 2250, and Dr. Marcus had already treated hundreds of patients, maybe thousands. They came from all over the Badlands, as far away as Cape May and even parts of Delaware. Most were doing better. Davy would have good days and bad, but his good days, which were far more than they used to be, proved to Marcus that his treatment plan was working. Erol was another story. He refused to take his medicine or work with Dr. Marcus. His mother was heartbroken and Erol's condition had advanced to the point where he was becoming dangerous.

The Peace Brigade, which was completely funded by the AP fishery works, beefed up surveillance on Erol after the warning from Dr. Marcus. After three months, the only violent thing they saw him do was bang his head repeatedly on a brick wall once or twice or shout at a passerby. Eventually, they eased up on Erol and got back to their normal routine. Erol freaked out a lot of people and was the subject of many young girls' nightmares but had done nothing illegal. He could be threatening, but he never stalked or physically touched anyone, at least that had been reported.

Jamison Gregory held the title of "Head of Security" for the AP fishery works. He was in charge of land security and oversaw the craurchin exterminations that occurred each and every day on Asbury Park's three land borders. A former highly decorated military man, he was extremely good at his job. A simple job in his mind. "I kill fucking craurchins. I kill them and I get paid to do it. I'm like the shepherd, and the fishery is the sheep. I protect the flock. The craurchins are foxes and wolves." He would often describe it this way when out with his friends. But when he stepped into his security control center, twelve hours a day, six days a week, that was where the joking ended.

He wasn't just efficient at seeing to the eradication of craurchins at his borders, but he often came up with new and inventive ways to increase the kill counts. He knew how vital it was to kill the cycle 1s and 2s in their reproductive stages. An individual getting paid for craurchin exterminations was not eligible for the kill point program. Especially when said men and women, like Jamison, had drones, fumigation chemicals, and a staff of over seventy people at his disposal. A corporation, however, could write off the number of kills for tax credits. To say Jamison saved the AP fishery a bundle was an understatement.

Jamie, as his beautiful wife Jenny called him, was a humble man. He didn't brag about his achievements and he didn't flaunt his wealth with extravagant toys and fancy jewelry. The company compensated him with a lush salary and annual bonuses. The Gregories lived in a large, neat house on the beach with their three children and Jenny's mother, Ada. The house had a lift system, but that was pretty much where the high-tech gadgets ended.

They lived a simple life and Jamie cherished his family time. Like many good fathers, Jamison had a special relationship with his oldest child and only daughter, Jamaica. Jamaica was a striking and intelligent twelve-year-old with dark, beautiful, caramel-tinted skin and long, curly, flowing dark hair. She had long, thin legs that she hadn't quite gotten used to, and was always tripping or falling down. Jamie absolutely adored her. They often walked the beach collecting seashells or hermit crabs for her youngest brother Georgie. In the summer, they walked into town for ice cream or strolled the boardwalk. Jamie spent lots of time with his two boys but always made time for just him and Jamaica.

"Daddy, Daddy, 'bout time you got home!"

"Sorry, Jam Bam, another rough day at the office."

"That's what you said last night!" Nobody could guilt him like Jamaica.

"I'll tell you what, how 'bout we get some frogurt later tonight?"

After dinner, Jamison played some catch on the beach with his three children and two dogs, Nautica and Anchor. They played until the sun set on the town behind them. It had cooled down some, and he sent the boys in with the dogs.

"Tell Mommy that the two Js are taking a walk, okay, guys?"

"K, Dad."

"Are you ready, weirdo?"

"Frogurt! Let's go!"

They picked up their tasty treats at their regular place, then walked up the block and across the street to Bruce Springsteen Park, where they sat on a bench by the manmade pond in the center. They were the only two in the park, as the day turned to dusk, or so they thought.

"Dad?"

"Yes, honey?"

"Dad, I don't like it here. Can we go home?"

"We just sat down. Don't you want to finish your dessert? Baby, are you having your nightmares again?" Jamaica nodded her head. "Still the same dream?" She nodded her head again and that's when he noticed Erol Windsong sitting on the bench across from them. *When did he arrive?* He was staring them down with those distant black eyes. Jamaica was shaking a bit and could not help but think instantly of her dream. It was always the same.

She was with her daddy, holding his hand as they walked the boards. She was a couple years younger than now, nine or ten. It was just starting to get dark. They were heading out to get a chili cheese dog. She let go of her dad's hand as she took a couple of steps toward a giant firefly she had spotted. It was really large, like the size of a baseball. She caught it and watched as the yellow light of the insect turned a very bright azure blue.

She turned to show her daddy, but he was gone. She turned to look down the boardwalk and realized she was standing in the middle of a very dark, heavily wooded park. She could see people in the town surrounding the park. They were going about their business, oblivious to her presence just a few feet away. She called for help, but no one could hear her. It was as if she was in a giant soundproof bubble. She tried to run but her legs were frozen in place. Suddenly, the giant fireflies were everywhere, lighting up the park with a bright, brilliant azure haze. She heard a noise from the pond behind her, splashing, then footsteps. She still couldn't move. The park and the town suddenly went totally black.

"Erol, stop staring. It's very rude," Jamie said calmly. There was no response from Erol. Jamie stood up and began walking toward him, then stopped when he realized Erol's eyes were not staring at them at all. They were affixed on the pond behind them. It all happened so fast. The splashing, the clumping of the 6 limbs up the embankment. The entire time Erol's eyes never blinked, never released their gaze upon the pond and the cycle 6 craurchin climbing up the embankment, heading their way.

"Jamaica, get over here! Quick!" he screamed.

He met her halfway and pulled her toward the park entrance, but the 6 was moving fast. He looked back at Erol and noticed he had a small craurchin in his hands. A cycle two or three. He appeared to be twisting its head as an azure blue, plasmatic light emerged from it. He pointed it toward the 6, which stopped dead in its tracks. But just for a moment. It was enough time. Somehow Jamie knew what he had to do. Without a thought, he pulled out his favorite weapon, the LZ-23.6 from his leg holster and projected the laser onto Erol's head. He pushed the button, and Erol's head exploded. The cycle 6 let out a high-pitched screech that could be heard for blocks. It screeched for what seemed like an eternity, frozen in place, and in apparent pain, as if it had been lasered as well.

Jamie used the opportunity to contact his security team, who dispatched four of his best drones. They would be there in five minutes. *Five long minutes,* he thought. He hushed Jamaica out of the park.

"Wait for me a block away! Up near the gazebo!"

"No, Daddy!"

"Yes. I've got this. I promise. Go!"

The 6 stopped shrieking, its gazed fixed on Jamie, and charged his way. Jamie knew he needed to evade the cycle 6 for about four more minutes. This would seem like an eternity, but would not be the first time he faced a craurchin alone. It would be the first time one on one with a 6, however. Jamie knew the 6 had two brains. And, he knew that he had to take both out. His first shot hit the shoulder, creating much damage, but far from stopping it. His second and third grazed the head, and the fourth connected.

"One brain down. One to go, motherfucker!" Jamie yelled at the enraged, screaming, thirteen-foot-tall monster, "Jo'dete, bitch."

He figured he had about two minutes before the drones arrived. The craurchin dropped from its upright position and chased toward him on all fours, pincers snapping at the air. *This mother is fast!* Jamie ran behind a stand of trees firing while on the run. It followed him. He continued his sprint. He would try to draw it back out to the center of the park, into the clearing, where it would be an easier target for the drones. He could hear them whizzing in the near distance. They were right on time. He cut out of the treeline toward the paved area at the center of the park. The cycle 6 was only ten feet behind him when the drones arrived. They took it out quickly. It lay dead only a few yards from good old Erol, or at least what was left of him.

"Are you okay, boss?" came a voice on his communicator.

"I am. Thanks, Joe! Nice job!" Jamie commended his drone operator.

"How's the other boss, boss?"

Jamie looked at the unharmed statue of Bruce. Two hundred and fifty years ago, they called him "the boss". He stood in the center of a meticulously pruned garden, guitar slung over one shoulder, one armed raised in a fist, red bandana on his head. Inscribed on the marble plinth upon which the boss stood, were the words "Greetings from Asbury Park." Below that was inscribed "Bruce 'The Boss' Springsteen born September 23, 1949, died April 23, 2044."

"Good one, Joe! But he's good, man. No damage. He's good."

He walked out of the park. A crowd was starting to gather around the entrance. They moved out of the way so the sanitation crew could come in and clean up, and Jamie used the opportunity to walk out inconspicuously. Jamie couldn't get the thought out of his head that Erol had set him up. It scorched his mind that he had controlled the craurchin somehow. He wasn't sure how it was done, but he knew this. There would be an investigation of course, and he would have to explain why he killed an innocent man, but he would worry about that later. He wasn't sure what he would say, but right now he needed to find and hold his daughter.

CHAPTER 25

VENTNOR CITY

Father Merrin: I cast you out! Unclean spirit!
Demon: Shove it up your ass, you faggot!
Father Merrin: In the Name of our Lord Jesus Christ! It is he who commands you! It is he who flung you from the gates of Heaven to the depths of Hell!
Demon: Fuck him!
Father Merrin: Be gone...
Demon: Fuck him, Karras! Fuck him!
Father Merrin: ...from this creature of God! Be gone! In the Name of the Father, the Son, and the Holy Spirit!
— THE EXORCIST

SOLDIERS OF THE NEW TERRITORY

"Qi, you need to hit the head. Aim at the area between the top rim of the shell and the bottom of the head when it's standing. Go for the top of the head when it's on all sixes. It will try to cover its head with its pincers when standing. It may burrow its head into the sand when all feet are on the ground. I've seen 'em do that under heavy fire."

Dante turned to the rest of the group as he made the point, his head burrowing into his own outstretched arms. He paused his lesson and looked out at the newest group of trainees.

"Is it true they have two brains? If so, do we have to kill both brains?" asked Qi. He was standing in the hot sand, barefoot, as only a seasoned shore local could do. Qi had bright, rosy cheeks and lots of freckles. Some would say he had a baby face. His long hair was mussed up and he wore camo shorts.

"I was just getting to that. Yes, the cycle 6s and we believe 7s have two brains—and yes, you have to kill both of them. Of course, if you decapitate it you will destroy both brains. Good question, Qi. Oh, and we don't go barefoot into a lair." Dante pointed at his feet, shook his head, and continued.

"They will always protect the brain. It is the most vulnerable area for the craurchin. Right, Khim?"

Khim was staring off into space. Again. For the last two weeks, it was happening more and more frequently. It started out slowly. At first, he was disengaged and unfocused, often asking Dante to repeat things, or forgetting what he was saying midsentence. It then advanced to where it was currently, namely, complete disorientation. He had also become nervous and withdrawn. Something was going on in that head of his. Was he concerned about Hakira's pregnancy? He didn't think so, but tonight Dante would call Hakira. She was scheduled to talk to the group this week and could observe him firsthand. But he wanted to warn her first. Dante suspected Khim's PCLS was creeping into the advanced stages.

"Khim?"

"Yes, Dante, that's correct. That is correct."

It was an absolutely spectacular late summer's day. The skies were clear, the breezes were warm, and the humidity was low. In the distant surf, the sun glittered off of the silky-smooth ocean. Dogs of all breeds played by the water, constantly sniffing the air for trouble while doing so. On the boardwalk, some locals were watching the activity on the beach. Dante and Khim were training the Ventnor group on South Troy Street beach. Gabe and Bryce were on the next beach, teaching drone operation and technology to the third group. You could see the drones buzzing over the Atlantic in the distant sky. Terrell's two brothers were keeping watch, one posted to the north and the other to the south.

This had been the routine for the last year and a half, and their work was starting to pay off. All along South Jersey Shore, as well as many points inland, people now had the skills and resources to not only extricate victims, but to prevent takings from happening in the first place. Lairs were being cleared, and citizens were encouraged to continue with the KP system, but to concentrate on cycle 1s and 2s. Of course, most Badlanders already knew how to kill a craurchin. After all, with the kill point system, and just to survive, killing them was an important part of daily life, part of their culture. But few knew how to defend themselves from a large 5 or 6, especially in a surprise attack—and surprise attacks and takings were becoming more and more common. Few had the skills Dante had, and cycle 7s were a completely different story. Even Dante had never faced a 7. Only a handful had even been seen by human eyes.

Team Dante (as they were now officially called) taught them how the craurchin lived, how it hunted, how it attacked and fought, as well as its genetics. The training started at 7:00 a.m. and ended at 5:00 p.m., six days a week for four weeks. During the final week, they brought in Hakira and Terrell. Hakira discussed early medical treatment for victims. The first critical actions to be taken—how to keep the victim warm and calm and how to do a transfusion with synthetic blood was covered. Terrell discussed how the craurchin thought, how it communicated with its cluster, and of course its number one goal in life—to become a cycle 8. On the very last day, Team Dante took the group out to clear a lair.

"Mr. Long, which is more effective, bullets or lasers?"

Sixteen-year-old Qi was really into the training. His mother, who had always told him that his name meant "life force" said that he was her life force and that he was born to protect people from harm. *Perhaps she is right,* he thought. The training these last few weeks had gone really well. In fact, he felt that Mr. Long was impressed with how quickly he was learning. He was actually enjoying himself and had a new mission in life, namely to be a part of Team Dante one day.

"Great question, Qi! We usually discuss this on orientation day, but we must have missed it this time. Both have their advantages and disadvantages. Lasers are much more accurate but will not cause as much internal damage as a bullet. Whereas a bullet will—" Dante noticed the group directing its focus to Khim, who was turned away from the group. He was facing the sea, talking to himself in unrecognizable words. Dante excused himself from the group and walked up to him for a clearer listen.

"Akabi da batba, datafa je dadoo."

"Khim? Khim! Hey Khim, buddy, what's going on?"

No response. Dante walked around to face him and saw that his eyes were rolled into the back of his head. All he could see were the whites, and it was double eerie because they were magnified from his thick glasses. Then, he noticed the blood stain on his gray t-shirt.

"Khim? Hey, I'm gonna lift your shirt." No response. He lifted his shirt and gasped when he saw it. The scar, from the craurchin's leeching of almost a decade ago, was swollen, inflamed, and bleed- ing. *Holy fuck. Is it pulsing?*

He spoke into his communicator. "Gabe, somethings up with Khim! I'm gonna send our group over with you guys."

"Sure, Dante, what's going on? Is he okay?"

"Those issues we were discussing the other night. They're getting worse, Gabe."

"All right, take care of him. We'll talk to you tonight at dinner."

THE GOOD DOCTOR

Dr. Marcus DiFillipo was tugging on his gray goatee as he hovered along on the upper tier of Route 76. He was very familiar with the three-hour drive from Pittsburgh to the New Jersey Shore. Even so, driving these days made him a little nervous, and of course when he was nervous, he tugged his goatee. Despite the numerous trips to his clinic in Asbury Park and more recently to the new one in Somers Point, he would never get used to how much the world changed once he had crossed over any of the bridges into New Jersey. In this case, it was the Walt Whitman Bridge. Like the flip of a switch, it went from normal to otherworldly.

The traffic along most of I-76 had been heavy but moving. It was laden with folks heading to their jobs, visiting friends, or going on vacations. It was as if most of the northeast coastline was not overrun by alien creatures, and there was not a devastating war going on. It only proved that if it was not happening in your back-yard, it was not happening. Going through Philadelphia had been slow and arduous but at least it moved—a little bit. The high-rises in the distance loomed ominously above the skyway that wrapped around Center City at the thirtieth story level.

The skyway, built over sixty years ago, was supposed to alleviate traffic on the highways around the city, and it did for a while, but certainly not today. He could see the massive traffic in the distance, as he switched to the middle tier of the Schuylkill Expressway and headed into south Philly. He then took the Walt Whitman Bridge exit and was cruising 120 miles an hour into New Jersey. As he sped deeper into New Jersey, that switch flipped.

Otherworldly, he thought *That's exactly what this is.*

In the oncoming lanes, there was moderate traffic heading into Philly, but heading into New Jersey, the lanes were virtually vehicle free. He cruised down the North-South Freeway, south toward the shore. When he exited onto the Atlantic City Expressway, the lanes were reduced to only one each way. The other six lanes were damaged, overrun with sinkholes, weeds, and even trees. The upper tiers had collapsed years ago, leaving large boulders and slabs of concrete with steel reinforcing bars sticking out, like the legs of large metallic spiders. Maintaining eight lanes was far too expensive for the gateway to the Badlands, with a war going on and all. The government kept only the two lanes open. One in and one out was the only way. These were for emergencies and the convenience of Badland residents.

People in the Badlands don't travel much, Marcus thought. *Mostly just to the drop zones.* Marcus sped south on the expressway toward Somers Point and his recently opened clinic. Many of the homes and commercial buildings along the highway were vacant, run-down, or burned out. Abandoned, rusted-out diesel engine cars could be seen on the once pristine suburban streets. The look and feel, when contrasted with a highly populated city like Philadelphia, was postapocalyptic. *And actually,* Marcus thought, *it is the apocalypse for most down here.*

About half the way to his exit, making good time, he caught a flash in his rearview camera. He looked down and saw it was a patrol vehicle, a New Jersey state trooper.

"Slow down and pull over nice and slow," came from his hover's sound system.

Marcus pulled over and waited for instructions. About five tense minutes passed and he was starting to get concerned, then he heard the robotic voice again.

"I scanned your vehicle, and I know you have a laser." Marcus did not like weapons, but he knew he needed one in the Badlands. Everyone down here carried.

"Open your door and lay it on the ground—slowly." In addition to the patrol car, Marcus noticed a drone was hovering above. He did as he was instructed. "Okay, I'm coming over to your vehicle. Be still, no sudden movements."

Marcus watched the large, broad-shouldered officer marching his way. He opened the driver side port and raised both arms out of the vehicle's skylight.

"Dr. Marcus DiFillipo? Permission to scan your retina?"

Marcus nodded as the officer moved his metallic scanner toward his left eye. He then studied his scanner for a few minutes. He seemed to be satisfied with what he was seeing.

"Thank you. Where are you heading?"

"To my clinic in Somers Point. May I ask why you stopped me," Marcus glanced at his badge, "Officer Devlon?"

"Well, these roads get very little use, except by Skulls and other unsavory types."

"Skulls?"

"Yes, this is one of the routes they use to bring in drugs. Thank you for your cooperation, have a good day. Oh—and be careful." With that, he walked back to his vehicle and hovered off in the opposite direction. Dr. Marcus was not surprised that he was an ArtEng, the artificially engineered prototypes many law enforcement agencies were using these days.

BECOMING DR. MARCUS

When overpopulation of craurchins along the New Jersey coast was officially identified in the early 2220s as a national crisis, Marcus was a minimally nerdy, innocent twenty-two-year-old woman named Marne, with a 4.0 GPA who was finishing up her bachelor of science in biology. She would move on in the fall to study psychology and organic chemistry and then advance to graduate school for the psychiatric medical doctoral program.

Right from the start, Marne took an interest in the craurchin dilemma. She was an avid reader and followed all of the scientific articles, white papers, and blogs written by Dr. Felix Sanchez. Actually, she was borderline obsessed with the problem and felt, even at the naïve age of twenty-four, that the government was not doing enough. They were not allocating enough money for the study of the craurchins and their impact on the environment and people.

"For Christ's sake, this is a full-blown alien invasion! They may appear to be non-thinking animals, but they are more than just another invasive creature screwing up the ecosystem. They are freakin' aliens!" she would tell anyone who would listen. Marne went on to graduate, receive her doctorate, complete her residency and two years later, in 2230, obtain her medical license. It had been the same year the war broke out and the same year the government pulled out of what would eventually become the Badlands.

In 2232, thirty-six-year-old Dr. DiFillipo received her first grant to study craurchin behavior. She put together a staff of four researchers and was granted a permit to house three cycle 3s and two cycle 4s in a giant, heavy-gauge wire mesh pen at her research facility in Youngstown, Ohio. Nine years later, Dr. Marne DiFillipo, now Dr. Marcus DiFillipo, had moved his research facility to Pittsburgh, Pennsylvania, and was receiving his third government research grant. In March of 2245, Marcus received a call from a hysterical intern.

"Dr. Marcus, a cycle 5 has gotten into the craurchin's pen! I can see Boris, Thor, and Scamp, but Hercules is missing! I think it ate him, but I don't see any remains! What do I do? *Oh fuck.* What do I do?"

Holding back a chuckle, Dr. Marcus tried to settle the young student and calmly told her with his soothing, steady voice, "Listen, under no circumstance do you enter the pen. Gather the other researchers and start reviewing the video. I'll be there soon. This may be the first cycling of a 4 to 5 caught on film."

Marcus now had a cycle 5 to study. This opened the doors to Marcus for all kinds of great research opportunities. Like a teenager on his first hover drive, he headed to the lab with his heart beating rapidly and a wide grin on his face.

The following year, Nathan Martelle was leeched while taking some fluid samples from Hercules, the one-year cycle 5. Nathan was one of Marcus's top researchers and unbeknownst to anyone, would open the doors to an entire new field of study for Dr. Marcus. On this fateful night, Hercules shot his dangerous toxin at the young researcher, who ducked out of the way. This wasn't unusual for Hercules, and those working with him often wore protective garb and safety glasses. Unfortunately, Nathan was wearing none of these, and when dodging the venom, he was blindsided by the tube, which came out of Hercules mouth and attached itself firmly to Nathan's lower stomach. While trying to remove the leeching tube, the cycle 5 paralyzed him with its venom. Nathan screamed in fear and writhed in pain until he passed out.

When he awoke, he shouted for help for about thirty minutes before his cries were heard by another researcher coming out for some fresh air. The researcher solicited the help of five others, and they anesthetized the creature. He was rescued, but the craurchin had taken two quarts of blood. The very next day, Marcus hired a cra-handler to keep the researchers safe, but poor Nathan was never the same. When he returned back to work several weeks later, he seemed okay. After a few months, however, something changed. He was often jittery. He sometimes found it hard to concentrate. He often talked about the strange thoughts that went through his head while being leeched by the large predator.

Dr. Marcus studied the communication patterns of his cluster and always felt that the craurchins he had in captivity communicated with each other. Many years later, he would write a controversial article for *Science Century 23* entitled, "Craurchin's and Telepathy – The Ultimate Form of Interspecies Communication." Several months after his leeching, Marcus began interviewing Nathan extensively and studied his brain patterns. Nathan, a talented researcher dedicated to science, threw all he had into the effort, working side by side with Marcus, looking for answers. It was becoming clear to Dr. Marcus that Hercules was communicating telepathically with Nathan. But how?

"I truly believe many of the thoughts running through your head are Hercules's, not just yours," Marcus told him early on.

"That could be. The dreams are often about a sort of metamorphous that the craurchin is going through, a changing if you will, and always very gray. This change is not a cycling, but something else altogether. Now why would I dream about that, and why so fuzzy? Perhaps Hercules is trying to hide them. The words are often unclear, but words just the same."

"Metamorphous?" Marcus's interest was indeed peaked.

"Yes, I feel like it is related to something dramatic that happens in a later cycle. An obvious physical change of some sort, more than just a size change. More of a complete anatomical change, but thinking back, and realizing they were not my thoughts and dreams, I now suspect they were Herc's and that he did not want me to see them."

As the years rolled by, Nathan's condition grew worse. Like a soldier with battle fatigue, he could not shake the stress caused by the trauma of his ordeal. Even worse were the voices, which were unwelcome thoughts, in his head. They lived there now and would not leave. Dr. Marcus DiFillipo, now author of his first best-selling book, felt responsible, and so it was now his mission in life to exorcise the demons from Nathan's head. The grants had ended and the funding was now coming solely from his books, articles, and speaking engagements. The DiFillipo Foundation was concentrating primarily on the study of the trauma and the psychological effects caused by leeching.

In 2241, Dr. Marcus put a name to the condition—PCLS, post-craurchin leeching syndrome. In 2256, after many years of hard work and research, with much of that help coming from a deeply damaged Nathan, Marcus felt he was closer than ever to a possible cure. Because Hercules was still in captivity, he could study both of them. He performed tests on Hercules and observed their effects on Nathan. And vice versa. Was there a link? Then one early evening, during a snowstorm in 2263, Marcus decided to remain at the lab instead of making the dangerous trek home. He had sent his staff home hours earlier.

"Jhon, before you leave, can you help me with these bodies?" They had just received a shipment of cycle 4 and 5 cadavers.

"We'll put three in the cold box and one of the 5s on the anatomy dissection table." Together they used a hover-cart to move the cadavers.

"Thanks, Jhon, now you get home safely." Marcus walked him to the lobby.

"Good night, Dr. Marcus."

As Marcus closed and locked the glass doors behind Jhon, he looked out the window at the snowflakes just starting to come down. For some reason, Marcus started thinking about how all of the creatures living out there, humans as well, would deal with the cold, heavy snow that would blanket Pittsburgh in the next couple of hours. Each would cope in their own way and most would survive. But not all. That got him thinking about how the craurchins survived not just severe weather but dangerous situations as well. He had observed it many times with his captive specimens, now two clusters of five each. The cluster would gather, huddle close, and form a defensive wall with the cluster's leader up front. He performed one study, with cra-handlers close by, where he advanced toward a cycle 3 in a threatening manner. Within minutes, the rest of the cluster and its king arrived. But there was something else— the entire cluster was blindfolded. On one occasion, Marcus had witnessed one of his cycle 5s allowing a 3 to leech her. And that's when the thought struck him.

The more a cluster king or queen leeches with its cluster, the stronger the bond between cluster members and their king or queen.

Marcus practically ran to the lab, where his cycle 5 cadaver was awaiting. He gowned up in his coveralls, donned his booties, gloves, mask and hairnet, then entered the lab. He took out his laser scalpel and cut the cadaver from the neck and collar, down the breastplate and belly, and all the way to the groin, watching the wallvid and careful not to hit any organs. The cadaver was already deshelled to make the dissections easier. He then split the soft rubbery skin and tissue apart, exposing the craurchin's inner organs.

Marcus located the leeching tube, and as he lifted it, realized it was not attached to either of the two stomachs. It appeared to be connected to the spinal column running up to the brain. He grabbed his laser from the table and cut the head in half being careful not to damage the brain. He split the skull apart and, sure enough, the leeching tube was connected to the brain. *How did scientists miss this?*

"Because it is infused with the spine," he answered aloud.

HIS MIND IS NOT HIS OWN

Aztec's number one objective was to keep Hakira calm. In her current state, having her soulmate break down was the last thing she needed. He knew that Marcus was Khim's only chance of getting his head in order.

"Hakira, you must be calm. For you and the baby. You know better than anyone that panicking will get us nowhere. I have contacted Dr. Marcus. Just get Khim to Somers Point! I'll meet you there."

"What did he say? Tell us what he said!" Bryce was struggling, along with Dante and Gabe, to hold Khim down.

Two hours prior, Khim had a total, violent meltdown. Being the last day of training, they had had the group of trainees on Shelter Island in Lakes Bay, where they were clearing a lair. They had taken out most of the cluster and were about to finish off the cycle 5 queen when Khim started freaking out. Observing him closely, one could see that he was having some sort of breakdown. First, he would yell, "Spare the 5. Spare the 5!" then he would start shooting at it with a shaky, almost spastic arm.

"No, no, no, no!" he had shouted. And then the shooting had occurred. His arm was shakier than ever, hitting trees, rocks, and water, and then he took out one of the dogs. Dante was charging him from the side as he took a shot at a young trainee, hitting him in the leg just as Dante tackled him to the ground. The rest of the team had taken out the 5, and here they were trying to calm Khim down, still on the island where other craurchins were no doubt living.

"We have to get him to Somers Point! I have no sedatives, so we have to either tie him up or hold him down during the trip!" Hakira was trying to remain calm, as she held both her hands on her substantial belly.

"Okay, on three, we lift him up and get 'em to the hover boat. One, two—"

When they arrived in Somers Point, Dr. Marcus was waiting for them. It had been a very difficult ride for the three men restraining Khim, and when they got to the clinic, he was still fighting them.

"I never knew Khim was so fucking strong!" Dante remarked.

"It's part and parcel of the PCLS. Hold him steady, I have a heavy sedative for him." With that, Marcus injected him in the arm. Within a minute, the struggling had subsided, and within five minutes, he was completely sedated.

"What's the next step, Dr. DiFillipo?" Hakira asked anxiously.

"So—" Marcus let out a long sigh. "Khim is in the late stages now. This may sound crazy, but soon the craurchin, wherever it may be, will take full control of his mind. Almost like a demonic possession. It may be for a few hours or a few days. It all depends on the individual."

"How so?" Bryce wanted to know.

"All of us humans have a variety of attributes both good and bad. Timidity, perseverance, stubbornness, empathy, belligerence, laziness, and so on and so forth." Marcus wagged his right pointer finger, emphasizing each attribute as he continued.

"Individuals with strong fortitude, strength in mind if you will, tend to fare better. My studies have proven that individuals with lower IQs, ADHD, or lack of concentration, depression, and high stress don't do well at all. Their minds are left wide open." Marcus took a deep breath then continued. "From everything I've heard from Jon," the doctor glanced over at Aztec, "Khim is both highly intelligent, and has always been very grounded. If this is true, he will be able to resist it longer than most—it's probably the reason he's lasted this long, but just for a while."

"And in the meantime, what do we do?" Hakira was rubbing her belly nervously.

"We basically have two choices. We could kill the craurchin that leeched Khim. With thousands, maybe even millions of them out there, I don't think that is feasible. Or, we replace his blood. It's called a total exchange blood transfusion, and it's just what it sounds like. I take out all of his blood and replace it with donor blood."

Dr. Marcus had a theory that the protein in the plasma in human blood, linked the craurchin to the human's thoughts when that blood flowed to its brain. The more blood a craurchin took from its victim, the worse the PCLS. Dr. Marcus discovered this years ago by experimenting with blood transfusions. He allowed a cycle 5 to leech a macaque monkey. The monkey later developed PCLS symptoms that came on much quicker and were much more severe than a human. Several weeks later, Marcus then gave the monkey a full blood transfusion, and within hours, the monkey started exhibiting signs of improvement. By week's end, it was back to normal. Marcus had the 5 who leeched Nathan killed that very same day.

"Do we have enough donor blood for the procedure?" Hakira asked. "Can we start soon?"

"Yes, and yes."

CHAPTER 26

MY BADLANDIAN HOME

Supposing that I should have the courage
To let a red sword of virtue
Plunge into my heart,
Letting to the weeds of the ground
My sinful blood,
What can you offer me?
A gardened castle?
A flowery kingdom?
What? A hope?
Then hence with your red sword of virtue.
—STEPHEN CRANE

MY BADLANDIAN HOME

Terrell, listen to me. You have this gift. You have this gift and you can't ignore it. How you will use it, I don't know, but I know you will do good things with it, Terrell. Embrace it.

On this balmy night, Terrell thought about the words that his mother had uttered to him as she had been leaving for the far-away Heartland hospital. It was early April of 2274 and soon the hot weather would be here. Terrell sat on his back porch, taking in the complete and total darkness. The only light was from the glaring, full moon and some candles burning in the kitchen. The wind ruffled his recently grown-out beard and afro. It felt good. He was now close to six foot three. He was taller than both his brothers and his father. His mother would have been very proud of her boy and his evolution into manhood. When he had heard those words that she spoke to him so many years ago, he hadn't realized it would be the last time he would see her again. The last time he would hear her sweet, soothing voice. At the time, he hadn't fully grasped what she was trying to tell him. Now he did. At the time, he had known he had a gift. Now, five years later, he knew exactly what she was trying to tell him. He knew as surely as the sun rose in the east and set in the west.

Total darkness settled over everything. Over a year ago, the government started shutting the street lights off at 9:00 p.m. to save energy. There was talk at the committee meetings of purchasing a solar generator, but that still had not happened. The government had also issued a curfew and put limitations on water and electricity usage. The town desperately needed to do something. And soon. Last year, he and his father and brothers demolished the house behind the Williams' homestead as part of a program to make Cape May safer.

An empty structure could be a haven for trouble, M.J. had told them. *A cover for unwanted intruders both human and alien.* The more open land, the less chance for craurchins to lurk in the shadows.

So, they knocked it down. Now, sitting here watching the brilliant moon and stars shining over the black Atlantic Ocean, he had an awesome view of the beach and vast ocean beyond. On this night, Terrell could hear the quiet, meditative crashing of the breakers in the distance, and Einstein sniffing around at the edge of the yard. He and his brothers had just spent the last three hours watching bootleg videos from the twentieth century. The tenth and final century of the second millennium. Robin Williams, Richard Prior, and his favorite, George Carlin. Later on, they were going to listen to some Led Zeppelin and Dr. Dre on their dad's antique CD player.

My God what a time in history, Terrell thought. *Stand-up comedy. Amazing music. Why on earth would the Heartland out-law this art?* Prior to the videos, Zak and James had smoked some old-school weed purchased from the Skulls.

The Skulls were considered by many to be wicked, but they were only filling a void. Alcohol and marijuana were banned in the Heartland proper, and after two centuries of being legal, Terrell could not understand why. He didn't smoke or drink but understood why others felt the need—release, joy, escape. He saw nothing wrong with those options.

The door creaked open and his brother Zak stepped out onto the porch with his dog Petro. He lit a safecig, which he inhaled deeply, and then sat down next to his youngest brother. Petro ran off toward Einstein at the far end of the yard.

"Is all well in your Badlandian home?"

"All is well in my Badlandian home," Terrell answered with a smile. It was their secret greeting, the title of a poem their mother had written.

"What's on your mind, my not-so-little bro?"

"Just thinking about things." Zak thought Terrell seemed a little melancholy.

"That was a damn shame about that incident at Casa Azteca. I'm not sure why I've been thinking about that lately," Zak commented.

"I don't know. It was over a year ago. Maybe because it was so horrible." Terrell had a seashell that he was using to scoop up sand and pour onto his bare feet. The cool sand felt good between his toes. "I think about it a lot. I think of all the deaths at the hands of craurchins and evil men. At least they weren't leeched." He continued with the sand and shell, never looking up at his brother.

"Does the delegation still think it was McNimble?" Zak asked.

"Oh, we know it was McNimble. He may not have physically released the craurchins, but he was behind it!" Terrell finally looked up. Zak got his attention.

"My friend Laz has a vidwall and he said he heard a report on Liberty News, claiming the Skulls were behind it."

"How the hell did Lazzie get a vidwall? What a freakin' dweeb!" Terrell said laughing.

"He saved KPs for almost two years, that's how. So, what do you think? Were the Skulls involved?" Zak pursued.

"All of the men involved, two in the boat and one in the truck, were trappers that worked with the Skulls. They weren't official members, but they contracted with the Skulls. Did you know the Skulls supply craurchins for matches up and down the east coast? But McNimble knows these men as well, because he sponsors all of the matches in AC, hence the connection," Terrell explained.

"So, he figured the men would be videoed, identified, and linked to the Skulls."

"Yes, and Liberty backed it up."

"But?"

"But Aztec and the Skulls are cool. They both know the truth."

"That McNimble planned and financed the attack?" Zak asked.

"Yes."

"And what are they planning to do about that?"

"I'm not privy to that. None of us are."

Zak decided to steer to the topic that he thought was causing his little brother so much anxiety. It was a sensitive subject but needed to be addressed.

"Terrell, are you still hearing the voices?"

"I'm trying."

"You're trying? What do you mean *you're trying*?"

"Oh, I *need* to hear the voices. I *strive* to hear the voices."

"You want to have PCLS?"

"Oh no, they don't control my mind. I control theirs."

"How so?"

There was a long silence. Zak decided Terrell would answer when he was ready. He figured Terrell was obviously thinking things through, deciding if he should share what was in his incredible, beautiful head. Terrell sat still, staring at the black ocean. Then he looked at Zak with an intensity and desperation Zak had never seen before in his youngest brother.

"The craurchin that leeched me was killed, but when she was terminated, her cluster, those that survived the rescue at the lair, still had access to my thoughts, because they shared my blood. But they are weak. They cannot control me. I control them, especially the lower cycle ones. Sometimes, I feed them false thoughts, false information."

"You control *them*?"

"Yes. I can usually get into their heads. They try and block me, but when I get through, I know their thoughts. I'm not even sure if *thoughts* is the correct word. I know what they know. Bak0o had a large cluster that included more than just the craurchins that were at her lair. She has many relatives all around the cape." Terrell sneezed a couple of times, he had had a cold for a few days now, then continued. "They are trying to hide something from me and I'm going to find out what it is. Something to do with the eighth cycle."

It had become more and more clear to Terrell that the aliens had a cohesive plan. A big part of it was to colonize the Jersey shore, but the other part, the part that happened at cycle 8, he had not yet figured out.

"We've talked about this before. Something momentous happens at cycle 8, correct?" It wasn't lost on Zak that Terrell had just called out his leecher-craurchin by name. *They had fucking names?*

"Yes."

"But nobody knows what."

"The craurchins do and the dogs do." They both looked at Einstein and Petro sniffing away in the backyard. Terrell wanted to explain.

"Did you know I can read dogs as well? Well, not their thoughts, more like their emotions. It is communicated in colors. Reds, blues, yellows, greens and blacks. For example, shades of yellows and blues form patterns in my head that I know represent happiness. Sharp, bold reds when craurchins are nearby or pose a threat. I'm still learning."

"Incredible!" Zak believed him beyond a doubt. "What about black?"

"I saw black from Einstein, just before Bak0o almost killed him."

There was another long moment of silence. *What surprise will he have for me next?* Zak thought. After a while, Terrell looked up at Zak. The intense look on his face both surprised and frightened Zak. He wasn't ready for his little brother to become a full-fledged adult.

"Zachery. I've had long talks with Dr. Marcus and his theories, and my intuition, my gift as mom called it, align. Craurchins are born with this intuition. Their one goal in life is to survive until cycle 8. Dogs just sense it. I do know this, and I know it from the chatter I hear in the cluster's heads. At cycle 8, there is an amazing metamorphosis both anatomically and intellectually."

"What else have you and Dr. Marcus talked about?" Zak wasn't sure he wanted to know.

"Lots of stuff. Leeching. PCLS. Craurchin anatomy. Did you know that Adam and Eve, if still alive, will reach cycle 8 in the next ten to twelve years? And the first generation of their descendants will be close behind them. That thought terrifies me."

"Because whatever happens at 8 will make them more dangerous?"

"Extremely dangerous. I believe it will be the start of the craurchin takeover!" There was another long period of silence. Again, Zak knew his younger brother was thinking things through. Finally, he spoke.

"Zak, there is something I must do and I need you to help me. I need you to trust me."

A BOLD DECISION

"If CraTek is killing the 5s, 6s, and 7s, isn't that a good thing? We don't want them to make it to 8, no?"

"Correct, Dr. Marcus, but you have to look at the big picture. Let's just say CraTek was allowed to continue and eventually wiped out all of the 5s, 6s, and 7s. That would be a good thing, and it would forestall craurchins, at least most of them, from hitting cycle 8 for at least another eighty years," Terrell pointed out.

"The problem is," Aztec cut in, "that the smaller craurchins are being allowed to thrive. In fact, CraTek is actually working on accelerating their reproduction. Eventually—"

Dr. Marcus cut Aztec short. "Eventually, the Badlands will be completely dominated by craurchins. It will literally be one big, giant craurchin ranch. I get it, Aztec. But I agree with Terrell, the first problem is curtailing the metamorphosis to cycle 8."

"Ideally, we want to do both," Terrell added. "Let CraTek continue to harvest the 5s, 6s, and 7s, and somehow we'll kill the 1s, 2s, 3s, and 4s ourselves. I'm not sure how we do that. We know CraTek won't stand for it. We also have to figure out how and where they are accelerating reproduction. Are they cloning them? If so, that is something that has to be shut down!"

"My contacts know what's going on with the harvesting, and they've located the de-shelling facility, but still nothing on the acceleration program. CraTek tags certain 1s, 2s, 3s, and 4s for the program, but that's all we know. So far," Aztec continued. "If we find the lab where CraTek is doing this, what do we do? Bomb it?" he said sarcastically. He answered himself. "Maybe. We could release the information to the media, but it would only gain sympathy from the east and west coasts who can do nothing. We all know where the Heartland stands."

In the Heartland, the media, which was sanctioned by the government, was extremely anti-Badlands. Years of propaganda and negative press had led most of the people of the Heartland to believe that the problems of the Badlands, which by this point were stretching further and further up and down the east coast, were of the Badlanders' doing and thus the Badland's problem.

The common, brain-washed, God-fearing Heartlander considered most Badlanders to be filthy, godless, drug addicts and alcoholics. There has always been a group to focus hate on in

America, and in the twenty-third century, it was Badlanders. They were the most recent targets in a long history of racism, bias, and fear mongering. From enslaved Africans in the eighteenth and nine-teenth century, to the Jews, Irish, Italians, Afro-Americans, homo-sexuals, and transgender people in the twentieth century. From the jailing of Japanese Americans in 1942 to the jailing of immigrant children and cops killing Black people in the late 1900s and early 2000s, to the extermination of specific dog breeds in the 2100s. There was always someone or something to be the focus of our fear and hate.

But for some reason, craurchins, invaders from another world, were not a focus of that fear and hate. Why? Because they were believed to be America's next great commodity?

"I need to go now, but we'll meet again next week?" Aztec finished his drink. "You guys feel free to stay and continue. I have to pick up Phoebe. Terrell, will you be staying the night or shall I get you a ride home? Hell, you can borrow one of my hovers if you want."

"Thanks, Mr. Penndleton, but I'm gonna stay. Dweezle and I are gonna hang out later. You would let me borrow one of your personal aircraft vehicles?"

"Well, Terrell, I didn't teach you how to operate a PAC-V for nothing."

"I'll be here another hour or so. Let's reconvene in a week, Aztec," Marcus added.

"Terrell and I have some additional matters to discuss."

Aztec embraced his friends, then headed to the rooftop, to his vehicle. When he left, Terrell and Marcus continued the conversation.

"Dr. Marcus, I thought about what we discussed last week and I want to do this."

"Terrell, like we discussed, I think this could work. Hell, I'm sure it *will* work. But I don't feel comfortable doing this without your father's consent. It's unethical and your father will never forgive me."

"He would never consent. *Never*. But he doesn't understand the situation we are all in—and by all, I mean the entire country. Hell, the entire world!"

"I know, son, I know." Marcus stroked his white goatee with his thumb and forefinger as he stared out into space.

"Doc, you have no choice. *We* have no choice. Let's discuss the details. We do my leeching in your Pittsburgh facility and we do it with a cycle 5. Dante, Zak, James, Kim, Bryce, and Gabe have already agreed to help. Because my brothers are involved, you can say you assumed Dad knew as well."

"I don't know, Ter. I feel I'm deceiving your father, and I don't like it."

"You would absolutely be deceiving him. And, so would my brothers and I, but when GAOB0o starts her metamorphosis and we have done nothing to stop it, you will have to ask yourself if the deception of one man was worth it. And the answer is a very simple—yes—especially once you see what that metamorphosis looks like. My mother told me I had a gift and that I needed to use it for the good of all of us. She is the one that we must be true to."

CHAPTER 27
WHAT GOES AROUND

There's just a little fashioned karma coming down
Just a little old-fashioned justice going round
A little bit of sowing and a little bit of reaping
A little bit of laughing and a little bit of weeping
Just a little old-fashioned karma coming down
Coming down coming down just a little old-fashioned karma coming down
It really ain't hard to understand
If you're gonna dance you gotta pay the band
It's just a little old-fashioned karma coming down
— "LITTLE OLD-FASHIONED KARMA," WILLIE NELSON

THE CALVARIA

"Hey, boss, I just got a call from a friend. You're not gonna believe this!" Skeet was the bartender at the Skull's Clubhouse and the Calvaria, as well as Sarge's personal assistant. "Vidwall on, Liberty Network," Skeet shouted at the far wall centered on the bar.

"What gives, Skeeter?" Sarge was president of the Wildwoods branch of the Skulls. He was not happy, not happy at all.

About thirty men were seated at the bar, Sarge included. The rest of the club was on assignment, namely delivering craurchins to south Florida to be used in craurchin-gator death matches. This latest entertainment craze was incredibly popular in the sunshine state, a land that was just starting to see cycle 2s and 3s.

The group at the bar was listening to music, smoking real cigarettes, and talking loudly. There was another group playing old-school billiards and darts in the back. A few couples were dancing to an old R&B song from 1970. The Calvaria was very smoky and smelled like pickled eggs and stale beer.

"Everybody shut the fuck up. It's coming up now!" Skeet announced. "Music off."

"*And tonight, we are reporting on that tragic story in the Ocean City Badlands. As we reported early yesterday evening, a cycle 6 craurchin attacked and killed two people on the estate of Liquorjuana founder Jonathon "Aztec" Pendleton. Even though there was formidable security at Casa Azteca, two craurchins, a cycle 5 and 6, breeched the estate. The 5 was killed before it could do any harm, but the 6 killed a security guard and a young woman working on the estate. Well, we have now learned that the craurchins were deliberately released onto the property. Drone video revealed the release of the cycle 5 from a suspect in a truck at the main gate, and the release of the 6 by two men on a boat offshore. All three men were identified as handlers and members of the notorious Skulls skimmer gang out of the Wildwood Badlands. Police say the motive was a dispute over liquor distribution in the Badlands. Officer Devlon of the New Jersey State Troopers stated that—"*

"Are you fucking kidding me?" Sarge shouted at the screen. He slammed both fists on the bar top. "What the fuck!"

"Sarge, I thought we resolved that issue. What the fuck are they—"

"We did! Skeet get me Aztec on the line. I need that video."

"Will do, boss, private or speaker?"

"I'll take it in my office."

Sarge grabbed his moonshine and stormed off into his office. He actually preferred Aztec's cognac, but if he was going to be pushing his club's booze in the Badlands and elsewhere, he wanted to actually develop a taste for it. Perhaps even improve it. He was sitting at his desk tapping his fingers on its surface impatiently. *"What the hell is going on here?"* he thought. His club was as badass, actually more badass, than any, save perhaps the Helter Skelter out of Philly, but they did not play that way. If you had a problem with the Skulls, you tried to settle it nonviolently. If you couldn't resolve it or you crossed them, then God fucking help you. He thought he had settled with Aztec. As he was pondering his conversation with Aztec, Skeet's face popped on the vidwall.

"Hey, boss, Aztec is on."

Seconds later, Aztec's earnest face appeared on the wall. Sarge could see that he was in his office at Casa Azteca. Good, he was taking the call seriously.

"Hey, Sarge, it's all lies. It's a setup."

"Go on. I'm listening."

"We're pretty sure it's McNumb Nuts and we are looking into a connection to the craurchin handlers. He's got the motive, and he's egotistical enough to think he can get away with it. Also, we know he's got very strong ties to the Liberty Network. For God's sake he's been doing political favors for them for years. If he asked them to report that Earth was flat, they'd do it."

"Aztec, let me see the drone video."

"That's why I'm calling."

"You called me? Didn't Skeet call you?"

"No. But I'm sure he was about to. Here's the video."

Together they watched the video taken at the gate to Casa Azteca. They watched a very muscular man with a long red beard unloading a cycle 5 from its cage. The man's entire body, including his bald head, were covered in tattoos.

"That's Scurge. He supplies me craurchins, but he is not a Skull. McNimble would know of him for sure."

DON AND DUSTY

"Dusty? Dusty, where are you?" Don had been in the wine cellar for what, an hour? A day? It was nighttime, Wildwood had no streetlights that worked, and he was in a cellar three feet below grade. It was truly the darkest darkness. He heard whimpering in the corner. *Where was that fucking lighter?* He thought he might have dropped it in his panicky retreat from the boardwalk.

"Dusty!"

He crawled on his hands and knees, on the cold concrete floor, totally blind, feeling his way in the direction of the whimpers. God, his stomach hurt. Still. Don had candles (compliments of his favorite souvenir shop) spread all around the perimeter of the small cellar. He would light them when he hung out there and read the old comic books he had collected over the years. When he got to Dusty, the sweet dog was lying on his side panting.

"What's up, boy? You okay?" he said, stroking the dog's body and feeling for the possible source of his whimpering. *Maybe he heard something.* "Did you hear some—"

That's when he felt the wet, warm hole on the top of his dog's hind leg. "Oh no, Dusty, no." He scooped the canine up from the floor and made his way to exit, banging his head two or three times along the way. He ran out into a rainy black night, knowing exactly where he was going. It was the only place he could go.

When he arrived at the Skull's clubhouse, it was 2:05 a.m., and the boys were still going strong. He had sprinted the entire way, 22 blocks, with Dusty in his arms. He was drenched from the rain, his lips were turning blue, but he hadn't a shimmer of a care for that. He had to get help for Dusty.

Hang in there, boy. Hang in there, boy. Hang in there. He was missing one of his shoes, sweating profusely, and covered in blood. He could hear them partying from outside the Calvaria, even though all the doors were closed. When he opened the front door and walked in, no one noticed him right away. But then someone did.

"What the fuck! Who are you? What's in yer fucking arms? Is that a fucking craurchin?" yelled a large, very tattooed man with a long, black braided beard, and long, black hair tied in a ponytail. He pulled a blackjack from his back pocket. He was wearing cut-off jean shorts and a sleeveless leather coat. The coat had over a dozen tiny red skulls sewn on each collar. They represented human kills. He was barefoot and heading rapidly toward Don.

"Hold up, Slam! That's a dog in his arms not a craurchin! Holy shit, is that Dungy Don?"

"M-m—my dog. He—he's hurt!" Don was struggling to catch his breath. "Please help him, Sarge—please, I beg you!"

Sarge was as tough as they got. He was a bearish man with a perpetual five o'clock shadow and sparkling blue eyes. He had a deep voice that stopped folks in their tracks and made them listen. But even he could not bear the loss of a dog in the Badlands. He walked up to Don and took the dog from him. He felt for a pulse. He felt nothing. He laid Dusty on his back, turned his head, and put his ear on the dog's heart. Again, he heard nothing.

And then, he did something that surprised everyone in the club. He gave the dog chest compressions. Still nothing happened. He then walked over to a dirty, bloody, and very upset Dungy Don and looked him straight in the eyes with all the kindness he could muster.

"Don, Dusty is gone."

"No!"

"Don, how did he get shot? Where—" Sarge stopped when he noticed Dusty's blood wasn't the only blood on Don. There was a large stain on his lower body. His hip.

"Don, you're bleeding!" Don didn't answer. He was hugging his dead dog. Crying.

"I said you're bleeding, Don."

"I don't care."

"Mango, Shianne—help me with him! Don, I need to know who shot you."

"I don't care," he repeated, still crying.

"Who *the fuck* shot you and Dusty?"

"CraTek," he said and then passed out.

"COMES AROUND" TIME

The Cross Examination was ridiculously busy again this weekend. More craurchin death matches, more drinking and fighting. To make matters worse, that fucking bartender Janson didn't show up for work once again. *Time for a new bartender,* Doug thought. *Two strikes yer out when you work for me. I don't care what your excuse is.* Luckily Sheryl was there. Reliable, sexy Sheryl lit up the place.

This was to be one of the most anticipated fights of the year. A double header. First up a 1,700-pound white alligator from Florida would be fighting a twenty-two-foot long Burmese python, also from Florida. The winner would be fighting Menoetius, the reigning king. Menoetius was a 2,000-pound cycle 7. He was also known as Adam, husband of Eve. He was the only 7 ever seen. Scurge had trapped him in the Eagle Bay marshes just northwest of Brigantine over a year ago, and he hadn't lost a fight since. He would be fighting for McNimble. Unbeknownst to anyone, save the cycle 7, the

Leviathans, and Scurge, he planned to free him from the cage right after the fight. Scurge would help ensure that he could continue his journey toward cycle 8, and with the Leviathans, take out as many of the ten thousand people in attendance as possible and get the 7 to safety.

"Yo, Stinger, I need two hundred KPs on the snake. The python's gonna take care of business tonight, yo!"

"No KPs asshole. Cash only."

Doug looked at his communicator. Still an hour to go before show time and the Cross Exam was packed. There was a time when that would have excited him to no end, when all he saw were dollar signs and KPs out the wazoo. But, lately he just didn't care. He just wanted to go home and soak his feet. At forty-five, he was already tired of this shit. He was ready to make a move. He knew the religious fucks in the Heartland were not for him, but neither were the low-life drug dealers, pimps, gang members, and the like. Perhaps a tropical island somewhere would suffice. An island far away without craurchins. He was thinking about his options and making drinks for thirsty customers when suddenly his already shitty night, got five times shittier. Scurge just walked in.

Did the bar literally just go silent for a second or two?

"Hey, Scurge," a few patrons muttered. Scurge just grunted.

Doug and most of the regulars noticed that he never came in with Sally anymore. Not since that night. The night that Charles Corbin showed up. Since that night, he had actually grown meaner. As if that were possible. There were rumors that he murdered Sally, but nobody dared to ask around or report anything. Best not to get involved. See no evil, hear no evil. Scurge walked around the bar to Sheryl's side, thank God, and sat next to Ivanka, a skinny dope fiend with several teeth missing, Scurge's current piece of ass.

"Hey, Sheryl, we need whiskey, hon," Ivanka half shouted. She turned to Scurge. "You want anything else, baby?"

"No. I'm good. Give me a bump, bitch."

"Sure thing, Scurgie. Here go. Oww!" Scurge had pinched her hard enough to bruise her leg. "The next time you refer to me as Scurgie, you lose more teeth."

"Sorry, hon, here you go." She poured out two white lines of powder on the bar top. A really long one for him and a shorter one for herself. On the walls all over the CE, the fight flashed on. McNimble's bloated face was on the screens, getting ready to start the opening ceremonies. While he was snorting the powder off of the dirty bar top, Scurge saw a shadow on the bar and felt the presence of something large behind him.

"Hey, Scurgie, how's it going, buddy? Well, would you look up there—it's everyone's favorite mayor, Mayor McNumb Nuts. Speaking of numb nuts, how are yours hanging, bud?"

The large mass towering above Scurge was roughly six eleven and 370 pounds, all solid muscle, sweat, and veins. He wore cut-off jeans, faux suede sandals, and a leather vest. He had the familiar Skull's logo on the back of the vest. On his head, he wore a red bandana wrapped around his shoulder-length brown hair. The long, red-dyed hair hanging from his chin was the only facial hair. He had no tattoos and no piercings.

"Hey, Lane, what brings you to the Cross Exam?" Lane was the Skull he worked with for his craurchin deals and most of his other business with the Skulls. He had never had a problem with Lane. *Why is he talking to me like this? On my turf?*

"See my friend over there?" Lane asked. A large, heavyset man sitting directly across the bar from them raised his glass when he saw Lane pointing his way.

"Well, Bullfrog over there was the lucky man who got to deliver those two reptilians up on that there wall. We heard this would be a good spot to watch the match. I hear you delivered the 7. Hey, Sheryl, get my bud here a drink. Okay, catch up with you later."

He started off toward the other side of the bar then stopped, turned around, and walked back to Scurge. "I almost forgot. We need a cycle 6 and 5 by this Wednesday."

"I've got you covered. I'll have them."

As the night rolled on, Scurge and Ivanka continued to snort the white powder and drink straight bootleg whiskey. At one point he was going to walk over and confront Lane. Maybe sucker punch him in the balls just to send a message, but the two men were no longer there.

"Come on, slut. It's toilet room time." Ivanka followed him in, bottle of white powder in hand. They each did a bump off the back of their hands. She turned on the spigot, ran her fingers under the water, and then dripped some of it down her snorting nostril. She turned around and started kissing Scurge, and he turned her around violently and pulled her shorts and panties down to her ankles, pushed her head down, bending her over the sink. He then dropped his jeans and penetrated her from behind. He was just getting into his rhythm when the door burst open, smashing against the wall.

402

"Get the fuck out of—"

"Zip it, Scurgie!"

A large fist, about the size of a honeydew, smashed him in the face. Lane's fist. He saw red bubbles pop from his nose, and he spit out two teeth as he staggered back into the side wall, knocking the paper towel dispenser off the wall. It fell to the floor with a loud bang that echoed throughout the toilet room, but Scurge stayed on his feet and charged Lane, pants still down to his ankles, fist flying. He managed to connect a few and drew blood from Lane, but this only infuriated Lane.

By this point, Ivanka had scurried out of the way, pulling her shorts up as she hopped toward the door. Bullfrog caught and steadied her, and then physically directed her out of the toilet room, giving her a hard shove back toward the loud bar.

"Hey!" he called to her. When she turned to look at him, he put his index finger to his lips. "Shhh."

Lane shielded Scurge's punches and when he had an opening, grabbed each wrist and manhandled them into Scurge's face repeatedly, knocking out another tooth. He then lifted him off his feet and charged him, like a blocking dummy, into the wall. Scurge crashed through the old-school gypsum wallboard, landing inside the wall cavity and wedged between two six-inch metal studs.

"That was for those two innocents. What happens next is for everything else. Hey Bull, check this out."

Bullfrog walked in and laughed hysterically at what he saw. Struggling to release himself from the wall, feet sticking out and kicking away and arms struggling to find a stronghold, was Scurge.

Stuck in the wall. His face was almost unrecognizable, his pants were down to his ankles, and his penis was still erect.

"That motherfucker likes this! Fucking sicko!" The Bull pulled out his twelve-inch blade.

"Unfortunately, this is your last warning, Scurge. I'm going to leave you with a reminder that you will never forget." And with that Lane walked out, leaving Bullfrog to finish the job and, in the process, unknowingly saving hundreds, probably thousands of lives in the arena at the Monarch Hotel and Casino.

CHAPTER 28

THE CYCLE 7

*Haunched like a faun, he hooed
from grove of moon-glint and fen-frost
until all owls in the twigged forest
flapped black to look and brood
on the call this man made.
No sound but a drunken coot
Lurching home along river bank;
stars hung water-sunk, so a rank
of double star-eyes lit
boughs where those owls sat.
An arena of yellow eyes
watched the changing shape he cut,
saw hoof harden from foot, saw sprout
goat-horns; marked how god rose
and galloped woodward in that guise*
— "METAMORPHOSIS," SYLVIA PLATH

THE WALL

By 2275, CraTek had harvested most of the 5s, 6s, and 7s in the Wildwoods and were preparing to move their operation to the shores of Stone Harbor and Cape May. In preparation for the next craurchin population explosion, and subsidized by the government, they started building a wall about a year prior. The Wildwoods were now a little safer due to the dramatic decrease in 5s, 6s, and 7s but the population of the smaller aliens had doubled. And so, the wall. Keep the craurchins boxed in between the Jersey mainland and the Atlantic Ocean.

The plan was to build the first leg of the wall on the eastern side of the Garden State Parkway, running over fifty miles, stretching from Cape May to Atlantic City. That would be Phase I. Work had already begun in the Wildwoods, but there were unexpected problems. Namely the Skulls.

"Boss, we've got another situation. There's been some more sabotage at the wall."

"I do not need a situation, Janes. What happened, did they burn another concreter vehicle?" Rusty Cohms was not in a good mood. His craurchin shell yields were down again this month and now this *fucking* wall. He was dressed business-military casual, wearing field pants, marching boots, and a perfectly pressed short-sleeve fleece shirt. A chain around his neck adorned a gold cross.

"They destroyed a half-mile of wall at Mill Creek. Basically, we build a mile of wall and they destroy a half-mile. At this rate, the project completion date will be five years behind schedule." Janes, reporting directly to Cohms, was managing the wall project.

408

"Mill Creek is one of the vital crossover points. How do these fuckers know to hit that? How do they know this information? There must a mole. We'll address that, but right now we not only need to double security, but we need to go on the offensive. We go right after the Skulls. Put them out of business."

"Sir, we don't know for sure it's the Skulls. We have no proof that they committed any crimes. My expertise is construction. I have no military or policing experience, but I do know construction, and I know that this extra security will kill the budget."

"Do you doubt for a second that it's the Skulls? Besides, this is the Badlands. We'll beg for forgiveness later. Fine, you just worry about construction and staying on schedule. CraTek will provide the budget. Leave the Skulls to me, Janes. I have contacts. Mercenaries. The Skulls won't know what hit 'em!"

Cohms couldn't have been more wrong. The Skulls not only knew what he was planning, but they were preparing to outmaneuver him. Cohms would not know what hit *him*. Three years ago, the Skulls started bribing CraTek workers to provide intel. Thank you, Aztec. The workers were happy to oblige. They also had several of their own embedded spies, gathering information every day.

"So Cohms is bringing in mercenaries?" Sarge had a sly grin on his face and looked more animated than usual.

"The private contractor is a company called Alleviant, Inc. Some of their fighters are former U.S. Marines who fought in the Cairo Campaign of 2250. Some are just yahoos. There'll be about twenty-five of them hitting the Calvaria II. We haven't nailed down the exact time, but we have an unconfirmed date."

"Twenty-five? That's it?"

"Don't get cocky, boss. They have the best weapons and technology short of the U.S. military at their disposal. To say they're formidable is an understatement!"

"Point taken, Lane, but we've got better intelligence. That advantage is everything."

Over the last two years, the Skulls had tripled in size. They had moved into a new, much larger clubhouse, procured better weapons and technology, and most importantly had gained the trust of the Badlands. In a short period of time, they had morphed from a group of thugs and outlaws, at least that's how they were perceived by most, to a kind of Robin Hood, fighting for the rights of those who couldn't. Most of the new recruits were sons and daughters of the Badlands. They also had connections and treaties with many of the other clubs.

These clubs and gangs had popped up over the last decade or so, up and down the east coast where the craurchin populations were growing. The spies they had embedded in CraTek did everything they could to gain intelligence and obstruct the harvesting operation and construction of the wall. And the spies came from many of the clubs besides the Skulls, so the network was strong and hard to tie to just one group. The entire operation had been well planned by Aztec, Sarge, and some silent partners that were very well connected.

"Boss, I need to have a word with you. Shit, this is some good news. We've got to have a drink." Lane ducked behind Sarge's desk, opened his bottom drawer, and pulled out a bottle of scotch and two plastic cups.

"Shit—Lane that's my best stuff! This better be fucking good!"

"You know, my father taught me a lot of things. But one thing he often told me was that revenge and patience could be the best

410

of friends. Well, if that's true, then this is the epitome of that phrase. Our patience has finally paid off."

Sarge hadn't seen Lane this excited since the birth of his daughter. It was amusing to see such a large, strong man excited, like a little boy who was just given a new toy. He sipped his scotch.

"How so, Lane? Shit, give me the news!"

"You know how we got Diamond Dave employed on the CraTek harvesting squad?"

With the help of Aztec, they had created a brand new, iron-clad identity for Dave, Gordon Fisher, upstanding citizen with a flawless resume.

"Yes, Gregory Fisher, wasn't it?"

"Gordon Fisher. Well, he used his background in construction to get transferred to the wall team about a month ago. He was working the southern part of the wall and as luck would have it, he crossed paths with our friend from Atlantic City and seized the opportunity."

"COMES AROUND" TIME FOR ROGER

McNimble was deeply invested in CraTek's harvesting and de-shelling operation. He invested money. He invested time. And most importantly, he invested influence. He used that influence to quiet CraTek critics, bribe Heartland bureaucrats, pull in additional investors, and buy off corrupt New Jersey politicians.

Three weeks after Fisher began working on the wall, luck would have it that McNimble was taking a group of investors on a tour of the construction, and to his section of the wall nonetheless!

The wall was constructed using the latest poured concrete technology. Forms and reinforcing were no longer required, and the concrete admixture had a super accelerator, that cured the concrete in one-eighth the time. A special vehicle called a concreter formed and cast the concrete formula all in one pour. Because of the reduction in labor and the fast-curing concrete, structures could be erected in half the time, with half the labor. The wall was ten feet thick and thirty-five feet high.

Craurchins were climbers, but halfway to the top, there were solar-powered zappers that prevented their ascent. Atop the wall were guardrails on each side of the ten-foot wide boardwalk. This boardwalk was for security vehicles and tourists. That's right, when complete, the public could actually use the walkway as an observatory for craurchin watching, yet another way for McNimble to exploit the Badlands.

Fisher had been working Section B.5.83, when he saw the group of three men and two women approaching from about four sections north of him. He recognized the chunky bald man leading the group. Roger Mc-fucking-Nimble. *Are you kidding me?* he mouthed.

McNimble had almost been at the end of what for him, was a very busy day. Earlier he had taken the group of wealthy businessmen to the de-shellery plant where they had seen the process of extracting dead craurchins from their shells followed by a lavish lunch in the executive suite of his hotel. They ate snail's escargot and lobster tails with champagne. Afterward, they had flown to the Wildwoods for a tour of the harvesting operation where they wore gas masks during the fumigation process and drove in the beach trovers for the body pickups. Then, off they went for some drinks and now, the wall. Afterward, there would be a five-star dinner at McNimble's top-rated restaurant in AC.

Fisher had just finished pouring a section of wall with the concretor machine. It was cordoned off from the completed side with yellow flashing border-boards. "Caution do not cross" flashed in bright red letters. Acting on instinct, Fisher quickly moved the north border-boards six feet south. He was calm and self-aware, and made sure nobody was watching. McNimble's group was too far away to realize what he was doing. To them, from their distance, it was just a worker making some adjustments. He then climbed into his vehicle, sat back in the seat of the cab and waited as the group approached.

The weather that day had been made to order. It was early August, and even though the beach was many miles east, the marshland view from the top of the wall was amazing. Below, salt marsh aster, narrow leaved cattail, salt marsh bulrush, and spike grass waved in the slight, warm breeze along with a mish-mash of hundreds of other plants and trees. There were also many craurchins scurrying about looking for crabs, snails, mussels, and fish eggs. It was low tide and the smell was a little rough to those not acclimated. As McNimble approached, Fisher could not help but think about his sister Nefertiti and her two orphaned children. His niece and nephew. He missed her every day. Roger was a good five paces ahead of the group, his fat cheeks and chins bouncing as he plodded excitedly along. Fisher could hear him addressing them.

"And this was built with state-of-the-art construction techniques. The best technology to date. Perhaps this young man up here in the—"

He was ten feet away.

"Hey, you, excuse me."

Five feet away. Fisher pretended not to hear him.

"Sir! Hey, son, I'm talking to you, boy. Jeez, for fuck's sake."

Two feet.

"Hey, you!"

McNimble stepped into the uncured concrete and instantly sank in, up to the top of his chunky thighs. The others stopped. The closest man, an investor named Barnibus MacAfee, almost followed Roger in, but quickly halted and maintained his balance. They all gasped in horror as he sank down further, making a kind of *klump* sound as he descended up to his ample waist. He was screaming with the high-pitched voice of a school girl.

"Help! Fuck! Fuck! Help!"

"Oh my God!" one well-dressed woman screamed. "Somebody help him!"

Not one of them attempted to pull him out. Within a minute, he was buried to his chest and screaming in a panic for help. Fisher lowered the dipper arm of his vehicle in a feigned attempt to save him.

"Grab on!" he yelled, knowing full well it was too late. McNimble's arms were already locked in the rapidly curing concrete. McNimble could feel his limbs crushing as the concrete solidified. Another minute went by, and his screaming turned to gurgling as his neck went in, then chin, then nose. His eyes were large and wide. Then, one last *klump*, and just like that, he was gone, forever a part of the wall.

"Good riddance." Diamond Dave AKA Gordan Fisher whispered to himself. "Bye bye."

GAOB0O, 2275

GAOB0o, also known as Eve, sat in her lair, underneath the Townsends Inlet Bridge. Her twenty-foot frame stretched out on the embankment, in the shady sand, up near the top of the concrete pier, upon which the corroding steel tower rested. The inlet was one of the places that the locals didn't bother to clear because the population was just so numerous.

Today, the small beach was populated with thousands of craurchins of all sizes and cycles. It was a wavy, virtual sea of craurchins on the hot sand. They were enjoying the sun rays pelting the backs of their shells with its joyous heat. You could tell which ones were members of what cluster. It was like the queen bee in a hive, surrounded by her colony. The queen stood out—larger, grander, and in obvious command. On the beach, the multitude of clusters consisted of a dozen or so smaller craurchins, among the 5s and 6s. They were all sub-clusters. Eve was the queen bee of this hive.

She had occupied this lair for decades, and she knew she would have to move on to a safer place. And soon. Trouble was heading her way and from both directions. The boy was looking for her, and she had her cluster looking for him. Her mate, BAEGo0, known to the humans as Adam and Menoetius, had died recently at the hands of an Earth predator. A big white alligator. He had big plans that were foiled when his servile was put out of commission. Together, she and BAEGo0 had reproduced over a hundred children, and their children, over a hundred more. And so on.

She was over 150 years old, weighed almost a ton, and had a shell that could resist a small nuke. Her eyes were large and had deep, bright yellow iris and scaly lids. The four horns on the top of her head were four feet long and twisty, with a sharp point at the ends and barbs all around from tip to shaft. She would fondly remember her days here on the inlet. She had had many close encounters, but had always managed to elude the humans when necessary. Her many leechings were always easy picks, devoid of putting herself in danger. She lived smart most of her long life and survived the fumigations, the extermination campaigns of 2220, the depletion of food sources, and the huntings. But now she faced the harvesting and de-shelling.

Because she was the mother of all the craurchins from Cape May to Long Branch, she knew much. She had ears spread up and down the coast. She knew of the harvestings in the Wildwoods. Of CraTek. She knew of the wall. She knew of the rescues. She knew of Jamison Gregory in Asbury Park. Of Dr. Marcus. Of Aztec Pendelton. Of the delegation. She knew of Terrell Williams, and she knew he was the only one who could find her.

She recalled, with much pride, how the long plan was working so well. How from the early years of eluding the radiation and stowing a ride to earth, to the population of the beaches of the Jersey coast, their plan was coming to fruition. Soon, the colonization would begin.

My children, the hours are growing short. And my time is growing near. In a decade, my metamorphosis will begin, but now I must find a safer lair. I'll need all of your help to get there.

The craurchins, clustered for a mile along the beach, all stopped to hear her words. They all knew where she would be going, and it would be their job to make sure she got there safely. She and Adam were the first to arrive on this planet, and now, with Adam gone, she would be first to reach cycle 8.

When my hour comes, the attack on the eastern shores will begin. The invasion on the west is getting started as my counterpart cycles soon to 7. Soon the humans will evacuate those beaches as well. The most important thing we can do is keep me alive so that I can lead you to our ultimate goal. The most important thing right now, right here, is stopping the boy.

Somewhere, many miles away, GAOB0o knew the boy was shuttering as his name was being thought, in unison, by every craurchin within a fifty-mile radius.

Made in the USA
Las Vegas, NV
10 December 2021